The Happiest Little Town

Barbara Hannay writes women's fiction, with over twelve million books sold worldwide. Her novels set in Australia have been translated into twenty-six languages, and she has won the Romance Writers of America's RITA award and been shortlisted five times. Two of Barbara's novels have also won the Romance Writers of Australia's Romantic Book of the Year award.

Barbara lives in Townsville with her writer husband and enjoys being close to the Coral Sea, the stunning tropical scenery and colourful characters, all of which find their way into her popular stories.

barbarahannay.com

ALSO BY BARBARA HANNAY

Zoe's Muster
Home Before Sundown
Moonlight Plains
The Secret Years
The Grazier's Wife
The Country Wedding
The Summer of Secrets
Meet Me in Venice
The Sister's Gift
The Garden of Hopes and Dreams

BARBARA HANNAY

The Happiest Little Town

MICHAEL JOSEPH
an imprint of
PENGUIN BOOKS

MICHAEL JOSEPH

UK | USA | Canada | Ireland | Australia
India | New Zealand | South Africa | China

Michael Joseph is part of the Penguin Random House group of companies
whose addresses can be found at global.penguinrandomhouse.com

First published by Michael Joseph in 2022

Cover images: theatre © Vectorpocket/Shutterstock.com;
bus © Dzm1try/Shutterstock.com; landscape © HappyPictures/Shutterstock.com;
flowers, stars and butterflies © K N/Shutterstock.com
Cover design by Laura Thomas
Typeset in Sabon by Midland Typesetters, Australia

Printed and bound in Australia by Griffin Press, an accredited
ISO AS/NZS 14001 Environmental Management Systems printer

 A catalogue record for this
book is available from the
National Library of Australia

ISBN 978 1 76089 943 1

penguin.com.au

We at Penguin Random House Australia acknowledge that Aboriginal and Torres Strait
Islander peoples are the Traditional Custodians and the first storytellers of the lands
on which we live and work. We honour Aboriginal and Torres Strait Islander peoples'
continuous connection to Country, waters, skies and communities. We celebrate
Aboriginal and Torres Strait Islander stories, traditions and living cultures;
and we pay our respects to Elders past and present.

For Milla

PROLOGUE

It wasn't the happiest of beginnings. Tilly tried to pretend it would be okay, that somehow, miraculously, everything would turn out for the best, but the rain soon dampened her foolish hopes. The rain, the winding road that climbed into the mountains, twisting and curling like a snake, and the giant trees hanging over the bitumen, their leaves dripping, blocking out the sunlight. The gloom of it made her more wretched than ever. And disgustingly carsick.

She knew her mum wouldn't have wanted this. Her mother would never have dreamed of sending her precious only child away from sunny Cairns, away from her circle of friends and her school where at least a couple of the teachers were cool. And her mum certainly wouldn't have sent her to the boring old Tablelands where there was nothing but farmland and hardly any shops, and absolutely nowhere for kids to hang out.

Everyone knew the cafés up there only served tea and scones and were full of boring, wrinkly old folk. And it was always raining.

She might as well be heading for Mars. Actually, Mars would probably be way more interesting than a pathetic little nowhere town like Burralea.

Tears burned her eyes and threatened to spill, but she'd been crying for weeks now and she didn't want Jed to see her crying again, although he deserved to feel bad. He should feel guilty as hell, seeing as he planned to dump her with some unknown woman and just abandon her.

CHAPTER ONE

Five days earlier . . .

For the first time in months, possibly years, Kate Sheridan was happy. Happy with an over-the-top joyousness that had her bounding out of bed every morning and looking forward to each new day.

Admittedly, her bubbling emotions were probably eighty percent excitement and twenty percent nervousness, but it was wonderful to feel alive and hopeful again. And it was all thanks to the van.

Amazing really, that a divorcee in her early fifties should feel so utterly thrilled about a second-hand, almost six-year-old former tradie van. But Kate had such wonderful plans for renovating her van's interior, as evidenced by the layout designs crammed into her notebook, and the oodles of pictures saved to her Pinterest page.

Countless hours she'd spent in research, watching YouTube videos of the most gorgeous renos, reading books and blogs and listening to podcasts about the process. She'd had doubts, of course, *huge* doubts about her handywoman skills, but she'd been encouraged by the discovery that plenty of other women had managed this fanciful endeavour solo.

The messages about getting started were nearly always the same. *Don't be overwhelmed. Just take it slowly, step by step.*

Already, Kate had taken the first of these steps, bravely stripping the van's insides and having a side panel replaced with one that would allow her to sleep across the van rather than lengthways. And, having padded the walls with insulation, she'd begun the challenging task of lining them with tongue-and-groove timber.

This ambitious task was only half finished. Kate had needed to seal the timber first – two coats on either side – before hammering the panelling together with a rubber mallet, wood glue and patience.

The occasional bent board had proved a nightmare, but she'd learned to discard these, rather than agonise over getting them to fit, and she was already loving the transformation. A timber interior gave her little van an enchanting air of timeless charm.

She also had a host of exciting plans for overhead cupboards, racks and shelves. She'd even found a little triangle of ancient stained glass in a second-hand shop that she planned to incorporate into her design.

Although her project was still in its infancy, Kate allowed herself to dream about hitting the road and heading off . . . somewhere . . . anywhere . . .

Possibly because she'd lived in North Queensland for most of her life, she especially liked to picture herself in the wintry south, cosy in her beautiful, timber-lined van and sipping a mug of luscious hot chocolate as she gazed out at a stunning vista of sea and southern skies. Oh, the freedom!

Of course, Kate still faced a huge mountain of work ahead of her. Right now, the little garden shed that came with her rented cottage was stacked to the rafters with pieces of timber in every length and thickness, as well as finds from op shops. And that was without the carpenter's tools, including jigsaw and a nail gun, both of which Kate actually knew how to use, thanks to a series of useful tutorials on YouTube.

Kate was determined to create the cutest outfit on four wheels. Then, she would set off on the adventure of a lifetime, the adventure she deserved.

Her spirits took a small dive, though, when she looked out her bedroom window to find her van shrouded in misty rain. Again. For the third morning in a row. If this weather kept up, which it probably would – this was autumn in the Atherton Tablelands, after all – she would have to erect a tarpaulin to work under.

Not a problem, Kate told herself as she swung out of bed, shoved her feet into slippers and pulled on her dressing gown, knotting the sash firmly to emphasise her determination. She couldn't be put off by a little drizzle. After all, the farmers in these mountains spent their entire lives stomping around in mud and rain, and at least it was cool up here, which was a welcome change after the steaming heat and humidity of Cairns.

Besides, she thought, as she spooned oatmeal into a saucepan, the rented cottage she'd found was a charming stopgap. Perched on a hillside a few kilometres out of Burralea, it offered gorgeous views of rolling green countryside. Bonus, it was cheap, and it wasn't too far from the hardware store.

Anyway, Kate couldn't have stayed in Cairns. It was just too horrible with everyone talking about her behind her back, and giving her pitying looks. She was sick of being *poor Kate*.

The entire city seemed to know the sordid details of her ex-husband's fall from grace, including the fact that Stan had run away to Cambodia, where there was no extradition agreement with Australia, which meant he'd be almost impossible to extract. To add to the disgrace, Stan had taken off with his former business partner's wife, plus far more than their fair share of the company's profits.

This ghastly news had been front-page headlines in the *Cairns Post*, and splashed all over the internet, as well as being gossiped about on the local TV and radio stations.

Throughout the shameful debacle, Kate's friends had been amazingly supportive, which was very sweet of them. Bringing her comfort food and buckets of wine, they'd even abandoned their own families as they'd sat with her, telling her not to listen to all the gossip. But although Kate had divorced Stan a good two years before this latest scandal erupted – and had believed she was well shot of him – she'd still had to face the stares in the supermarket, the whispers and shocked glances.

She'd grown tired of hanging onto a tight, brave smile, while thanking people for their sympathy, when all she'd really wanted to do was to angrily agree that yes, her ex was a lying cheat and a womanising conman. And yes, it was just appalling that one of Cairns's most popular tourist operators had not only lost his wife to this prick, but had been so financially stripped that he'd been forced to sell his charter boats, leaving his tourist business in tatters.

The emotional turmoil of being linked via gossip to her infamous ex had been far, far worse than the divorce. It didn't help that Kate had felt a fool all over again for having once loved this man. She'd lost count of the hours she'd lain awake until 4am, battling regrets for the choices she'd made, primarily the major life choice of marrying a charming guy with sparkling green eyes and an off-kilter moral compass.

She'd been quite certain she had to get away.

'But why would you move to the Tablelands?' her daughter Pippa had demanded over the phone when she'd heard Kate's plans.

'Why wouldn't I?' had been Kate's immediate response. 'It's beautiful up here.'

'But you don't know anyone.'

That was the general idea. A clean slate. Freedom. Anonymity and starting over.

Already, Kate was loving the rural vibe – the fresh air and farmlands, not to mention the lakes and rainforests, and the slower-paced lifestyle. These days, instead of driving to a multi-storey car park and traipsing through a massive shopping complex, she bought almost all her fruit and veg from farmers' markets, or from small individual shops with friendly staff always ready for a chat.

'Can't you move here to Townsville?'

'You don't need me in Townsville. You've got David. And your job and your friends.'

'But what if we have a baby?'

This silenced Kate for a moment. 'You're not pregnant, are you, Pipps?' She hoped she didn't sound too unenthusiastic, as she imagined babysitting expectations interfering with her travel plans. Please, no. Pippa was only twenty-five after all, and she and David weren't even married, although Kate was well aware that young people these days quite happily planned for parenthood with no thought of a wedding.

'No,' Pippa admitted. 'I'm not pregnant. But David and I have been talking about it.'

'Well, then.' Kate was only a little ashamed of the wave of relief that washed over her. She loved both her daughters, of course she did, loved them fiercely. And it was for the girls' sakes that she had stayed with selfish, sly Stan for all the years their daughters had lived at home, which on reflection had not been her smartest decision, but had seemed important at the time.

'Let's not get too ahead of ourselves,' Kate said now. 'I've found a rather sweet little cottage to rent. It's not far from Burralea – and anyway, I've had enough of the heat in Cairns,' she added as an extra excuse. 'Working on the van is quite hard physical work and it's so much cooler on the Tablelands. I'll be able to get the refit done a lot faster.'

'And then you'll just take off.' There was no missing the reproach in her daughter's voice.

Well, yes. Kate understood that her van renovation and travel plans had come rather out of the blue for her daughters. It certainly wasn't the sort of project that would have even remotely interested their father. Stan wouldn't have had the patience. Which was possibly why Kate had embraced it with so much enthusiasm.

At least her younger daughter, Chelsea, was too busy getting on with her brilliant legal career in Brisbane – and her even more dazzling social life, by all reports – to worry too much about either of her parents.

'I won't be gone forever, love.'

Call her selfish, but now that she'd sold her house, paid out the mortgage and was doing up the van on a sensible budget, Kate was completely in love with her new, free and unencumbered status.

For the first time in a very long time, she was doing exactly what she wanted. And she was happy.

CHAPTER TWO

It happened at a rehearsal in front of the entire cast – such a simple fall, but so embarrassing.

Olivia Matthews, with her usual top-notch skill and flair, had finished her two-hander scene with Peter Hubbard, a pleasingly talented actor who, by day, worked as an accountant in Burralea. Peter, as directed, had exited stage right, and Olivia made her departure via the front stairs.

She remained in character, which was her custom, and it should have been a simple matter to descend the short flight of wooden steps to join the rest of the cast, who were scattered about the Burralea Community Hall on metal chairs or folding camp stools, some chatting, others studying their lines, but most watching the stage.

In Olivia's youth, which was now a regrettably distant memory, she had been a professional actor, appearing on television and on stage in NIDA's Jane Street Theatre – and yes, the Burralea Amateur Players knew all too well that they were extremely lucky to have her in their midst.

Olivia still took pride in her ability to throw herself, mind, body and spirit, into just about any role, and tonight she'd embraced the dignified, nose-in-the-air haughtiness of Lady X with her customary high level of energy.

Unfortunately, Olivia was perhaps just a little *too* deeply in character on this occasion. Just as she reached the bottom step, with her nose still angled snootily to the ceiling, she somehow missed her footing, her ankle twisted beneath her and she lost her balance.

She found herself flat on her back on the dusty floor, unable to move, with her right foot at an impossible angle. Stunned, she was aware that something was very wrong. And she had never felt so helpless.

Of course, the players rushed to her aid, which was very sweet of them, but it was disconcerting to realise that their goggle-eyed stares and shocked gasps were directed at her groin. Only then did Olivia understand that her skirt was up around her hips, so that her thighs and knickers were on full display.

Good grief. She couldn't even remember which knickers she was wearing. Please let it be the black silk, or the ones with the purple roses and not that old, faded pair with the tear that she'd been meaning to throw away.

Fortunately, Josie, the director, arrived quickly on the scene. A thin, plain woman in her sixties, with dyed auburn hair cut into a bob and a dead straight fringe, Josie was both sensitive and practical, and now she hastily pulled Olivia's skirt back into place. But by then the entire cast had gathered around and would have most certainly scored an eyeful of Olivia's pale, elderly thighs and 'granny knickers'.

Olivia had barely processed this ignominy, before burning pain and rising panic cancelled all other thoughts.

'Are you all right?' someone called.

'Where do you hurt?' enquired another voice. 'Did you hit your head?'

'Can you sit up?'

So many stupid questions.

'Give her a moment,' commanded Josie, who had been a school deputy principal before she retired and was now kneeling beside Olivia and taking her hand in her own. Despite her plainness, Josie had fiercely intelligent blue eyes and now she offered Olivia a gentle smile. 'Don't try to move just yet,' she said.

This was welcome advice. 'It's my ankle,' Olivia managed to say, although she realised that her head was also spinning and her heart was pounding.

'Yes, I can see that your ankle's starting to swell.' Josie gave her arm a sympathetic pat. Then, turning to the others, she issued a command in her best director's voice. 'Hamish, check the fridge out the back. See if there's any ice.'

'And here's a pillow,' said someone else.

Olivia recognised the new voice as belonging to Margot, who ran the local hardware store and helped with building the theatre sets. Kneeling on the other side of Olivia, Margot slipped a satin covered cushion beneath her head. 'How's that?' she asked.

Olivia tried to smile her gratitude. At least she was no longer quite so close to the wooden floorboards that hadn't been mopped in a while.

'Shouldn't the cushion be under her ankle?' another voice cut in. 'I'm sure I remember they told us in first aid classes you need to elevate the injury.'

Promptly, the cushion was transferred to Olivia's now screaming ankle, while her head was once again lowered to the floor. She knew everyone was doing their best and she might have tried for a grateful smile if she hadn't been so distracted by the pain, plus a new and totally unwelcome question that launched her almost into a sitting position.

Will I still be able to carry on as Lady X?

She had to continue in the role, surely? The show must go on and the play would fall to pieces without her. The part of Lady X was made for her.

'There, there,' Josie murmured, pushing her gently back down.

'But the rehearsal —' Olivia protested.

'Don't worry. You need to lie still for a bit. Give yourself a chance to get over the shock.'

'Here's the ice.' Hamish, son of a local dairy farmer, appeared now, waving a plastic ice block tray.

'For God's sake, Hamish,' cried a scornful young female voice that could only belong to Heidi. 'You can't wrap a plastic tray around Olivia's ankle. Put the ice in a plastic bag or a tea towel or something.'

Exhausted suddenly, Olivia closed her eyes and let the comments circle above her, and at last a towel holding cooling ice was wrapped around her burning ankle.

'She'll need to see a doctor.'

'Obvs.'

'But I don't suppose we should bother Dr Reilly at this late hour.'

'No, best take her to Atherton Emergency.'

Olivia's eyes snapped open. 'I don't need to go to the hospital.'

'Of course you do.'

This last comment was delivered by a commanding, deeply masculine voice that Olivia instantly recognised as belonging to Rolf Anders. Good grief. How long had Rolf been here?

She turned to see him standing a short distance away. A beefy fellow with rusty hair and a greying beard, Rolf Anders was a local author, a writer of considerable fame, actually, who had chosen to live on the Tablelands. He had a beautiful house down by the lake and had actually written *Next Stop Mars*, the playscript they were currently rehearsing.

Olivia had always been comforted by the fact that such a successful artist had chosen to live here in the Far North, way out of the southern cities' limelight. Not only had she valued his friendship, but his presence gave credibility to her own choices that she knew many people, including her own family, had questioned.

Rolf rarely graced these amateur rehearsals, but now he came closer and stood, with his hands comfortably plunged in the pockets of his corduroy trousers, as he offered Olivia a reassuringly sympathetic smile. 'I'd be happy to take you over to Atherton Emergency,' he said.

Olivia did appreciate his offer, although the last thing she wanted was a trip to hospital. 'Thanks, Rolf, but I'm sure all I need is to rest up for a bit. It's bound to be just a strain.'

This, of course, prompted others to join in again.

'A pretty serious strain by the looks of that swelling.'

'Could be torn ligaments.'

'And at your age —'

Olivia glared in the direction of the young female who had dared to mention her age. She'd always gone to great lengths to preserve her looks and she didn't care to be reminded of the danger of falls for elderly women. And she most definitely did not need to hear this from smug, teenage know-alls like Heidi McLellan.

But now Rolf had moved even closer and was speaking with a quiet authority that silenced the others. 'I'm sure you should have that ankle looked at, Olivia.'

'Absolutely,' agreed Josie. 'As soon as you're feeling up to moving, we'll help you out to Rolf's car.'

Olivia hadn't the strength to argue and she knew she'd already taken up too much precious rehearsal time. But she hoped that when she had Rolf on his own she'd be able to persuade him to simply drive her home. Surely, all she needed was a hot cup of tea and bed rest?

Unfortunately, Rolf wasn't buying this option.

'Don't fret, Olivia,' he said, after he and Hamish had more or less carried her outside and she was finally settled on the back seat of his Range Rover with her leg elevated as comfortably as possible. 'Apart from the players' genuine concern for you, they have a responsibility to make sure you have a proper medical assessment.'

'But it's not as if I'm planning to sue the theatre. I wouldn't dream of —'

'Duty of care, my dear. Not so much a matter of indemnity, as a simple duty of care.' Rolf spoke gently but firmly as he tucked a blanket around her and then snapped her seatbelt in place. 'And I feel partly responsible. I wrote the damn scene that had you exiting via the stairs.' A moment later, her door was closed and he was behind the wheel and starting up the motor.

It seemed she had no option . . .

Normally, she enjoyed the short trip from Burralea to Atherton, sweeping across wonderfully fertile farming land which, depending on the season, might be green with new crops, gold with ripening grain, or a rich, dark red with newly turned earth. It was a different story tonight, however, with a heavy mist rolling in, shrouding the landscape and showing little but the headlights of the oncoming traffic.

Closing her eyes, Olivia told herself to relax, to accept her fate. There was little she could do for now.

But she had never been one to give in easily. 'They'll give me a moon boot, or something,' she said, projecting her voice to reach Rolf in the front. 'I'm sure I'll be able to keep rehearsing.'

'It's hard to know, isn't it?' he replied over his shoulder while he concentrated on navigating the mist-drenched road. 'But I suspect you'll be told to rest.'

For heaven's sake. Resting would almost certainly mean staying at home and missing rehearsals. And, sadly, despite their amateur nature, the Burralea players' rehearsals were the highlight of Olivia's week. Not that she liked to admit that her life had shrunk to such a modest low.

With this thought, more negativity arrived and she even found herself wondering if the young players might be secretly delighted if she was out of action. *While the cat's away . . .*

But surely they wouldn't be pleased? They knew how invaluable she was.

Somewhat desperately, she tried again. 'I guess ankles only take a couple of weeks to heal, wouldn't you think?'

She saw Rolf's broad shoulders lift in a shrug. 'Let's hope so.'

It wasn't the reassurance she needed.

CHAPTER THREE

Kate was in the van, drilling three neat holes into metal, a task requiring exact precision. Her concentration was fierce, as was the scream of the drill, which was, no doubt, why she didn't hear a vehicle approaching up the track.

The first Kate knew of her visitor was when she turned to find a stranger filling her doorway, and she got such a shock she almost dropped the drill. She may have even cried out.

The intruder was male, tall and big shouldered. A Viking of a fellow, with a wild blond beard and even wilder fairish hair.

Aghast, Kate brandished the drill at him like a weapon.

'Hey!' the stranger cried, holding up his hands in self-defence. 'Sorry if I startled you.'

'Of course you startled me.'

'I did knock,' he said, as if that small gesture had given him the right to invade her private domain without an invitation.

Kate wasn't impressed. She waved the drill again, indicating that he should back out of the van. Which he did, at last, but with some reluctance, carefully ducking, so he didn't bang his head.

He was aged somewhere around forty, she guessed, and dressed in a loosely hanging flannel shirt, battered jeans and work boots. His forearms, exposed by rolled-back sleeves, were covered in elaborate tattoos and his nose was crooked, as if it might have been broken at some time in his past. But now that Kate had calmed down, she could see he wasn't planning to attack her, so she set the drill down and followed him outside.

It was raining again, or perhaps, more correctly, *still* raining. Luckily she had erected a tarp over the van. Beyond that sheltered space, she could see his vehicle standing in the drizzle, a dark station wagon splattered with mud from the churned-up track.

'So what do you want?' she asked cautiously.

He took a moment to answer. Actually, he seemed to grimace as he set his hands on his hips and drew a breath. 'This is kinda awkward,' he said. 'But I'm delivering your ward.'

'My *what*?'

'Your ward,' he said. 'You've been named as her guardian.'

Kate shook her head. The guy was talking gibberish. 'I'm sorry,' she said. 'You've got the wrong address. I don't have a ward. I'm not anyone's guardian.'

The look he gave her now was almost pitying. 'You're Kate Sheridan? You were married to Stanley Sheridan?'

Now her knees threatened to give way. What the hell? Could this really be something to do with Stan? Surely, after all this time, she'd earned immunity from any fallout his actions caused.

'I divorced Stan over two years ago,' she said, just managing to edit the pleading note from her voice and replace it with a sterner tone.

'Yeah, but in this case, I'm afraid that doesn't really count.' The stranger shrugged and sent her a faint, sympathetic smile. 'The name's Jed, by the way. Jed Larsen.'

He paused, waiting for Kate's response, but she was too tense to grace his introduction with so much as a nod. Undeterred, he continued. 'You see, Stan Sheridan has a daughter and —'

'He has *two* daughters,' Kate cut in, but her head was reeling now and she reached behind her for the van's door handle for support. 'I'm their mother. Both our daughters are fully grown adults and they certainly don't need a guardian.'

Just the same, Kate was grateful that Pippa and Chelsea were now safely out of the district. They had been as embarrassed as she was by their father's behaviour, but their emotions were complicated by the very fond memories they still held of their dad.

Despite Stan's faults, which were now so glaringly obvious, he had been a fun and loving father, especially when the girls were little. He'd taught them to swim, had dabbed soothing lotion on their chicken pox scabs, and given them fun adventures, like the time he'd taken them on a memorable ride in a hot air balloon, with Kate watching fearfully from the ground way below.

'Hot air being Stanley's forte, of course,' Kate's mother, who'd been waiting with her, had muttered out of the side of her mouth. She had never been a fan.

Even in those early days when Stan had played the role of Dream Husband and Father, with an endearing ability to make everyone laugh, Kate's mum had been suspicious.

At the time, Kate had been angry with her, reverting to the touchiness she'd been prone to in her teenage years. 'I can't believe you're being a stereotypical, fault-finding mother-in-law.'

But, unfortunately, her mother had been right to distrust Stan. Even back then, he'd been conning Kate and their daughters, sneaking away for liaisons with other women that he'd camouflaged as business trips, which he'd also somehow managed to get those silly women to pay for. And lately, of course, all the stories of his past misdemeanours had been circulating around Cairns more wildly and loudly than ever.

These unhelpful realities were haunting Kate now as her unwelcome visitor nodded.

'The problem is,' he said, 'there's also a third daughter and she's only thirteen. She had a different mother, of course. There's a good chance your ex might not even know about her, but Stanley George Sheridan's name is most definitely on her birth certificate.'

So what? Kate wanted to scream. Given Stan's numerous affairs, it was more than possible that he'd fathered another child – half a dozen other children for all she knew.

'But this girl still has nothing to do with me,' she cried, so angry now she was shouting.

'I'm afraid she does, actually.' Jed flicked a frowning glance to his vehicle and when Kate followed his gaze, she realised, with a sickening lurch of her stomach, that someone was sitting in the front seat. Through the misty drizzle, she couldn't quite make out details, but the person seemed to have long dark hair.

Was this the girl? Supposedly, Stan's thirteen-year-old daughter? Had this Jed guy actually had the gall to bring her here?

Kate's blood seemed to drain from her body. She sank onto the van's step, feeling both faint and ill. Surely this was some kind of nightmare? Any minute now she'd wake up and find herself bliss-fully alone – just her, the van and a shed full of handywoman tools on a misty hillside.

But when she blinked her eyes open, Jed Larsen was still stub-bornly in front of her.

'Look,' he said. 'I know this has come out of the blue.' He did sound sympathetic, but that wasn't any help.

Kate covered her face with her hands, wishing she could use sheer willpower to make him vanish.

'It's a pretty complicated situation that I need to explain,' he said next. 'Maybe we could . . .' He gestured now towards her house.

No way was she inviting him into the cottage. What was he expecting? A nice cup of tea? A cosy conversation and a chance to

enjoy the warmth of the potbellied stove that she'd lit before breakfast to counter the chill, damp air?

Kate wasn't normally inhospitable, but to invite this guy inside
her home would mean inviting his passenger as well, and if the
passenger really was Stan's daughter, Kate wasn't ready for an introduction at such close quarters, thank you.

'I don't see why you need to explain anything to do with my ex,'
she said haughtily. 'He isn't even in the country anymore.'

'Yeah, but that's part of the problem.' As if Jed Larsen sensed
that he needed to get his story out quickly before Kate lost the last
remaining shreds of her patience, he hurried on. 'Ange, the girl's
mother, died recently.'

A strangled sort of gasp broke from Kate now and of course
she felt instantly sorry for both the girl and her unfortunate mother.
She couldn't help glancing towards the car again. The passenger's
head seemed to be bowed. She was probably looking at her phone.
She was a teenager, after all.

'Ange never married,' Jed said. 'She didn't really have many boy-
friends before she met me, and I'd only been with her for a little
more than a year before she had the accident.'

'A car accident?'

'Yeah.' His mouth pulled tight and he looked genuinely sad, then
he gave a sigh. 'So the kid's pretty much an orphan.'

'Yes,' Kate whispered and she couldn't deny it was a desperately sad situation. A girl with no mother and a scandal-mired,
cowardly runaway for a father.

Just awful. She felt truly sorry for the girl, who was currently
sitting alone and just a few metres away, no doubt wondering what
the hell was happening. But Kate still couldn't see why she needed to
be involved. Not now, not when she'd finally started to heal, when
she was making a new life for herself.

Damn you, Stan. You're supposed to be well out of my life.

I served my time with you. I stupidly gave you my love and loyalty for far too many years. And now, after all the ways you've caused me pain, I'm supposed to be free, detoxifying myself.

Kate couldn't take care of the girl. She couldn't possibly give up on her goals, her wonderful plans to set off in the van and travel wherever the urge took her. No one with any heart could expect her to throw those dreams away while she picked up the pieces after yet another of her ex-husband's many misdemeanours.

It was too much to ask. Impossible. Kate was finished with teenagers. She'd served her time dealing with the moodiness and arguments, the broken hearts over boys, over pimples, over school results. She'd found it hard enough before, and she'd loved her own daughters deeply, but to go through all that again with someone else's child. With Stan's daughter . . .

There had to be other people who could take this girl in. Didn't Ange have family?

'The thing is,' Jed said next, 'Ange named you in her will as her daughter's guardian.'

Kate gaped at him, and for what felt like an age, she couldn't speak, couldn't really even think. 'But that's ridiculous,' she finally managed. 'We've never even met. Why on earth would she do that?'

Jed sent another wistful glance past the van to the house, but when Kate showed no interest in shifting, he gave a resigned sigh and folded his arms across his chest, almost hugging himself as he tucked his hands under his armpits. 'According to Ange's lawyer, she made her will some years back – back when you and Stan Sheridan were still married. Happily married, as far as an outsider like Ange could tell. And as Stan was Tilly's father —'

'Tilly?' Kate interrupted. 'Is that the girl's name?'

He nodded, gave a small shrugging smile, then continued. 'Apparently, the way Ange looked at it, Stan was Tilly's father and you, as his wife, were the mother of *his* other daughters – Tilly's half-sisters. So if anything happened to Ange, she wanted Tilly to be with you guys. It meant she would at least have a family.'

'But – but surely Ange – Angela —' Kate was stammering and she had to pause, take a breath and try again. 'Surely she must have known about the divorce. She must have realised that Stan and I weren't the happy-ever-after couple she'd imagined. Didn't she change her will?'

'Apparently not.'

'But why the hell wouldn't she?'

'That's a question I can't answer. But it seems people can be a bit slack about updating their paperwork.' With a sheepish smile, Jed added, 'I can't talk. I don't even have any kind of will.'

Oh, God. So this nightmare was *legal*? Kate couldn't hold back a groan. It was like she was sinking into quicksand and had nothing to cling to. As if she'd found herself inside a trap, but every time she tried to search for a way out, her mind slipped and slid.

A woman she'd never met had named her – in a last will and testament – as her child's guardian. It was utterly bizarre. Preposterous. But although Kate was no expert in such matters, it also sounded horribly possible and legitimate.

Then again, how could she be sure this guy, with his wild beard and bikie-gang aura, was telling her the truth? One thing was certain – she needed to have a very serious talk with the lawyer he'd mentioned.

'You'll have to give me this lawyer's contact details,' she said.

'Of course. I made sure I brought them with me.' Jed looked pleased with himself as he felt in his shirt pocket and drew out a white business card. Stepping forward, he handed it to Kate. 'And I'll fetch Tilly now,' he added.

'No, you won't.'

Jed had already swung in the direction of the car, but now he turned back, frowning.

'I – I'm not sure it would be helpful to meet Tilly just yet.' Kate hoped she didn't sound as panicked as she felt. 'Let me talk to this lawyer first.'

Even before she'd finished, Jed was shaking his head. 'Sorry, that's not how this works.'

A ghastly chill slithered through Kate. 'What do you mean?'

'I have to leave Tilly here with you now. Today.'

'But you can't. That's nonsense. She's been living with you until now, hasn't she?'

'Yes.' There was a flash in Jed's eyes that might have been pity. 'But I've scored a new job in the west – headquartered in Perth – and I'm flying out of Cairns first thing in the morning.'

Thud.

It was like receiving a knockout punch. Kate flinched, then closed her eyes as she dropped her head into her hands. This could not be happening. Not to her. Not now.

'You can't do this,' she bleated. 'You can't just abandon the girl. Aren't you – aren't you – more or less her stepfather?'

'Not really. I certainly can't keep her.'

'Neither can I.'

Jed was shaking his head. 'Seriously, she shouldn't be with me.'

'Why not?' A sickening thought struck. Surely this guy hadn't behaved inappropriately with Tilly?

On cue, he flung out his arms. 'Take a look, lady. I'm a forty-year-old, inked-up male, with long hair and a broken nose. More than once I've been pulled over by the cops simply because they didn't like the look of me.'

Unfortunately, Kate could believe this. Jed had certainly scared her when she'd first seen him.

But still . . . that didn't mean . . .

'Please understand,' he said, more gently. 'There's already gossip in the flats where we've been living. A bloke like me living with a thirteen-year-old girl who's not my daughter. No relative at all. How long do you think it'd be before the police turn up, jumping to conclusions? Probably with Child Safety in tow.'

Oh, good grief. A ghastly sense of doom descended on Kate, cold and suffocating. And then a bright idea struck. 'What about her grandparents?'

Again Jed shook his head. 'Ange ran away from home when she was seventeen. And now her dad's dead – a drug overdose – and her mum's brain's so addled, she's in an institution.'

Help.

'Tilly's a good kid,' Jed went on. 'She doesn't deserve all this shit that's happened in her life.' He grimaced. 'She and her mum were very close.'

Kate groaned.

Jed sighed. 'I don't have a bloody clue how I can do any more than I already have. I probably should've just let the lawyer sort it, but there's next to no money in the estate, so she'd been making noises about flicking the problem to Children's Services.'

'That seems logical.'

Jed, however, shook his head. 'Ange told me she had a bad experience in foster care. She didn't want to take that risk for Tilly.' His Adam's apple bobbed as he swallowed. 'So here Tilly is. I've found you and it's your turn now.'

CHAPTER FOUR

'It's just a chicken casserole, but I've divided it into smaller portions and they should freeze well.' Josie's smile was hopeful as she let herself in through Olivia's unlocked front door bearing several plastic containers.

Olivia was sitting in an armchair in her sunny front room with her injured ankle resting on a hassock and her crutches propped against a nearby bookcase. She hoped her smile was sufficiently appreciative as she wondered how in heaven's name she would fit these containers into her already full-to-bursting freezer.

In just the few days since her accident, an astonishing number of good-hearted locals had arrived on her doorstep with offerings of food. It was very kind of them, and Olivia was quite humbled by their generosity, but the only freezer space she had was at the top of her fridge – and already she'd been given three chicken casseroles, a vegetable lasagne and a tuna bake, not to mention two date loaves and a lemon drizzle cake.

The locals were all keen to help and there had even been talk in the neighbourhood of creating a roster of good folk designated to stay with Olivia day and night.

'We want to make sure you're okay, that you don't have another fall,' Deidre from the house on the corner had told her.

Olivia had quickly quashed that idea, however. She was afraid Deidre was rather too much of a gossip. Within no time the entire village would know the contents of her pantry, what brand of toothpaste she used and, no doubt, the precise details of her underwear drawer. Besides, even if that judgement was a bit harsh, Olivia had been living on her own for too long. She prided herself on her independence and she couldn't bear the thought of non-stop vigilance.

She'd possibly been a little too brusque when she'd rejected Deidre's proposal, however, and so she tried to tone down her reaction this time.

'This is so kind of you,' she told Josie. 'Thank you.'

'Only too happy to help.' Josie was always bright eyed, but today she had an extra glow about her, as if she thoroughly enjoyed her role as good Samaritan. 'I'll just take these through to the kitchen,' she said. 'Can I put them in the freezer for you?'

'Ahh . . . if you could put them in the bottom part of the fridge for now, thanks.'

'All of them?'

'Yes, please,' Olivia responded firmly, worried that a glance into her chock-a-block freezer might burst Josie's feel-good bubble.

'Whatever you say.' With a shrug and a glance that clearly questioned Olivia's choice, Josie disappeared down the short hallway and Olivia heard the fridge door opening and closing. A beat later Josie was back. 'And what else can I do for you while I'm here? A spot of housework?'

Already her eager eyes were darting around the room and back down the hallway. But housework was another area that had been taken care of and the cottage was pretty much gleaming and spotless.

Just yesterday, Father Jonno had sent a team of happy helpers from the local Anglican church to dust, mop and polish and generally take over in a manner Olivia had found barely tolerable, even though she knew she should have been grateful.

Actually, despite the intrusion, Olivia *was* grateful. She was jolly lucky to be part of such a caring community, and she had phoned Father Jonno to thank him. She had also phoned Rolf Anders, who had been quite the knight in shining armour on the evening of the accident. Even the sweet but impossibly young doctor who had seen to Olivia in Emergency had been thorough and gentle and sympathetic. Faultless, really.

So yes, she was very grateful and, unfortunately, although she didn't like to admit it, she was still in quite a deal of pain. She'd found that just learning to manage a pair of crutches was surprisingly difficult. Using them took an unexpected degree of physical strength.

Josie, meanwhile, was still hovering. 'Maybe I could water the pot plants on your kitchen windowsill?' she suggested.

This was one task Olivia could actually manage, with just one crutch and the sink cupboards for support, but she was supposed to keep the ankle elevated as much as possible, and if it made Josie feel better . . . 'Well, yes,' she said. 'Thank you. I'm sure they'd appreciate a drink. Actually . . .'

'Yes?' Josie had been about to disappear again, but now she turned back, her expression still eager.

Olivia was uncomfortably conscious that she and Josie needed to discuss rehearsal plans for Lady X, but the conversation was likely to be awkward. 'How about we have a cup of tea?' she said.

'Of course.' Josie smiled. 'That was going to be my next suggestion. I'll water the plants while the kettle boils.'

'Lovely. You shouldn't have any trouble finding things. The tea, sugar and mugs are all there on the bench. Oh, and there's a date loaf in the cake tin if you'd like some of that.'

'Perfect!' Once again, Josie disappeared, leaving Olivia to ponder on the delicate conversation to be negotiated. She wished she didn't feel so tired and anxious. The ankle had caused her sleepless nights, and she'd had far too much time to worry over the prognosis she'd received from the hospital. Her sprain wasn't especially complicated, they'd told her, but given her age, the healing would take several weeks at least.

They couldn't give Olivia any assurance that she'd be back to normal by *Next Stop Mars*'s Opening Night. But the very thought of not appearing in this production brought a ghastly, clawing kind of panic. It was impossible. There had to be a solution.

Closing her eyes, Olivia drew deep, slow breaths and wished she'd kept up the calming meditation exercises she'd learned at yoga classes all those years ago. From the kitchen came the sounds of the kettle being filled and then humming to life, the gentle chink of teaspoons and china mugs and the lid of the ancient cake tin being prised open.

'Here we are then.' In no time, Josie was back with a tray bearing their mugs, milk jug and sugar bowl, as well as plates with buttered slices of date loaf.

When she set these carefully on the coffee table, Olivia forced a grateful smile.

'You only have a little milk, don't you?' Josie said. 'And half a teaspoon of sugar?'

Olivia nodded. Over the years, the players had shared so many tea and coffee breaks at rehearsals, they all knew each other's preferences.

With Olivia's mug and date loaf set in easy reach beside her, Josie settled into a well-padded cane chair. Thin and birdlike, the woman seemed smaller than ever now, surrounded by the overly plump cushions. 'Forgive me,' she said as she crossed her skinny legs, 'but I haven't really asked how you are.'

'I'm doing really well,' Olivia lied.

Josie frowned, not even trying to hide the doubt in her all-too-knowing eyes. 'Honestly?'

Regrettably, it was much harder to put on an act in real life than it was to deliver scripted lines on the stage, especially when Olivia knew there was a good chance Josie had already grilled Rolf Anders for details of their trip to the hospital.

Nonetheless, Olivia did try to be convincing. 'I'm fine,' she said. 'I just have to keep my leg elevated until the swelling goes down.' And then, quickly changing tack, 'How did the rest of the rehearsal go the other night? Were you happy with everyone?'

'Oh, it went really well, actually. We were worried about you, of course, but once the cast settled down, we concentrated on one of the robot scenes.'

'Right. That was a good idea.' Olivia managed another smile and sipped at her tea, while she tried to think of other distracting questions.

But, of course, Josie wasn't to be diverted. 'So,' she said, with a carefully sympathetic smile, 'Rolf tells me you'll be out of action for some time.'

Olivia desperately wanted to protest. She was sure the doctors had been exaggerating. It was ridiculous to suggest that such a tiny stumble could render her helpless for so many weeks. But she couldn't deny that she did feel incredibly feeble at the moment and – God help her – she *was* seventy.

Until now, she'd never really felt her age, thanks to the care she'd taken with diet, exercise and skin care, plus the fortunate genes she'd inherited – and a hairdresser who kept her silver hair shiny and stylish.

But Josie was waiting for an answer and Olivia reluctantly gave up and nodded. 'Yes, that's right. I'll be hobbling around for several weeks at least.'

'You'll probably miss the play,' Josie suggested super gently.

'I can't.' This protest sounded far more desperate than Olivia would have liked, but her emotions were too raw and she couldn't pretend. If only she could leap out of her chair and stomp around to show how upset she was.

'Olivia, my dear. You might not have a choice.'

'But I won't be on crutches for all of that time. Once the swelling goes down I'll probably have a moon boot.'

'That should certainly be easier in terms of mobility,' Josie admitted. 'But still . . .' She paused, as if unwilling to state what she clearly considered to be obvious.

'Couldn't Lady X wear a moon boot?' Olivia cried, thrilled by this sudden, genius solution that had arrived like a gift from the gods of the theatre. 'It could add a comic touch.'

'Sweetheart, you know it's not that kind of play.'

'But that's nonsense, Josie.' Rolf's play was totally original and whacky. *Downton Abbey* meets *Star Trek*.

'It's the first time Burralea has ever produced a world premiere, so it can be any kind of play we want it to be,' Olivia protested. 'For heaven's sake, Josie, use your imagination. Speak to Rolf. He can fiddle with the script. Add extra comic lines to accommodate the moon boot.'

To Olivia's dismay, the look Josie bestowed on her now was one of unmistakable pity.

'Your mobility might be still quite limited. But don't stress. We don't need to make a decision right now,' Josie said soothingly. 'Let's see how you progress over the next week or so.'

Miffed and slightly alarmed by her own outburst, Olivia responded more meekly. 'Yes, of course.'

'But in the meantime – just as a precaution —' Josie's face twisted into a pained smile. 'I'm planning to ask Margot to learn the lines for Lady X.'

'Margot? Margot *Cooper*?' This time Olivia almost dropped her tea mug. She'd never heard anything so ridiculous. 'But Margot's not an actor.' Margot and her husband ran the local hardware store.

Margot was on the theatre's committee. She was very good at liaising with the local council or with tradesmen and she worked on the sets. But while she might be clever with a hammer and chisel, she wasn't an actor's toenail. How could she possibly play Lady X? Apart from a lack of acting ability, she would look so wrong with that terrible frizzy grey hair, her permanently flushed face and double chin.

More frantic questions circled.

Aren't you bitterly disappointed that I might not be available? You know Burralea has never had another actor of my calibre.

Shouldn't you consider shifting the date for Opening Night?

Watching her carefully, Josie said, 'We all know that no one can fill your shoes, my dear Olivia, but still, you might be surprised. There've been odd occasions in the past when Margot has filled in at rehearsals, and I've always thought she read rather well.'

CHAPTER FIVE

Kate was still fuming as she followed Jed Larsen to his station wagon. How dare he just dump this kid on her and then plan to take off? How dare he leave her with absolutely no option but to offer the girl a bed for the night?

She'd been set up, well and truly. Cripes, she didn't even know for sure if this child was truly Stan's daughter.

Was this going to be the hellish pattern of her life? To be constantly hoodwinked by men, who were perfectly happy to dump their crap on her, wreck her plans, and then sail off to follow their own whims without a backward glance?

Kate would have loved to throw a tantrum, to yell wildly as she told Jed off. Actually, she might have put on quite a spectacle if she hadn't been so conscious of the passenger, still waiting in the front seat, still with her head bowed, with her long black hair hiding her face – hair that Kate couldn't help noting was much darker than anyone else's in their family.

Even as they drew close to the vehicle, the girl didn't look up. But at least the rain had stopped.

Jed opened the passenger door. 'Hey, Tilly.'

She had been busily tapping on her phone, typing with her thumbs in that clever way that teens managed with ease, but now she quickly closed the app she'd been using, turned the phone over and set it in her lap. She was wearing frayed denim shorts and an oversized striped top that slipped off her shoulders, revealing the straps of a purple tank top, or possibly a bra. Her skin was olive and tanned – again, quite different from the pale Celtic complexions of the rest of the Sheridan family.

Very slowly, the girl looked up and Kate saw her eyes, and then she knew. Holy crap, she had to be Stan's child. Her eyes were a sea of misery, but they were also the exact same shade of green as Stan's, with that same crystalline clarity. And if she ever smiled, which currently seemed unlikely, her eyes would almost certainly sparkle just as his did.

Damn, damn, damn.

'So, this is Kate,' Jed was saying and he seemed to be the only one smiling. 'Kate, this is Tilly.'

'Hello, Tilly.'

The girl didn't bother to reply. She just stared at them blankly.

'Right. Let's get your things out of the back.' Jed spoke in the jollying tone teachers used with kids setting off on school excursions. Then he called over his shoulder, 'You might need to give me a hand, Tilly. You've got so much stuff.'

With obvious reluctance, the girl unclipped her seatbelt, and as she emerged from the car, Kate was surprised to realise how small boned and delicate she was. Those genes must have come from her mother, along with her dark hair and olive skin. Kate and her daughters were all quite tall with strong, swimmers' shoulders.

Despite her small frame, Tilly was able to heft an enormous, bulging pack onto her back, while Jed lifted a huge suitcase. 'Perhaps you could grab a couple of those boxes?' he said to Kate.

So all these cardboard cartons filling the back of the station wagon belonged to Tilly? They seemed to contain a jumble of books, magazines, pots, pans and crockery. There was even a plant in a hanging basket. It was pretty clear these were the bits and pieces of someone's life.

Tilly's mother's life?

Kate stood for a moment, just staring, her throat becoming painfully choked as she considered the deeper implications of these items that, clearly, had been untidily shoved into whatever receptacles were available at the time.

This was Tilly's world. Transported here. And the poor kid had probably been given no more choice in the matter than Kate appeared to have.

How unfair life could be.

But don't go soft, Kate warned herself and she blinked to make sure her eyes were clear of tears. Of course, Tilly's situation was incredibly sad. If Kate allowed herself to think about this from the girl's point of view, she could easily come unstuck.

But there had to be someone else out there who was far more suitable to care for Tilly than she was. Someone who had kids Tilly's age. Someone who wasn't trying to make a new independent life, who hadn't thrown their whole heart and soul into a brand new dream project.

'Are you okay there?' Jed called. He looked impatient. No doubt, he was keen to empty his car and head off.

Kate picked up one of the cartons. There was no spare room in the shed, so she was going to have to find space in the cottage. The laundry, perhaps? With luck, she wouldn't have to store this stuff for too long.

First thing in the morning, she would make contact with Angela's lawyer. And she would probably ring Children's Services or Child Safety or whatever, as well. She'd make sure someone with authority understood upfront that they needed to find an alternative caregiver for Tilly.

It was preposterous to think that she could be named as a guardian by a person she'd never met and then be automatically obliged to take on such a massive responsibility.

'Just push the door open,' she called to Jed and Tilly who had reached the end of the rain-puddled, flagstone path and were waiting on the cottage's doorstep. 'There's a mat inside. If you wouldn't mind wiping off any excess mud?'

Jed opened the door, then stepped back to allow Tilly in ahead of him, and Kate let out a heavy sigh. She had no idea how she was going to negotiate the next twenty-four hours. She felt totally inadequate for dealing with a young girl who'd recently lost her mother, had absolutely no experience of helping a teenager to cope with such profound grief.

At least she could concentrate on practical matters, and the spare room where Tilly would sleep tonight was in a reasonable state. There were clean sheets in the linen press and a warm patchwork quilt, so she could certainly provide overnight accommodation.

The potbellied stove was still pumping out a little warmth, Kate noticed, as she joined the others in the lounge room where Tilly was looking around cautiously. The girl probably found the cottage old-fashioned with its multi-coloured rag rugs and sensible terracotta floor tiles that didn't show the mud.

Kate rather liked the rustic vibe, however. A feature wall in this front room had been painted a deep matte pink and long windows let in plenty of light, while the kitchen opening off this area had bright yellow walls and snowy white cupboards. The cheerful colours were a pleasant antidote to the grey clouds and frequent mists outside, but Kate didn't expect Tilly to appreciate such details.

She nodded down the central hallway. 'The suitcase and backpack can go into the second room on the right. But we'll probably have to put the boxes in the laundry for now. That's at the far end of the hall on the left. Actually, when you get the other boxes, you'll find an external laundry door at the other end of the house.'

Kate didn't offer Jed afternoon tea.

When he said goodbye to them, he kissed Tilly's cheek and gave her shoulder a pat. 'You'll be okay, won't you, buddy?'

Tilly remained quite still, however, her expression unreadable. Kate wondered how long she and Jed had known each other. How long had the two of them been alone together? She realised she wasn't even sure how long it had been since Angela had died. It was too late to ask such questions now.

The rain had started again and was heavier than ever, as he drove off. Kate stood, watching his car head down the track and disappear into the clump of rainforest that closed in over the driveway, then she shut the front door and turned to Tilly. *Okay, I suppose I can do this.*

She wondered if Tilly drank tea. 'So, how about I —'

'What are you doing with that van?' The question – the first sentence the girl had uttered in Kate's hearing – was fired as a definite challenge.

Kate swallowed a gulp of surprise. Tilly was clearly no fool and this was her reconnaissance. She was sussing out the situation she'd been landed in, no doubt thinking ahead and trying to understand her options.

'I'm renovating the van,' Kate told her.

'Doing up the insides?'

'Well, yes.' No point in evading the truth.

'So you can travel?'

Kate was about to answer again that yes, she definitely planned to travel, but the girl's face silenced her. What was that look? Panic? Fear? Desolation?

A terrible battle stormed in Kate's chest. She knew she mustn't weaken. She deserved the van. It was her safety net, her cocoon from which she planned to emerge like a butterfly. She loved having this goal, her own goal and no one else's.

But it seemed suddenly too cruel to declare to this unfortunate kid that yes, of course she was taking off on the trip of a lifetime.

'I – I haven't quite decided,' she said instead.

* * *

The place was even worse than Tilly had expected. Not a boring little house in a dreary, boring street in a totally dreary, boring town, but a shack stuck all by itself on an empty hillside, in the middle of nowhere. And it looked out into nothing but misty rain. No other houses in sight, no neighbours. Just awful cows, heads down, eating grass in the rain.

Help! she wrote to her group of girlfriends on WhatsApp, who were now her only lifeline to sanity. *I've ended up in Shitsville. And she hates me. I can tell.*

Run away, was her friends' advice and Tilly was very tempted to take it. All she wanted was to be back in Cairns with her besties. But she baulked at the thought of trying to run all the way back down that massive mountain, certainly not in the dark. And there was no point in running to anywhere else on the Tablelands where she didn't know a single freaking soul.

Of course, it would be hopeless to try to call for an Uber or taxi up here. Tilly knew she would probably have to hitch a ride and she wasn't quite desperate enough to risk something so dangerous just yet.

But if she kept feeling as bad as she did right now, she might have no choice. First chance she got, she would check out the bus timetables.

Only problem . . . if she made it back to Cairns, would any of her friends' parents be prepared to take her in?

CHAPTER SIX

Out of habit, Margot woke when the first grey light of morning began to slip around the edges of her bedroom curtains. And as usual, her husband, Jack, was already up, out in the kitchen, rattling about, preparing to head off early to their hardware store. Jack always found plenty to do at the store before it opened for customers, leaving Margot to wrestle with the kids and get them off to school before she joined him.

It would be another ordinary day for her, a day of unpacking the latest deliveries, of stacking shelves and double-checking the orders, of helping customers to decide which drill they needed, or how much shade cloth would cover their bush house. A day like all the others. And yet Margot felt different.

For a moment or two, still foggy with sleep, she couldn't quite think why she felt happier. Then, like sunlight breaking through clouds, she remembered.

Lady X! Oh, my God. Margot was so suddenly flooded with amazed delight, she almost laughed out loud, and once again she was reliving the astonishing events of the previous evening, which had begun when Josie phoned to tell her that poor Olivia was going to be out of action for quite some time.

The fact that Josie had even bothered to discuss this news was a surprise. Margot had never been a member of the cast and was usually only consulted about the management side of the theatre – plumbing or electrical issues, maintenance of the equipment, helping to build sets.

'It means we're going to need another Lady X,' Josie had added and then, after a small pause, 'I'm thinking you might be perfect.'

'Me?' Margot had exclaimed, so shocked that the old-fashioned saying about being knocked over with a feather had suddenly made perfect sense.

Josie laughed. 'Why not?'

'You know very well I'm not an actor.'

'I think you could be, actually. You have a very expressive face and you're always so wonderfully attentive to your customers. You know how to read people, Margot. And you have filled in for us at rehearsals on occasions.'

'Only at rehearsals if someone was sick.'

'Yes, I know, but you always handled it well. I notice these things. Anyway, it's just a thought. Why not have a go?'

Margot could think of a host of reasons why she shouldn't attempt such a foolish endeavour, beginning with the obvious fact that her role at the theatre was to hammer together sets, splash paint where needed, or even, perhaps, sew on a last-minute button.

Sure, she loved the Burralea Little Theatre, loved being part of the buzz and the fun. She loved that opening night excitement when the curtain rose, even though she was watching from the wings. Loved the company, the camaraderie. But Margot was a team player, a behind-the-scenes person. She could never dream of being centre stage and she certainly couldn't imagine taking on such an important role as Lady X. That part had Olivia Matthews written all over it and no one else could possibly fill her shoes.

'I wondered if you might be free to come round to my place,'
Josie had said next. 'We could have a nice quiet little evening to
ourselves, relax with a glass of wine perhaps, and just try a short
reading to see how you feel.'

Put like that, it had sounded almost doable. Most evenings,
once Margot had fed the family, the kids disappeared into their
bedrooms, hopefully to finish their homework, while Jack settled
in front of the telly, often nodding off before his favourite cop show
ended. Margot was usually busy putting through loads of laundry.
They were unlikely to miss her.

And so she had gone. Josie only lived three streets away and
Margot had walked, wrapped in a woollen cape to ward off the
cool autumn chill. Josie was married to Hector, a scientist – a
biologist, actually. They had moved to the Tablelands after he'd
retired, to enjoy the bountiful natural wonders in the region. Hector
seemed to spend half his life away on field trips, studying birds or
searching for tiny endangered mammals, which was possibly why
Josie had become so deeply involved in the theatre.

Their house, set back from the street behind a lilly pilly hedge,
was a low-set timber cottage with a deep front verandah. A simple
design, and yet Margot had always found it surprisingly appealing and artistic. She suspected that Josie had spent a great deal of
time scouring antique shops to find the perfect pieces of furniture
and artwork.

The lounge room was almost like a stage set, with wonderful
old armchairs and deep sofas, standard lamps with gorgeous, exotic
shades, potted palms, and walls covered in bookshelves and marvellous paintings.

It wasn't a particularly cold night, but a gentle fire flickered in
the grate, adding to the atmosphere, and classical music played
softly in the background. Margot felt herself relax as Josie invited
her in and she sank into a comfy chair upholstered in velvet.

A glass and a half of red wine later, having enjoyed a convivial conversation, mostly about their families, Josie had handed Margot a few pages of script.

'Why don't you read this through while I put the kettle on?' she'd suggested – gently, no pressure.

Well, Margot thought, there was no harm in just reading a few pages to herself, was there? It was a section of the play that hadn't been rehearsed yet, or at least, not in Margot's hearing.

At first, as she read Lady X's part, she could only hear Olivia's strong, authoritative voice, but as she settled back into the plush cushions to read it through again, she began to hear other ways those lines might be delivered.

Lady X needn't be quite so snooty, really, need she? If an actor like Noni Hazlehurst, for example, had been playing that part, she might have been a little warmer, perhaps.

Josie reappeared. 'I should have asked. What would you prefer? Tea or coffee? Or perhaps hot chocolate? I'm rather a fan of peppermint tea at this time of night, but I can make anything, of course.'

'I'd be happy with peppermint,' Margot assured her, quickly crushing her initial urge to choose hot chocolate.

'All right then.' Josie glanced at the pages in Margot's lap. 'And what do you think of that scene?'

'Oh . . .' Margot wasn't quite sure what to say. 'It's interesting. Rather witty. Rolf's such a good writer.'

'He's wonderful, isn't he? Maybe we could read it together when I come back with our tea?'

Margot was instantly anxious about reading aloud and she downed the last of her wine in one hasty gulp, hoping to fortify her nerves.

But when Josie came back, she found there was no need to be scared. They read through the scene together, sipping tea, stopping to chat about a clever piece of dialogue. And when Josie suggested they try out different voices and styles – just for fun – somehow, rather miraculously in the midst of it all, Margot stopped fretting. She realised this was actually quite enjoyable and she found herself wanting to add a little punch and personality to her delivery.

Looking up from the page, she saw Josie beaming at her like the midday sun.

'That was marvellous,' Josie said and deep inside, Margot knew she meant it.

I'm going to be on the stage, Margot told herself now as she threw off the bedclothes. It was still rather amazing to remember that this astonishing impossibility was truly going to happen.

As if by magic, Josie had unearthed skills Margot hadn't even realised she possessed. This morning, she was almost floating as she climbed out of bed, donned her dressing gown and slippers and made her way past Bridie's and Nate's bedrooms.

Aged thirteen and twelve, Margot's children had become highly skilled at sleeping in. 'Morning!' she called to them. 'Time to get up!' And as she knocked on their doors, she was aware of an uncharacteristic sing-song note in her voice.

In the kitchen, she began to assemble their favourite ingredients for porridge – oats, cinnamon and dates, with slivered almonds. Wrapped in happy reverie, she wondered what sort of costume she might wear in the play, and she wondered, too, if she should talk to her hairdresser again about the de-frizzing options they'd discussed long ago, which Margot had shrugged off as being unimportant.

Now that she was, literally, stepping into the limelight, she needed to take more care with her appearance. She should probably try to lose a little weight. Goodness, it was wonderful to have a goal. Really, just too exciting for words.

Margot couldn't remember the last time she'd spent a morning thinking about herself. Usually, she was fussing over the kids, worrying about whether Bridie had put enough effort into her latest school assignment, whether Nate would make it into the soccer team or end up as a reserve again, sitting on the bench and trying to pretend he didn't care.

She had to give this pair another two calls to get them out of bed, but that was nothing unusual.

'And make sure you're dressed before you come to the table,' she called, even though they knew this was the rule.

The porridge was well and truly simmered and she was finishing their lunches as they appeared in their school gear, their faces still sleepy, their hair unbrushed.

Margot ladled porridge into bowls. 'Can you grab the honey from the pantry, Bridie? And, Nate, can you get the milk?'

'Can't we have brown sugar?' Bridie demanded grumpily.

Margot had been trying to transition them to having honey on their porridge, but this morning she didn't want a row. 'Oh, all right. But not too much.'

Plonking herself onto a stool at the kitchen bench, Bridie helped herself to an overly heaped spoonful of the rich brown sugar, and the look she sent her mother was challenging at first, then puzzled. 'Are you okay?' she asked.

'Of course. Why?'

'You seem like you're in a weird mood.'

'Well, I'm not. I'm fine.' Margot was at the sink now, rinsing out the porridge pot before putting it into the dishwasher.

'Have you already eaten your porridge?'

'I'm not having any this morning.' Margot had been reading about skipping breakfast as a form of intermittent fasting and now seemed the perfect time to start.

'And you're all sort of chirpy,' Bridie declared.

Was it really so obvious? Margot wasn't ready to share her news with her children. To speak about the Lady X part too soon might be tempting fate. Olivia could have a miraculous recovery and reclaim her right to the role.

Besides, Bridie and Nate were unlikely to be impressed. Or worse, they might even view the prospect of seeing their mother on stage as hugely embarrassing. Or hilarious.

Glancing through the kitchen window, Margot could see a beautiful, clean blue sky and the sun was shining on her hibiscus bush, making its golden blossoms glow. 'Well, I'm just glad that it's stopped raining,' she told them.

As if, said the look in Bridie's eyes. Nate didn't look up from his porridge.

CHAPTER SEVEN

The sun was shining, but Kate felt ragged, having barely slept a wink overnight. Talk about tossing and turning! She'd practically worn holes in the bedsheets, agonising over the injustice that had befallen her. And this morning, despite having indulged in a long, hot shower, she doubted that even a second mug of coffee could restore her spirits.

What on earth was she going to do about the teenager in her spare room?

Of course, there were practical steps she could take. She would ring the lawyer, once she'd figured a way to do so out of Tilly's hearing, but she had an uncomfortable feeling that the woman wouldn't be very helpful. She would probably try Child Safety as well, but again, she was uneasy about how that might play out. Uneasy, too, about how she would feel if Tilly was packed off to a foster home.

Of course, she told herself, there were oodles of wonderful foster parents and for sure there'd be a special couple just waiting to welcome the girl into their home.

But she couldn't shake off Jed's parting words.

Ange told me she had a bad experience in foster care. She didn't want to take that risk for Tilly.

Kate wished this didn't bother her. She'd been trying hard not to mind and had told herself it wasn't her problem. But at some point in the early hours, she'd woken from a horrific dream in which *she* had been the mother who had died, and once again Stan had scarpered. But this time it was *their* girls, Pippa and Chelsea, who'd been left behind, as young teens. With no one.

After she'd woken, this unsettling scenario had continued to haunt her and she'd dissolved into tears, burying her face in her pillow to muffle her sobs. Since then, she'd been troubled by a guilty conscience, an inner voice that was getting louder, poking at her more sharply, and making her utterly miserable.

Now, it was almost eight o'clock. It was a beautiful day outside and Kate drew a deep breath as she carefully knocked on Tilly's door. On the previous evening, their conversation had been minimal. Neither of them had been in a chatty mood, so Kate had suggested they have their simple pasta supper on their laps in front of the TV.

Tilly had visibly relaxed at this suggestion, but pretty soon after the meal, she'd taken off for a shower and then disappeared into her bedroom. They hadn't spoken since. The girl had appeared to be asleep when Kate had tried to say goodnight.

'Are you awake?' Kate called to her now. 'Can I come in?'

There was a muffled response.

Inching the door open, Kate found Tilly in bed, propped up by pillows, phone in hand, as if she'd just finished sending a message.

'Good morning.' Kate smiled. 'How'd you sleep?'

Tilly made no attempt to produce an answering smile. 'Okay.'

'I've made coffee. Would you like a cup?'

'No, thanks.'

'How about tea?'

Tilly shook her head.

Patiently, Kate asked, 'What would you like for breakfast?'

'I don't know,' came the sullen response. 'Toast?'

'Of course. And how do you prefer it? With Vegemite? Avocado?'

For the first time, a spark of interest gleamed. 'Avocado would be good.'

A 'please' or 'thank you' might have been nice as well, but Kate reminded herself that Tilly was probably feeling even more miserable than she was. 'Right then,' she said, managing another smile. 'If you'd like to get up, I'll have it ready for you in five minutes.'

Tilly, dressed in her frayed denim shorts and another long-sleeved T-shirt, with her hair brushed and hanging in a shiny curtain past her shoulders, looked a little brighter as she came into the kitchen. And her face had a rosy, freshly washed glow. Clearly, Ange had taught her daughter good grooming habits.

'It's stopped raining,' Tilly commented.

'It's actually a beautiful day outside,' Kate replied.

Crossing to the kitchen window, where the hanging basket Tilly had brought with her now hung from a curtain rod, the girl looked out at the spectacular view. The cloudless sky was washed clean and beneath this ran fold upon fold of green hillsides and valleys, the silver glint of a curving creek – verdant beauty that stretched forever to distant blue ranges.

All of Kate's previous visitors had raved about this view and Kate wondered if Tilly might make a comment, but although she spent a good, long moment staring out through the window, she was frowning as she turned back.

'Don't you bother with a garden?' she asked.

Kate blinked. *Of all the cheek.* Her first impulse was to put Tilly in her place, but she was trying to start the day on a pleasant footing, so she found herself offering excuses. 'Oh, I'm just renting.' *And I hadn't planned to stay long.* 'Do you like gardens?' she asked.

'I guess.'

Kate looked again at the hanging basket. 'Did your mother have a garden?' She was pretty sure Jed had mentioned that Angela had also been renting.

Now Tilly nodded. 'Mum had tons of pot plants. All kinds of pots.' Pulling her phone from her pocket she quickly tapped the screen, then held out a photo. It showed a smallish balcony made absolutely beautiful with lush palms in pots, bromeliads in baskets, herbs, bright petunias. A truly impressive collection.

'That's so lovely,' Kate told her. 'Where are those plants now?'

'Jed left them with Mrs Kettle, our neighbour.'

Oh. Kate wasn't sure what to say. The poor girl had lost so much. Her mum, her home, these beautiful plants. She could feel the weight of Tilly's grief sinking through her own body and she felt compelled to change the subject before the moment overcame them.

'All right, then. Here's your breakfast.' She had conscientiously mashed avocado with a little lemon and salt and pepper. 'Would you like a light sprinkle of chilli flakes?'

Tilly shrugged. 'Sure.' Then, a beat later and very faintly, 'Thanks.'

Kate had also made a helping for herself and as she sat opposite Tilly at the kitchen table, she mentally debated whether she should try to start a conversation, or simply tuck in. To dine together but in silence felt distinctly uncomfortable, but she was still dithering to find a suitable opening line when her phone rang.

Pippa's name showed on her screen.

Kate couldn't believe the way she tensed. *Not now.* Normally, she loved a phone chat with Pippa or Chelsea, but this morning the timing couldn't have been less helpful. She was tempted to ignore the call. Pippa could leave a message. But Tilly was staring rather intently at the phone and at the last minute, Kate swiped to accept, jumping up from her seat as she did so.

'Excuse me,' she told Tilly, and then, turning away from the breakfast table, she headed for the far side of the room. 'Hi, Pippa.'

'Hi, Mum, guess what?' Her daughter sounded unusually excited.

Oh, the irony! A strange, choked laugh broke from Kate. She could have asked the exact same question. *Guess what, Pipps? I'm having breakfast with your half-sister. Yeah, the sister you never knew you had. Don't worry, I never knew about her either.*

'I can't imagine,' she told Pippa instead. 'What's up?'

'You're going to be a grandma.'

Wham! Kate gasped. 'You're pregnant?' Surely this was one surprise too many?

Just in time, she remembered that a more appropriate maternal response was required. 'That – that's wonderful, darling.' But Kate was terribly afraid she sounded more horrified than happy and she was very aware that a wide-eyed Tilly was listening to every word.

Opening the kitchen door, she stepped outside, gently closing the door behind her.

Pippa, meanwhile, was gushing with excitement. 'I know,' she was squeaking. 'It's amazing, isn't it? I can't quite believe I have an actual little human inside me.'

Neither can I, thought Kate, and she leaned back against the door jamb, feeling weak.

'I know it's a bit too soon for us to be starting a family,' Pippa went on. 'We're supposed to be saving for a deposit on a house, but that can always come later.'

'Mmmm,' Kate replied, too dazed to say more. After yesterday's shock and her sleepless night, she was struggling to take in this news. 'I – I guess so.'

'You're happy for me, aren't you, Mum?'

'Yes, Pipps, of course. It's wonderful.' This time Kate made a concerted effort to sound positive, but she couldn't help asking, 'And I guess David's excited about becoming a father?'

Her question was met by silence.

Kate frowned. 'Pippa?'

'Of course David will be thrilled,' came the response, but there seemed to be a nervous note in Pippa's voice. 'I know he will be.'

'You mean you haven't told him yet?'

'I'm going to, Mum. I'll tell him tonight, just as soon as he gets home from work. I'll make his favourite dinner and everything. But I've only just done the pregnancy test and I – I wanted to tell you first. Women understand these things better than men, don't they?'

'I – I suppose.' Realising that Pippa was looking for moral support, Kate added more warmly, 'Sure. Of course.'

'But David's going to be a wonderful father,' Pippa added more confidently. 'And I know he'll be over the moon.'

Kate wished her daughter didn't sound quite so nervous. She told herself she was imagining things. David had always been sweet and thoughtful, the perfect boyfriend. The baby news might come as a shock to him, but he would support Pippa, no question. 'Well, that's lovely then,' she said. 'And more importantly, how are you feeling?'

'Oh, I'm fine. I don't even have morning sickness at the moment, but it's early days, I guess.'

'You'll see a doctor, won't you?'

'Yes, Mum, obviously.' Her daughter sounded a tad exasperated now, a familiar echo from the teenage years, when both Pippa and her sister had routinely bristled at any form of motherly interference.

'Of course. I know you'll be sensible,' Kate placated. 'And I hope you have a lovely celebration this evening.'

'Thanks.'

They said their goodbyes and Kate let out her breath on a heavy sigh. Beyond the fence, her neighbour's Friesian cows were carrying on as they always did, slowly, steadily chomping at tufts of damp grass. Lucky cows!

Damn it, all Kate had asked for was a little space, a little freedom, but it seemed fate was determined to hold her down. First Tilly, now the news that she was to be a grandmother, with all the expectations that entailed. Bullets were flying from every direction.

She looked towards her van, standing just a few metres away, patiently waiting under the tarp, and then she looked beyond it to the quiet hills that were either dotted with more cattle or striped with rows of avocado trees. For a few blissful weeks, this had been her world, serene and peaceful, her happy place, inspiring her with confidence and with plans for adventure.

Now.

Now, she had been named as a thirteen-year-old's guardian and she was about to become a grandmother and, for certain, her daughter would plead with her to move closer to be available for babysitting.

Kate supposed she could resist this latest pressure, at least for the time being. The baby wouldn't arrive for another nine months and Pippa would have some kind of maternity leave. But that still left Tilly. Perhaps, though, with careful questioning and research, Kate could find a solution for the Tilly dilemma.

One thing was certain – she couldn't give up on her dreams.

By the time Kate returned to the kitchen, Tilly had finished her toast and was at the fridge, helping herself to a glass of fruit juice. She turned as Kate entered and her green eyes held a distinct challenge. 'Was that your daughter?'

Kate was tempted to refuse to answer her. She hadn't planned to share info with Tilly about her half-sisters. But she supposed Jed

Larsen might have told the kid about Pippa and Chelsea and she was probably desperately curious.

Kate gave in. 'Yes, that was my daughter Pippa.'

'Where does she live?'

'Townsville.'

Tilly looked solemn as she absorbed this. 'And you have another daughter, don't you?'

'A-huh. Chelsea. She's in Brisbane.'

'They're my sisters.'

'Half-sisters, yes.'

The girl was standing very still. She'd made no attempt to drink the juice and she was clutching the glass in two hands, clutching it so tightly, in fact, that her knuckles showed white.

Kate couldn't imagine the emotions storming through the poor kid. For that matter, she also couldn't imagine how Pippa and Chelsea might react to the news that they had a half-sister. And a thirteen-year-old to boot.

'Do I look like them?'

Oh, God. Suddenly, this was getting way too hard. Kate's eyes and throat were burning and she feared she might burst into tears. She was too aware of her recent dream, too conscious of Tilly's tragic situation. It was impossible to remain distanced and impassive.

She tried for a smile, but it felt rather wobbly. 'There's not a strong resemblance,' she said. 'Although Chelsea has green eyes like yours.'

At this, Tilly's green eyes widened and Kate knew she must be wondering exactly who was responsible for the striking colouring. *Please don't ask me about Stan. I couldn't handle that now.*

'What do they do?'

It took Kate a moment to compute this new question. 'Pippa and Chelsea?'

'Yes.'

At least this was easier to answer. 'Pippa's an occupational therapist. She works mainly with old folk. In nursing homes. And Chelsea's a lawyer, just starting out.'

'So they're brainy.'

'They did well at school, yes.'

Tilly's solemn expression continued as she digested this information.

Watching her, Kate couldn't resist asking, 'Do you like school?'

'Sometimes.' At last, Tilly took a sip of her drink and Kate remembered that her own avocado toast would now be cold. Crossing back to the table, she picked up a slice and took her first bite.

'What are the schools like up here?' Tilly asked.

I have no idea. A corner of the toast wedged uncomfortably in Kate's throat. She swallowed and it seemed to scrape all the way down. The pain did nothing to ease her tension, but it was time to set Tilly straight.

'Look,' she said. 'Before we start talking too much about schools, I need to ring your mother's lawyer. You must understand, this has all come out of the blue for me. I'm not sure I . . .' It was the worst moment to hesitate, but Kate couldn't quite finish this sentence.

Now it was Tilly's throat that jerked and her green eyes glistened with tears. 'You don't want me.'

Help – help – help.

'I knew this would happen.' The girl's voice was shaky now. 'When I saw how you were doing up that van, I knew you probably had all kinds of plans to take off.'

'Well, yes – I . . .' While she was floundering to find the best way to answer this challenge, Kate was distracted by a sound coming from outside. The purr of a motor.

Looking towards the window, she saw a mud-splattered yellow tradie's van making its way up the track. *Flint the Sparkie* was written in spiky black letters on the van's side.

Damn. She'd totally forgotten that she'd arranged for an electrician to come today.

She needed advice about the wiring in her van and had decided she wanted help from an expert, rather than relying on the info on various blogs and websites. She'd found Liam Flint's number in an old phone book that the owner had left in the house.

Now, as Tilly stood waiting for an answer, the van came to a stop and a man climbed out – tall, middle aged, with dark curly hair and dressed in khaki overalls. He was the last person Kate wanted to see.

Or perhaps he was the perfect excuse to escape.

* * *

As soon as Kate headed outside to talk to the tradie, Tilly was already composing another message to her friends.

I know she's working out how to get rid of me. But she's not going to tell me. She's going to keep me hanging . . .

No question, Tilly's life totally sucked.

She'd thought it had been bad before – after the accident and everything. But at least then, even in the darkest depths of that terrible time, she'd had her friends and a couple of kindly teachers at school and they'd more or less known what she'd been going through and had tried to show that they cared.

Even Jed had done his best – all through those first days of helpless heartbreak and crying, and later, during the horrible weeks that had followed. He'd taken Tilly to the movies, and had cooked Mexican tacos almost as good as her mum's, and had let her go for sleepovers at Zara's. He'd even sat down and talked with her about her mum whenever she'd needed to.

Now, she had none of that. No friends, no school, no Jed. Just this Kate woman who already had two perfect daughters and who was trying to work out how to get rid of her.

It was so effing unfair. Just awful to realise that nobody here could have any idea of the bleak and bottomless loneliness that swamped her.

Tilly was tempted to scream and smash plates. Throw stuff. Too bad if it made Kate hate her. Kate already hated her anyway.

Scowling through the window, Tilly watched Kate outside with the tradie. The two of them were standing there in the yard together, chatting away, and Kate was smiling at him. He was tall and big shouldered and she had to tilt her head back to look up at him. She was pointing to the van and waving her arms around.

And she didn't look at all worried and tense now, not the way she looked whenever she talked to Tilly. She seemed happy and worked up in an excited kind of way, like the van was the most interesting thing in the world.

Or maybe it was the guy who was so interesting. Whatever. Just watching her smile like that made Tilly sick. And sadder and madder than ever.

Her fingers closed around the glass she'd been holding and she was gripped by an urge to smash it down on the kitchen countertop. Except that she kinda knew deep down that smashing a glass might feel good, but it would only make everything else worse.

Then again . . .

Tilly cast a despairing glance around the kitchen, at the breakfast things still on the table. The dirty plates and mugs. Place mats that needed wiping. Toast crumbs on the kitchen bench, and a scattering of avocado skins and lemon halves. Spilled coffee grains.

She thought about her mother's clean and sparkling kitchen. Her mum had always loved to keep everything super neat and tidy, totally uncluttered.

'Tidy home, tidy mind,' Tilly's mum had liked to say, but her mum had worked as a cleaner in other people's homes so she'd known how disgustingly messy some people could be.

Still, her housekeeping tips had pretty much filtered through to her daughter. And right now, Tilly had nothing better to do. So maybe it wouldn't kill her to tidy up this kitchen.

Just for the hell of it.

Or just for her mum.

CHAPTER EIGHT

Wednesday night, rehearsal night, had for years now been Olivia's favourite night of the week. Even in the quiet times of the year when the Burralea players weren't auditioning or preparing for their major productions, a core group would gather in the community hall on these weekday evenings.

Sitting around an ancient silky oak dining table, they would read through scripts, sampling different types of plays and taking turns to try various parts. Most evenings they also brought something to eat – a pizza, cheese and crackers, slices of quiche – and with the addition of wine, the evening could become quite social.

Josie was always there of course, along with Peter and Hamish and Heidi and Derek, and sometimes Margot would be there, quietly painting a piece for a set, or mending a costume or taking care of the washing-up. They all knew each other's foibles, and despite this, for the most part, still managed to enjoy each other's company.

In recent years, for Olivia, these players had become the closest thing she had to a family. Like true theatrical types, they even greeted each other with hugs, and heaven knew they were the only hugs Olivia received these days.

Tonight, of course, the players would be in full swing rehearsal mode. And Margot would be strutting on the stage playing Lady X. Olivia's mind boggled at that unlikely prospect. Meanwhile, here *she* was, at home alone. With her foot up, still resting the blasted ankle, having eaten yet another heated-up serving of chicken casserole, and watching some silly quiz show on television.

Olivia's one consolation was the glass of whisky at her side, a hefty dram of a particularly fine Scottish single malt that Rolf Anders had brought her. Dear Rolf. He really was a sweet and thoughtful friend. Olivia knew that the local gossipers could never understand why his wife had divorced him. He'd confided in Olivia, however, that Lisa had never forgiven him for giving up a thriving business as a builder to become a writer.

No doubt Lisa had regretted this decision later when Rolf proved to be a hugely successful author. But by then he'd moved to the Tablelands and, for a while, rumours had been flying thick and fast that he'd had an affair with Emily Hargreaves, the owner of the local newspaper. Olivia had never questioned Rolf on this delicate point, but like most newspapers in small country towns, the *Burralea Bugle* had now sadly folded and Emily spent most of her time out west on her husband's cattle property. Rolf, on the other hand, had made many trips back and forth to America.

He'd set his latest blockbuster novel in Washington, DC, and subsequently, new rumours were rife about a romance with a glamorous woman in the diplomatic corps. Olivia knew this rumour to be true, actually, and she was pleased for Rolf, even if the affair was necessarily long distance. But now, musing along these lines, she couldn't help remembering her own time in America. So long ago, almost fifty years now, and yet her memories of moving to Southern California to join Michael were still painfully intact.

Her desire to become an actor had been actively supported by her family, who'd always been involved in the arts. Her father had been a jazz pianist, her mother a potter of some renown, and her sister, who'd been a talented viola player, had scored a spot in the Australian Chamber Orchestra. So when Olivia had set her sights on studying at NIDA, her parents had given her every encouragement.

She'd met Michael Carruthers in her first year. In his youth, he'd been even more devastatingly handsome than he was these days and from the moment Olivia had first set eyes on him, she'd been smitten. It wasn't until their second year that they'd become lovers, and then in their third and final year they'd both been the stars of their drama class.

Olivia had scarcely been able to credit her good fortune when she'd been cast with Michael in *Romeo and Juliet*. That year, they'd been the golden couple. No one in theatrical circles had doubted that they were destined for huge careers abroad. London, Broadway, Hollywood. They could take their pick.

Oh, the excitement of that glorious final season in Sydney. Olivia's life had been enchanted. With Michael she'd rented a loft apartment in a converted warehouse. It housed the tiniest possible kitchen, but had an enormous bed under a sloping ceiling. So romantic. And at the theatre there'd been deafening applause, flower-filled dressing rooms, parties and champagne, not to mention the constant flash of cameras whenever Olivia and Michael appeared in public.

For aspiring young stars, that season had been the perfect launch. Olivia had been foolish enough to dream that she might be the next Katharine Hepburn or Meryl Streep and she couldn't wait to arrive in Los Angeles . . . City of Angels . . .

Until Fate intervened.

No, don't think about that. Stop right now, before you end up in a ridiculous mess.

Perhaps the universe was listening to her plea, for at that very moment, a sudden knock sounded on Olivia's front door.

'Who is it?' she called sharply, knowing that most of her friends would be busy at the theatre, and hoping she wouldn't have to drag herself out of her chair.

'Rolf,' came the reply.

'Oh, Rolf.' Her voice lost its sharpness immediately and of course she promptly got to her feet and reached for the crutches. 'Coming,' she called. And, really, only a few steps were required to open the door to greet him.

The evening was chilly and Rolf was wearing a bulky jacket and blue and green tartan scarf. 'How lovely to see you,' Olivia said. And then, with a cheeky smile, 'You haven't brought me another bottle of Laphroaig, by any chance?'

Rolf laughed. 'Sorry, no. Have you already finished the first one?'

'Good heavens, no.' Olivia also chuckled. 'It was my poor attempt at a joke.'

'Well, I *have* brought chocolate-coated ginger.' As Rolf came through the doorway, he produced a box wrapped in glamorous emerald foil.

'Oh, my.' Olivia recognised hand-crafted chocolates from a local dairy. 'How perfect.'

'I knew you were stuck here and missing another rehearsal tonight and I thought you might need cheering up.'

'Rolf, that's incredibly sweet of you.' Olivia was deeply touched and she felt almost choked up as she gestured to a chair. 'Take a seat, won't you?' Then, seeing his gaze drift to her whisky glass, she added, 'Actually, before you get comfortable, you might like to fetch yourself a drink?'

He grinned. 'Why not?'

'Wonderful. You should find whatever you need in the kitchen.'

'And how about I also bring you a top-up?'

Olivia eyed the thin layer of whisky left in her glass. 'Just a little one, perhaps.'

With another smile, Rolf disappeared and was back in no time with a crystal glass and the Laphroaig bottle, plus a little dish filled with fresh ice cubes. After the drinks were organised and he'd shed his jacket, which he hung on the coat-stand by the door, he settled comfortably into one of Olivia's cushion-lined cane lounge chairs.

'So, how's the ankle?' he asked politely.

'Oh, thanks for asking, but it's much the same. Such a nuisance, although I suppose I should be grateful that I don't need surgery.'

'There's that,' Rolf agreed.

'It's just as well, as I'm afraid I don't have private health insurance.' Strangely, Olivia felt comfortable admitting this to Rolf. She knew it was silly to try to hide the reality of her straitened means, but she would hate anyone else at the theatre to know how very carefully she had to manage her meagre funds. Whenever she needed to go to Centrelink, she always parked in the Woolworths car park and hoped no one noticed her slinking across the road.

Now, carefully, she asked, 'Did you call in at the rehearsal?'

'Just for a moment or two.'

When Rolf made no further comment, Olivia had to try again. 'I suppose you know Josie has cast Margot in the Lady X role?'

He nodded.

'And . . . have you seen Margot on stage?'

'Only briefly.'

Their gazes met and held, but Rolf's expression remained inscrutable. Olivia suppressed her urge to sigh. 'I'm not going to ask —'

'That's very wise of you, my dear.'

It wasn't quite the response she'd expected or needed, and now she wasn't sure how to react. Perhaps Rolf and the rest of the players had together decided that she should calmly accept Margot as her replacement. But none of them could have any idea how hard this was for her.

A small silence fell, and Olivia and Rolf both took sips of the wonderfully rich and delicious scotch.

As Rolf set his glass down, he said, 'I think you mentioned once that you knew the actor Michael Carruthers?'

Good heavens. Why now? Tonight of all nights? Olivia had been trying so hard to forget.

'Yes,' she said eventually. 'Why do you ask?'

'I made a quick trip to Sydney last month. There's been some interest in *Next Stop Mars* and —'

Olivia couldn't help interrupting. 'But the Burralea performance will still be the world premiere, won't it?' Even if she could no longer be on stage, this arrangement was sacrosanct, surely?

'Yes, yes, of course. Don't worry, that's a given. But I was talking to theatre folk down in Sydney.' Rolf gave an easy shrug. 'And Michael Carruthers happened to be involved in one of the discussions.'

'You didn't mention me?' There was no way she could hide her tension.

'Well, at the time, you were still playing Lady X, so yes, your name did come up.'

'Oh.' Olivia sat in stunned silence. Dazed. Of course, she had kept an eye on Michael's career. In Australia he was still a well-known name and she had seen him countless times over the years on both big and small screens. 'How – how is Michael?' she asked, wishing she didn't sound so cautious, almost frightened.

At least Rolf seemed quite relaxed. 'It might be an unfair comment, but I thought he was showing his age.'

'Well, yes.' Olivia eyed her useless foot and gave a wry smile. 'Age catches up with all of us eventually, doesn't it?'

Rolf, who wasn't much younger than she or Michael, smiled sympathetically. 'Didn't you tell me once that you two were at NIDA together?'

Olivia frowned. Had she told Rolf that? 'I suppose I may have done,' she admitted. 'It's true. And I was in Hollywood for a little while when Michael was there, too.'

'Really? I hadn't realised you spent time in Hollywood.'

Oh, Lord. Why on earth had she mentioned *that* place? Now, Rolf would realise that Michael had soared to stardom in the US, while her own career had never got off the ground.

Nervous now, she reached for the scotch glass, needing a fortifying sip. Nevertheless, the relentless memories came flooding back.

'Olivia.' Rolf was leaning forward, his elbows resting on his knees, as he watched her with an intense, worried frown. 'I seem to have upset you.'

'No,' she protested, giving a swift wave of her hand in an attempt to brush his concern aside. 'I'm all right. I'm fine.' But she was *nowhere near* all right. She was falling apart, remembering those terrible six months before she'd finally travelled to LA . . . when she'd stayed behind in Australia. Alone.

Olivia had never dreamed that an IUD could fail, and three months had passed before the exact reason for her missed periods had been diagnosed. Michael was appalled. They couldn't put off their plans for Hollywood. She would have to terminate the pregnancy.

For Olivia, that had been impossible. She could never destroy a life that she and Michael had created. Despite her shock and although the baby could not have been more than a few inches long, she had known almost straight away that she loved it.

Michael had pleaded with her, had put up every possible argument. The agents in LA were impatient and timing was all important. This chance in Hollywood might never come again. Olivia, however, had been equally stubborn. In the end, he'd headed off for America on his own, while she'd stayed behind, hiding away in an aunt's house at Katoomba in the Blue Mountains, where she'd given birth to a beautiful baby boy.

Oh, dear heaven. In the years that followed, not a single day had passed without her remembering precise details of that dear precious babe. His little eyes, slate grey, staring and unfocused. The small frown furrowing his brow. His dark hair still damp. The perfect little fingers and toes. The tiny birthmark on his neck like a bird in flight.

'Olivia. I'm sorry. I *have* upset you.'

Olivia blinked and was dismayed to feel dampness in her eyes and to read deep concern in Rolf's face.

'No,' she said quickly. '*I* should be apologising. I was just side-tracked for a moment. Remembering . . . something . . .'

Thank heavens she had a lifetime of acting to draw on. Now, she managed to flash a smile to Rolf. 'Why don't we open those chocolates you brought and you can tell me what Michael's up to these days.'

She knew Rolf was reluctant to drop the subject of her time in Hollywood, but he was too considerate to push her when she wasn't ready to confide. As she unwrapped the box and they bit into delicious nubs of chocolate-coated ginger, he told her instead about the new role Michael had landed with the Sydney Theatre Company. And then about the astonishing possibility that *Next Stop Mars* might be performed in the Sydney Opera House.

'And who knows where it will go from there?' said Olivia.

Rolf nodded. 'I honestly wasn't expecting a huge fuss, but word's out that Carruthers might be playing Lord X and now my agent says his phone is running hot.'

This news stung Olivia far more than it probably should have. But for the first time in decades, she and Michael were connected to the same play. However, he would once again be the toast of the theatre world, while she was left behind in the shadows.

She was determined, though, that she mustn't let her personal pain sour her recognition of Rolf's success. 'You have another hit on your hands,' she said. '*Next Stop Mars* will be as popular as your books. Maybe even more so. They might even make it into a movie.'

'Don't let's get ahead of ourselves,' said Rolf. 'But Carruthers could certainly attract a lot more attention for the play.' His face twisted in a wry smile. 'He's a huge talent and can be very charming, but I have to confess, Olivia – I haven't totally warmed to the guy.'

She wasn't sure whether to laugh at this comment, or cry. Instead, she asked Rolf what he was going to write next and he obligingly bounced a few ideas around. Throwing spaghetti at the wall, he called it. Testing ideas to see which ones might stick.

Olivia found this surprisingly interesting and fun. They had a few laughs and she even threw in a few ideas of her own and, to her surprise, Rolf actually took out his phone and made note of one or two of her suggestions.

Thus, the evening rolled along so pleasantly that she almost stopped thinking about the rehearsal going ahead without her. By the time Rolf left, she was feeling mellowed by his good company and the two scotches she'd downed. Perhaps, tonight, she would sleep well for a change.

She kept herself busy for the next little while, hobbling about on her crutches and getting ready for bed. But once she was settled with the pillows just so, a glass of water and her current bedtime reading at her side, the bedside lamp glowing softly – the relentless memories returned.

Michael. Los Angeles. Tinseltown . . . shiny, bright and unreal.

By the time Olivia had joined Michael in LA, he'd already been there for six months and had landed a role with a major production company. He was also deeply embedded into the Hollywood culture.

Nevertheless, he'd seemed pleased to see Olivia. He'd actually told her that he still loved her, but even with his huge acting talent, he hadn't been able to make this sound convincing, and he certainly hadn't been willing to discuss the subject of the baby son she'd left behind.

Of course, this hurt Olivia deeply. Giving her baby up had been the most agonising decision she'd ever made. Her parents and even her kindly aunt had felt it was for the best, however. As fellow artists, they'd been keen for Olivia to pursue her brilliant career, and they were sure the baby would go to a good home, to people who really wanted him.

Michael wasn't prepared to listen to any of this, while Olivia had wanted to protest, to make a scene, to force him to feel her pain, to understand the gut-wrenching sacrifice she'd made. But Michael had given her no choice. From the start he'd made it clear that he'd never wanted the pregnancy to go ahead. The baby was her problem. End of story.

Despite this tension, he'd been happy enough for Olivia to move in with him, and he'd taken her with him to all the glittering parties he was invited to. But by then, he was well entrenched in these glamorous circles, and it was patently clear to Olivia that there were other women in his life.

It was LA in the early seventies, after all, and Michael Carruthers in Hollywood was more astonishingly attractive and sexy than ever. And, of course, the women were all impossibly beautiful and threw themselves at him without shame.

Despite the distress this caused, Olivia would never blame Michael's behaviour for her own lack of success in Hollywood. She knew her problem had not been a lack of looks or talent, but more a lack of momentum. The choice she'd made before leaving Australia had continued to haunt her, disintegrating her usual confidence and pizzazz.

Amidst the dazzle and excitement of Hollywood, she'd been listless. No doubt these days her condition would be recognised as depression.

And now, remembering those bleak and dark days, Olivia shivered. She pulled the doona higher, and opened the novel she'd planned to read. But the pages held no interest this evening and the doona didn't seem to offer any warmth. The cold was inside her.

Don't think about it. But she was lost. Helpless. The tortuous thoughts kept spinning.

Perhaps the hardest thing – the cruel reality she'd never quite been able to accept – was that her son had never tried to find her. But it was so foolish to keep wondering. He would be well and truly middle aged now and if he'd ever been interested in finding her, he would have done so years ago.

Resting her head once more on the pillow, Olivia closed her eyes. And, as she had so many, many times in the past, she steeled herself to be stronger. She could never forget her baby, but she could block out that winter in Los Angeles when she'd felt hurt and helpless, with no one to talk to. It was time to think positively once again, to remember that she had, at least, been sensible enough to break away from Michael and move on with her life.

Olivia had, in fact, escaped quite quickly away from LA and over the next couple of decades she'd worked in the UK, mostly in regional repertory theatres. Here, she'd been gradually, thankfully, conscious of a sense of healing. She'd had a few affairs along the way and they'd been fun for the most part. But then she'd met Gerald Northey, an actor from Yorkshire and an absolute darling.

Such happy years she and Gerry had enjoyed together – a later-in-life romance that she had never expected but had found quite perfect. Olivia always felt stronger whenever she remembered

Gerry's gentle good humour and cheeky smile, the sense of deep companionship she'd shared with him.

After he'd died from a heart attack, she had come back to Australia. It was almost time to retire and she'd travelled around the country, mainly through regional towns, preferring, for her own very good reasons, to keep away from the metropolitan cities. And yes, Michael Carruthers's return to Sydney had been one of those reasons.

Somewhat to her own bemusement, Olivia had finally chosen to settle on the Atherton Tablelands in Far North Queensland. The rolling hills had reminded her of the Yorkshire Dales where she and Gerry had been so especially happy. And in quaint and pretty Burralea, she was now contented enough with her humble cottage and garden. Although she might have died of boredom if it hadn't been for the little theatre.

These days, Olivia's connection to the theatre was so deep in her veins, she feared she might not survive without it. For her, each season and each new play was a chance to step into a new world, where she could, for a few months, spend time being someone else, at least in her imagination.

She relished every aspect of the theatre – learning new lines, turning up for rehearsals where she could drop occasional subtle hints to Josie, although the woman was a surprisingly competent director for such a little, out-of-the-way place.

And Olivia especially looked forward to the building excitement that always gripped the players as they neared Opening Night. The costume fittings, the dress rehearsals, the interviews for news stories, although these were now, sadly, published in the *Cairns Post*, rather than their local paper.

And it was always fun to see the placards on lampposts and on a noticeboard in the post office, or in the bakery's front window. But the little theatre wasn't merely a source of joy for herself. It gave the whole town something to look forward to. In the street, in the supermarket, people would smile, or send a wave, or even ask about her upcoming role.

Small town excitement was sufficient for Olivia Matthews these days. But she couldn't bear to be left out.

She *mustn't* be left out.

CHAPTER NINE

Burralea was a picture-postcard town, Kate had decided – the old-fashioned sort of town that tourists loved, with quaint cafés and a rather grand, central two-storey pub. A town with gardens spilling onto footpaths and lampposts decorated with flower-filled hanging baskets, but a tiny town where very little happened, as far as Kate could tell.

There was, at least, a small supermarket, a bakery, a newsagency and a hardware store, so the place catered for most of her needs, and Kate had never minded before that she hardly knew anyone here. Being a newcomer had given her privacy, and these days obscurity was her friend.

She hadn't planned on being in the district long enough to settle in. But this morning she was aware there were serious drawbacks in keeping to herself.

Now, having left Tilly to choose something for their lunch from the Burralea bakery, Kate ducked into the hardware store. She felt a little uncomfortable about cornering Margot Cooper with her new problem, but the woman had always been helpful and friendly whenever Kate had popped in to buy gear for the van. Wood glue, varnish, self-tapping screws, whatever she'd needed, Margot always seemed to have good advice about the best choices. And anyway, she was pretty much the only person Kate knew in Burralea. And Kate needed advice about Tilly.

The whole issue had pretty much reached a climax when Kate had arrived back in the house after her prolonged chat with the electrician. Her head had been buzzing, first with Pippa's baby news and then with Liam Flint's suggestions for wiring the van and managing wi-fi and overhead lighting. Not to mention the electrician's engaging manner and his heartening enthusiasm for her project.

All of which meant she'd been somewhat distracted when she'd come into the kitchen. But then, woah!

Tilly hadn't merely tidied the kitchen. She'd washed the dishes, dried them and put them away, had wiped the countertops and left the sink gleaming as if it had been polished, with a shininess far brighter than Kate had ever bothered to achieve.

Even the floor had been swept.

Kate was quite overcome. She knew very well that neither of her daughters would have voluntarily produced a clean-up like that when they were thirteen. She'd always had to beg and bribe Pippa and Chelsea just to keep their own bedrooms respectable.

Now. This. Spotless perfection.

Kate had tried to imagine how Tilly must have felt when she'd embarked on this surprising task, unasked. Chances were, she would never know, but she'd interpreted the pristine kitchen as a silent plea – a plea that had pierced Kate's heart.

For heaven's sake, Tilly was only thirteen and she was com-pletely alone in the world, apart from a ratfink, absentee father and two half-sisters, all of whom she'd never met. And in that moment of painful clarity, Kate had realised she had no choice. She would have to find a way to help the kid.

First, though, she had needed to clarify the situation with Angela's lawyer. Christina Paxton was the name on the card Jed had given Kate and this was also the person who quickly answered Kate's call.

'Yes, I've been expecting to hear from you,' Christina said.

'I couldn't ring straight away. I thought it might be awkward if Tilly was listening in,' Kate told her.

'Where's Tilly now?'

'In my house. I'm outside in my van.'

'Okay, I'll try to be brief.' And the woman was thoroughly businesslike as she went on to explain. 'Now – it's fortunate that Angela prepared a will and it's great that she named you as guardian.'

Kate was about to jump in with a 'but' when Christina continued.

'But you can't actually leave a child to someone,' she said. 'They're not a piece of property.'

'Of course they're not.' This was good to hear, and yesterday Kate would have jumped at the chance of a possible loophole. But now —

'Your best option,' Christina said, steamrolling on, 'is to ask the Family Court to make an order, naming you as the person who has parental responsibility.'

Parental responsibility. The words had an ominous ring. 'There's no other alternative?' Kate asked.

'You mean you'd rather not take on this responsibility?'

'I'm still coming to terms with the idea.'

'That's understandable.'

'But I know her mother didn't want foster care.'

'No, Angela's intentions were rather clear in that regard.'

'And there doesn't seem to be anyone else.' Kate looked around her van at all the work she'd done, the panelling, the shelves. 'So what's involved in getting this court order?'

Christina explained that the court would need Stan's consent for the order, or every evidence that they had tried to get him involved.

'Of course, you could just go with no court order and leave it as a casual arrangement,' Christina admitted. 'In those situations, the schools usually just roll with it. The only problem might be if someone complained. That's unlikely, but a possibility, I guess. And down the track, if Tilly wanted to get her licence, or a passport, she'd need a legal guardian.'

'I see.' Kate had thanked Christina and asked if she could think this over. After that, she'd gone in search of Tilly. She'd found her in her bedroom, lying on top of the neatly made bed with her eyes closed. There was no sign of any scattered belongings and her bags seemed to be packed and ready for imminent departure. As Kate tiptoed into the room, she could see tears seeping from beneath the girl's dark lashes.

She spoke quietly. 'Tilly.'

There was an emerald flash as Tilly opened her eyes, and her expression was fierce.

'Thanks so much for cleaning the kitchen,' Kate said. 'It was such a lovely surprise. You did an amazing job.'

Tilly's response was a one-shouldered shrug.

Carefully, Kate lowered herself to the edge of the bed. 'I've just been talking to your mother's lawyer,' she said next and she could immediately sense the way the girl stiffened. 'She confirmed everything Jed told me about your mum's will. Angela named me as your guardian.' After a beat, she said, 'She also explained that we need to apply to the Family Court to make this official.'

At this, Tilly launched bolt upright, her eyes wide with fear, her cheeks suddenly drained of colour. 'But you don't want to. You want to send me to a foster home.'

Kate shook her head. 'You're not being sent anywhere,' she said gently.

'What do you mean?'

'I mean you're staying here. With me.'

'But you don't want me.'

Kate inwardly winced as the guilty charge hit home. 'I never said that.' She tried to smile, but wasn't very successful. 'I'll admit I was shocked when Jed turned up without any warning. But now . . .' She paused, hunting for the right words. She could hardly admit that she was taking Tilly in against her will and because she could find no alternative. 'I'd like you to stay here.'

Oh, help. She'd done it. She'd spoken the fateful words out loud. And those words were surely as binding as any public vow. She was committed.

Tilly, however, was frowning at her. 'But what about your van?'

Yeah. Good question. Kate stamped quickly on the rising panic that threatened. She couldn't abandon her dreams. She wouldn't. She mustn't.

'I'll certainly keep working on the van,' she said carefully. 'And, well, maybe we'll just have to see how things pan out. One thing I've learned since I started the renovation is that it's best to take things one step at a time. So, for now, as I see it, the first step for us is finding out about the best school for you.'

Kate hadn't really been expecting a smile, or a hug of appreciation, but she was making a magnanimous gesture, after all. Tilly's reaction, however, could only be described as a kind of dismal resignation, which hadn't been exactly heartening.

At least, this morning in the hardware store, Margot greeted Kate with her customary warm smile.

The shopkeeper had been transferring tins of paint from a trolley onto shelves. 'Hi there,' she said. 'How are you today, Kate? How's the van coming along?'

'So, so.' Kate tilted her hand from side to side to suggest her uneven progress. And then, taking a step closer and lowering her voice, she added, 'But, if you don't mind, I need a little advice about something totally unrelated to the van.'

'Oh?' Having neatly positioned three tins of paint just so, Margot turned to give Kate her full attention. 'So, how can I help?'

Kate swallowed. 'It's just that I believe your children go to the local high school?'

Margot's eyebrows lifted at this, which was hardly surprising. 'That's right,' she replied cautiously.

'Sorry. I know this is out of the blue, but I saw you with your son and daughter the other day and – and . . .' Kate swallowed again, even more nervously. 'And now I have a young girl staying with me. Well, I'm going to be caring for her, actually. For – for the next little while.'

'Goodness.' Margot quickly tried to cover her obvious surprise with a polite smile. 'How nice.'

'Yeah.' Kate was still getting used to her rash decision.

'Well, my kids go to the local high school,' Margot said. 'And it's great. They're getting good results and I'm very happy with them there.'

This was good news, at least. Kate nodded. 'This girl, Tilly, is thirteen and she's in Year Eight, but she knows no one and —'

'My Bridie's in Year Eight!' Margot broke in with a broad grin. 'She has a lovely group of friends.' Then she frowned, as if stopping to give this some thought. 'It's a pity I'm not free in the afternoons, I'd invite you both over for afternoon tea, so the girls could meet. You'll have to come around for dinner instead.'

'Oh, I wouldn't want you to go to any trouble.' Kate was very conscious that Margot worked in the shop all day. Surely, the last thing she needed was having to cater for extra dinner guests?

Unfortunately, Kate was also uncertain about how Tilly would behave. The girl had shown no sign that she was looking forward to making new friends. She still spent most of her time on her phone, Snapchatting with the friends she'd left behind in Cairns.

'Oh, it won't be any trouble,' Margot responded, chuckling. 'Don't expect anything too flash, though. My meals are never in the gourmet category.'

'Gosh, it's very kind of you.' Kate was hovering between feeling awkward about the intrusion and grateful for the woman's warmth and generosity. 'Let me bring a dessert then.'

'How lovely. That's wonderful.' Margot beamed. 'It's a deal.'

'I should warn you, though,' Kate added. 'Tilly's going through a rough patch. Her mother died not so long ago.'

'Goodness.' Surely they weren't tears in Margot's eyes? 'The poor love.' She reached out her hand, but didn't quite touch Kate's arm. 'That can't be easy for you?'

'No,' Kate admitted. 'Tilly's – she's a distant relative and she's had to move up here from Cairns. I'm afraid she's struggling to settle in.'

Margot nodded. 'Don't worry, I'll warn Bridie and Nate to cut her a little slack. What did you say her name was again?'

'Tilly. Tilly Dent.'

'Cute,' Margot said with a smile. 'That shouldn't be hard to remember.'

They set a time for dinner the next evening, and after thanking her again, Kate left her to continue stacking the paint tins.

'Bridie?' Tilly repeated with a derisory snort. 'What kind of parents call their daughter Bridie? Haven't they heard of feminism?'

It was probably just as well that Kate was driving and staring straight ahead, which meant that Tilly couldn't see her expression.

'What are your friends in Cairns called?' she asked.

'My best friend's name is Zara. And then there's Betsy and Frankie and Raven.'

Kate smiled and was tempted to respond that Bridie's parents were almost certainly of the same ilk as those who called their daughters Tilly or Raven or – Frankie. Loving. Contemporary. Looking for something a little different.

'I think Bridie's a pretty name,' she said instead. 'It's like Emily or Lucy – just an old name that's back in fashion. I don't think it's supposed to have anything to do with actual brides.'

Just the same, Kate was surprised to hear a thirteen-year-old voicing concerns about feminism. It certainly showed how little she knew about this new generation of teenagers. 'It's very good of Margot to invite us,' she said. 'I hope you won't be snooty or critical.'

Tilly merely sighed.

CHAPTER TEN

That evening, everyone made an effort. Tilly could see that Kate and the girl, Bridie, and her mother were all trying to make her feel welcome. But she couldn't help wishing it was Zara's house in Cairns that she was walking into.

She and Zara would have headed straight down the hall to Zara's bedroom to listen to music. In that haven of purple walls draped with glittery strings of lights, they'd have chatted away madly about the usual problems of zits and split ends, about clothes and school, and whether they believed the suss claims the supposedly popular girls made about their escapades with boys.

Meanwhile, Tilly's and Zara's mums would have planned something simple for dinner, even possibly takeaway, so they could hurry straight to the deck for pre-dinner wine and a happy gasbagging session, with their feet up on the railings, almost as carefree as their daughters.

Remembering these nights, Tilly could almost hear the tinkle of her mother's laughter in the air, and as she and Kate walked up to the modest little house in Burralea, she was hit by a horrible whack of loss and longing. Fortunately, there was one thing that managed to distract her. A chimney.

Tilly had never seen a stone chimney on the outside of an ordinary timber house before. And once they were inside the house, which again was quite ordinary, with timber floors and somewhat shabby, out-of-date furniture, she saw that the main lounge room wall was home to a proper open fireplace. This was also made of stone, while logs of firewood were neatly stacked in a brickwork alcove beside it.

Sadly, the evening wasn't quite cold enough to call for a fire, but Tilly could imagine bright flames leaping and flickering on wintry nights, making the room wonderfully cosy and romantic. And that thought was intriguing enough to lift the worst of the heavy gloom from her, at least while the introductions were made.

Bridie was a rather tall and skinny girl, with mousy, curly hair that Zara would no doubt suggest needed a good colour treatment. She had a nice smile, though. And her mother was like a lot of mothers Tilly had seen on parent–teacher nights, a bit frumpy and plump, but pleasant and friendly. She insisted that Tilly must call her Margot and not Mrs Cooper, which was kinda cool.

There was excitement all round when Kate produced the tiramisu she'd made for dessert. So, all in all, they got off to a reasonable start.

Bridie's dad had remained in an armchair, watching TV with the sound turned low. But when his wife called his name, he rose and nodded to Kate and Tilly, and he said, 'Good evening,' politely, if somewhat distantly.

Tilly had been hoping he might be a chatty, smiley kind of dad, the sort who came forward to shake hands and perhaps crack a silly joke. But at least he was a visible, flesh-and-blood father, who actually lived under the same roof as his kids. Neither she nor Zara had been that lucky.

Bridie's brother, Nate, was also there, but he was hanging back in the hallway and looking mega shy and awkward. Tilly couldn't help flashing him a quick smile of sympathy, but it seemed to make him blush.

After that, she wondered if Bridie might take her to her bedroom, but apparently dinner was pretty much ready to be served. So they all sat on hard wooden chairs around a dining table, while Margot set off to the kitchen to fetch a lamb casserole.

An uncomfortable silence fell then and, once again, Tilly couldn't help wishing she was at Zara's house, giggling and gossiping and listening to music. More often than not, their mums would let them eat dinner in their bedrooms. Sitting cross-legged on the bed, or on the floor with a massive pile of cushions, they would watch a movie on Zara's laptop, with one of the mothers occasionally popping in just to make sure they weren't watching porn.

Lost in memories of those happy evenings, Tilly felt her phone vibrate in her pocket. It was sure to be Zara, sending a message, and she was desperate to check it, but Kate had given her strict instructions about phone etiquette for this evening. It took huge self-control to ignore it, but Tilly was saved by Bridie asking her a question.

'Do you play guitar?'

Tilly shook her head. In Cairns she'd played cello in the school orchestra, but her mum couldn't afford to buy her an instrument of her own, so she'd had to borrow a school cello for practice at home. The cello was another thing she'd had to leave behind.

Bridie tried again. 'What about sport? I play netball.'

Tilly shrugged. 'I play soccer.'

'So do I,' piped up Nate, from across the table.

'I'm not very good at soccer, though,' Tilly felt compelled to admit.

'Me neither,' the boy responded with a shy grin.

'Oh, Nate, you're a fine soccer player,' his mother insisted a little too loudly, as she came back through the doorway carrying a steaming casserole pot, which she set on a round cork tablemat. 'You just need more confidence.'

Tilly saw the doubtful face the boy pulled and she couldn't help sending him another discreet smile. When he blushed again, however, she thought maybe it was time to hold back on the sympathy.

Bridie, who'd been watching this exchange, posed a new question. 'So, what *do* you like, Tilly? Boys?'

Tilly guessed the girl's patience might be wearing thin. After all, this was mostly a charade to keep the adults happy. 'I like books,' she said. 'And music.' And then, 'Most things really.' Although she certainly wasn't prepared to air her opinion on boys.

Margot was serving up plates of lamb chops floating in a sauce loaded with carrots and peas. And as the plates were passed around, Kate posed a question of her own. 'So if you like books, Tilly, do you also like English at school?'

'Sure. It's probably my best subject.'

'That's great.' Kate looked particularly pleased.

Tilly shrugged. Her mum had always been more interested in her marks for Maths and Science, convinced they would lead to the best jobs. 'What's the big deal with English?' she asked.

'It's more or less my line of work,' said Kate. 'Writing and editing.'

'Really?' For some reason, Tilly hadn't thought of Kate as a working woman. She'd assumed she was retired, or simply that she didn't need to earn a living. She'd been renovating the van, after all, and planning to travel.

Until I landed on her doorstep.

With that thought, Tilly was anxious all over again.

'I've got to say you have the perfect job for the van life, Kate.' This came from Bridie's father, as Margot dished up the final plate. 'With emails and wi-fi and everything, editing work would be so easy to take on the road.'

Oh, God. Tilly held back her cry of dismay, but this conversation was scaring the hell out of her. She realised now that the chunks of time Kate spent at her laptop were probably for her work. And Bridie's parents were making it all too clear that everyone knew about Kate's dreams for her van.

And worse, it seemed Kate even had the perfect job to make that lifestyle complete. Which could only mean that Tilly was in the absolutely wrong place. She'd ruined Kate's plans.

Deep down, Kate must hate her.

If only she could run away. Right now, at this very moment. It wouldn't be exactly easy, though, when everyone around the table was staring at her.

* * *

As Kate drove out of Burralea, along quiet, dark, country roads, Tilly, having initially fiddled with her phone, spent the trip slumped in sullen silence with her head pressed against the passenger window.

Kate was disappointed and somewhat embarrassed that Tilly hadn't even pretended to enjoy the evening. The discussion about Kate's work and the van had obviously bothered the girl. Kate had seen the instant flash of fear in her eyes, and she'd pretty much clammed up before the meal began.

The kid was so insecure. She must be on tenterhooks the whole time, waiting for Kate to ditch her.

And I came so close to doing exactly that. Could Tilly tell? *Am I really that bad at putting my own needs on hold?*

Uncomfortably, Kate found herself battling an old memory, a time years ago, when her daughter Pippa had come home from hockey practice all excited because she'd nominated her mum to be their team's manager. Which meant turning up to every game with spare jerseys and water bottles and oranges cut into quarters.

Back then, Kate had been working five days a week for a tourist magazine and her Saturdays were precious. She usually did the supermarket shopping after dropping Pippa at hockey. But when she'd told Pippa there was no way she could take on this managing role, her daughter had been devastated. She'd read it as outright rejection.

'You're always doing stuff for Chelsea's ballet,' she'd wailed.

This was true. Kate enjoyed making ballet costumes. She'd even made costumes for other kids in Chelsea's dance class if their mothers hated sewing. But hanging around every single hockey game held no appeal for her at all, and Stan couldn't be relied on as a backup.

Kate had always felt guilty about that decision, however, and she wasn't sure that Pippa had ever really forgiven her. The smallest choices could have a huge impact on kids.

Not that grown-ups were immune from the after-effects of other people's decisions. Until a few days ago, Kate had been totally focused on a post-Stan life of freedom with no commitments. Now he'd managed to snare her yet again.

But Kate knew it was toxic to look on Tilly as a problem inflicted by her ex, and as the road dipped down to a narrow bridge across a creek, she tried to start a conversation. 'Bridie seems like a nice girl,' she said.

'Mmmm,' was Tilly's limited response.

'I'm sure she'll help you to settle in at school.'

'Yeah. Maybe.' Tilly didn't sound convinced.

'You enjoyed meeting her, didn't you?'

Tilly sighed. 'She's okay, but I didn't enjoy finding out that everyone here knows you're supposed to be heading off in your van.' For the first time on this short journey, Tilly turned to Kate. 'I s'pose you'd already told them I'm a huge problem, getting in your way.'

'Of course I haven't. Tilly, I'd never say that. The only reason Margot knows about the van is because she works in the hardware store where I buy my tools and timber. But I'm sure she never meant to imply that you were a problem. No one suggested that.'

'They didn't need to say it out loud. Anyone with half a brain could work it out.' Tilly slumped even lower in her seat. 'I'm not going to that school.'

Oh, Lord, thought Kate. *I was silly to even attempt this.*

Of course, she'd known it wasn't going to be easy. Teenagers were difficult at the best of times, but a lonely and grieving teen was so much more complicated.

If she countered Tilly with an *of course you're going to school* comment, Tilly would snap back and they'd end up fighting. Trying another tack, she said carefully, 'Maybe you'd like to see a counsellor then?'

Tilly stiffened. 'No way.'

'But counsellors are specially trained. They have . . . special insights.'

'You reckon? They sent me to a counsellor at my old school. After Mum's accident and – and everything. All she wanted to do was quiz me about Jed.'

'Jed?'

'Yeah, she was sure he must be trying to have sex with me.'

Kate remembered now that this kind of suspicion was a major part of Jed's reason for bringing Tilly to her. 'She wasn't very helpful then?'

'Effing useless.'

CHAPTER ELEVEN

'So, I'm finally here for that de-frizz you've been telling me I need.'

Tammy, Burralea's popular hairdresser, beamed at Margot. 'Great decision.'

'I know you've been suggesting it for ages and I keep telling you I'm too busy.'

'A-huh,' agreed Tammy, whose own hair was currently deep aqua and styled in trendy, shaggy layers.

'But now, I'm going to be . . .' Margot hesitated. She still felt nervous about telling people that she would actually be appearing on stage.

'But now you're stepping into Olivia's shoes,' Tammy supplied.

'Oh, so you've heard?' Margot knew she shouldn't be surprised. The whole of Burralea had probably heard this news by now. And no doubt they were all shaking their heads and rolling their eyes.

'Josie was in here yesterday,' Tammy explained, gentling her voice as if she'd sensed Margot's sudden tension. 'She likes to keep me up to date with theatre news, especially as I'll be helping her out again with the hairdos and wigs.'

'Yes, of course.' Margot offered a lopsided smile to Tammy's reflection in the ornately framed salon mirror. The players were all hugely grateful for Tammy's hairdressing and wardrobe skills. 'My problem is, I'm still in a bit of a panic about the whole thing.'

Tammy patted her shoulder. 'You'll have to stop that. Josie says you'll be wonderful.'

'Really?' Margot, desperate for an honest answer, kept her gaze locked with Tammy's.

'Absolutely,' Tammy said without flinching.

Phew. Margot let out the breath she'd been holding. 'Well, that's very nice of her.' She managed a small smile. 'Actually,' she went on, as Tammy began to gently brush her tangled hair. 'I'm still wondering if it's worth trying to fix my old mop. Maybe I should just go for a wig for Lady X.'

Tammy frowned. 'Well, a wig's certainly an option for that role, but I guess that's up to Josie. She'll have the final say.'

'Well, yes, of course.'

'But wouldn't you like to have your hair looking really nice anyhow?'

Margot gave a helpless little laugh. 'Is that even possible?'

'Of course it is, woman. Don't be so down on yourself.' Tammy stopped brushing and, as her gaze met Margot's in the mirror, she gave a concerned smile. 'But I do understand why you might be a bit nervous about standing in for Olivia – it's kind of like standing in for —'

'Judi Dench?' Margot supplied.

'Well, yes, I guess.' Tammy chuckled. 'Or that snooty old bird in *Downton Abbey*. I forget her name.'

'Maggie Smith?'

'That's the one, yeah.'

Margot groaned. 'And those two women just happen to be dames, because they're such bloody brilliant actors. Far out, Tammy, now I'll be more nervous than ever.'

'Oh, sorry, sweetheart.' Tammy gave Margot's shoulders a reassuring squeeze. 'Look, you really have to stop worrying. Josie's no fool. She wouldn't have faith in you if you were a dud. She wants the performance to be as good as possible. I'm sure you're going to be fab.'

'Thanks, I think.' Margot was grateful for the affirmation, even though her confidence was still rather fragile.

Tammy winked. 'After all, it's only the Burralea players. Not Broadway.' And then she grinned. 'Besides, I'm going to make your hair *beeyootiful*.'

Crossing to shelves on the wall behind the counter, she selected a couple of products. 'This is a chemical relaxant,' she said, holding up a bottle. 'It'll smooth that frizz and add lots of gloss.'

'I could certainly do with gloss.'

'This is the one for you then. It'll give your hair a lovely gleam and make it look really healthy.'

'Sounds just what I need,' said Margot. 'Let's do it.' Even if Josie did decide she should wear a wig for the play, it was time she started taking proper care of her hair. With luck, it might even boost her rocky self-esteem.

It was just two nights later at the next rehearsal that Margot's self-esteem faced a major test. All week, she'd been working hard at learning her lines. Having bravely delivered the news of her acting debut to her family, she'd received their slightly stunned but sincere approval, and then she'd called on Bridie and Nate for extra help in the kitchen and laundry in the evenings.

Admittedly, Margot had also bribed her kids with a raise in their pocket money, just to make doubly sure she got the extra time she needed. But now, at least, each evening, as Bridie and Nate attended to the dirty dishes or loaded clothes into the washing machine before disappearing to their rooms, Margot was able to lock herself away in the small room they used as a home office and work on a block of her playscript.

Even Jack had pitched in to lend the kids a hand, dragging himself away from the television, which was a downright miracle. Seemed he was as stunned and chuffed about his wife's promotion as she was. Mind you, Margot knew that the players didn't expect her to have the script down pat just yet, but she was keen to show them she was no slouch, and she was pretty happy with her progress.

On rehearsal night, she even made sure she got to the community hall on time, instead of a few minutes late as had been her habit in the past. Better still, her hair was looking just as glossy and healthy as Tammy had promised. *And* she'd been able to tighten the belt on her jeans a notch, which meant she was already losing weight. Yay!

Actually, Margot was feeling so upbeat that she almost skipped as she locked her car and crossed the road to the rehearsal. The Burralea Community Hall was an old, modest barn-style building, built of corrugated iron with rows of windows down each side and a wide, double front door, through which the lights from inside spilled, showing up the faint, misty rain that touched her cheeks as softly as a powder puff.

She heard the happy ripple of voices inside and quickened her step. She was so looking forward to this evening and letting every-one see how conscientious she'd been. Until one, well-enunciated voice stopped her in her tracks.

Olivia.

What was *she* doing here?

Despite her warm clothing, Margot shivered. Had Olivia mirac-ulously recovered already? Had she returned to reclaim her rightful part in the play?

Don't panic. It's okay, Margot told herself. *You always knew you were only a stand-in. And it was an interesting experience.*

Perhaps she also felt just the teensiest bit relieved that she wouldn't have to perform on stage after all. The Burralea players knew she was really just a backstage person, like Tammy. Building the set and caring for the props were her responsibilities. Always had been, always would be, and it was best to stick to where she belonged.

Having thus prepared herself for probable disappointment, Margot stepped from the dark footpath and up the three concrete steps into the brightly lit hall. Here, as she'd expected, most of the players were gathered around Olivia. The woman was seated on an ordinary wooden chair, but she managed to look majestic, despite the crutch at her side and her foot encased in a moon boot.

Her hair and makeup were as perfect as ever and she wore a vivid turquoise silk scarf, thrown about her shoulders with careless, artistic flair. It seemed, to all intents and purposes, that Lady X was back.

'Ah, Margot,' Olivia announced when she saw her, and a certain note in her voice suggested she'd been waiting for this moment. Her smile was ever so reserved, and the expression in her dark eyes cautious. Watchful. The players around her seemed to sense this too, as they turned to watch Margot's approach.

For Margot, this woman's sudden focused attention was far worse than being on stage. But somehow she managed to take a deep breath and hurry forward with her arms extended to give Olivia a welcoming hug. 'It's so lovely to see you, Olivia.'

'Thank you, my dear.'

'How are you? How's your ankle?'

'It's healing well, thank you, although too slowly for my liking.' Olivia's mouth twisted in a resigned sort of grimace. 'But at least I don't have to keep my leg elevated all the time now and I'm much more mobile.'

'That's good news.'

'Yes. I've just been telling these lovely people that I should be fine on stage.'

Even though Margot had been schooling herself not to mind, disappointment arrived, sharp and cruel. With great difficulty, she forced herself to smile. 'That's wonderful.'

'Yes,' agreed Olivia. 'Such a relief.' And now a gleam shone in her eyes, quite possibly a gleam of triumph.

Margot cast a frantic glance around the hall, searching for Josie, who must surely have given her approval to this decision. But there was no sign of their director. Chances were, she was out the back, attending to some administrative detail. And now, Margot supposed that she should go backstage, too, to find out about sets or scenery that needed her attention.

'Wow, Margot,' a voice commented suddenly. 'I love your hair.' It was the young teenager Heidi, whose own white-blonde hair was styled into a super trendy, blunt-ended bob that happened to be perfect for her role as an AI.

'Oh? Thanks.' Margot had been so side-tracked by Olivia, she'd almost forgotten about her newly glossy, smooth hair.

To her surprise, others joined in with compliments.

And then Josie appeared. 'Hello, everyone,' she called. 'Are we ready for our warmups?'

There was no time to quiz Josie as the chatter died away and the players spread out in the cleared space in the middle of the hall. Olivia got to her feet and joined them, complete with her crutch and moon boot.

Margot tried not to watch how Olivia was managing as they went through their usual warmup exercises – rolling their necks around, then forward and from side to side, before rolling their shoulders, then circling their arms. She could see Olivia out of the corner of her eye, however, and she had to admire the way the woman had a good go at everything, although she couldn't quite manage raising her arms above her head and then leaning to one side to stretch her ribcage.

But that was okay. Josie had always warned them to only do what they could comfortably manage, and they soon moved on to breathing exercises.

'Well done, everyone,' Josie announced after they'd completed their forward folds and had shaken everything loose. 'Right. I think we'll start with Act Two this evening. So we'll need Hamish and Heidi waiting and ready in the wings, and Peter and Margot on stage.'

'Me?' Margot couldn't help exclaiming.

Josie smiled at her and nodded. 'Yes, that's right. You're in this scene.'

But – Margot wanted to cry as a flash of cold panic ripped through her – *but what about Olivia?*

'Excuse me!' As if on cue, an imperious voice called out from behind them.

Margot could sense everyone else turning with her to find Olivia standing at her most regal, despite the crutch and boot.

'It's been very good of Margot to fill in for me,' Olivia said now. 'But as you can see, I'm quite mobile, and I'd like to resume my role, moon boot and all. I honestly believe I can pull it off.'

'You mean pull the boot off?' called Derek, one of the cheekier youngsters.

Dignified as ever, Olivia ignored him. She kept her gaze fixed on Josie and the tension in the hall was almost suffocating as the two women eyed each other.

An entire ice age seemed to pass before Josie replied.

'Olivia,' Josie said at last, in a tone that could only be described as placating. 'It's wonderful that you're here tonight to give us your support, but I think you should allow yourself at least one more week to recover.'

There was no missing the flash of dismay in Olivia's eyes and

Margot was sure the woman would launch a protest. Around her, the rest of the cast remained frozen and silent, as if they were all holding their breaths.

At last Olivia's mouth quirked in a complicated little smile, and she lifted one shoulder in a shrug. 'Of course,' she said with excessive demureness. 'Over to you, Margot.' And then, with her shoulders back and her head high, she returned to her chair with the magnificent dignity of a queen resuming her throne.

'Okay, then.' Josie gave a small clap of her hands and gestured to the required cast members to head for the stage.

Margot, however, felt sick. Even though she'd rehearsed this scene at home and she knew almost all the lines by heart, her legs were so suddenly weak she wasn't sure they would carry her. It didn't help that Peter Hubbard was already waiting on the stage, and Heidi and Hamish were sending her sympathetic smiles, as if they knew how scared she must be.

Oh, help. Margot knew, in that moment, that she'd been fooling herself to dream she might be able to act. She was a woman who worked in a hardware store. She knew about hammers and paint-brushes and hose connections. Not acting.

How on earth had she ever thought she could do this? There was no way she could get up there and perform Lady X with Olivia Matthews watching her.

'Come on, Margot,' called Josie, who was now at the edge of the stage.

Stomach in knots, Margot pulled the script from her shoulder bag and began to walk forward on trembling legs. As she neared the stage, she set her bag on a chair and, reluctantly, she kept going, clutching the script tightly.

Somehow she managed to climb the short flight of steps to the stage, but her heart was beating so fiercely she could hear it thumping in her ears.

Josie smiled as she drew closer. 'You'll be fine,' she murmured.

Margot shook her head and replied in a whisper. 'I don't think I can do this. Not with Olivia down there.'

'Of course you can. Don't think about what might go wrong. I have every faith in you.' A hint of sympathy gleamed in Josie's bright eyes as she murmured from the corner of her mouth, 'Just remember to breathe. We don't want you swooning.'

Swooning? The old-fashioned word jolted Margot. She had memories of novels she'd read where the 'fairer sex' had fainted and swooned. She'd always thought them so ridiculous.

Remembering this now, she almost snorted. She felt the tension in her shoulders give way and with that, the terrible, paralysing spell was broken. She continued onto the stage to the spot where she was supposed to stand and looked down at her script. In this scene, Peter had the opening lines, which he delivered now with his usual urbane smoothness. And Margot responded.

She didn't need to look at the script. Not for that opening line, or for any of the others. In this scene, Peter's character, Lord X, wasn't coping at all well with their bizarre circumstances in the spaceship and Lady X was doing her best to cheer him up.

With no formal acting training, Margot could only draw on her experience as a wife and mother and as a shopkeeper whose customers often came to her with their dilemmas – a broken windowpane, a leaking toilet, a rusting downpipe. This evening, these experiences held her in good stead. And as long as she focused on Peter and refused to let herself think about anyone else, she managed. It was far from a brilliant performance – Margot knew that – but it also wasn't pathetic.

Josie seemed pleased. She only interrupted them twice with directing suggestions, and it was only when the scene was finished that Margot allowed herself to look down to the chairs where the other players were waiting for their turn.

Olivia's chair was empty. She had disappeared.

CHAPTER TWELVE

There was nothing about Tilly's new school that she liked. Everything was pathetic, beginning with the horrible red and yellow uniform. She couldn't imagine the warped brain that had come up with that disgusting colour combination. The woman in the uniform shop had tried to call the colours maroon and gold, but changing the names couldn't fix the way they looked.

In Cairns, Tilly's uniform had been a tasteful blue gingham. Admittedly, at the time she'd never really appreciated it, but she'd give anything to be able to wear it now.

Sadly, though, the uniform was only part of her problem with this school. Everything about it felt wrong, no doubt because Tilly wasn't merely missing her mum, but her home, her friends and the world she knew, the only world she'd ever known.

Okay, so maybe her home in Cairns had only been a ground floor flat in a six pack with the tiniest garden imaginable, but Tilly had always been happy there. And Cairns was a city of sunshine, with palm trees and bright tropical flowers, mango trees and fruit bats and the salty tang of the sea.

In Cairns, she'd had neighbours who'd known her all her life.

And even after she'd lost her mum, she'd still had Jed, impressing the hell out of her friends when he picked her up from school on his Harley-Davidson. Tilly had thoroughly enjoyed staging those moments in front of an audience of schoolmates, taking her time to tuck her hair inside her helmet, then climbing onto the motorbike behind Jed and giving him the thumbs-up before he rocketed off.

But although she missed everything about her old life, the thing she hated most about the new school was that she was also the 'new kid'. She felt as if everyone was staring at her like she was some kind of freak animal in a zoo.

It had been bad enough in Cairns when she'd been the kid whose mother died. Now she wasn't just motherless, but a *new kid* as well, *and* she'd arrived mid-semester, which made her newness extra obvious.

Bridie Cooper had tried to be friendly. Tilly understood that the girl was doing her best. She'd introduced Tilly to the other kids in their class and no one had been bitchy or mean. But Tilly was certain that they not only knew about her mother's death, but also about her being dumped on Kate, and even if they tried to be nice, there was a hesitancy and an awkwardness that just felt *wrong*.

I can't stand this. I hate it here.

Tilly had written several versions of this message in her Snapchat texts to Zara, and her friend's responses were always the same.

Run away.

So now, after ten unhappy days on the Tablelands, Tilly had decided to do just that. She'd texted Zara to warn her of her arrival, and then she'd checked the bus timetables and planned her escape.

At the end of the morning break, while all the other kids wandered back to their classrooms, Tilly stayed in the toilets. She'd left most of her schoolbooks at home to make room in her bag for a few extra clothes, pyjamas and toiletries, and she quickly changed out of her uniform into jeans and a long-sleeved T-shirt, a boring grey one that shouldn't attract attention.

As the school grounds grew quiet while classes resumed, she stealthily made her way behind a row of bottlebrush trees till she reached the gate at the bottom of the sports field. From here she calmly exited the school grounds and kept walking.

Phew.

She reached the bus stop with time to spare and the only other people waiting there were an old couple sitting on the wooden bench in the tiny roofed shelter. They both had snow-white hair and were dressed in matching moss-green hand-knitted cardigans. They nodded and smiled at Tilly, but they didn't ask her any pesky questions, so that was good. She only hoped that nobody from school had seen her leaving.

At last, a bus appeared, rounding the corner, and Tilly's stomach tightened. Last night she hadn't slept much, she'd been too excited about this daring plan, and this morning she'd been so sick with nerves she'd had trouble keeping her breakfast down. Luckily, she had both cash and a debit card. Jed had put an extra two hundred dollars into her account before he left, so she had plenty of money to cover a bus fare to Cairns. But what if the driver took one look at her and told her she should be in school?

Tilly forced herself to think positively. In a few minutes she would be inside the bus, seated near a window towards the back, and then they'd be off, travelling across farming land that spread over low, rolling hills and plains. She'd be yawning at the paddocks of grass dotted with cattle and the fields filled with tall ripening corn. And as they drove across the Tablelands to Tolga and then Mareeba, she would no doubt be impatient with the boring scenery.

Everything would improve when they reached Kuranda, and the farmlands and eucalyptus gave way to dense rainforest. There, massive trees draped with twisting vines would crowd the edge of the road and, finally, the bus would wind back down the mountain range to Cairns. With luck, Tilly would arrive before the school lunchbreak ended and Zara would skip afternoon school to be with her. They might even go to a movie.

Tilly let the old couple get on the bus first. It was a bit of a struggle for the old man, but he eventually made it up the steps with his wife's help. The driver wasn't quite as old as they were, but his hair and moustache were streaked with grey and he seemed to know them. He had a bit of a chat with them about the old man's new hip. The couple were travelling to Cairns for a check-up at the hospital.

Then it was Tilly's turn. Drawing a deep breath, she forced herself to smile and to look relaxed. 'A one-way ticket to Cairns, please.'

The driver narrowed his eyes at her. 'Do you have ID?'

ID for a simple bus trip? Panic flared until Tilly remembered her library card, which still showed her Cairns address. 'Will this do?' she asked, whipping it out of her purse.

The driver peered at it and then grimaced. 'No date of birth. How old are you, miss?'

Tilly almost upped her age, but sixteen-year-olds could get their own driver's licence, so surely she could ride on a bus at thirteen? 'Thirteen,' she said.

'Thirteen?' The driver frowned. 'Okay, I'll need your Unaccompanied Child Form, signed by a parent or guardian.'

Horrified, Tilly gaped at him. 'I haven't got one.'

The guy shrugged. 'Sorry. No form, no travel.'

'But I *have* to get to Cairns. It's really important.'

He shook his head. 'That's the law, I'm afraid. This isn't like a school bus, you know. If you're thirteen, you can't just take off and travel on your own. Not without a permission form signed by an adult.'

Somehow, Tilly choked back the sob that filled her throat. She didn't think she could bear this last-minute disappointment. It didn't help that she could see the elderly couple watching her with obvious sympathy and concern.

Pressing her lips tightly together to hold everything in, she turned to step down from the bus and pushed her shoulders back, hoping she didn't look as totally crushed as she felt.

The bus doors closed and her tears began to fall as it pulled away from the curb. She couldn't bear to watch it disappear. What the fuck was she going to do now?

* * *

The second time Liam Flint arrived at Kate's place, her greeting was ultra-polite, almost cool.

'Good afternoon.'

'Hey there,' he responded with a radiant grin that made her want to smile right back at him.

She curbed this impulse, of course. She'd been rather embarrassed, remembering the way she'd behaved during Liam's previous visit. For heaven's sake – alone in the van with him, while having a supposedly sensible discussion about solar panels and off-grid options, Kate's real life had momentarily melted away. Despite the turmoil that had been happening all around her, with Tilly's arrival and Pippa's news of a grandchild on the way, Kate had found herself gripped by a giddy and girlish impulse to grin and *almost* flirt.

It didn't help that Liam Flint had praised her van and her handywoman skills to the skies and, obviously, it had been way too long since she'd been alone at close quarters with a sexy man. She'd been caught off guard by his good looks. But how pathetic was that?

Kate was *over* men. Totally. She hadn't been on a single date since her divorce. Okay, so maybe there'd been times when she'd felt very lonely, but she'd also been well and truly burned by Stan. And while she wasn't the only woman in the world to have chosen the wrong life partner, most people hadn't made as spectacularly bad a mistake as she had.

Today, with Liam Flint once again on her doorstep, she forced herself to remember that first meeting with Stan all those years ago, at a girlfriend's birthday party. How easily he'd bowled her over with his sparkling smile and flattering compliments.

'You're so lovely, you make me wish I could write poetry.'

Yuck. But then, Stan had been clever enough to know the dangers of actually trying to attempt poetry, especially as Kate was a professional writer and could sniff a trite piece of verse at fifty paces. Pity she hadn't been equally as wary of his smile.

Given that history, though, Kate couldn't quite believe she might spare a second glance for an electrician dressed in workmanlike overalls and bearing a toolbox. But perhaps a big-shouldered tradie, with wavy, slightly too long hair and smiling dark eyes should not be permitted to spend his days visiting the homes of lonely women.

According to Margot, whom Kate had carefully interrogated, Liam was a divorcee, which came as no surprise. Margot had added, however, that his reputation as an electrician was top-notch, so for the van's sake – yes, truly, for the *van's* sake – Kate had organised this second visit.

She'd been careful this time, however, and she'd asked him to come in the afternoon when Tilly was due home on the school bus. With this safety precaution in place, she was determined there'd be no unnecessary smiling.

Problem was, Liam Flint had an extremely distracting vibe. While he quizzed Kate about her decisions on wi-fi and lighting over her kitchen sink, the air in the van seemed to hum and buzz, making her stiff and awkward.

Mid-conversation, Liam stopped and frowned at her. 'Is something the matter?'

'No,' came her automatic and quickly fired response. But the answering disbelief in Liam's gaze warned that she absolutely had to set the record straight, pronto. 'Okay,' she said bravely. 'I may as well be upfront and admit it. You make me feel – a bit vulnerable.'

'I'm sorry.' His frown deepened. 'You feel threatened?'

'No, not threatened.' Kate swallowed. *What the heck. Just spit it out.* 'Look, I'm a divorcee, living on my own, and I guess I'm worried I might accidentally smile – or say or do something that makes you think I'm flirting.'

A small silence fell as Liam digested this. 'And that's a problem?'

'It is for me.' She was relieved that he didn't expect an explanation and she couldn't bring herself to look at him again, so she had no idea if he was amused, or bewildered, or if he thought she was just plain crazy.

But then, he said smoothly, 'No need to worry. If I get the impression you're flirting, I'll just ignore it. I'll know you don't really mean it.'

His voice conveyed a gentle tease as he said this and Kate couldn't help smiling.

'Good,' she said. 'Glad we've got that sorted.'

Liam turned his attention to his toolkit now and selected a set of pliers. His hands were strong, and slightly rough. Workman's hands. 'But really, you don't need to worry,' he added. 'I only sleep with women who play hard to get.'

Naturally, Kate had beat a hasty retreat, which she hoped was also dignified, despite her flaming cheeks. At least she'd had an excuse so that the ridiculously embarrassing conversation hadn't been the only reason she'd needed to leave. Her editing tasks had been piling up while she'd turned her attention to getting Tilly settled.

Now, as she reached her cottage and heard the reassuring screech of Liam's drill coming from the van, she made herself a mug of tea, settled at the end of her kitchen table and reopened the file on her laptop with the latest manuscript she'd been working on.

Kate had begun her working life as a journalist, mostly with newspapers and magazines, and when she'd been offered a position as subeditor, she'd discovered that she enjoyed supervising the layout of pages and she had a surprising talent for checking the accuracy of other journos' writing.

Since the rise of online publications, however, opportunities to work with print media had been rapidly diminishing, especially in regional areas. These days, almost all of Kate's work was done online as a freelance editor, via her laptop. Mostly, she worked on manuscripts submitted by writers who wanted to self-publish their non-fiction books, although she'd worked with a few fiction authors as well.

She enjoyed helping them to polish their writing and make their message clearer. She had even set up a blog where she wrote articles for aspiring writers about style and structure, punctuation and grammar, and she answered their questions. She'd called the blog *Minding Your Ps and Qs* and it had proved to be a good point of connection for attracting new clients.

The best part, of course, was that this job was portable and the hours were flexible. So yes, Margot and Jack Cooper had been spot-on when they'd commented that this was the perfect job to support Kate's van renovation and travel plans – a point that had not been lost on Tilly.

Tilly. Kate sighed. Things hadn't really improved since the girl had started at her new school. On the first day, Kate had been ready and waiting with home-baked brownies for afternoon tea, and she'd greeted Tilly with her warmest smile. But when she'd enquired how the day had gone, Tilly had merely rolled her eyes and continued with a pouty teen face straight on to her room where she'd firmly closed – but not quite slammed – the door.

Okay. Enough. Kate couldn't afford to spend any more time agonising over the clash between her personal dreams and her grieving ward's needs. She had to get on with this work.

It was sometime later and Kate was deeply immersed in a former newspaper colleague's intriguing crime investigation, when her phone rang. Annoyed by the disturbance, she almost didn't bother to answer it, until she recognised the caller as a teacher from Tilly's new school.

Please, no. Don't tell me Tilly's misbehaving. Kate was almost wincing as she tapped her phone to accept the call. 'Hello? Kate speaking.'

'Oh, Mrs Sheridan, it's Imogen Kirk here. I'm Tilly's English teacher and I'm also her year coordinator.'

'Yes?'

'Is Tilly at home?'

'Excuse me?' Kate frowned and checked the time on her laptop screen. It was only 2.45pm, too early for the school bus. 'I'm sorry, no, Tilly's not home yet. But I don't understand. Why should she be here? Isn't it too early?'

Even as Kate asked this, she feared it was a foolish question.

'It's just that Tilly hasn't been at school since mid-morning,' the teacher said. 'She didn't have permission to leave and none of her classmates seem to know where she might be.'

'I – I . . .' Kate's mind whirled as she struggled to think straight. How could this have happened? Where could Tilly be? 'Are you telling me you have no idea where she is?' Her question probably sounded like an accusation, but that was too bad. Surely the school was responsible for keeping tabs on their students?

'Tilly hasn't reported for class since morning break,' Imogen Kirk replied. 'And as far as we can tell, she's nowhere on the premises.'

'Really?' A pointless response, but Kate was fighting panic.

'I was hoping you might know where she is.'

'No. I'm sorry. I haven't a clue.' Kate was almost whimpering now, as her imagination threw up untold horrors.

'I didn't want to alarm you unnecessarily. I wouldn't normally jump to report a possible truancy so quickly,' the teacher said next. 'But I know Tilly's situation is unusual. And Bridie Cooper seems worried. She told me she tried to ring Tilly on her mobile, but couldn't get an answer.'

Kate didn't find this especially surprising. Bridie and Tilly hadn't exactly gelled. But where on earth could Tilly be? Had she taken off? Tried to run away? Where could she go? As far as Kate was aware, Tilly didn't know anyone on the Tablelands. Did that mean —

Oh, God. Was this a matter for the police?

'Hopefully, I'm overreacting,' the teacher said next. 'Tilly could just be dodging class and she might turn up again in time to catch the bus home. We'll have teachers at the school bus stop on the lookout and I'll certainly let you know as soon as I hear anything.'

'All right. Thank you.'

Imogen Kirk rang off and Kate sat staring at her phone, too numb to think straight. But then, knowing she couldn't ignore this, she gave herself a shake, found Tilly's number and tapped to connect. As she listened to it ringing, she closed her eyes. She even found herself shooting up a quick prayer, but the only response was Tilly's recorded voice.

Hiya. Can't take your call, so leave a message if you like.

'Tilly.' Kate heard the fear in her voice and tried to calm down. 'I hope everything's okay. Can you please give me a call and let me know where you are?'

After that, she wasn't sure how long she sat, just staring at the phone, waiting and hoping, while her mind raced through alarming possibilities. Had Tilly run away? If so, where would she go?

Was Cairns the most likely place? But how would a thirteen-year-old travel that far?

Would she try to hitch a ride? And if she did, what if . . .?

Kate tried not to think about the what ifs, but they were impossible to stop. What if some creep picked her up? A rapist? A murderer?

Oh, help. She had to stop these wild thoughts. She wished there was someone she could speak to about this – just to offload momentarily. But there was little point in phoning her girlfriends in Cairns. They were all busy with work and their families, and what could they do?

The only person she really knew here on the Tablelands was Margot Cooper, and the poor woman would also be busy at work. And anyway, Margot's daughter, Bridie, was already trying to help the teachers.

A knock sounded at the door, startling Kate so that she jumped. She turned, saw Liam Flint, and realised she'd been so worried about Tilly that she'd forgotten he was still there in the van.

'Hi,' he said. 'Just letting you know I've finished the wiring for —' He stopped. 'Sorry. Are you okay?'

Kate wasn't sure how to answer. She didn't want to burden a man she barely knew with her problems, and just seeing Liam again brought back the flooding embarrassment of their most recent conversation. But she was so worried and stressed she couldn't help herself. 'No, I'm afraid I'm not okay. I – I've just had a call from Burralea High. Tilly's gone missing.'

'Tilly?'

'The young girl I've been caring for. She only started at the local high school last week. I knew she wasn't really settling in, but now . . .' Kate felt her face crumple and when she tried to speak again, her voice cracked. 'She's been missing since mid-morning.'

CHAPTER THIRTEEN

Kate ended up telling Liam everything. He seemed genuinely concerned and she had no one else to share her angst with, so it all came tumbling out – not just about Tilly's disappearance, but about Stan and the divorce and his subsequent scandal and how this daughter, whom Kate had never even known about, had been more or less dumped on her doorstep.

'I've known the poor girl was miserable here,' Kate said. 'She's grieving for her mother, and I've tried to be understanding, to say the right things and make her feel welcome. But I've obviously been a dismal failure.'

By now, Liam had helped himself to a seat at Kate's kitchen table, and she half expected him to mention the van and how unsettling it must have been for Tilly to realise that her guardian was planning a big adventure.

But he didn't mention any of this. 'You shouldn't beat yourself up,' he said instead. 'Sounds to me like you've been an absolute hero.'

'Not if Tilly's —' Kate stopped and bit her lip as she struggled for control. She kept seeing Tilly in some sleazy guy's car, terrified out of her wits. 'I'm so scared she's in trouble.' She shivered. 'I don't want to call the police.' She dreaded the thought of this. Somehow it would make everything too sickeningly real. 'But I suppose I really should.'

'Maybe you could try calling Tilly one more time?' Liam suggested. 'If she doesn't answer and you have to leave a message, you could tell her you're worried and you'll be calling the police. You never know, if she's just playing hooky, that might frighten her into calling you back.'

'Of course,' Kate cried. 'I can't believe I didn't think of that.' She was so grateful she could have hugged him. 'That's exactly what I'll do.'

* * *

For Tilly, it had been close to the very worst day ever. It was so tedious to be hanging around waiting. Zara hadn't been able to answer her phone during class time, but Tilly had managed a quick call in the lunchbreak, warning her friend that she wouldn't be on the bus to Cairns after all.

Zara's response had included a juicy swearword, which Tilly found encouraging. Somewhat nervously she had then dared to ask, 'Seeing I can't get the bus, do you think your mum might come up here to collect me?'

'Yeah, sure,' had been Zara's prompt response and Tilly hadn't liked to remind her friend that this would mean a three-hour round trip for them. 'But Mum won't be free until after four,' Zara added. Eleanor, her mum, worked as a receptionist for a group of GPs in Freshwater. 'And she doesn't like me to contact her at work unless it's urgent, so I should probably wait till school's over to call her.'

This was not good news. It meant Tilly had to fill in the rest of the day hanging around the few streets that made up the tiny town of Burralea. *And* she had to do so without being seen by anyone who might recognise her and dob her in. Even though she'd changed out of her school uniform, she had to be careful.

So far, she had spent time in the Burralea Library, but it was pathetically small, not much bigger than a caravan, so there hadn't really been enough shelving to hide behind. For lunch, she'd bought a sausage roll and an iced coffee from one of the cafés that had a garden courtyard, where she'd been able to eat at a table hidden behind a vine-covered trellis.

Then she'd spent what had felt like a very long and dreary afternoon sitting on a patch of grass in the small central park. Luckily it wasn't raining, but again, she made sure she was hidden by shrubbery, which meant she was sharing the space with ants and insects and even a lizard or two.

At one point a dog had come nosing around, perhaps just curious, but possibly hoping for food. He was a nice enough dog, some sort of bitser, and Tilly wouldn't have minded his company. But he had a collar and she was worried his owner might come looking for him, so she shooed him away. Besides, she was more of a cat person.

That was another thing about Cairns that she missed. She and her mum had kept a cat, a beautiful tortoiseshell called Josephine. Josephine was ancient, at least ten years old. Tilly couldn't really remember a time in her life when the cat hadn't lived with them, but when they'd had to leave the flat, Jed had talked her into offering Josephine to their neighbour.

'She's too old to move to a whole different environment,' he'd reasoned, sounding suddenly knowledgeable, as if he knew all about cats. 'Besides, you'd be pushing your luck to expect your new guardian to take your cat as well as you. And you know Mrs Kettle already loves Josephine.'

Tilly did know this was true. Elderly Mrs Kettle was a lonely widow and she'd been very happy to take Josephine in. Tilly comforted herself with the prospect of visiting the two of them when she got back to Cairns. And along with that thought, she entertained herself by imagining her new future with Zara and her mum.

Would she get to share Zara's bedroom with its wonderful purple walls and strings of lights? Would they have bunk beds perhaps, or would Eleanor find another spot for her?

One thing was certain – Tilly would keep whatever space she was given mega clean and tidy. Actually, she could volunteer to keep the whole flat clean and tidy and that had to be a bonus that Eleanor would appreciate.

But when she tried to actually picture herself squeezing into Eleanor and Zara's small flat, she felt her insides shrivel again with nerves. This time, she'd distracted herself by watching videos on TikTok on her phone, until she'd had to stop for fear of running out of battery.

Time crawled, but eventually, school was out for the day. This brought mobs of kids streaming through the little town, riding their bikes, or wandering along footpaths. Watching them from her hiding place, Tilly could see them dawdling, chatting and elbowing each other, laughing over shared jokes. From a distance, they actually looked nice and normal and happy, really, just like her friends in Cairns.

But that only made Tilly desperately homesick for Cairns and her own friends. She tried Zara's phone again and luckily, she answered quickly.

'Have you been able to talk to your mother?'

'Yeah. Just finished,' said Zara. 'Actually, Mum wants to talk to you, Tills.'

'Okay.'

'She'll probably call you in a minute or two.'

'Right.'

'So, I'll ring off for now.'

'Yeah, sure. So she's okay about coming up here to get me?'

'I – I think so. Love you, babe.'

'Love you, too.' Tilly hoped she was imagining that hint of caution in her friend's voice, and her stomach was suddenly so ultra-tight and sore, she feared she might throw up. Almost immediately, her phone rang again.

'Tilly. It's Eleanor here.'

'Hi, Eleanor.'

'Listen, sweetheart . . .'

Tilly cringed. She could sense this opening *had* to be the start of bad news and she didn't want to hear any more.

'I'm sorry,' Eleanor went on. 'I'm not sure how Zara got it into her head that we could take you in to live with us. But honestly, honey, it's just not feasible.'

As if she needed to emphasise her point, Eleanor sighed rather dramatically and Tilly wanted to scream.

'To begin with,' Eleanor quickly added, 'there's not really enough room in our little place. Sharing a room with Zara is okay for sleepovers, but I don't think it could work long term. And I hate to mention costs, but I'm not sure I could manage to care for two teenagers on my salary. But Tilly, the even bigger issue is that I need to respect Ange's wishes.'

'But Mum loved you and Zara.' Tilly could hear the tears in her voice, but she couldn't help them. She'd never felt quite so desperate.

'Tilly, your mum named this other woman, Kate Sheridan, as your guardian. It was in her will. I believe it's all legal.'

'But it's ridiculous.' Tilly could feel her world shattering and she no longer tried to hold back her tears. 'Mum never even met Kate.'

'Yes, I know. But honestly, sweetheart, Ange and I used to talk about everything – you know, if the worst happened – and I know she never expected me to take care of you, just as I wouldn't have expected her to take in Zara. I don't want to sound harsh, sweetie, but I think you need to give Kate Sheridan a chance.'

'She doesn't want me.'

After a beat, 'Did she tell you that?'

'She doesn't have to. I just know it. She's doing up a van and she wants to travel around Australia.'

This brought silence from the other end of the phone. *Thank God.* Finally, Eleanor understood how bad this was.

'Maybe . . .' Eleanor said carefully.

And Tilly held her breath. *Maybe I should come and live with you and Zara, after all?*

'Maybe Kate would be quite prepared to put those plans on hold – just for a year or two.'

Clunk. It was like having a jail cell door slammed in her face.

'Tilly?'

Yeah. Whatever. There was no point in continuing this conversation.

'Tilly?' Eleanor asked again.

'Yup?'

'I really think you should hang in there for a little longer. It's been a terrible time for you, I know. And changing schools is never easy, but why don't you give it another week or two with Kate? Keep in touch. Let me know how you're doing.'

'Yeah, sure.'

'And, sweetie, are you still there?'

'Yeah.'

'You'll contact Kate, won't you? She must be really worried.'

Tilly promptly hung up without even bothering to thank her.

She wasn't sure how long she sat on the grass in a miserable huddle, hugging her knees, while tears slid down her cheeks and afternoon shadows crept through the park, bringing a hint of night-time chill.

When her phone rang again, she didn't even bother to check the screen to see who was calling. She didn't want to talk to anyone, not even Zara. She hated everyone. It would serve all of them right if she just stayed here in hiding and got rained on and froze to death.

It wasn't long, however, before she wished she had packed a warm jumper in her bag. But she was supposed to be down on the coast by now, in warm, sunny Cairns, not up here in the cold, damp, crappy mountains.

She couldn't keep crying forever though, and eventually her tears reduced to an occasional sniffle. When she wiped her face on her sleeve and looked out, the schoolkids had all disappeared. They would be home by now, having afternoon tea, kicking balls in back-yards, maybe even helping their parents on their farms, riding quad bikes, tractors, even horses.

Tilly had never felt lonelier. Even after her mum's accident, Jed had been there, but now . . .

She shivered and realised she wasn't quite ready to die of exposure. Out of habit, or perhaps desperation, she reached for her phone, checking to see who that last caller had been.

Kate. And she'd left another message. This was the third time Kate had rung and the message would be the same as the others, but Tilly supposed she might as well listen.

* * *

Kate was pacing the floor, willing Tilly to return her call. She had oodles of editing work that needed her attention, but she couldn't concentrate on anything but Tilly's disappearance. Her overactive guilty conscience was making her feel especially wretched.

It was just awful to realise that Tilly had actually been planning this escape. The girl had left a stack of her schoolbooks on her bedside table, and she'd almost certainly done this to make more room in her schoolbag for clothes. Which meant that last night at dinner and this morning during breakfast, while Kate had chatted away about random, innocuous topics – sport, pop star gossip, the weather, anything to keep a thread of conversation alive – Tilly must have been nursing her plan to run away.

Now, having crossed the lounge room for the umpteenth time, Kate stopped at the window where the pot plant that Tilly had brought from Cairns hung. The trailing mandevilla looked impressively healthy with lush green leaves and beautiful crimson trumpet-shaped flowers.

Almost certainly, the girl's mother had cared for this plant and until this morning it had seemed important to Tilly. With a deeper stab of guilt, Kate also remembered the boxes, still stashed to one side of the laundry and filled with Angela's pots and pans, her books and crockery.

All of these things must be precious links to Tilly's mum, but the girl's need to get away had obviously been so strong she'd felt compelled to abandon them.

Which pointed to one glaring reality. Kate's efforts to make Tilly feel welcome had been totally pathetic. *I let the poor kid down.*

Kate knew Tilly was mourning the loss of her mother, so of course she should have tried way harder to reassure the desperately sad child that she was welcome and important. Certainly more important than any van.

For heaven's sake, how could she have been so caught up with planning overhead cupboards or choosing the right shade of chalk paint? The van was nothing but an old box on wheels and Tilly was a living, breathing human being. More than that, the child was a totally innocent victim of the cruellest of circumstances. Kate couldn't quite believe her thinking had been so warped.

Guiltily, she also realised that she should have told Pippa and Chelsea about Tilly. Heavens, she hadn't even rung Pippa back to chat about her pregnancy and to find out how David reacted to the news. Surely Pippa's boyfriend should have been the first to hear about the baby? Kate hoped everything was okay with them.

Right now, however, Tilly had to be her focus. Tilly was vulnerable and helpless and she was only thirteen – such a vitally pivotal age. *And*, the girl's mother had relied on Kate to provide love and support.

'I'm so sorry,' Kate whispered, swiping at tears as she set about pacing once again, with a background accompaniment from the electrician's hammering and drilling.

Liam had originally planned to come back another day to finish the job, but when he'd realised how worried Kate was, he'd offered to hang around, which was a big surprise. She wasn't used to that kind of backup from a guy, and this guy hardly knew her. She was grateful, though, just to know he was there, but she was sure he couldn't wait much longer.

Her bottom lip was practically raw from her chewing as she crossed the room yet again and reached the windows that looked out over grassy rolling hills. The sun was already slipping towards the west and making deep shadows in the valleys.

Before long it would be dark and Kate knew she couldn't wait till then. She was running out of time. Tilly wasn't going to phone back and she had no choice but to call the police.

She'd already added the number for the Burralea police station into her phone. Now, she was shaking as she drew the phone from her cardigan's deep pocket.

But before she could select the number, the phone rang suddenly, vibrating against her palm. She was so startled, she almost dropped it. Oh, dear heaven. Tilly's name showed as the caller ID.

'Hello!' Kate cried.

'Hi.' The voice was thin, almost unrecognisable.

'Is that you, Tilly?'

'Yeah.'

Thank God.

'Have you called the police?' the girl asked.

'Not yet,' said Kate. 'I was just about to call them. I've been so worried. Are you all right?'

'Yep.'

Kate's relief was so fierce, her legs almost gave way. Stumbling to the nearby sofa, she sank onto its broad arm, her lips trembling as she struggled not to cry. 'Where are you?'

'In Burralea. In the park behind the library.'

Good heavens. Kate had been battling terrifying visions of the girl being ferreted away by some ghastly man – to Cairns, perhaps. Or she'd imagined Tilly hunkering in a dark, dank rainforest, trying to hide and being scared out of her wits.

Now she wanted to ask a thousand questions, but Tilly had already answered the most important ones. She was all right and she was in Burralea. 'Stay right there,' Kate said. 'And I'll come and get you.'

'Okay,' Tilly replied, and then, after the tiniest pause, 'I'm freezing. Can you bring me a jumper?'

'She rang!' Kate's voice was close to a scream and she was still shaking as she stumbled outside to share the good news with Liam. 'Tilly just called.'

He was out of the van in a flash and met her halfway along the path.

'Tilly's okay,' Kate spluttered. 'She's in Burralea and she's fine.' And then, as her relief exploded, she burst into noisy tears. Which was possibly how she ended up with Liam's arm around her shoulders, being steered back towards the cottage.

In the doorway, however, she stopped abruptly and pulled away from him. She should be heading for the van, not into the house. 'I've got to go to her. Are the keys in the van?'

'Yes, but I've disconnected the battery, so I'll need five minutes or so to have it ready.'

'Oh.'

'We can take my van.'

Kate gave a somewhat dazed shake of her head. 'Don't you need to get home?'

'Not especially.'

Curiosity flared. Kate had no idea of Liam's living set-up, but surely it was too much to expect him to continue to help her? He'd already hung around way longer than he'd needed to. She fished in her pocket for a tissue, but couldn't find one, so used the backs of her hands to swipe at her tear-splashed cheeks. 'Are you sure you don't mind waiting here?' she asked him. 'At least you'd have time to fix the battery.'

'I'd actually feel better if I came with you.'

'But —'

'You've been pretty rattled,' Liam said. 'I reckon you should let me drive.'

It was his calm and quiet authority that silenced Kate. And in the hush that followed, she was aware of the toll of the afternoon's stress. She had to admit she did feel rather exhausted and she certainly didn't want any delays. She needed to get to Tilly *now*.

If she was honest, she didn't have the strength to argue with Liam Flint. Even so, it felt weird to accept help from a man she'd only recently met. She'd been so used to standing on her own two feet.

'Okay,' she said. 'Thanks.' And then she remembered Tilly's request. 'Oh, and I have to fetch a jumper for her. And maybe a scarf. She's freezing.'

In no time, they were heading down the track and Kate had to admit she was grateful to simply slump in the passenger's seat, nursing Tilly's jumper to her chest, while Liam took charge behind the wheel.

The happy reality was slowly sinking in. Tilly hadn't been abducted. She was okay.

As they crested the final hill and saw the rooftops of Burralea in the distance, she turned to Liam. 'Do you have kids?'

To her surprise she saw a sudden tightening of his jaw, followed by a jerky motion in his throat as he swallowed.

'No,' he said. 'No luck in that department.'

Kate wasn't sure how to respond. She could only guess there must be more to this story, but she didn't like to pry. Fortunately, Liam seemed to recover quite quickly. Almost immediately, his demeanour was as calm and collected as ever, making her wonder if she'd imagined the tension. And now, after turning at an intersection, they were heading down the final slope towards Burralea.

'So, I've been thinking you should give yourself an easy night,' Liam said. 'Have you tried the Burralea pub? I can't imagine you'd be cracking your neck to cook dinner tonight and they do pretty good meals. The dining room's nice and cosy, as well. There's a fireplace and I reckon they'd have a fire burning on a nippy night like this.'

Kate couldn't deny that the thought of not having to cook dinner was very appealing. She wondered if Liam regularly ate at the pub and then reminded herself that it was time to stop wondering about him. Now. This very minute.

* * *

Tilly dreaded seeing Kate again. She knew she would be in all sorts of trouble. It had been bad enough dealing with the disappointment of Eleanor's rejection, without the inevitable questions and lectures she would now have to face from Kate.

The evening mist was once again closing in and it was so depressing to know she had no choice but to stay here and go back to that house on the hill, with the van outside, always reminding her of the huge sacrifice Kate was making.

The last thing she expected was to see one of her teachers walking across the park towards her. It was Mrs Kirk, her English teacher.

Oh, cripes. Now she would cop it. For sure she was about to get a serious revving. Maybe a suspension. Although Mrs Kirk wasn't too bad, actually, as teachers went. Not young, but not old either, the kind of teacher who kept kids in line without having to be too strict. She had long auburn hair and was a bit arty looking. This afternoon she was wearing a long skirt and boots and a flowing knitted cape that made Tilly more conscious than ever of her own lack of warm clothing.

'Hello, Tilly,' she said as she came closer.

'Hello, Miss.'

'I was just heading home when I saw you here, so I had to come and check you're okay. You weren't at school this afternoon.'

'No.'

'You know we've all been worried about you.'

This didn't sound like a revving. Not yet, at any rate. Just the same, Tilly dived into defensive mode. 'I called Kate – Mrs Sheridan – the person I'm living with. She knows I'm here and she's coming to get me.'

Mrs Kirk nodded. 'Yes, Mrs Sheridan rang me as well, to let me know.' Dropping her head slightly to one side, she smiled, but Tilly recognised it as the careful kind of smile adults used when they wanted to ask an awkward question.

'Tilly, you are comfortable about living with Kate Sheridan, aren't you?'

'Comfortable?' Tilly couldn't help frowning. It was a pretty weird question. 'Yeah,' she said. 'Her place is comfortable.'

Mrs Kirk frowned. 'I wasn't really talking about physical comfort. Not just a roof over your head and food to eat.'

'Oh.'

'I know you're dealing with a lot of personal unhappiness. I just wanted to make sure that – that your new living arrangements – and Mrs Sheridan's behaviour – aren't adding to your worries.'

Here we go. This teacher was just like the school counsellor in Cairns, trying to find out if Kate was some kind of weirdo. Tilly couldn't help feeling a bit guilty, especially considering how deeply upset Kate had sounded on the phone just a few minutes earlier. 'No,' she said decisively. 'No, I've been upset because I'm missing everyone in Cairns, but Kate's fine. She's good.'

For a scant second, Tilly wondered if she should mention the van issue, but Kate was now her only refuge, her only alternative to going into foster care. And she *had* been very vague about her actual plans for the van.

'Well, that's good news,' Mrs Kirk was saying, and this time her smile was brighter. 'So, we'll see you at school tomorrow?'

Tilly nodded. 'Sure.' She almost asked if she was in trouble. Surely she'd have to be punished for wagging school? But the teacher hadn't sounded too angry, so it was probably best to stay quiet.

Mrs Kirk had barely left the park before Flint the Sparkie's van pulled into a nearby parking spot. To Tilly's surprise, Kate emerged from the passenger seat.

Kate seemed a little cautious as she approached and Tilly was tense again, waiting for a lecture.

'Here you are,' was all Kate said, and she handed over a thick woollen jumper, which Tilly quickly hauled over her head. Kate had brought a scarf with her as well – one of her own, pale cream, luxuriously soft and fluffy as a cloud, and Tilly was so grateful for the blissful warmth, that she didn't bother to question why the electrician had also come to collect her.

Yet another surprise came moments later, when he joined them, and instead of going mad on Tilly, Kate introduced him as Liam Flint.

'Liam's suggested we should all have an early dinner at the Burralea pub,' Kate said and it was only then Tilly noticed how tired and strained she looked, not at all the laughing flirt she'd been on that other morning when the electrician had arrived to work on the van.

This evening Kate was very pale, with no makeup, rather messy hair and with raw shadows under her eyes. Actually, her eyes looked a bit pink, as if she might have been crying.

Had she really been *that* worried? Tilly knew her own mum would have been sick with worry if she'd thought Tilly had run away. But Kate? *Really?*

Tilly wasn't sure what to say, but no one seemed in a talkative mood. Without any more fuss, not even one reprimand, they headed out of the park and crossed the road to the old timber pub.

Inside the pub, on the ground floor, was a massive dining room with gleaming timber floors and lots of tables and chairs scattered about. A grand staircase led to a floor above and a stone fireplace had a proper log fire burning, even though it wasn't quite winter yet.

The whole scene was old-fashioned and quaint, but Tilly found it strangely comforting, like the soft scarf she kept close to her neck, even though she was no longer cold. They chose a table near the fire and Liam Flint bought drinks from the bar – a beer for himself, a glass of red wine for Kate and a lemon, lime and bitters for Tilly. It was a new taste for her, kind of grown up and different, but nice.

When she was offered a menu to choose from, she was allowed to select whatever she liked, so she went for battered fish and chips and a sticky date pudding for dessert. Her mum probably wouldn't have approved, but neither Kate nor Liam raised an eyebrow.

The food came quite quickly and after Tilly's lonely and uncomfortable day, it tasted amazing. Better still, the dining room with its cheerful fire was so cosy, she could sense the tight knot of misery that she'd been battling for days gently beginning to unravel.

CHAPTER FOURTEEN

Imogen Kirk loved the drive home to the farm, leaving Burralea township behind and literally heading for the hills. Most afternoons, once classes had finished, she was kept busy with any number of tasks – attending staff meetings, coaching debating teams, feeding assessment results into the school's database, to name just a few – and it was often dusk before she got away.

By then, the colours of the sky were the mellow pink and gold of a medieval fresco and as Imogen followed the road climbing westwards, the sun's softening rays lent the steeply grassed slopes a velvety quality. For nearly twenty years, she had lived in these hills and she still marvelled at how lucky she'd been when the Queensland Education Department had sent her so far north. Having grown up in Brisbane, Imogen had never expected to spend her adult life at the other end of the state, but after just a few years of teaching in the south-east, she'd applied for a transfer.

She'd been happy to go anywhere, just for fun, but she'd pictured herself on the Darling Downs, or maybe in the Wide Bay region. Instead, the Education Department had sent her sixteen hundred kilometres away to the Atherton Tablelands. And here, she'd met

Jamie Kirk, a quiet, big-shouldered dairy farmer.

With his rustic looks and smouldering smile, Jamie had seemed to the young English teacher as if he'd stepped straight from a Thomas Hardy novel. *Far from the Madding Crowd*. Her very own Gabriel Oak – without all the tragedy – much to her parents' relief.

Imogen and Jamie had been married in Burralea, in the little white wooden church on the hill. And they'd been ridiculously happy, even though the dairy industry had presented testing times in the years that followed. It helped that Jamie loved the farming life, never minded the early rises, and he'd met the industry's challenges head on. He'd been quick to introduce technology to the milking sheds, and he'd also diversified to grow top quality pasture for hay, which was in high demand in southern states with much lower rainfalls.

As for Imogen, she adored living perched on one of Queensland's highest hilltops and waking each morning to a spectacular view. Admittedly, this view was frequently shrouded by mist or rain, and Jamie would already have left their bed for the milking sheds.

Nevertheless, she'd always looked on their home's isolation with a sense of romance – their very own castle in the clouds – even though, in truth, the house was quite ordinary – three bedrooms, with a tin roof and weatherboard walls.

For most of the time Imogen had lived here, the timber walls had been stained brown and the roof painted green, a colour scheme that blended with the hills and the muddy tracks worn by the cows' daily journeys to and from the milking sheds. But a few years back, their daughter, Eve, who'd still lived at home at the time, had begged her father to change the house's colour scheme.

Grey had been the in-trend colour. Almost every house that had been 'done up' in Burralea had been repainted in some shade of grey.

Jamie had resisted. 'We don't need to follow the latest fad. Grey's boring.'

But he couldn't deny that their house needed a new coat of paint. Imogen had toyed with the possibility of pale primrose, but Jamie had totally baulked at anything so twee, so they'd gone with Eve's choice after all. These days their home was graced by soft, dove grey walls, a snowy white roof and white window trims, with a shiny black front door and black and white striped awnings on its western windows. Even Jamie had agreed it looked fresh and smart and uplifting. And in spring, surrounded by rivers of blooming agapanthus, it actually looked rather romantic.

But even without tarting up the house, life had been good for the Kirks.

Imogen was forever grateful that Jamie had been happy for her to continue with her teaching, and working in secondary schools had made her very aware of how fortunate her own family was. Their kids, Eve and Hamish, had grown up with boundless fresh air, incredible freedom, a cosy home, food aplenty, an unending supply of books and, perhaps more importantly, happy, healthy parents.

But this evening, as Imogen rounded the last bend, saw the house up ahead and the milking shed, with the evening star shining in a purple twilight sky and the silhouettes of the last straggling milkers dawdling and munching at verge grass on their way downhill, her thoughts were consumed by a youngster who wasn't nearly as fortunate as her own two.

Tilly Dent.

What a worrying day it had been, not knowing where Tilly had got to. Even poor Bridie Cooper had been beside herself, as if she'd somehow felt responsible. And Kate Sheridan had been stressed to the eyeballs.

Thank God Tilly had finally turned up and seemed okay. Okay on the surface, at least. But Imogen sensed the girl was seriously troubled.

Imogen had only met Kate, the guardian, briefly, when Tilly first arrived at the school, and the woman had admitted she was still coming to terms with her new and unexpected responsibilities. From every angle, this was an unusual and tricky situation. This afternoon, however, Tilly had been quite emphatic that her guardian was not adding to her problems and Imogen was grateful that she could relax on that score.

And now, she was home at last. She drove into the garage beside the house, lugged her heavy bag of books from the back seat and made her way indoors. As always, muddy gumboots were lined up by the back door, but Imogen merely wiped her own shoes carefully on the rubber mat and continued inside.

The kitchen welcomed her – warm and bright and smelling deliciously of roasting chicken. How wonderful. Imogen had been half-expecting that she would have to rustle up a quick stir-fry.

Jamie was there, too. Her steady, dependable, sweet and sexy Jamie, finished with the day's tasks, freshly showered, greeting her with a hug and a kiss and the offer of a glass of red.

Why not? Imogen was sure she'd earned one.

'This is a lovely surprise,' she said, nodding towards the oven as she accepted the glass. 'Did you put the chicken on?'

'No, that's all Hamish's work.' Her husband smiled. 'He's off to another rehearsal this evening and I think he felt in need of mean-ingful sustenance.'

'Fair enough.' Imogen loved that their son had joined the local little theatre. Hamish's personality was a true mix of both his parents. He'd always enjoyed helping his dad on the farm and although he was currently having a gap year, he planned to study Veterinary Science when he followed his sister to Townsville's JCU.

But Hamish also shared Imogen's love of books and the theatre, and he was rehearsing with the Burralea players for their new production of a Rolf Anders play, and thoroughly enjoying the experience from all accounts.

Now, she bent to peer through the oven door. 'Are my eyes deceiving me, or has Hamish included vegetables in this meal?'

'Potatoes, pumpkin and brussels sprouts, apparently.'

'We've brought him up well,' she said with a grin.

'Seems maybe we have.'

It was so good to be home and, with their dinner sorted, Imogen had the perfect opportunity to kick off her shoes and follow Jamie into the lounge room to relax. But some nights it was hard to switch off. She couldn't stop thinking about Tilly.

'Actually, where is Hamish?' she asked.

Jamie shrugged. 'Not sure. Probably in his room.'

She set her glass aside, untasted, on the coffee table. 'There's something I need to ask him. About the theatre group.' When her husband looked puzzled, she added, 'It's to do with an issue at school today. Won't bore you with the details and I won't be long. I'll be straight back.'

Leaving Jamie comfortably settled in his favourite armchair, she hurried down the hall to Hamish's room. No surprise that her son was playing a game on his laptop, which he managed to do while sprawled on his bed with his feet up the wall. How many times had she asked him not to do that?

Of course, there were marks on the wall. But then, Imogen knew that once Hamish headed off to university at the end of the year, she might not clean those marks away. She was pleased that both her kids wanted to go to uni, but she wasn't looking forward to the empty nest her chicks would leave behind.

When she knocked, Hamish looked up quickly, then paused his game.

'Hey,' he said.

'Hi, there. Thanks for putting dinner on. It smells fantastic.'

'No worries.'

'And excuse me for interrupting,' Imogen added as she took another step into his room. 'I just wanted a quick word – sounding you out, really, about the theatre group.'

'Sure. What do you want to know?'

'There's this new kid at school.' Now Imogen helped herself to the chair beside her son's desk, which remained pretty much abandoned these days. 'Her name's Tilly. She's only young – thirteen – and she's going through a really tough patch. She just moved here recently, hardly knows anyone. But she's in my English class and we were reading a play in class the other day. You know, with the kids reading out loud and taking parts. And I thought this girl was amazing. I couldn't help noticing how she slipped straight into character. Did it so naturally, as if, for a little while there, she forgot about her own sad situation.'

Hamish nodded, seeming to understand. 'So you reckon she'd go well in the theatre group?'

'Well, I think it's a possibility. It might help her to feel more settled and she's certainly got talent. I could suggest it to her. See if she's interested. But I wanted to sound you out first. What do you reckon?'

Hamish shrugged. 'I'd say yeah, why not? I guess the only problem is we're well underway with *Next Stop Mars*. I'm not sure Josie would be all that keen to change the cast around at this point. It's been tricky enough replacing Olivia.'

'Yes, I can imagine.' Imogen had been surprised to hear that the Burralea hardware store's Margot Cooper had stepped in to fill Olivia's role. It was rather an intriguing choice and Imogen was curious to see how it turned out.

'I guess there's always room for another robot in the play,' Hamish mused. 'Probably wouldn't give her many lines though.'

'Still, it might be fun. A diversion.'

'You want me to ask Josie tonight?'

'No, it's okay, thanks mate. It might be best if I speak to Josie first and explain the situation. And Tilly might not be interested, of course.'

'Sure. Okay.' Already, her son's attention was wandering back to his screen.

* * *

As soon as Liam Flint dropped Kate and Tilly back at the cottage, he headed straight for Kate's van to reconnect the battery.

'I won't hang around. You both need a good night's sleep,' he told them.

'Thanks so much for your help!' Kate called after his tall, retreating figure, but somehow, the thanks felt inadequate and she was strangely disconcerted that he was making such a hasty exit.

'No worries,' he called back, giving a brief wave.

It was very dark now, with no house or vehicle lights visible, and the half-moon overhead almost totally hidden by clouds. Kate could barely see Liam.

'Goodnight,' he called again. ''Night, Tilly!'

'Goodnight,' Tilly and Kate called together, but already he had lifted the van's bonnet and was getting on with the job.

'He's nice,' Tilly said, as the tinkering sound of metal on metal reached them through the darkness. 'I've been pretending to myself that my dad is like him.'

Oh, Tilly.

'My dad's not that nice, though, is he?'

Kate heard the mix of tension and hope in the girl's voice and she struggled to find the best way to answer. 'Well,' she said. 'When it comes to looks, Stan – your dad – isn't as dark as Liam. He has green eyes. Just like yours.'

'Really?'

'Yes, he has very sparkly green eyes,' Kate told her. 'And he's a great smiler. And he can be very charming. That's how he won me in the first place.'

'Wow.' Tilly was stock-still as she absorbed this news. 'Mum never told me about his eyes. She wouldn't tell me anything, really.'

'That's probably not so surprising,' Kate said gently. 'I suspect Stan probably charmed Angela, too, and then he would have let her down badly when he took off. She might have been deeply hurt.'

'Yeah, I guess that's probably how it was.' Tilly gave a small sigh, then lifted her schoolbag onto her shoulder. 'Anyway, I thought you said Liam wasn't your boyfriend.'

'He's not,' Kate retorted sharply, caught out by this sudden change of tack, and glad of the darkness as she felt her face heat. Flicking the torch on her phone, she pointed it downwards to light the path to the house. 'Liam was here today, working on the van, finishing the wiring.'

'And driving you into town and having dinner with you.'

'He stayed because he could see how upset I was. About you.'

It seemed Tilly had no response to this. As Kate opened the front door and switched on lights, she told herself that she was grateful that Liam had backed away so promptly now. She couldn't afford to be thrown off course by his thoughtfulness. She couldn't afford to be distracted by any man. Stan had taught her that lesson the hard way.

And tomorrow she would ring Christina Paxton, the lawyer, and tell her to go ahead with the application for that court order. And if Child Safety needed to come and check Kate out, she'd go through that as well. Tilly needed certainty. Security.

As for the van . . . one step at a time.

Turning her focus back to Tilly, Kate smiled. 'I'm sure you must be ready for a nice hot shower.'

'That would be great.' But now that they were inside the brightly lit house, Tilly dropped her gaze and fiddled with the strap of her schoolbag, and when she looked up again, her expression was shy. 'I'm sorry, Kate. Sorry about today. I didn't really think about how worried you might be.'

Kate felt her heart melt. 'I'm just so relieved that you didn't come to any harm.' Impulsively, she reached out, as if to hug Tilly, but a wary flash in those green eyes warned that Tilly might not be ready for such a motherly response. Kate patted her shoulder instead.

'I'll grab that shower,' Tilly said, and she looked a little weepy as she headed down the hall.

Watching her, Kate could feel her own emotions fraying. She flopped into an armchair, trying to calm the storm inside her – the memories of Stan, her worries about Tilly, her sympathy for the girl's poor mother. And hovering also in the mix – Liam Flint's surprising involvement.

This afternoon, Kate had been too stressed to question his decision to hang around. But he hadn't shown the slightest sign of flirting and once he'd realised how worried she was, he'd seemed genuinely concerned for her. Later, after her exhausting and stressful afternoon, she'd found his suggestion of dinner at the pub both practical and incredibly appealing.

The meal had been almost *too* cosy and enjoyable, though. Apart from the pleasure of a warm and inviting dining room, with a crackling fire and the tempting aroma of hot dinners wafting from the nearby kitchen, there'd been a deceptive intimacy with the three of them together, almost like a family.

And then there was the way Liam had smiled at Kate across the table. At one point his smile had been quite – there could be no other word for it – *heated*.

But surely her imagination had been playing tricks?

Liam hadn't been coming on to her. She'd been looking her worst in her oldest jeans and a hastily dragged-on jumper. She hadn't bothered with makeup, hadn't even taken the time to do her hair properly. And yet . . .

That smile . . .

Kate was still shocked by the way she'd reacted. She'd almost forgotten those helpless yearnings. Surely, she hadn't come into Burralea this evening to rescue Tilly, only to find herself distracted by their male companion?

One thing was certain, she had to be careful. Very, very careful.

* * *

As the lights of Burralea shimmered in the darkness ahead of Liam, he decided to head back to the pub. He wasn't ready to go home and spend another evening alone. He needed a drink in the bar, surrounding himself with chatter and laughter. Most of all, he needed a distraction.

In the past few hours, he'd spent way too much time thinking about Kate Sheridan. At first, working away in her van, he'd been amused by how flustered she'd been as she'd delivered her awkward anti-flirting claim. Hell, Liam was used to harmless banter with clients, playing into popular myths about tradies and lonely women, and he'd enjoyed teasing Kate when he'd told her he only slept with women who played hard to get.

The joke had landed on the other foot, though, when he realised he couldn't stop thinking about Kate. He'd already developed a healthy respect for her handywoman skills. A woman doing a solo renovation on an entire van was damned intriguing. Kate not only knew how to use a screwdriver, but a nail gun *and* a circular saw, and Liam found this idea crazily sexy.

Of course, he also hadn't missed the appeal of her slender body. But today there'd been something else – a touching vulnerability combined with arresting dark eyes and a soft and sweet mouth.

And then, that light in her eyes. The look that from any other woman usually meant she was chatting him up.

These details had been haunting Liam before Kate had even mentioned her arsehole ex-husband, or the girl who'd gone missing, which was when he'd suddenly found himself way too invested in her plight and wanting to offer assistance. He couldn't help but admire Kate for taking this kid on. Couldn't help being sympathetic to her dilemma – caught between getting the van ready for her big adventure and shouldering the responsibility of another woman's kid.

Hell. His ex-wife, Simone, hadn't even wanted the bother of having their own children, let alone someone else's. Just once, while Liam had been away working on a mine site, Simone had tried to babysit for one of her friends, but as soon as the kid even looked like crying, Simone had been on the phone to her mother in a panic. And, of course, Gail had abandoned a dinner party to rush to Simone's aid.

So yeah, full marks to Kate. Liam had been impressed by the way she'd forgiven Tilly for the fright her running away had caused, offering the kid warmth and support this evening rather than lectures.

And he had to admit, there was something about Tilly that had sucked him in too. The kid had looked dead scared when he'd arrived with Kate at the park, but there was also a gutsiness about her, an admirable dignity in the way she'd accepted their help without a huge post-mortem of her failed attempt to escape.

Tied to this episode, however, was the uncomfortable reality that Kate's complicated family issues sure as hell justified her choice of keeping Liam at bay. And the last thing he wanted was to stuff things up for her. Which was why he'd made a neat exit as soon as he'd delivered Kate and Tilly safely home and reconnected the battery.

Now, his task was to clear his head. To reset.

'Sparkie, old mate, good to see you!'

It seemed Liam was in luck. As soon as he stepped into the noisy bar, he was greeted by Rolf Anders, comfortably perched on one of the stools and grinning and waving to him.

Rolf was a local, but he was also a novelist and a highly successful one at that. Before he'd turned to a writing career, however, Rolf had been a builder, a fellow tradesman, and from this common ground, he and Liam had formed a solid friendship.

'Great to see you, too.' Liam pulled up a stool next to Rolf. 'Last I heard, you were in Sydney.'

'Yeah. I had a couple of weeks down there, talking to theatrical types mostly.'

'The big smoke's always interesting. Did you have a good time?'

'Couldn't wait to get back here.'

Liam grinned. He didn't entirely believe Rolf, but he also wasn't especially surprised by his response. Rolf had built himself a spectacular home not far out of Burralea, in an idyllic setting among tall pines and overlooking beautiful Lake Tinaroo. It was the kind of fantasy most people only dreamed of.

Liam's own home was a modest cottage on the edge of town, his ex having well and truly fleeced him. But his divorce from Simone was another story he didn't want to dwell on tonight. 'Can I get you another of those?' he asked, nodding to Rolf's almost empty glass. 'Scotch, isn't it?'

Rolf's response was an even broader grin. 'Thanks, mate. Won't say no.'

Liam ordered two scotches and felt himself relax. This was just what he needed – a good, smoky dram and a friendly conversation with a diverting companion.

'Such fortunate timing,' Rolf said as the barman set their drinks in front of them. 'I've been meaning to get in touch with you, Liam. The local little theatre's putting on a play I wrote and I was wondering if you might be able to help with a little fancy lighting.'

Liam lifted an eyebrow. 'How fancy?'

'Oh, nothing too out of the box. The Burralea players have a tight budget, of course, so it'll have to be fairly simple. I guess I'm just hoping for a bit of atmosphere. A few LED lights here and there. This play's set in outer space, you see. It mostly takes place on a spaceship heading to Mars.'

'Wow, that's different.'

'I know, I know . . . it's nothing like my novels, but I was in the mood to try something totally new.'

'And why not?' Liam asked, but then he frowned. 'I'm afraid my knowledge of theatre lighting is fairly basic.'

'But you helped with the council's Christmas pageant last year and that was bloody brilliant.'

'Well, thanks. And yeah, I've had *some* experience. When I was living in Brisbane, I worked for a while with a corporate events manager and he put me through a quick design course. I guess I can manage basic programming of lights, that sort of thing.'

'Which means you'd be perfect for this job.' Rolf was beaming now. 'Poor Josie went into a total flap when I tried to talk to her about the lighting. I wasn't asking for anything too outrageous, but it seems lighting and sound are her biggest headaches. She has willing helpers, but it's all so technical these days, they can't keep up.'

'Yeah, it can be a challenge. But as long as the individual lights are all matched up to the lighting board, it shouldn't be too difficult, even for non-techie types.'

'If you could do that for them, so they could manage by pushing levers up or down, they'd be over the moon, I reckon.'

Liam savoured another smoky sip of his scotch, knowing he could be about to surrender his precious spare time for the next few weeks. His thoughts flashed to Kate and the unexpected pleasure of sharing a cosy meal with her.

Yeah, but that wasn't going to happen again. And hadn't he already decided he needed a distraction? On a reckless impulse, he said, 'Sure. Shouldn't be too hard.'

Rolf's eyes shone. 'So you'll lend a hand?'

This time, Liam didn't hesitate. 'Why not?' He gave a small chuckle. 'I guess you're in luck. You caught me at the right moment. I'm also in the mood to try my hand at something different.'

'That's brilliant!' Rolf's grin was wider than ever as he raised his glass to clink against Liam's.

'Have you already worked out the set design?' Liam couldn't help asking.

'Only in very broad terms. Margot from the hardware store is pretty experienced and she has a few ideas for the spaceship's bridge. Glass desks at right angles, workstations built out of cardboard and painted silver, that sort of thing. But I'm thinking that anyone on a spaceship to Mars will see the stars and planets in great brilliance.'

'Yeah, and the view out the portholes or viewing screens would change during the voyage.'

'Exactly.' Rolf looked genuinely excited now. 'The local audience would go apeshit if we could manage something like that. Tell me what you're thinking. Remember, we don't have to be totally accurate and try to match up the real world constellations with what our voyagers might see.'

'Just off the top of my head, I reckon I'd go with LED lights. If we poked holes in fabric, for example, I could wire it up with little lights. As many as you like, I guess. Constellations. Whatever.'

'Perfect.' Rolf gave an enthusiastic nod. 'Nothing as intense as the Milky Way, of course. Just a general impression, I guess.'

'Then again,' added Liam. 'It could be fun to throw in a few familiar constellations like the Southern Cross, or even some of the zodiac groups.'

'Cancer the Crab. Taurus the Bull.' Rolf threw up his hands in enthusiastic delight. 'Brilliant. But I'm more than happy to leave that up to you.'

'I guess, with a little careful programming, the patterns could change.'

'You can do that?'

'I can give it a damn good go.'

Rolf slapped his thigh. 'I love you, mate. I'll tell Josie she can rescue my lighting project from her too-hard basket.'

CHAPTER FIFTEEN

Olivia wasn't surprised to discover Josie on her front doorstep. She'd been expecting, or rather *dreading*, a conversation about the previous week's rehearsal.

She was more than a little embarrassed about the way she'd left the hall so abruptly. It was poor form – Olivia had known that – but if she'd stayed, everyone would have seen the hugely embarrassing tears streaming down her face.

Until that moment when Margot had stepped onto the stage and delivered Lady X's lines so competently, Olivia hadn't realised how fragile her own ego was. Suddenly, she'd felt as if her very sense of self had been snuffed out. Which was ridiculous, of course. A complete overreaction, but Olivia hadn't had a hope of holding back her tears.

That night, as she'd struggled home, she'd been fighting those tears all the way. Tears of self-pity, of anger. Tears of envy. And loneliness. Such a bewildering cocktail of emotions.

Ever since then, Olivia had felt lost, consumed by a dreadful emptiness, shuffling about her little house, sunk in a depression almost as bleak and deep as those long ago, dark days after she'd first arrived in Hollywood. It was so very hard to accept that she was no longer indispensable to the Burralea players.

Even more painful had been coming face to face with the grim realisation that without her involvement in the little theatre, she was nothing but a lonely old woman. This was, however, the glaring, obvious truth. Olivia had no partner, no children, no grandchildren.

Yes, there'd been willing helpers popping around since her accident, but Olivia had dismissed them as soon as she'd been allowed to move about, assuring them that she didn't really need help with meals and housework. So even those kindly visits had dropped off.

For the most part, her loneliness was of her own making, of course. She knew this, and she knew she had tried to buoy herself out of her funk. She'd hoped that reading might at least lift her spirits and she'd turned to her old favourites – Mary Wesley, Maeve Binchy, Georgette Heyer – but even these gifted storytellers hadn't helped her to feel any better.

Now, heaven help her, here was Josie, looking as small and unprepossessing as ever, but with her intelligent eyes shining as bright as search lights from beneath her dyed auburn fringe.

Olivia could guess why Josie had come. Despite her friendly overtures, Josie's responsibility was first and foremost to the theatre and she wanted to make certain that Olivia would not cause any trouble about Margot stepping up for Lady X. Which was fair enough. The only problem for Olivia was that she couldn't be sure she had the inner fortitude to take part in this conversation with the necessary grace and goodwill.

But she had no choice and she would have to do her best.

'Josie, dear.' As Olivia opened the flyscreen door, she was grateful that she remembered to squeeze her cheek muscles to produce a smile. 'Lovely to see you.'

'You, too, Olivia. How are you?' Josie held up a brown paper bag. 'I come bearing croissants.'

'From the bakery? How thoughtful.' Olivia had heard about Camille, the new French girl who'd started working at Ben Shaw's local bakery. Apparently, she'd caused quite a sensation with her delicious croissants.

'Actually, *I* have a fresh jar of blueberry jam,' Olivia responded, pleased that she had made the effort last weekend to limp to the park at the end of her block where the local farmers and artisans sold their wares at the monthly markets.

And now, to her surprise, the very thought of company and a luscious croissant filled with beautiful blueberry jam prompted an unexpected lift to her spirits. Oh, dear, was she really so fickle?

Olivia suggested Josie follow her through to the kitchen, as it was so much easier to sit at the little table there than trying to ferry tea things on a tray up and down the hall. Fortunately, the sink and benches were relatively tidy, and it was a pleasant enough room with its pretty, old-fashioned dresser showing off her best blue and white china. Better still, her kitchen caught the morning sun and the pot plants on her windowsill were thriving, adding to the agreeable atmosphere.

After her first sip of hot, sweet tea, Olivia, feeling bolder, decided she wouldn't wait for her visitor to find the right opening. 'Josie,' she said, diving straight in. 'You mustn't worry that I'm going to put up any resistance.'

Josie's normally wide eyes almost popped now, no doubt with shock, but she quickly gave a guilty little smile, as if she realised she'd been caught out. 'I assume you're talking about Margot?'

'Yes, of course.' Olivia saw no point in beating about the bush. 'Margot's quite competent as Lady X.'

'She is,' Josie agreed. 'And given time and experience, I think she might even be more than merely competent.'

'Perhaps.' Having begun so magnanimously, Olivia wasn't prepared to pile on the enthusiasm too thickly. She pushed the plate of croissants towards Josie. 'We'd better eat these while they're still warm.'

An affable silence fell then as they carefully slit the pastries open and helped themselves to the jam. Then there was the bliss of first bites.

'Oh, my goodness,' Olivia said as she swallowed the divine buttery flakes. 'That's not a taste you'd expect to find in Burralea.'

Josie laughed. 'No, I guess not.'

They happily munched a little more and Olivia took another sip of her tea. *So far, so good.*

As Josie set her cup down, her expressive face was filled with empathy. 'So, my dear, apart from the wretched ankle, how are you finding things, generally?' With another, carefully gentle smile, she added, 'I know it's hard for you, not being part of the production.'

'Well, yes, I can't pretend I'm enjoying my time out.' Olivia allowed herself a small sigh. And then, because so many thoughts had been boiling inside her, she couldn't help continuing. 'To be honest, I've even found myself thinking I should have joined a choir instead of the theatre. At least then I'd be able to hide in the back row, blending my voice with everyone else's, and no one would have minded about the damn moon boot.'

'Goodness.' Josie looked more amused than sympathetic. 'Things can't be that bad, surely? I'm sorry, but I can't see our Olivia ever hiding in the back row of any production, hoping to make herself invisible.'

Olivia might have taken offence at this, but there was something about the way Josie had said 'our Olivia' that touched her in the most unexpected way, rendering her silent.

'I've been very aware that this accident has been tough for you,' Josie went on to say next. 'And, actually, I've been wondering if you might be interested in a little side project?'

'Oh?' A small spurt of excitement flared in Olivia's chest. A little side project must surely mean another play, something to start working on for a production later in the year. 'A side project does sound interesting. What is it?'

'It's a little different,' Josie said cautiously. 'Imogen Kirk from the high school approached me.'

'Hamish's mother?'

'Yes. She mostly teaches English and she has a young student in one of her classes – a girl who's just moved here recently. It's all rather sad. The girl's mother died and there's no father in the picture and she's been sent to live with a guardian. I think the guardian's an extended family member. At any rate, the kid's finding it all rather difficult.'

Where was this leading? Olivia wondered how on earth this sad story could have anything to do with her.

'The thing is,' Josie said next, as if she'd sensed Olivia's unspoken questions, 'Imogen believes this girl has acting ability, so she sounded me out about having her join the little theatre.'

'I see. But you're only weeks away from production.'

'Yes. Imogen knows this, of course, and she's warned the girl that it would be too late to score a decent part, but apparently she still seems quite interested.'

Olivia frowned. 'I'm sorry, but I don't see how this has anything to do with me.'

'I was thinking along the lines of a few extra lessons for her – one on one – a little mentorship from you, perhaps.'

Good heavens. Olivia had never seen herself in a mentoring role. She was a performer, not a teacher. What was the old saying? *Those who can, do; those who can't, teach.* 'How old is this girl?' she asked tightly.

'Thirteen, I think.'

Now, Olivia couldn't hold back her dismay. 'Josie, you've got to be joking. I can't work with teenagers. I know absolutely nothing about them.'

'But you've had so much experience.'

'On the stage, yes, but not as a teacher, and certainly not with children. And think about it, Josie. Seriously, do you really think a thirteen-year-old would want to take lessons from an old crone like me?' Olivia was certain she had nothing in common with Gen Z, with their permanently attached phones and their fingernails all painted in different colours. They were almost like another species. 'I'm quite sure I couldn't help this girl.'

'But look at the way you've helped Hamish and Heidi. And Derek, for that matter.'

Olivia blinked. 'Do you really think I've helped them?'

'Of course.'

'Oh.' Olivia hadn't even realised Josie was aware of those discreet suggestions she'd made to other members of the cast from time to time. She'd tried to be careful, not treading on their director's toes. 'Actually,' she added now, as a bright idea struck, 'if you think my input might help, I'd be more useful giving Margot a few coaching sessions, wouldn't I?'

'Possibly.' But Josie didn't look so confident now as she leaned back in her chair and crossed her arms tightly. In fact, she looked as cornered as a bad poker player, and she dropped her gaze, then seemed to take a breath – for courage? – before she finally looked up and spoke. 'The thing is, Margot's already having extra coaching. We had a special Zoom session last night for her and Peter with Freddie Sinclair.'

'Who's Freddie Sinclair?'

'He's a rather big-time director, actually. Rolf Anders met him in Sydney when he was down there recently and he's producing *Next Stop Mars* at the Opera House.'

'Oh, yes. Rolf mentioned that was going ahead.' An unwelcome shiver skittered down Olivia's spine. She'd been trying not to think about Michael Carruthers playing Lord X down in Sydney. That news had only made her more deeply depressed about her own extraction from the play. 'So – this tutorial – or whatever it was,' she said, wishing she could deflect her attention from Michael and Sydney and this Freddie fellow. 'Was it all conducted over the internet?'

'Yes, we had a Zoom session last night at my place.' Josie's eyes were once again shining and animated. 'I thought it would be a boost for Margot's confidence. And it was pretty amazing really. Here we were in Burralea, with Margot and Peter delivering their lines in front of my computer. And there was this wonderful director giving them feedback from Sydney. Technology really is fantastic, isn't it?'

'Quite,' said Olivia faintly. 'And – and you didn't mind?'

'I was thrilled,' Josie said, but then she frowned. 'Why would I mind?'

'I thought it might be disconcerting to have another director interfere with your vision?' Olivia had always taken such great pains not to cross this line herself.

'Heavens, no,' exclaimed Josie. 'I'm fully aware that I'm very much an amateur. It was wonderful to have Freddie's professional feedback. He was ever so encouraging.'

'Well.' Once again, Olivia remembered to squeeze her cheek muscles. 'That's a satisfactory result for you.'

'Yes, it was wonderful.' Josie stood and began to clear the table.

'Don't worry about those things,' Olivia responded perhaps a touch too snappily. 'I can manage.'

'Oh, let me help a little.' Josie carried the plates, cups and saucers to the sink deftly and efficiently, as if she'd spent half her life waitressing in cafés. Then she picked up her handbag and slipped the straps over her shoulder. 'Thanks for the cuppa.'

'My pleasure. And thank you for the croissants.'

As Josie reached the kitchen doorway, she turned back. 'So, will you give some thought to whether you'd like to help Tilly Dent?'

'Tilly Dent?'

'The young girl I was telling you about.'

'Oh, of course.' Olivia toyed with the idea of asking if there'd be any payment. A little extra cash always came in handy.

Again, Josie was one step ahead of her. 'I imagine it would probably be on a voluntary basis.'

This was more or less a challenge for Olivia. Of course, she was prepared to be charitable. After all, it wasn't as if she had anything else to do with her time. And who knew? If she really tried, she could probably dredge up a few useful exercises from long ago classes. Or she might even think up a few ideas of her own. It could be interesting to try to put the most important things she'd learned about acting down on paper. And if she was stuck, there was always information on the internet.

'Well, all right,' she said quickly, before she had time for second thoughts.

* * *

'The Burralea Theatre? Really?' Bridie rolled her eyes as if she couldn't quite believe what Tilly had just told her.

Tilly gave a defensive shrug. 'I need to do something besides school and I quite like acting.' With another shrug, she added, 'I'm not all that into sport.'

It was lunchtime and Tilly and Bridie were both eating tuckshop lunches. They'd chosen hotdogs slathered with tomato sauce, knowing they would never be served these at home.

Almost a week had passed since Tilly's attempted runaway and, apart from another longish chat with Mrs Kirk, this time in her office, there'd been very little fuss made about her disappearance from school. Tilly knew she'd been lucky to get off so lightly, and she was slowly coming to terms with the fact that she was going to be stuck here in Burralea for the foreseeable future.

Bridie had been extra nice to her – incredibly nice, really – and Tilly was grateful for the way the girl had reached out, especially as Zara had sent a Snapchat saying that perhaps they shouldn't write to each other for a while.

This message had gutted Tilly. She'd found it on her phone after Liam had dropped her and Kate home, and she was sure Eleanor had made Zara write it, but that knowledge hadn't helped.

Tilly had thrown herself onto her bed and wept into her pillow and she might have cried all night, if Kate hadn't come in and found her.

Kate had been rather lovely about it. She'd called Tilly sweetheart and had given her the biggest hug. 'I'm sorry you feel so miserable,' she said. 'I know it must be terribly hard for you, having to come here to a strange new place, with none of your friends. But I really do care about you, Tilly. I'm here for you, honey, and I promise I'll help you every way I can.'

It was the first proper hug from an adult that Tilly had received since her mum had died. Jed had been too cautious to hug her when she'd been upset. He'd just given her hair a scruff to show that he'd cared and Tilly had pretended to hate it.

To her surprise, just feeling Kate's warm arms around her and holding her so very close *had* helped.

'You must miss your mum so much,' Kate had said gently. 'Would you feel comfortable telling me about her? I'd love to know more.'

Tilly hadn't been sure where to start. It was impossible for anyone else to understand her special bond with her mum, but she did feel an urge to try to share a little of this with Kate. 'For a long time it was just Mum and me,' she said. 'Just the two of us. Mum worked really hard during the week, so she could have the weekends off to be with me. Not that we did anything especially exciting, but we always went shopping on Saturday mornings. First we'd look up all the specials and we'd make a list and we'd be really careful about only buying the things on our list. We needed to know exactly how much it was going to cost, you see. And then, if we had money left over, we'd eat out for lunch – usually sushi. And on Sunday mornings we did yoga in the park.'

'Yoga?' Kate sounded surprised.

Tilly gave a smiling little shrug. 'I know it sounds lame, but it was actually pretty cool fun. The park was down on the water-front and we'd go early before it got too hot. Not just Mum and me, a whole group of people – old, young, all ages – and we'd go to a café together afterwards for coffee and milkshakes. Mum said yoga helped keep her strong and flexible for her work. She was a cleaner, you see.'

It was good to feel safe about telling Kate this. Some of the bitchier kids in Cairns had teased Tilly about her mum's 'cleaning career', but she could sense that Kate wouldn't look down her nose at such a humble job.

'Mostly Mum worked in other people's homes,' Tilly said. 'But two days a week she worked in the hospital – still as a cleaner. That's where she met Jed, after he fell off his motorbike.'

Kate smiled. 'That almost sounds like something that might happen in a movie.'

'I guess.'

'And at some point Jed moved in with you?'

'Yeah, but not for ages.' Now Tilly was also smiling. 'I knew Mum was worried about upsetting me. I had to spell it out to her that it was fine by me, if she wanted her boyfriend to move in full time – just as long as she and I could still have our Friday nights at Zara's.'

Of course, the mention of Zara had set Tilly crying again and Kate had stayed with her that night until she'd fallen asleep.

With Kate nearby and the lamp turned low while a Spotify soundtrack played softly, Tilly had felt herself relaxing, just as she had in the pub, and for the first time in ages, she'd slept soundly.

The next day at school, Mrs Kirk had been extra nice to her and Bridie had gone out of her way to be friendly, and this school hadn't seemed quite so bad after all. Since then, Tilly had even been looking forward to giving Mrs Kirk's suggestion of the Burralea Little Theatre a go.

Just last year in Cairns, Tilly's English teacher had entered her and a few other kids in an eisteddfod. They'd had to recite poetry and Tilly had won first prize in her age group. She'd been presented with an engraved cup with her name on it. Now the cup was somewhere in the boxes in Kate's laundry.

But here was Bridie, suggesting that joining the local little theatre was a pretty dumb idea.

'What's wrong with the little theatre?' Tilly asked her.

Bridie pulled a face. 'Well, for starters, it's full of oldies. I mean, my mum's in it.'

Jeepers. Tilly tried to imagine Bridie's mega ordinary mum acting on stage, but somehow the picture wouldn't gel.

But then Bridie shrugged. 'Hamish Kirk's in it too though, and he's pretty cool.'

'Is he related to Mrs Kirk, our teacher?'

'Yeah, he's her son. He was a senior here last year. He's kinda hot, actually. And there are other kids,' Bridie admitted. 'A fair few kids, I guess, at least when they do their Christmas musical.'

Tilly quite liked the idea of a Christmas musical. 'Well, I suppose I can at least try it out,' she said. 'If I don't like it I don't have to keep going.'

***

Kate was genuinely pleased that Tilly was keen to follow up on her teacher's suggestion of trying Burralea's little theatre group. She offered to go along to the first rehearsal, in case Tilly decided after five minutes that she needed to escape, but the girl had been happy to be dropped off.

'And even if I hate it, I'll stay till the end,' she told Kate. 'I won't try to sneak away. Promise.'

Burralea was such a tiny town it was almost deserted in the evenings, but at least there were quite a few cars parked outside the old barn-like community hall where the theatre group met. Lights streamed from the hall's windows and doorways and Tilly seemed quietly excited as they pulled up. She'd chosen to wear ripped jeans and white sneakers, with a black and white striped T-shirt, and a black pullover draped around her shoulders.

'This should be okay, shouldn't it?' she'd asked Kate when she'd emerged from her room to give a quick twirl.

'I'd say it's perfect.' Kate had been pleased to be asked, while also thinking the girl had definite fashion flair.

Now Tilly crossed the footpath and mounted the steps leading into the hall, then paused in the doorway to turn back and wave to Kate.

'Have fun,' Kate whispered, and she realised that she meant it. Sincerely. In her heart, she was now committed to this kid. There was no going back, and she felt strangely okay about taking on this huge responsibility.

Not that she'd totally given up on the van. Last week at the pub, she'd even discussed that problem with Liam and Tilly. As they'd sat around a table having dinner, almost like a regular family – a concept that Kate still found both incredible *and* dangerous – she'd explained that she was determined to finish her renovation goals. She couldn't bear to give up halfway through a project. But for the time being, she was prepared to put her travel plans on hold.

Maybe she would rent the van out and make a little money on the side. Or maybe she would simply use it to accommodate any extra guests. Kate *had* almost suggested that she and Tilly might take off together for the summer holidays. They could rearrange the sleeping area, change the double bed into twin bunks, and then they could head south.

But she'd feared the girl might think being stuck in such a small space with a fifty-something was the worst idea ever. For now, at least, Kate had alternative options.

'And you're more important than the van,' she had told Tilly later that night, when she'd found the poor kid weeping her heart out over a distressing message from her friend Zara. 'I hope you believe that I don't resent you. I'm here for you, Tilly. You can trust me on that, I promise.'

As Kate said this, she could feel a corner of her heart still give a little whimper at the thought of setting aside the promise of freedom. And if she was totally, brutally honest, she still resented Stan for leaving her with this burden. But she also knew she could never feel good about herself, could never live with her pesky conscience, if she didn't give Tilly her total support.

Fortunately, in the week since then, Tilly had seemed pleasingly calmer, and her mood had definitely perked up after she and Kate had spent an evening unpacking the boxes in the laundry, deciding what might be useful or decorative and what should be stowed away, or even dumped.

Kate could only guess how deeply emotional this task must have been for Tilly, but the kid had been keen to get started and, for the most part, she'd seemed to enjoy rediscovering treasures salvaged from the only other home she'd even known.

The most exciting find was a small silver cup. Tilly gave a little squeal when she discovered it, first lifting it triumphantly high and then hugging it to her chest.

'Is that a trophy?' Kate asked.

Tilly nodded. 'I won it at the eisteddfod.'

'Wow! That's wonderful! Let me see.' Kate held out her hand. The cup was engraved.

Tilly Dent

Junior Speech and Drama Championship

11–14 years

'How amazing is that?' Kate knew all too well how big a deal this was. She could still remember Chelsea's dancing eisteddfods and the huge family excitement the one year she'd won a trophy. 'You clever girl,' she told Tilly and then she gave her another hug, the second hug in a matter of days, before fetching a special microfibre cloth to dust and polish the trophy properly. 'I think this deserves to go in the lounge room, don't you?'

They set it in pride of place on a shelf on the bright pink wall, then returned to the business of unpacking.

There were gardening tools – a hand trowel, a weeding fork, secateurs and a small rake – which they put into a wooden crate to be stored in the shed outside. And crockery, which Kate was happy to make space for in her kitchen.

'Mum liked to use the bright flowery plates for breakfast and the plain white ones for dinner,' Tilly explained.

'So you can start the day with a smile?' Kate suggested. 'And finish with sophistication?'

Despite the shrug Tilly gave at this, she looked pleased. 'And we should definitely use Mum's wok,' she declared, as she dived deeper into a box.

Angela's wok was obviously very good quality and Kate made a silent vow to upgrade her stir-frying skills. Then they came across a little wooden box, quite old with a Chinese painting on the lid and also on the coasters inside. The paintings were faded and worn and scratched.

'I think these were my grandmother's,' said Tilly. 'But Mum wouldn't tell me much about her, except that she was born in Hong Kong and she met my grandfather there. He was an English sailor, and they somehow ran away together, then ended up here in Australia.'

'Well, you should definitely keep this box to remember her,' Kate said, but she was also remembering the grim story Jed Larsen had passed on about how Angela had run away from her drug-addicted parents when she was seventeen. Which was, of course, another reason to take good care of Tilly now.

In many ways it had been a relief to have reached this point of acceptance. And the decision had proved timely when a woman from Child Safety turned up on Kate's doorstep the very next day, brimming with officialdom and a raft of interview questions. Luckily, she had deemed Kate to be a suitable carer, so that was another hurdle behind them.

This evening, however, after dropping Tilly off at the theatre, Kate had a different family issue to deal with and it involved making two rather difficult but important phone calls.

She'd been waiting for the right moment to contact her daughters with the news that they had a half-sister. She hadn't wanted to ring them during the day while they were at work, but then, in the evenings, Tilly had been with her.

Admittedly, Kate was aware that she might have been finding excuses for not contacting Pippa and Chelsea earlier. She did feel a tad guilty, but she told herself she had still been shell-shocked. Or perhaps Stan's misbehaviour had taught her that family ties might be safer when they weren't so tightly bound.

Whatever the reason, the time for finding excuses was over. Tonight, Kate knew she couldn't put this task off any longer.

She was nervous, though. This news was huge. She figured Chelsea would probably cope okay, but she was anxious about ringing Pippa. Her elder daughter had never been particularly secure and was already touchy about her mother's move to the Tablelands.

Heaven knew how Pippa was going to react to this new revelation. Kate was hoping she could distract her from a too over-the-top reaction by focusing more on her pregnancy.

It seemed, however, that the universe was one step ahead of Kate. She had just reached home and was barely out of her vehicle when her phone rang, and it was Pippa's name that lit up on her screen.

'Hey, Pipps,' she said as she locked the van. 'You won't believe it, but I was just about to ring you.'

'About time, Mother dearest. You must be feeling pretty damn guilty.'

'Excuse me?'

'When were you going to bother telling your daughters about this kid you've adopted?'

Kate couldn't hold back a small groan. 'That's exactly why I was about to ring you,' she said as she set the key in her front door. 'But I haven't adopted her.' Kate used her elbow to close the door behind her. 'And anyway,' she said as she turned on lights, 'how did you hear about Tilly?'

'I had a message from Jessica Booth. Remember her? She was in my class at school and she married Brett Jones from Burralea. Jessica and I are friends on Facebook.'

'Facebook?' Kate repeated, aghast, as she imagined her private life splattered all over social media.

'No need to panic, Mum. Jessica sent me a direct message. Nothing public. To be honest, I almost didn't bother reading it. I'd had enough from her when she was pestering me about Dad and all the dirt about him in the papers. Today, she was full of how you've taken this kid in. Far out, Mum, I can't believe it.'

'But I —'

'How could you? You knew I was hoping you'd move here, closer to *us*. And now, instead, you're starting on a whole new family up there.'

'Hardly a family, Pippa.'

'But this girl – this teenager – she's living with you, isn't she?'

'Yes.'

'And you're her guardian?'

'It's not official yet.' Kate lowered herself into an armchair. 'But yes, I'm taking care of her.'

'And you didn't think this news was worth sharing with your daughters?' With each question Pippa's voice was growing shriller.

'I'm sorry, Pippa. If you want to have a proper conversation about this, you're going to have to calm down.'

'It's pretty hard to calm down about something so hurtful. It's almost like Chelsea and I don't exist for you anymore.'

'Come on, that's a bit harsh. I said I'm sorry and I can explain.' Kate kicked off her shoes and tried to settle more comfortably in her chair. 'It all happened out of the blue and I really didn't have many options, but this girl – her name's Tilly – is your half-sister.'

'My *what*?' Now Pippa was screeching and Kate had to hold the phone away.

'Your half-sister,' Kate repeated with excessive patience. 'Stan, your dad, is her father.'

'Holy shit.' This was little more than a whisper now and then Pippa was silent, no doubt trying to digest this latest shock delivered by her father.

As calmly as she could, Kate explained. She told Pippa it was more than likely that Stan had never known about Tilly. She also told her about Angela, Tilly's unfortunate mother, about the will she'd left and Jed Larsen's unexpected arrival, as well as the subsequent conversations with the solicitor.

Not surprisingly, Pippa had a host of questions. What was Tilly like? Had Kate told Chelsea yet? Did this girl look like either of them? Was Tilly short for Matilda? And what about Kate's van? What was she going to do with that?

Patiently, Kate answered this avalanche. It took quite some time. Yes, she would phone Chelsea this evening. No, Tilly wasn't a shortened form of any other name, and apart from her green eyes, which were just like Stan's, she was quite petite and dark and looked distinctly different from the rest of the family. As for the van, there was still a big question mark hanging over that.

Eventually, Kate managed to steer the conversation back to an important question of her own. 'I was actually keen to hear how you are, Pipps. Are you keeping well? And how did David take the news about the baby?'

These quite reasonable questions were met by a rather disconcerting sigh and then silence.

'Pippa? Are you there? Is everything all right? You're keeping well, aren't you?'

'Yes, yes. I'm fine, thanks. I'm fighting fit. I don't even have morning sickness. Not yet, at any rate.' But a new kind of impatience had crept into her daughter's voice, almost as if this was a topic she would prefer to avoid.

'And David?' Kate persisted. 'He's happy about the baby?'

'Not really.' Now there was another pause and another sigh, while Kate's stomach began to churn. 'He says we should have waited. He reckons we haven't saved enough yet. We should save for the deposit on a house before we start a family.' Pippa made a scoffing sound. 'Like that's going to happen before I reach menopause.'

'Oh, dear,' Kate murmured, hoping she sounded supportive, although she couldn't help feeling sympathy for David. He'd always come across as very sensible and steady, the complete opposite of Stan. And from what Kate had gleaned, it did seem as if Pippa hadn't really involved him in this pregnancy plan – until it was too late.

Shades of her father? Kate quickly dismissed that thought.

'I'm sure David will be excited once you have your first scan.'

'Fingers crossed.' Pippa didn't sound very hopeful.

At least Kate's phone call with Chelsea was, as expected, a little easier.

Her younger daughter did know about the new member of Kate's household, having received a very agitated call earlier in the evening from her sister, but she didn't take umbrage with Kate. And once Chelsea had recovered from the surprising news that Tilly was actually her half-sister, she was bursting with curiosity and wanted to know all about her.

'Can you send me a photo?' she asked. 'And maybe we can Zoom or FaceTime?'

Kate suspected that Tilly was equally curious about her half-sisters and FaceTime was probably the best option. 'I'll sound Tilly out,' she told Chelsea. 'But I think she'll be keen.'

'We're all the family she's got, poor kid.'

'Yes, more or less.'

'Actually, I have a better idea!' Chelsea sounded quite excited now. 'Pippa and I should come and visit you. If we could both wangle a long weekend, I could fly to Townsville and then we could drive up to the Tablelands together. I reckon we could do the round trip in a long weekend.'

'Oh, that would be lovely. A proper girls weekend.' Kate was already picturing her daughters' arrival and she could feel excitement bubbling inside her. It would be wonderful to have her girls here to actually meet Tilly in person, all four of them bonding, sharing meals, talking late into the night.

Someone might have to sleep on the sofa, but that should be okay. No, wait – Kate could get the bed in the van ready. She'd always loved the happy buzz of house guests, the dinner table conversations, the cosy companionship.

'I don't expect David would mind if Pippa had a weekend away,' Chelsea was saying now. 'But if he's gone all sensitive and fatherly now that they're pregnant, he could always come too, I guess.'

'I guess.' Kate wasn't sure what Pippa had discussed with her sister regarding her pregnancy, so she refrained from adding any further comment.

'It might take a week or two to organise,' Chelsea added. 'I'm a bit tied up at the moment.'

'That's okay. Sort it out with Pippa and let me know. I'm pretty free for the foreseeable future.'

As their phone call ended, Kate let out a deep, happy sigh, marvelling at how the simple prospect of bringing her newly blended family together could make her world feel so suddenly right.

CHAPTER SIXTEEN

Hamish Kirk had the same dark red hair as his mother, but that was pretty much where the resemblance ended. His hair was styled in a trendy undercut, with a sweeping fringe that almost reached his eyebrows and accented his high cheekbones.

He was also quite tall and he might have looked rather intimidating, if he hadn't had such a friendly smile. Tilly was grateful for that smile as he came forward to greet her when she entered the community hall somewhat shyly.

'Hey, there, I'm guessing you must be Tilly.'

She nodded. 'That's right.'

'I'm Hamish.' He held out his hand. 'Welcome to the not very famous Burralea players.'

Tilly was often shy around guys, so she was grateful that Hamish had rescued her and hadn't left her hanging about in the doorway like a bad smell. She found it surprisingly easy to smile back at him and shake his hand. Which was a strangely skin-tingling experience. She'd rarely shaken anyone's hand. It was something adults did.

Hamish was dressed in black jeans and a grey pullover with

crossed swords on the front and Tilly noticed that he had a tattoo of an old-fashioned sailing ship on his wrist and he wore an earring. She wondered if he saw himself as some kind of modern-day pirate.

But she didn't have long to wonder about this, as Hamish looked back over his shoulder to the people scattered about the hall. 'I'll introduce you around,' he said. 'Have you met our director, Josie Weston?'

'No, not yet, although I think Kate, my guard – the woman I live with – spoke to her on the phone.'

'Come on then. There's Josie.' Hamish nodded to the far side of the room, where two women were in the middle of a rather animated conversation. Then he abruptly set off and Tilly hurried to keep up.

It was only as Tilly got closer that she realised one of the women was Bridie's mother. Mrs Cooper seemed to have done something with her hair – tonight it was swept up – and she was also wearing dangly earrings. She certainly didn't look anywhere near as drab and mumsy as she had on the evening Tilly and Kate had gone to her house for dinner.

The other woman broke off talking, as Hamish and Tilly drew closer. 'Hello there,' she said, even before Hamish could introduce her. 'You must be Tilly Dent.' This woman was small and thin, but her eyes were incredibly expressive, with an almost mischievous gleam, even though she was merely saying hello.

'This is Josie,' Hamish quickly inserted. 'And Margot.'

Tilly nodded to them, and Margot gave her a friendly grin. 'Lovely to see you here, Tilly.'

But Tilly didn't have time to respond before Josie hurried on. 'Now,' Josie said brusquely, almost as if introductions were a waste of time. 'I don't know if Imogen Kirk has explained, but we already have a play underway and we're getting close to production.'

Tilly gave another nod.

'If you'd like to be involved, though, we could probably find you a small role, as one of the robots. I'm not sure there'd be many speaking lines.'

Again, Tilly nodded. Of course, she hadn't been expecting to land a major part in their play, but she was somewhat taken aback at the thought of being a robot. 'That's sounds cool,' she said. 'Or I can just watch, if you like.'

Josie smiled. 'I'm sure you'd have more fun if we found you a part. And did Mrs Kirk mention the possibility of a coaching session with Olivia Matthews?'

'No, I don't think so.'

Beside Tilly, Hamish made a sound that might have been muffled shock, or even dismay. Turning, Tilly saw a hasty glance flash between Hamish and Josie, but she couldn't read it.

'See me before you leave tonight and I'll explain about the coaching,' Josie said. 'It could be a wonderful opportunity. Meanwhile, Hamish can introduce you to everyone else.'

Tilly would have liked to ask Hamish about this Olivia woman, but he was already moving away and in no time he was introducing Tilly to other theatre members, rattling off their names. Heidi, Derek and Shelley, who all looked to be around Hamish's age – and then others whose names Tilly couldn't quite take in. They all seemed friendly, though, so that was something.

There was barely time to chat, but Tilly managed to ask Hamish a quick question that was bothering her.

'Do you know anything about this coaching Josie mentioned?'

'With Olivia?' he said. 'Not really. I mean, Olivia's a very good actress. She's been a professional in her time and she's given me some useful tips, but I haven't had a one-on-one session with her.'

'What's she like?' Tilly asked, remembering that glance between Hamish and Josie.

Hamish didn't answer straight away and his expression was hard to read. 'As I said, Olivia's a very good actor. She's had masses of experience and she's probably a very good teacher. She had a fall and injured her ankle pretty badly, so she had to bow out of this production.'

'Is she kind of old?'

'Yeah.' Hamish shrugged. 'Quite old, actually.'

Tilly wasn't sure she liked the sound of this. Coming to the little theatre was one thing. She was prepared to at least give it a go. Going to an injured old lady for one-on-one coaching was something else entirely. But she didn't have time to mull over this possibility. Josie was calling them into the middle of the hall for warmups.

These were a new experience. At Tilly's old school in Cairns, the teacher who'd coached the kids for the eisteddfod had merely focused on the best way to deliver the lines in their set poems. There were no physical exercises. Now, Tilly really enjoyed doing spine rolls and neck stretches and then all different kinds of breathing exercises, finishing up with saying funny tongue twisters.

Then the rehearsal of the play began. First up, Bridie's mum was on the stage with Heidi and Derek, and Tilly watched in fascination as the woman she'd met as a shy, ordinary mother transformed herself into a rather snobby, bossy woman they were calling Lady X.

She couldn't help grinning. Margot was great.

Hamish was in the next scene and Tilly found herself riveted. Even without special lighting effects, the colour of his hair, the chiselled line of his cheekbones and the way he moved all created an impact. Tilly had heard of stage presence. Watching Hamish Kirk, she was sure she now knew exactly what this meant.

The play's story seemed intriguing, too, but they weren't rehearsing the scenes in the correct order, so Tilly found it rather hard to follow. After a while, there was a break. Josie stopped the actors on stage, then called a few of the players into a huddle. They seemed to be discussing where and how they should move the props and scenery.

Hamish, who wasn't needed, came and sat beside Tilly. 'You were great,' she told him, hoping she didn't look too fan-girly.

'Thanks. I can explain the play's storyline if you like.'

'Yes, please. It was a bit hard to follow.'

'Sure. As you could probably guess, it's set in the future.' Hamish spoke fairly quietly, so as not to disturb the others, and Tilly had to lean in. 'It's about a family who've inherited loads of money – billions – but they have next to no common sense. Anyway, they buy a trip to Mars to escape the climate catastrophe that's happening on Earth. But they're used to having servants and they're pretty hopeless at anything practical, so they boss the robot servants around and treat them like sh— dirt.'

'And Margot's called Lady X?'

'Yeah. The robots are more or less clever AIs. They've been programmed with a certain understanding of history and politics and they've given her the name Lady X. They refuse to call her anything else and we never find out what her name was on Earth. Peter plays her husband and he's Lord X. And then their kids are Prince Y and Princess Z.'

Tilly laughed. 'That's very strange, but it sounds fun. So I take it you're one of the AIs? What's your character's name? C-3PO?'

Hamish grinned cheekily. 'I'm Galahad.'

'Oh, yes. I heard someone call you that. So the humans are called X, Y and Z and the robots have regular names?'

'Yeah. Impressive names, I reckon. Heidi's another robot and she's called Daphne and Derek's Cedric. Actually, there's a really clever twist midpoint in the play when the robots take over. And then both the Xs and Y and Z have to be their servants.'

'Wow. That's awesome.' Tilly frowned as a new thought struck. 'Except it's a bit too much like what's probably going to happen in the future in real life.'

'Nah. Don't worry. I won't give away spoilers, but there's

another twist before the end, so it finishes on an upbeat note. I'll lend you my script if you like, or Josie might have a spare one.'

'Okay. I'd love to read it.' Tilly wasn't sure what sort of play she'd expected a small country town like Burralea to produce, probably something quaint and old fashioned. This futuristic space setting was so different. So totally random. 'How did Josie find the script?'

'One of our locals wrote it, actually. A guy called Rolf Anders.'

'You're kidding me. Someone from Burralea?'

'Yep. Serious. He's actually a well-known author. He normally writes novels, but he decided to try his hand at a play.'

'Wow, that's amazing.'

'Yeah. Rolf's a fucking genius.' Hamish winced. 'Sorry about the language.'

Tilly wasn't sorry. She hadn't heard anyone swear since she'd left Cairns and it was strangely comforting to hear it from someone as nice as Hamish. 'No fucking worries.' She sent him a sheepish grin.

* * *

Kate was already waiting outside in her van when the rehearsal finished. She saw a group of young people coming out of the hall onto the footpath, chatting and laughing, Tilly among them. It was such a relief to see that Tilly was also laughing and looking very much a part of the group.

Kate hadn't been sure about this little theatre idea, but it would be wonderful if the group helped Tilly to feel more settled. She flicked her headlights to get the girl's attention, remembering from her own daughters' teen years that a parent turning up in the midst of their friends could be a huge embarrassment.

Tilly saw her and waved, shared a few parting words with her new companions and then came hurrying down the footpath.

Kate thought she looked a little flushed and excited, although that might have been the nippy night air adding rosy circles to her cheeks. But there was a definite sense of satisfaction about Tilly as she settled in the passenger's seat and fastened the seatbelt.

'So how was it?' Kate had to ask.

'It was awesome,' the girl said. 'They're all really friendly.'

Kate smiled as she remembered Tilly's parting words. *And even if I hate it, I'll stay till the end.*

'And they're doing this amazing play set in outer space.'

'That sounds interesting.' Kate breathed more easily as she edged away from the curb and headed back down the street. With Tilly's enthusiasm coming hot on the heels of her phone chat with Chelsea, it seemed that life might be picking up on several fronts. 'Did they give you a part in the play?'

'A small one.' Tilly giggled. 'Guess who I'll be?'

'A character in outer space? I have no idea. Maybe an alien?'

'A robot.'

Kate couldn't help chuckling. 'That should be an interesting costume.'

'I guess. I'm not sure. They didn't talk about costumes tonight. They talked about sets, though, and I'm afraid I kind of dobbed you in. I hope you don't mind.'

'Dobbed me in how?'

'Well, it was me and Bridie's mum, Margot, actually. She's usually one of the main people who builds their sets. But she's busy with acting now. She's filling in for this other woman, Olivia, who had an accident. She fell off the stage or something. Anyway, they're looking for someone else to help with building the set and I – well, Margot and I both said you were really good at that sort of thing.'

This time Kate's smile took a rueful tilt. Here she'd been, making sure she kept a discreet distance from the players, while Tilly had been happily dragging her into their midst. 'But I've never built a set.'

'You're not mad, are you?'

'No,' Kate said, concerned by the sudden anxious note in the girl's voice. 'Just trying to understand.'

'Well, you've done all that work on this van. Lining the walls with timber and making those shelves and cupboards and everything, and I reckon that's probably way harder than anything they're going to need for their set.'

'What kind of a set is it?'

'A spaceship. I think Margot said something about how you've got the right kind of saw for cutting portholes, or whatever.'

'Hmm. I wouldn't be doing this on my own, would I?'

'No, of course there'll be others.'

'Do you have any idea how much time it would involve?'

'I'm not totally sure, but I think people just come in on the same nights as the rehearsals and they work on the sets in this room out the back. The hall gets used for different things on other nights. Choir practice and table tennis and stuff.'

'I guess I could ring Margot and get the details from her.'

'So you're not mad?'

'No, Tilly. I'm not mad.' To Kate's surprise she realised she was telling the truth. It might be fun to meet a few locals while hammering in a nail or two.

CHAPTER SEVENTEEN

Olivia wasn't sure who was more nervous – herself, or the young person who'd been delivered to her doorstep. She knew, for her own part, she was ridiculously tense. Twice during the preceding week she'd almost rung Josie to cancel this meeting.

A septuagenarian and a teenager had so little in common. Olivia was quite sure the girl was only coming to her under duress.

She had tried to prepare by reading a few articles on working with teenagers, and she'd even thought about taking the drastic step of consulting Margot Cooper. Margot was a mother of teens, after all, and she was at least familiar with the Burralea theatre's mindset and goals.

But when it came to actually contacting Margot, Olivia's pride got in the way. She hated to expose any personal deficiency, especially to the woman who was her replacement on stage. Now though, as she greeted the girl, Tilly, she felt regrettably underprepared.

Nevertheless, Olivia had never been a quitter – except for that one time years ago when she'd abandoned her Hollywood dreams. Given most challenges, she generally squared her shoulders and stepped up to the mark. Today, she tried not to hobble with her blasted moon boot.

'Tilly,' she greeted the girl, offering a smile that felt a shade too careful. 'Come on in.'

Tilly was still in her school uniform and she certainly didn't look thrilled to be there, but at least her nails were free of paint, her face was stud free and she hadn't rolled her skirt up at the waist to show off her thighs, so that was something.

The girl paid a discomforting amount of attention to Olivia's moon boot, however. Hadn't anyone taught her it was rude to stare?

Oh, well, best get this show on the road. Olivia had decided their session should take place in the little sunroom at the front of her house and she'd already set up the coffee table with a platter of almond croissants and a jug of lemonade with clinking ice blocks and glasses.

Tilly's eyes widened when she saw these. 'Are we having afternoon tea? I thought this was a drama lesson.'

'I imagined you might be hungry after school.' Olivia wondered if she'd gone too far – trying to be a grandmother, rather than a drama coach. 'And I wasn't given any clear instructions, so I thought this initial meeting should be a reconnaissance.'

At this, Tilly frowned.

'A chance to get to know each other a little,' Olivia explained awkwardly.

'Oh, right.'

'Take a seat, won't you?' Olivia gestured to one of the padded cane chairs. 'And have you sampled the croissants from the local bakery?'

'No.'

'Then you must try one.' Olivia had made a special trip to the bakery, knowing that the almond croissants were dainty and delicious, perfect for afternoon tea. 'They're rather special.'

'Thank you.' The girl sat carefully at the front of her chair as she took a croissant and the paper napkin Olivia offered.

'Would you like some lemonade?'

'Yes, please.'

As Olivia handed a filled glass to Tilly and then settled into her own chair, she wondered if she would ever be able to nudge this conversation past questions that rendered two-syllable responses. 'It seems you have a couple of fans,' she said. 'Imogen Kirk and Josie Weston both spoke very highly of you.'

The girl pulled a face, as if the compliment made her uncomfortable. 'It's probably just that they feel sorry for me.'

Olivia frowned. 'Because?'

'Because I'm new here.'

'Ah, yes, settling into a new place can be hard.' There was no point in avoiding the obvious subject. 'And I was very sorry to hear that you lost your mother recently.'

Tilly nodded and for a moment her expression became so miserable, even scared, that Olivia was terrified she would send the girl into tears. *I'm making a hash of this.* Clearly, a quick change of topic was needed.

'But getting down to business,' she said, adopting a more efficient tone. 'Josie would like me to give you a little private coaching.'

'Yes.' Tilly had finally taken a nibble at her croissant. 'This is amazing by the way.'

'Yes, they're quite delicious, aren't they?' Olivia smiled. 'And I believe you've been to a rehearsal at the local theatre?'

'Yes, just one.'

'And you've also done a little acting at school?'

'Just reading parts in class. And I recited a poem at the eisteddfod last year.'

'And you enjoy these activities? You like acting? And being on stage?'

Tilly nodded. 'Yeah, it's fun.'

Olivia paused before she asked her next question. It could be a waste of time and she might easily be disappointed with the response. But there was something about this girl – something more than her interesting looks, which weren't conventionally pretty, although her shiny black hair and smooth olive complexion were an attractive combination. And her eyes were quite a remarkable shade of jade. No, there was another quality that intrigued Olivia, a sensibility so subtle and fleeting it could easily be missed. 'Have you ever given any thought as to why acting might be fun?'

She supposed the girl might say that she simply loved being on stage, loved performing.

Tilly didn't take long to answer. 'Because I get to be another person?'

'Ahh.' Olivia knew she was beaming with delight. She couldn't have received a more satisfactory answer.

* * *

Kate had barely arrived home after dropping Tilly off for her drama lesson when she heard the rumble of a vehicle coming up the track. She was pretty sure she recognised that particular engine and a quick check through the kitchen window showed that her hunch was correct. A yellow van with *Flint the Sparkie* on the side emerged through the trees and her heart began an instant, silly thumping.

She couldn't imagine why Liam Flint might be calling on her, or how he'd managed to drop in on the one afternoon that she was home alone. Of course, the sensible thing to do was to head straight out to his van to deal with whatever business he'd come to discuss and then wave him on his way.

Instead, for some inexplicable reason, Kate found herself dashing to the bathroom to check her reflection in the mirror. And by the time she'd tidied her hair and added a quick swish of lip gloss – only because it was handy, right there on the bathroom vanity – Liam was already knocking at her front door.

Deep breaths. Calm down. Really, Kate couldn't believe she was so flustered. It didn't help that she'd thought about this man way too often during the past week, remembering his thoughtfulness, his kindness to Tilly and, most of all, remembering *that smile* . . .

'Hi,' he said when Kate arrived, slightly breathless, at the open front door. He held up a package. 'That REDARC dual battery system we ordered for your van came through. I was already out this way, so I thought I'd drop it off.'

'Oh.' The disappointment that hit Kate now was almost as dizzying as her initial excitement. Of course Liam was here on business. He'd explained to her the importance of this special dual battery system that he'd ordered from South Australia. It would enable her to charge up her laptop, her lights, her stove et cetera, without draining the van's engine battery. What on earth was wrong with her?

She held out her hand for the package, but when Liam gave it to her, he didn't let it go. And when Kate looked up at him, she saw a shimmer in his eyes that stole her remaining breath.

But this was silly. So preposterous for the two of them to be standing in a doorway, both clinging to a package and staring at each other.

She forced herself to concentrate on the reason for his visit. 'Were you planning to install the battery this afternoon?' She wasn't sure there was enough time before she had to collect Tilly.

'Actually, no.' He did have the grace to look ever so slightly abashed. 'But I was driving past here and I thought I'd let you know it arrived.' Almost immediately, however, he smiled. 'How are you anyway?'

'I'm fine, thanks.' It was a lie. Kate was a fluttery mess. And yet she knew she couldn't afford to feel this way. Not about Liam, not about any man. Of course, she was very grateful that Liam had waited with her last week when she'd been so worried about Tilly. And, yes, it had been a sensible idea to stay on in town for dinner, but that didn't mean . . .

'And Tilly?' Liam was asking now.

'Yes, she's doing well, thank you. She seems much more settled.' Kate decided it would be wise not to mention that Tilly wasn't at home right now.

'That's great.'

Finally, he let go of the battery, but instead of stepping away, he remained firmly in the doorway with a bulky shoulder propped against the frame. The light in his eyes was still there and his mouth betrayed the merest hint of amusement.

'Was there something else?' Kate asked, deliberately looking past that dangerous smile to the hills and the sun sliding steadily westward.

'Well, yes, I was thinking that congrats are in order.'

'Congrats?' She frowned at him. 'I don't understand.'

'You've done particularly well at resisting your urge to flirt.'

Kate knew Liam couldn't miss the flare of heat in her cheeks. Mortified, she glared at him. 'I can assure you, any flirting urges died long ago.'

And standing here now, feeling several versions of flustered and awkward, Kate reminded herself she should be thankful that her new responsibilities as a guardian had provided both her and this electrician with a serious and unavoidable distraction.

Now the only sensible thing to do was to thank Liam Flint for the battery, bid him good afternoon and close the door firmly. In his face, if necessary.

As Kate reached for the door handle, however, she found herself asking, 'What exactly are you driving at? Why drag up that flirting nonsense now?'

Liam stood for a moment, his grey eyes watchful, as if he was weighing up the best way to answer her. At last he said, 'Flirting seems to be the new F word for us, doesn't it?'

Somehow, she managed not to smile.

'But I guess I've been thinking that an urge to flirt is an indication —'

Now Kate raised a hand to silence him. She had to put a stop to this. 'Everyone knows that flirting is *usually* assumed to mean that a woman *might* be trying to attract a man's attention. But that's the last thing I was —'

Now it was Liam who interrupted. 'I was going to say that it's often a sign that the attraction is already in place.'

Kate's jaw sagged. How dare he?

'And before you get too mad with me,' he continued smoothly, 'it works both ways. Although, with blokes, it might show up as finding any excuse to call in.' The glint was back in his eyes and he nodded to the package in Kate's hand.

Face aflame, she dropped her gaze. She couldn't let this happen. Okay, so her body might be screaming one particular message about how happy she was to see Liam again, but her head knew with certainty that she couldn't afford to make another mistake.

'But it's quite possible that this bloke is out of practice at the whole flirting scene,' Liam was saying now. 'So, don't worry, he won't hang around.'

With that, he offered another devastating smile followed by a saluting wave, then did an about-turn and headed back down the path, leaving Kate clutching the battery in one hand, the door handle with the other, and her centre of gravity in shreds.

* * *

It was a very different speech and drama lesson from Tilly's previous experience. In Cairns, her teacher Mrs Jackson had mostly just given her instructions about how to deliver her lines. *Stop fiddling. Big voice. Big eyes. Give me a better 't' on latest. Now, we need a smug, smarty-pants face.*

The first difference was that this teacher, Olivia, who said she would prefer not to be called Mrs Matthews, was really quite old. She wasn't wrinkly, exactly, but her hair and her eyebrows were silvery white and she moved very carefully with the big boot thing on her foot.

So far, in this lesson, Olivia had not yet taken out the *Next Stop Mars* script, so she hadn't paid any attention to the few lines Tilly had to deliver. Instead, she'd been talking about what went on in an actor's head when they tried to be someone else. What was going on in their body?

'The message the audience receives isn't just about the words you're saying, Tilly. It's all about the behaviour underneath the scene.'

'The way I move?' asked Tilly.

'The way you move. The way you stand still. The expression on your face. How you act in the gap between the words.' Olivia smiled. 'Silence on stage can be very powerful.'

Tilly nodded. 'That's when you have to show emotion?'

'Among other things, yes.'

'My teacher in Cairns told us to think about something in our own lives that made us feel a certain way.'

'Yes, that's called method acting.' Olivia lifted an eyebrow. 'Did it work for you?'

'Sort of. I mean, it's easy enough to think of something that makes me happy.' Or at least it had been easy enough back when she and Zara were still great friends. 'I'm not sure it would work now, though. I mean, if I'm supposed to be sad, I'd have to think about something really sad that's happened to me. And then I'd start thinking about my mum – and I —'

Even just trying to explain this to Olivia made Tilly's voice crack and her eyes sting. 'I just couldn't.'

'No,' Olivia agreed gently. 'That would be very difficult. Too difficult, I'm sure.' The woman's face was a mirror of Tilly's sadness now. Even her eyes had a teary sheen and Tilly supposed this was because she was a very good actor. After all, everyone had said she was, although Tilly couldn't help wondering if Olivia was actually remembering something terribly sad that had happened in her own life.

Olivia even looked away for a moment and seemed to give herself a little shake, but when she turned back to Tilly, her smile still held a tremor of sadness. 'For most of us, there are certain things we can't afford to think about when we're on stage.'

Tilly nodded, relieved that she and her teacher agreed about this.

'The approach I prefer is slightly different,' Olivia went on to say next. 'It's a technique I learned in the UK, where an actor decides on the character's objective for the scene. In other words, we think about what the character wants to achieve. Do they want to make another character laugh? Or cry? Are they trying to uncover a secret? Or reveal a secret? Then, once we've worked that out, we need to ask ourselves, what should the character be thinking about? And then, finally, what they might be feeling.'

'I see,' Tilly said, although she didn't quite get it. 'My character's an AI, a robot with artificial intelligence, and I reckon she's mostly just thinking about how annoying the humans are.'

Olivia chuckled. 'I'm sure you're right. And what might her goal be?'

'She's probably trying to work out a way to annoy them back.'

'That's highly likely.' Olivia looked pleased. 'So, once you've decided on the goal and the thought processes, you think about the emotion your character might be feeling. Take the emotion you've just described – if you think about the word "annoyed", what do you feel?'

'Um. I'm not sure. Like I need to frown?'

'That's not a bad start. Now try saying the word out loud and take careful notice of your body as you do so.'

'Annoyed,' Tilly responded dutifully.

'Do you feel anything?' asked Olivia. 'What's happening in your body? Is your jaw tightening? Does the back of your neck feel a little stiff?'

'Annoyed.' Tilly said the word again, this time paying more attention to any sensations inside her. She grinned. 'You're right. I *did* feel annoyed in my jaw and in the back of my neck.'

Olivia smiled brightly. 'That's the ticket.'

'But would my AI character feel emotions?' Tilly asked next. 'She's not a human being. Pretty much a robot. With a chip in her brain.'

'Ah, yes.' Olivia's eyes widened. 'And that difference between humans and artificial intelligence is actually the essence of this play, of course. The script gives the actors a wonderful chance to highlight that small, but important gap. It's quite fascinating really.'

'But how do I do it?' Tilly knew Olivia wouldn't want her to just walk around like a robot. Nevertheless, she jumped out of her chair and began to march around the small front room, stiff legged, stiff backed, arms jerking, speaking out of the side of her mouth. 'I – AM – A – ROBOT.'

'Is that what Josie wants you to do?'

'I don't think so.' Tilly offered a sheepish smile. 'I'm not sure. I haven't actually rehearsed my scenes with her yet. But Hamish is an AI and he's not especially stiff. Not as stiff as I was just then.'

'No, I think, for this play, the difference needs to be more subtle. But I'm no sci-fi expert.' Olivia smiled again. 'I must ask Rolf what he intended. He's the man who wrote the play.'

'Yeah, Hamish told me about him.' Tilly was tempted to share Hamish's glowing description of the writer, complete with the swearing, but she didn't want to shock the elderly woman.

'For the time being,' Olivia went on. 'Do you think you could imagine what it's like to have no emotion at all?'

Tilly didn't need to ponder this question for long. 'Yeah. I can, actually. I was like that after my mum's accident. I mean I . . .' She stopped, overcome by a shiver, as unwanted memories came crashing back. And before she could stop them she was reliving the shock of that terrible day, the terror and unbearable grief.

Worse had followed – a harrowing night during which Jed, after comforting Tilly through her storm of crying, had then locked himself in his bedroom and stayed there for hours, bawling. The memory of a grown man crying, as if his heart had been ripped from his chest, would haunt Tilly forever. *Oh, crap.* If she wasn't careful she'd start crying again now.

Anxious to fight these tears, she tried to explain. 'The only way I could stop the sadness about Mum was to stop feeling anything. I – I just made myself – empty.'

'Oh, sweetheart.' Olivia also looked on the verge of tears. 'You poor little mite.' And then, she was pressing three fingers to her quivering lips, as if she was holding back a sob.

The sight of this somewhat snooty and stand-offish old lady looking so moved was a curve ball Tilly hadn't seen coming. This wasn't supposed to be happening.

Not now. Not now. Don't start crying. Stop remembering. Stop feeling. Be a robot.

But a huge tsunami of emotions was building inside Tilly and she was terrified she would break. Until she heard Olivia's voice again.

'Everyone's grief is personal and I wouldn't dream of telling you how you should feel, my dear. But long ago, I was given a drop of wisdom I found helpful. If you focus on your own inner strength, you can learn to live with a terrible loss.'

Inner strength?

The unexpected words landed inside Tilly. Took hold.

Could that be me?

She had never really thought of herself as strong, but she knew that her mum, despite her small frame, had shown all kinds of strength – lugging vacuum cleaners and mops and buckets through other people's homes all day long, then coming home to cook dinner and make sure Tilly had done her homework.

Their neighbour, Mrs Kettle, used to say: 'She's a tough little nut, your mum.'

'Take a deep breath, Tilly.'

Obediently, almost as if she was mesmerised, Tilly drew a huge, shuddering breath, and then another, deeper and stronger. As the air flowed into her lungs and then slowly out again, she felt herself growing calmer. Amazingly, after another breath in and out, the need to cry began to ebb.

Inner strength.

The words were like an echo. A gong. Even without saying them out loud, Tilly could feel a response deep within her. *Inner strength. Inner strength.*

Hell, yeah. Strength could be an emotion too and when Tilly concentrated, she really did feel as if her spine was a little straighter, her head a little higher.

How freaking amazing was that? It was like being handed a new way to think about herself. Her life might be crap, but she, Tilly Dent, could still be strong. A tough little nut. A warrior princess.

Who knew? If she kept thinking about *inner strength*, she just might be okay after all. Maybe this old bird knew a thing or two.

'Now,' Olivia said, in a gentle but back-to-business voice, 'if you're feeling better, we might take a look at this script.'

CHAPTER EIGHTEEN

Kate blamed her hormones. Women in their early fifties were notoriously all over the place hormonally and this had to be the logical explanation for the way Liam Flint kept invading her thoughts, and her dreams. Waking up yearnings she'd almost forgotten, in a body she'd assumed was safely dormant.

Lately, Kate's nights had been torture. But even in the cold light of day, when she was supposed to be editing an impressive memoir about life on a remote Cape York cattle station, her normally reliable focus kept drifting Liamwards. Way too many times she'd relived that heart-sparking moment when he'd arrived on her doorstep with the battery.

And like a CD set to repeat, Kate had also kept hearing the conversation that followed . . . Liam's admission about attraction working both ways . . . and his surprising confession that the visit was just a lame excuse . . .

It's quite possible that this bloke is out of practice at the whole flirting scene. So don't worry, he won't hang around.

Having lived for so long in the shadow of Stan's lies and brash overconfidence, Kate had lost any sense of trust in the male gender.

It was always safest to remain on guard. How could she trust a man on such brief acquaintance? She didn't even know why Liam was divorced.

Just the same, Kate found herself wishing she'd been a tad more receptive when Liam had called. After all, an attractive man, the right age and marital status, who'd already shown himself to be both sweet and caring *and* non-predatory, had found an excuse to turn up on her doorstep when she was home alone. And she'd been as welcoming as a prickly echidna.

No wonder Liam had hightailed it out of there. And yet, Kate knew for sure that any of her girlfriends would scream at her for throwing away such a perfect chance for a little romance.

Now, the chance was gone. Lost. And it wouldn't come again. The man had his pride, after all.

Damn. Kate let out a loud groan as she closed her laptop and gave up on the editing. Hopefully, she'd be in a calmer frame of mind in the evening and she could work on this project then, staying up till midnight or later, until she finally fell asleep from sheer exhaustion. In the meantime, she would distract herself with a day of hammering, sawing and drilling.

It was two nights later and Kate had finally calmed down, or at least she told herself she had, when she drove down Burralea's main street and saw a yellow van parked outside the theatre. Instantly, her inner chaos returned times ten.

'What's he doing here?' she demanded, as she swung her van too sharply into a spare parking space, banging a tyre into the kerb in the process.

'Who are you talking about?' asked Tilly.

Kate pointed across the street. 'The electrician.'

'You mean Liam? Your friend?'

Kate glared at her. 'Did you know he was going to be here at your rehearsal?'

'I guess. He was here last week. He's helping with the sets. Something to do with the lighting, I think.'

'And you didn't also think to tell me?'

'Didn't I?' Tilly asked, all innocence as she unsnapped her seatbelt, no doubt keen to escape her neurotic guardian and get into the hall.

'So you happily roped me in to work here without thinking to mention that Liam would be here as well?'

Tilly reached for the doorhandle. 'You said you were going to ring Margot. Didn't she tell you who else would be here?'

Kate winced. She hadn't got around to ringing Margot and had decided to just turn up anyway. After all, it was the Burralea Little Theatre, not London's West End.

'Anyway,' added Tilly, 'you said Liam's not your boyfriend.'

'He's not.'

'So, what's the big deal? I didn't tell you the names of half the people who were here last week.'

Uncomfortably, Kate realised Tilly was right. This was no big deal. Unless a midlife crisis counted. Problem was – the mere sight of Liam's van had brought back the myriad distracting thoughts and embarrassingly X-rated dreams that she'd been trying to erase from her memory. 'I just got a surprise, that's all.'

'Yeah, right.' Tilly opened her door. 'And I'd better get going, or I'll miss the warmups.'

'Yes, sure. Have fun.'

'You too.' Over her shoulder, Tilly shot Kate a cheeky grin. 'By the way, there's a side door you can use to get to the workroom at the back.'

Which Kate read as teen code for: *don't wander into the middle of our warmups and embarrass the hell out of me.*

* * *

'Kate, how lovely to see you.' Margot was as friendly and welcoming as ever, rushing forward to greet Kate when she came into the workroom, via the side door, as instructed.

Margot was also barely recognisable. Her hair, which had once been a rather sad and greying frizz, was now shiny, smooth and chestnut in tone and swept into a glamorous updo. Large golden hoops swung from her ears, and she was wearing a noticeable amount of eye makeup, and a long, stylish cardigan in a flattering rosy pink. Clearly, Margot had adjusted her image to match her new position as a stage actress and the new look jolly well suited her.

'I'm so glad you could join us,' Margot said. 'Oh, and I see you've brought your jigsaw, that's wonderful.' She laughed. 'I sell these things, but I've never actually used one.'

'Well, I have to warn you, I've never worked on a theatre set.'

'No, but you had never renovated a van before either, and yet you're doing an amazing job by all accounts.'

Kate wondered who had reported this? A hasty glance around the workroom showed no sign of Liam, but the space was so crowded with removable walls and pieces of furniture covered in dust sheets, she supposed he could be anywhere.

'I thought I'd give you a bit of a run-through before I'm needed at the rehearsal,' Margot said next. 'Has Tilly told you the setting is a spaceship?'

'Yes. She's rapt with the whole idea. But I wasn't sure if a spaceship setting made things easier or harder when it came to building props.'

'Each play presents its own challenges. And when you're working with a low budget, you need to boil the set down to its very essence. For us, it's usually the absolute minimum we can get away with to convey the idea.' Margot waved an arm towards large sheets of plywood attached to timber frames. 'These are mostly flats we've used in previous shows. We'll need to repaint them for *Next Stop Mars*, and we've settled on white, black and silver for our basic colour scheme.'

'Sounds good.'

'Hopefully, by the time we're finished, there'll also be touches of glass, shiny metal and maybe a hint of purple.' Margot pointed to two huge frames covered in black cloth. 'And these will become our starscapes.'

'Starscapes?'

Margot's grin was close to a smirk now. 'It may be a word we invented, but that's what we're calling them. We want our actors to be able to look out of their spaceship and see the wonders of the universe. Liam Flint is going to poke tiny holes in this fabric and wire them up with little lights. We're so excited. We investigated buying readymade LED star cloths to give the illusion of outer space, but they were far too expensive. And now Liam's solved that problem for us.'

'Wonderful.' Kate had no doubt Liam's contribution would be truly significant, but she couldn't quite see where she fitted into this scenario.

'But to make it a little more authentic, we decided we needed a few portholes for the set and maybe a viewing screen for the spaceship's bridge,' Margot said next.

'Ah,' said Kate. 'And that's where my jigsaw comes in? For the portholes?'

'Yes. Geoff here has drawn up a rough plan.' Looking around the room again, Margot frowned. 'Or at least I thought he was here. Geoff?' she called. 'Are you still here out the back?'

A small gnome-like figure, complete with rimless, round glasses, suddenly popped out from behind a huge cupboard. 'Yep,' he called, giving them a wave. 'I was just hunting down the spare G-clamps.

Liam's going to need a few more of these for fastening those extra lanterns to the bar.'

'Oh, good,' said Margot. 'Well, this is Kate. I was telling her you've worked out where you want those portholes.'

'Yes, yes. Goodo.' Geoff placed the clamps he'd been collecting into a cardboard box, which he set on a nearby table, then came forward, hand extended. 'Good to meet you, Kate.'

'You, too, Geoff.'

They were shaking hands as a new voice called from another doorway. 'Margot, you're wanted on stage.'

'Oh, oh, there's my cue. Sorry to love you and leave you.' Margot didn't seem at all apologetic and Kate sensed she was eager to head for the stage. 'Geoff, can I leave Kate in your good hands?'

''Course.'

An hour later, Kate surveyed their work with satisfaction. Having shown her his rough sketches, Geoff had helped her to lay the flats carefully, resting them on several sawhorses, and then he'd produced a round and – thankfully – clean garbage tin lid to use like a massive cookie cutter, providing an appropriate circular shape. Geoff had then held this in place, while Kate drew its outline on the masonite with a marker pen.

She'd been rather worried the noise of the jigsaw might annoy the players, but Geoff had assured her that with the connecting door closed, they'd be well insulated. So, she'd cut the portholes and then she and Geoff had tacked together another large rectangular window frame for the viewing platform.

It was companionable work. Geoff chatted happily, giving Kate a potted history of his life. He was a retired butcher and he and his wife had been born on the Tablelands and lived here ever since. Their daughter had moved to Cairns to work as a receptionist in a dental surgery, and their son was now working for a butcher at Tolga.

'So, he's only a fifteen-minute drive away from our place. Can't get rid of him,' Geoff joked.

He was intrigued when Kate told him about her van and her eventual travel goals, and he asked a host of questions, making the hour pass pleasantly. But in all that time, and despite the noise they created, Kate hadn't caught any sight of Liam.

Eventually, her desperate curiosity got the better of her. 'Geoff? The electrician, Liam Flint. He's here tonight, isn't he?'

'Sure, he was here earlier. I think he's inside now, watching the rehearsal with Josie and Rolf. They're going through the script and putting the lighting plan together.'

'Ah, yes, right. Of course,' Kate said, although this possibility had never occurred to her.

'You can go through to the players, if you'd like to see him.'

Her foolish body zapped at the very thought of seeking Liam out in public. 'No, it's okay.'

'Actually. I reckon it must be close to half time. Everyone will break for a cuppa around now.'

As if this had been a cue, Margot reappeared in the doorway. 'Oh, wow!' she exclaimed, hurrying forward somewhat precariously on high, wedged sandals. 'What a great job you two have done. Those portholes are perfect. And you've made the window frame, too. Josie's going to be thrilled.' Grabbing Kate's arm, Margot gave her a little tug. 'Come and have a cuppa. You've totally earned it.'

Kate found herself pulled through a side doorway into the front section of the community hall, where she could now see the stage, framed in the time-honoured way, by claret red velvet curtains. To one side, there was also a small kitchen where mugs were lined on a countertop, along with boxes of teabags, a wide-mouthed jar of sugar and bottles of coffee and milk.

The players – all ages, shapes and sizes – were milling about, helping themselves to hot water from the urn, jiggling teabags, chatting, laughing. Kate was somewhat fascinated to realise that these ordinary-looking people in everyday jeans and jumpers, just like any local she might see on the streets of Burralea, would be transformed into vastly different characters once they were up on the stage.

In a corner, she saw Tilly involved in an animated conversation with a tall young chap with striking autumn-toned hair. She assumed he must be Imogen Kirk's son.

And she saw Liam.

Clunk.

The electrician was spooning coffee into a mug. He wasn't even looking Kate's way, had shown no sign he was even aware of her presence, so it was doubly ridiculous that her skin tightened all over.

'Grab yourself a mug,' Margot said as they reached the kitchen. 'Any mug except the one decorated with cherries. That shouldn't be out tonight. I'll put it away. It's Olivia's mug and she's very touchy about anyone else using it.'

'Olivia? That's the woman who's giving Tilly the coaching sessions?' Kate asked.

'Yes, Bridie told me about that arrangement. How's it going?'

Kate shrugged. 'Fine, as far as I can tell. Tilly wasn't too sure about it when I dropped her off, but she was happy as Larry when I picked her up.'

'That's great.' There may have been a momentary flash of surprise in Margot's eyes, but if there was, she covered it quickly with another of her warm smiles.

Kate helped herself to a green mug with a picture of a cow sporting a straw hat. 'This one's okay?'

'Yes, totally.'

She selected a teabag – lemon and ginger – conscious, in her peripheral vision, that Liam was now taking his turn at the urn.

'Tilly did well in her little scenes tonight,' Margot said now. 'She only has a few lines, but she made a good impression.'

'That's wonderful.' Kate was genuinely pleased.

'I suspect she's a natural. She has that certain something.'

Kate looked again to Tilly, but the girl was too busy laughing at something the Kirk boy was telling her.

'Kate, hi there.'

A familiar masculine voice sounded behind her, sending a river of warmth over her arms.

'Tilly told me you were here tonight.'

Swallowing to ease the sudden tightness in her throat, Kate turned. 'Hi, Liam.'

His manner appeared completely relaxed, in total contrast to her over-the-top tension.

'I forgot you two know each other,' said Margot. 'Liam, you should see the beautiful portholes Kate's cut for us.'

'I'd love to see Kate's portholes.' There was a hint of amusement in his smile. 'Then I'll know exactly where to position the lights on the backing cloth.'

'Here, Kate.' Margot held out a commanding hand for Kate's mug. 'Let me fill that for you, and then you and Liam can take your drinks out the back while you show him what you've done.'

It was like a clumsily manipulative scene from a playscript, and of course Margot's innocent intervention only served to ramp up Kate's extreme tension.

The tension continued once she and Liam were alone in the back room, but at least they both had their hot drinks to hold and sip, which helped to normalise the situation. And to Kate's relief, she managed to talk sensibly enough about portholes and starscapes and the fascinating scenario presented by this play.

They eventually exhausted these topics, of course. Which was when Liam said, casually, 'By the way, I need to make a time to come back to install your dual battery system.'

'Yes.' Kate made a concerted effort to ignore the sudden drumming in her chest. This was her chance to speak up. To apologise, perhaps. 'Any time that suits you.'

'I was thinking Friday? Mid-morning?'

'All right.' And then, before she lost her nerve, she added quickly, 'If you could allow a little extra time for – for coffee?'

Liam lifted a curious eyebrow.

'I thought – maybe – we needed to talk. Clear the air. Or whatever.'

She knew he was listening intently, but he made no immediate response. Clearly, further explanation was required.

'I wanted to apologise,' Kate said. 'I gave you the cold shoulder the other day. I was a little confused.'

'And how are you feeling now?'

'Less confused.' *And kinda desperate* . . . But that wasn't info to be shared in this venue, especially when she was doing her best to ignore vivid memories of her dreams. 'If you have time, that is. For the coffee.'

From the stage area, Josie was calling. 'Okay, everyone. Time to get back to work. We're moving on with Act One Scene Five.'

Liam's gaze met Kate's and his mouth tilted in the merest hint of a smile. He held out his hand. 'Friday it is. And I'll take that mug back to the kitchen for you now, if you like.'

'Oh, yes. Thanks.'

As she handed over the not quite empty mug, Geoff returned to the workroom. He nodded to Liam. 'Happy with the portholes?'

'Yeah, mate. They're perfect.'

'Josie wants all the internal walls of the ship painted white,' Geoff added, addressing Kate. 'Thought I'd get on with it now.'

'Sure,' she said. 'Want any help?'

'Love some.'

'I'll leave you to it then.' Liam favoured them with a parting smile, then turned to head back to the players. After three steps or so he stopped, looked back over his shoulder, locking his gaze with Kate's. 'And yeah, I'll definitely make time for that coffee.'

CHAPTER NINETEEN

Like so many places on the Tablelands, the track leading into Kate's place was magical. Part of an old railway cutting, the track had steep banks on either side covered in lush ferns and arching tree branches that met overhead, creating a tunnel, until it eventually curved and climbed into an open paddock with spectacular views of rolling green farmland and distant hills.

The sheer beauty of this had touched Liam every time he visited, although, in truth, this entrance was just one example of the stunning scenery throughout the region. It was the beauty that had lured him home.

Liam had been born in Herberton, his grandparents having originally moved into the area to mine for tin and gold. When the mining petered out in the eighties, Liam's dad had worked with the local porphyry stone company, installing beautiful stone walls and cobblestone paths throughout the north. Like many country kids, however, Liam had been itching to get away to the big smoke as soon as he could. The Tablelands were too quiet, too tame. Cows and pretty views and sleepy, easily forgotten towns.

So he'd headed south for the state's capital, hungry for crowded city streets full of unfamiliar faces, the buzz of busy traffic, lanes and lanes of vehicles all racing to get somewhere. The whole fast-paced, neon-lit, anonymous spectacle. City girls.

Decades of marriage and a messy divorce later, he'd travelled back to the north for a visit. He no longer had family ties to the region – his parents had both passed away and his sister now lived in western New South Wales, but the home of his youth had reached out and cast a spell. He'd found himself gripped by a fierce nostalgia for the cool mountain air, the majestic rainforests and the drifts of misty rain that lent the landscape an air of almost mystical enchantment.

Choosing to settle in a modest little place in Burralea, he'd established his business and kindled friendships both old and new. But as far as romantic liaisons were concerned, Liam had been cautious. He knew only too well that gossip in these small country towns spread faster than a possum up a rainforest cedar.

Even his brief encounters with Kate had set tongues wagging. Their dinner at the pub with Tilly had not gone unnoticed and more than one local had been keen to tell Liam about Kate's arsehole ex and the damage he'd caused in Cairns.

Not that Liam had needed to listen to gossip. Kate had already told him about her dodgy husband on the afternoon Tilly went missing. Knowing this, on top of everything else Kate had to deal with – including the difficult clash between her adventures in the van and her sense of duty to Tilly – Liam was uncomfortably aware that he'd probably stuffed her around even further by playing into the whole flirting scenario.

He was damned attracted to her, no doubt about that, but she'd made it clear from the start that she didn't want to fool around and there was no chance of anything more serious. Even if Kate's responsibility to Tilly kept her in one place for some time, she wouldn't let go of her plans for the van and Liam had no wish to step in the way of her goals for independence and freedom and the chance to go anywhere she chose. Solo.

This morning, as soon as he'd installed the battery system, he would join her for coffee as she'd coyly requested, but when it came to romance, he had only one option. He had to make it very clear she was off the hook.

This noble plan proved easier in theory than in practice. When Liam finished the installation, Kate met him at the door looking all kinds of gorgeous in a soft white jumper and skin-tight jeans, with her hair all silky and shining golden and her lips painted a lovely, kissable pink.

'Hi,' she said as she stepped aside to let him in. Her smile was shy, her eyes extra bright and her cheeks aflame. 'So all's good with the battery?'

'Everything's absolutely fine with the battery,' Liam assured her. 'You'll be able to run your fridge, stove, lights, computer – everything you'll need for camping.'

'Thanks, that's awesome.' An aroma of freshly brewed coffee reached him. Kate ran her palms down the sides of her jeans, as if she was nervous. Then she gestured to the living room where a low table had been set with mugs, a glass coffee pot and china milk jug. 'Come in and make yourself comfortable.'

'Thank you.' There was a sofa and two armchairs. Liam chose an armchair.

Kate sat in the middle of the sofa, poised like a hostess as she lifted the coffee pot. 'You don't take milk, do you?'

'No milk or sugar, thanks.'

'Right.' Carefully, she poured the coffee and set the mug on a coaster in front of Liam, then poured a mug for herself, adding milk. 'So,' she said before she'd even tasted her coffee. 'I don't want to take up too much of your time, but as I said the other night, I wanted to clear the air. I need to apologise for the clumsy way I treated you the other day.'

'It's okay, Kate. I understand.'

'Do you? Really?' Her smile took a wry tilt. 'Because I don't seem to understand myself. I mean, *I* started the whole flirting conversation, but I've been behaving like a ditzy character in a romance novel, dropping hints and then coming up with all kinds of silly excuses and driving the hero up the wall.'

Hero? Liam couldn't help smiling. And damn it, Kate was looking so nervous and anxious, he just wanted to take her in his arms and kiss all those worries away.

'The thing is,' she said next, sitting very straight with her hands clasped on her knees and her gaze not quite meeting his. 'I don't think I meant it.'

Liam's breathing hitched. This conversation wasn't heading in any of the directions he'd anticipated. 'Meant what exactly?'

'Any of it. I was really mad with myself after you left last week. I more or less rejected you, but I actually think I do need – ah —'

'Ah?'

'Whatever – whatever you had in mind.' The pink in her cheeks had deepened to crimson. 'I suppose I'm talking about a – a fling.'

Wham. This was a jaw dropper Liam hadn't anticipated. He could feel his noble plans for restraint slipping fast.

Now Kate looked up at him and her brown eyes shimmered. 'Is – is that what you were thinking?'

A fling? Hell, yeah. He checked the impulse to leap out of his chair. But this new situation also called for a change to his original strategy. 'I was thinking more along the lines of taking things one step at a time.'

Kate frowned. 'But usually there's a sense of where those steps are leading to.'

She was right, of course. And Liam suspected he could talk her out of this, if he wasn't careful.

Time for a totally new game plan. Coffee untouched, he launched to his feet. 'You know, there's only one way to find out.'

So, this was it? The big moment that Kate had tried, unsuccessfully, to imagine? She felt a flash of anxiety, which might have turned to panic if Liam hadn't been smiling and looking totally relaxed.

As she rose from the sofa, he came towards her, warmth in his eyes, his hand extended, looking every inch the hot tradie in a blue cotton drill shirt, low slung jeans and elastic sided boots. When Kate reached out, she felt his fingers wrap around hers, strong, slightly rough, non-threatening. Gently, he tugged her a little closer to him and then lifted her hand to brush his lips over her knuckles. Feather soft. Shiver sweet.

'That's the first step,' he said, and there was a smoulder in his eyes now. He held her hand as he drew her closer still and pressed a kiss to her forehead. 'And I guess this is step two,' he murmured against her ear.

Kate felt his shadowed jaw, masculine and rough against her cheek and, as he slipped his arms around her, she was gripped by a yearning she'd almost forgotten, a need coiling through her, arrowing deep, spreading heat.

By the time his lips reached hers, she was already dizzy, winding her arms around his neck and opening her lips to meet him, and then pressing close and still closer. Wow. Being kissed by this man eclipsed any old memories. This was a whole new experience. All wonder and novelty and delicious, hot intimacy.

When they stopped for air, Kate whispered somewhat breathlessly, 'If that was step two, I can't wait for three.'

Liam gave a soft chuckle. 'Would that be the sofa?'

She shook her head. 'I've a much better idea.'

Her room was ready and waiting. She'd already closed the curtains, lit a Glasshouse candle and made up the bed with clean sheets and pillowslips.

'Minx,' Liam said when he saw this, but he was smiling and drawing her in to him again, scattering tantalising kisses to the curve of her neck. *Ah, yes.* To the V of her shirt. *Yes, yes.* And then to her chin and, finally, her lips.

Fire built fast and fierce in Kate now, and she was sure her needs must be one step ahead of his. Then he slipped his hands beneath the hem of her shirt and she felt his fingertips skim the skin at her waist with barely there, teasing caresses.

Oh, help. At any moment, she would lose all sense of control.

But wasn't that what she wanted? Craved? This wonderful helplessness? This total surrender to longing and need? This chance to have a man's hand – not just any man, but *this* man's hand – there and *there* – where she hadn't been touched in so long?

Yes. Yes. Yes.

The final break in their control was simultaneous. Mutual. Now they ripped off clothes, their own clothes, each other's, desperate for skin against skin. No more barriers. Just falling together onto lavender-scented sheets, reaching and finding. Lost in discovery and bliss.

Luckily, Liam didn't need to rush away. Kate made another pot of coffee and this time they drank it companionably together on the sofa. She was all abuzz and glowing, but she felt shy again, too, somewhat self-conscious and dazed by the awesome intimacy they'd shared. Overwhelmed by all the questions that presented themselves now. The first being where the next step might take them.

'You're looking worried again,' Liam told her.

'Sorry. I guess I've only just realised how little I know about negotiating flings. Or about negotiating the aftermath, at any rate.'

He grinned. 'Now that we've flung?'

'Exactly.' She couldn't help smiling.

'I guess we just —' He filled in the gap with an easy shrug.

'Go back to one step at a time?'

'Something like that.'

Kate didn't want to mention emotions, or anything scary like falling in love, but she feared it wouldn't take much at all for this man to capture her heart. Chances were, he'd already stolen a fair chunk of it.

His expression was more serious now as he watched her. 'You mustn't worry that I might get too serious.'

Silly how this perfectly reasonable comment felt like cold water being thrown over her fantasies. After all, she had no plans to get serious either. 'That's – good to know.'

'I'm very aware that you have the van ready and waiting for you to take off as soon as you're free,' Liam said next.

Kate nodded.

He shot her a quick, searching glance. 'That's still your plan, isn't it?'

'Yes.' She hoped she hadn't sounded hesitant. 'Yes, definitely,' she added with a little more force.

'Then rest easy, Kate. If there's one thing I've learned from my marriage, it's not to force my company on a woman who wants her freedom.'

This was a surprise. Kate needed a moment to take in this news. What kind of freedom had Liam denied his wife? She realised she knew very little about his past. Had he been a control freak? It was hard to imagine.

Now she was desperately curious. 'Do you mind if I ask how that came about?'

'How my marriage collapsed in a screaming heap?'

'I'd like to understand – if you don't mind.'

'No, it's a fair enough question.' He rearranged himself on the sofa, long legs stretched in front of him, almost as if he needed to consciously relax before he recounted his story. 'We were in Brisbane. Or at least Simone was in Brisbane and I worked out on the mines. Mostly in central Queensland. Sometimes in WA.'

'Fly-in fly-out?'

'Yeah. The money was great and there was always plenty of work for electricians on mine sites. Simone was keen. She said she didn't mind me being away so much – not when it meant a flash house in a good suburb, expensive clothes and overseas holidays.'

'The good life,' said Kate.

Liam shrugged. 'Her idea of the good life.'

'And what did you want?'

'Oh, I was happy enough, at first. But after a few years, my interest in constant travel wore thin and I was hungry for more at-home time. *And* I wanted a family. I'd made good money, we had a fancy house in New Farm, and I'd had enough of the mines.' He let out his breath on a sigh. 'We had a huge row. Simone didn't want me to give up such a great job, but I resigned anyway. I'd had enough.'

This sounded pretty fair to Kate, but if it ended in divorce, his wife must have been furious.

'It was only after I was settled back in Brisbane with a nine-to-five job that I realised how serious Simone was about never wanting kids, ever. And she wasn't happy having me around the place every night either. She was too used to enjoying her own space and she loved going out with her girlfriends. Rock concerts, discos, night clubs. All the things she'd done when she was single.'

'Other guys?' Kate couldn't help asking, only too aware that Stan had never taken his marriage vows seriously.

'Probably,' said Liam. 'I could see the way we were heading. Each day there was more and more evidence that we couldn't make things work, so I didn't bother – or maybe I didn't lower myself – to ask about possible affairs. I know so-called recreational drugs were involved. And the last thing Simone wanted was to be sitting at home, having dinner and watching TV with boring old me.'

Liam, boring? What was wrong with the woman?

'You don't need the gory details,' he said next. 'That's the gist of it. A host of Simone's girlfriends were already divorced and they put her onto a really cunning lawyer who made sure Simone's cut was very generous.'

'That must have been painful.'

'Yeah. Wasn't pleasant, but it's behind me. To be honest, it feels good to have the length of this big state between us now.'

'I get that,' said Kate. 'I wouldn't mind if Stan wanted to spend the rest of his life in Cambodia.'

While he'd been talking, Liam had rested an arm along the back of the sofa. Now, he lifted a lock of Kate's hair and gently twisted it around his fingers. 'You're a beautiful, sexy woman,' he said. 'Today was amazing.'

'It was,' she agreed softly.

'I hope we can see each other again. But I promise I'm not going to start pestering you.'

'Thanks.' Kate had been wondering if they might snuggle close again, but Liam was sensibly bringing them back to reality. After all, she wasn't free for a relationship, not even for casual dating. She wouldn't like to leave Tilly here on her own, and the whole idea of babysitting was tricky with teens.

'We must keep in touch,' suggested Liam.

'Yes, sure.'

'And we'll probably bump into each other at the theatre.'

'Yes.' Suddenly emboldened, Kate asked, 'I was wondering if

you'd like to drop in for lunch some time?' Of course, she blushed profusely.

Liam's response was another of his irresistible smiles. 'That'd be great. Sounds like a plan.' He got to his feet.

'Maybe you'd like something to eat now?' Kate asked as she rose too. 'I'm sure it's past lunchtime.'

'Nah, it's okay, thanks. It's time I got back to work.'

'What's on your books for this afternoon?'

'Fire alarms in Topaz.'

She walked with him to the door, her imagination already anticipating a yummy goodbye kiss, but as they passed the kitchen, her phone, which she'd left on the counter, began to ring. *Damn.* 'I'd better get that.'

'No worries.'

The caller was Chelsea. 'Hi, Mum.'

'Chelsea, hi.'

'Just a quick call. Sorry we never got organised for that FaceTime with Tilly, but will you be free if Pippa and I came up to see you next weekend?'

Kate saw Liam, paused in the doorway, and she waved her phone at him, gave a helpless shrug. He sent her an answering wave, then turned and departed.

'Absolutely,' she told her daughter. 'Of course I'll be free. How lovely. I can't wait.'

CHAPTER TWENTY

'My sisters are coming here? To meet *me*?' Tilly couldn't quite decide if she was excited or scared when she arrived home from school to be greeted by this news.

In her private moments, she'd thought a fair bit about these sisters. At first, she'd secretly labelled them her 'ugly stepsisters', just for fun, until Kate had shown her a couple of photos that ruled out the ugly bit. And of course, Pippa and Chelsea weren't really stepsisters at all. Tilly found it rather daunting to know that she shared genes with these attractive and clever women. And it was amazing, but also sobering, to be told that they wanted to meet her.

Having grown up believing that her family consisted of no one except herself and her mum, she was still getting used to the idea that she wasn't entirely alone in the world. She'd never really tried to imagine her father, and she wasn't sure she wanted to meet him, given that Kate seemed to share the same low opinion of him that her mum had. But half-sisters were something else.

'The girls can only stay for the weekend,' Kate explained, as Tilly helped herself to orange juice from the fridge and then a Monte Carlo from the biscuit tin. 'Chelsea's flying up from Brisbane and she and Pippa will drive up here together from Townsville.'

'Pippa's pregnant, isn't she?'

'Yes. Only early stages, though.'

Tilly shot Kate a playful smile. 'You'll be a grandma.'

Kate was chopping carrots for a casserole and now she looked up and gave a helpless eye-roll. 'How strange is that? I'm sure I'm far too young.'

Really? Kate might not have grey hair and wrinkles, but she was hardly young. 'You'll have to think of a cute name for yourself, so they don't call you Grandma,' Tilly mused as she separated the two halves of her biscuit to reveal the icing. 'And I'll be an auntie. Is there such a thing as a half-auntie?'

'I'm sure you'd just be called Auntie,' Kate said, sliding the carrots to one side and turning her attention to a bunch of celery.

But Tilly was already imagining her avatar on Snapchat – an image of a girl with big green eyes and straight black hair sliced down the middle. 'No, I want to be Half-Auntie Tilly.'

'You might frighten the poor little kid,' Kate said, but she was smiling.

'Do they know if it's a boy or a girl?'

'Not yet. It's a bit too early. And Pippa and David may decide they don't want to know.'

'Where will the girls both sleep while they're here?'

'Good question.' Kate paused in her chopping and cast a quick glance down the hallway. 'The third bedroom only has a double bed and I'm sure Pippa and Chelsea are way past wanting to share.'

'I could always sleep on the sofa.'

'That's sweet of you, Tilly, but I was actually thinking that one of the girls could go in the van. I should have enough time to make it nice.'

Wow! The van would be a cool place to stay. Tilly almost volunteered herself for that space. But she supposed Kate's daughters should have the first chance. 'They might both want the van,' she suggested, wondering if grown-up sisters still fought over things like that.

Kate shrugged. 'They'll have to toss a coin for it then, I guess.' Then she frowned. 'I'll need to do some shopping though. I'll definitely need a new mattress. And perhaps new sheets and a rug.'

'What about a heater?' asked Tilly, conscious that the nights in these mountains were now quite seriously cold.

'Yes, a small heater would be handy, too.'

'Can I come shopping with you? I'm really good at looking for that sort of stuff.'

Kate's eyebrows lifted with surprise, but then, as she slid her chopped vegetables into a waiting casserole pot, she smiled. 'Sure. Tomorrow's Saturday, so we can go over to Atherton and have lunch in a café while we're there.'

'Cool.'

***

Olivia was looking forward to Monday afternoon when Tilly was due for her next visit and she was even planning what they might have for afternoon tea. Of course, she knew afternoon tea wasn't at all important. These meetings weren't supposed to be anything more than a drama lesson, or some kind of coaching session.

Josie had proposed these lessons as an opportunity for Olivia to pass on a few gems from her extensive stage experience to a promising youngster, although Olivia knew jolly well that it was more a strategy for keeping her occupied and out of Josie's hair. No big surprise there. Josie had been a high school deputy before she retired, so she'd had plenty of experience in juggling staff and allocating unpalatable tasks. Running a small town's little theatre company was probably a breeze by comparison.

Josie had certainly brushed aside Olivia's objection that she knew next to nothing about teaching. And now, Olivia understood how astute their director had been. Not only had Olivia rediscovered a good many aspects of her craft that she was keen to share with Tilly, but the girl had proved unexpectedly receptive.

Besides, teaching Tilly had given Olivia an excuse to avoid being roped in to help with other tasks at the theatre, such as making the props. Just this past weekend, she'd been in the newsagency where Heidi worked and the girl had spent important time that she should have devoted to other customers trying to rope Olivia into making the 'workstations' for *Next Stop Mars*'s spacecraft.

'You have so much spare time on your hands now and all you need is a couple of these magazine holders,' Heidi had enthused as she'd set fold-out, collapsible cardboard contraptions in front of Olivia on the shop's counter. 'You assemble them like this,' she went on, her black and silver fingernails flashing as she placed two cardboard holders together. 'Then you flip them on their sides, tape two of them together and Bob's your uncle.'

Heidi hadn't seemed at all concerned about the customers waiting with increasing impatience behind Olivia. 'They'll look great spray-painted silver and with electrical tape making black outlines around the edges. Josie reckons we'll need about four workstations for the spaceship's bridge.'

Olivia was sure these props would be perfectly effective, but in all her years on the stage, she'd never made a prop and she wasn't about to start. She'd explained this to Heidi, carefully and politely. And mainly for the benefit of the customers behind her, she added that she didn't really have spare time, as she was giving special tutorials to one of the theatre's newest members.

There'd been a brief, mutinous flash in Heidi's heavily made-up eyes, but then she'd meekly stowed her cardboard holders under the counter and got on with the job of serving everyone else.

Olivia, meanwhile, would have sailed out of the shop with her customary dignity, if her ankle hadn't still been somewhat tender, even though she was finally free of the moon boot.

After that encounter, however, Olivia had been extra conscientious about preparing her next session with Tilly and she'd been surprised by how much she'd enjoyed the reading and thinking and planning. But for her, an even bigger surprise about these sessions, and one Josie couldn't have foreseen, was that Olivia had also found herself emotionally invested in Tilly's sad situation.

Last week, Olivia had been clinging to her own emotional tightrope as she'd watched the poor child reliving the sorrow and grief that had followed her mother's death. Afterwards, looking back on that precarious moment, Olivia wasn't sure how she'd found the right words, but somehow she'd been able to soothe Tilly.

And that moment of sharing a shred of wisdom about finding one's inner strength had proved to be a two-way gift. While Tilly had calmed down, Olivia had been uplifted by the knowledge that she'd actually helped the child. And that sense of happiness, of feeling connected and needed, had buoyed her for the rest of the week.

* * *

'Pikelets?' Tilly exclaimed, when she arrived on Monday and saw the plate ready and waiting on Olivia's coffee table. 'Do they make those at the bakery, too?'

'No,' said Olivia. 'I made them.'

'Really? I don't think I've ever eaten a homemade pikelet. My mum was good at cooking all kinds of meat, vegetables and rice, but she hardly ever cooked anything sweet.'

Tilly's tastebuds were on high alert as she helped herself to a pikelet topped with butter and strawberry jam. 'Oh, my gosh, it's still warm.' She took a bite. 'And it's so-o-o delicious.'

Olivia laughed. 'Well, pikelets are dead easy to make. I'll have to show you some time.'

'Would you? Would you, really? Wow, that'd be awesome.' After a carefully timed pause, during which Tilly helped herself to a second pikelet, she asked sweetly, 'I don't suppose you could teach me today, could you?'

'Today?' Olivia repeated, eyes wide with obvious surprise. 'I'm supposed to be teaching you about acting. I thought we could look at Roald Dahl's *Matilda* and interrogate the characters together.'

'Well, yeah, that does sound pretty cool. But my sisters – my *half*-sisters – are coming next weekend. They're coming to meet me, actually.' Tilly cocked her thumb towards her chest to add a little dramatic impact to this announcement. 'I'd love to be able to cook something for them. Pikelets would be the best.'

Olivia frowned. 'Can't Kate teach you?'

'I'm not sure she knows how to make pikelets.'

'It's a simple matter of dropping a spoonful of batter into a pan.'

'Yeah, but she's so busy fixing up the van and cleaning the house from top to bottom.'

Olivia pursed her lips as she considered this proposition and Tilly realised that her tutor probably didn't like having her plans overturned by a little smart-arse. But Tilly had been wracking her brains for a way to impress the hell out of these super-impressive sisters and pikelets seemed perfect. She could already picture herself serving them up for afternoon tea.

'We could do *Matilda* next week,' she suggested demurely. 'And we don't have to tell Josie about the pikelets.'

This time, Olivia narrowed her eyes as she studied Tilly for an uncomfortably long moment. Eventually, her gaze softened and she even smiled. 'How about we compromise? An hour of *Matilda* and then you can whip up a batch of pikelets before you go. And you're right. We don't need to tell Josie, do we?'

* * *

The van looked so different now that the bed was fitted with a top-quality mattress and made up with new bedding. The pillowslips and doona were all in trendy colours of turmeric and navy blue, and a final touch was a colourful crocheted rug that Tilly had unearthed in a second-hand store.

At first, Kate hadn't been too sure about the rug, but she'd bought it anyhow, thinking Tilly could always use it in her bedroom if it didn't suit the van. But Tilly had actually proved to be quite a skilled op-shopper.

Apparently, this had been one of her mother's favourite pastimes, and on Saturday Tilly had found a dress, a pair of jeans and a hand-knitted Fair Isle jumper that cost next to nothing and looked great on her. And to Kate's surprise, now that the rug was in place, folded across the foot of the bed, it was a perfect fit for the handmade vibe of her van's interior.

Standing in the doorway, she felt a deep sense of satisfaction as she viewed her handiwork. Outside the afternoon was grey, wet and misty, but the van was cosy and inviting with its timber panelled walls, the little triangular piece of stained glass hanging in the window, the shelves she'd made, the storage nooks and hooks, as well as the lights and lamps Liam had installed.

There was still plenty of work to be done. The cupboards had no doors and there were no bathroom facilities, but the sink, stove and bed were in place and the wiring was finished. The basics were covered and the whole set-up looked very comfy and inviting.

Kate's satisfaction was tinged with sadness though. She had no idea when she'd be able to take off in this natty little home on wheels. And now, one of her daughters would be the first person to sleep in the van, to slip between those crisp new sheets in that snug bed with its luxurious, pillow-top mattress.

That's okay, she told herself, as she slid the van's door closed and ran back through the drenching mist to the house, knowing that it was nearly time to head back into town to collect Tilly. Only a very ungenerous mother would mind if one of her daughters was first to sleep in that bed. Heavens, Kate could still remember how incredibly excited she'd been about buying a cot and then little bunk beds for her babies. Pippa and Chelsea might be grown up now, but they were still her precious offspring. Of course she didn't mind.

And yet . . . she also couldn't help thinking that it might be all kinds of fun if she and Liam were the first to christen those new sheets.

Jeepers. This thought had barely been born before it blossomed and grew legs. A chuckle escaped Kate. Should she phone Liam? Send him a text? A quick message with a cheeky suggestion about a midday rendezvous?

She should probably wait until he was actually here before she showed him the bed in the van, but she was pretty sure he'd be keen. Anyway, he'd also worked on the van, so he'd more or less earned the christening rights, hadn't he?

Happy shivers rippled through Kate as she allowed herself to imagine the scenario that might follow if she went ahead with this invitation, mentally adding a few saucy details. Her phone was on the kitchen counter and it was an easy matter to tap through her contacts until she found Liam's number. Dare she?

Hell, yeah. She needed a little fun. She'd earned a diversion. A celebration.

As her finger hovered over Liam's number, however, maddening second thoughts and doubts crept in. Liam's words echoed in her head. *I promise I'm not going to start pestering you.*

She couldn't help remembering that she had been the first to initiate their 'fling' last week. And in the aftermath, she and Liam had both agreed they should be sensible and cautious about pushing their relationship too far too soon. Now, less than a week had passed. Wouldn't she seem a bit too eager?

Then again, last week had been beyond amazing and she couldn't imagine that Liam was going to object. Before she lost her nerve, Kate tapped the screen and her phone instantly connected. But even as she heard it ringing, more questions pinged in her head. Hadn't she learned by now that it was always best to play it safe?

'Hello, Kate.'

Liam's voice sounded in her ear, deep and warm and several versions of sexy. Kate could picture his smile, was remembering the thrill of his kisses and everything else that had followed. So-o-o-o tempting.

And yet, to her dismay, more arguments lined up in her head. Shouldn't she remember exactly *why* she'd worked so hard on that van? It was never meant to be a shaggin' wagon. Her big goal was travel and freedom. Uncomplicated freedom. And she'd already had one major roadblock dumped in her path. She'd be reckless to add to her obstacles.

Perhaps more importantly, she needed to remember Liam was free to have any woman he wanted. Flings were all very well, but Kate was the type who fell in love. She could end up getting hurt.

She could still remember the pain of finding out about Stan. The first time. The second time. Too many times . . .

'Oh, Liam,' she spluttered, feeling totally torn. 'Sorry. That must have been a pocket bump. I didn't mean to ring you.'

'Oh? Well . . . okay.' Did he sound disappointed? It was hard to tell. 'Anyway, it's good to hear from you. How are you, Kate?'

'I'm fine, thanks.' Just hearing his voice, she could feel herself giving in. It wasn't too late and it would be dead easy to go ahead and invite him anyway.

By the way, while we're talking, how would you feel about . . .

Oh, help. She really should have given this more thought. It was true what they said about fools rushing in. 'Actually,' she continued quickly, before she weakened again. 'I'm in a bit of a hurry right now. I have to pick up Tilly from Olivia's and I'm running late. Gotta go. Sorry.'

She hung up before she made the ridiculous mess any worse. But already, she could feel the shame of her dithering gathering around her like cold mist, shutting out warmth and light.

* * *

'I was wondering when your birthday is.'

'My birthday?' Tilly was in the process of using an egg-flip to slide another perfectly browned pikelet onto the plate beside the stove, but she almost dropped the precious delicacy as she turned to Olivia in surprise.

'Sorry.' Olivia looked a little embarrassed now. 'I suppose you must think I'm a nosey parker.'

'No, it's okay.' Tilly carefully tucked the clean tea towel over the pikelets in the way Olivia had just taught her. She didn't add that no one up here had asked about her birthday.

Even when Tilly had enrolled at her new school and had filled in her date of birth on the forms, Kate hadn't paid any particular attention and certainly hadn't commented. Kate had checked with Tilly about periods and stuff, but birthdays hadn't been mentioned. Tilly assumed she'd been too distracted by her own worries at the time. 'It's actually not far away, on the fifteenth.'

'The fifteenth of this month?' Olivia crossed the kitchen to a calendar on the side of her fridge that she held in place with a magnet shaped like a flowerpot. 'That's a Wednesday. Goodness, it's Wednesday next week.'

'Yeah. A rehearsal night. I think we'll be getting close to dress rehearsals by then.'

'You'll have to have a cake,' Olivia said.

Tilly smiled. 'That'd be nice. But are you sure?'

'Why not? It would be fun.'

Tilly's meetings with Olivia were on Mondays, but she wouldn't mind in the least having a birthday cake two days early. It was pretty amazing that this old lady would bother with a cake when Tilly wasn't even her grandchild. And Tilly supposed she *should* pluck up the courage to mention her birthday to Kate. Kate was her guardian, after all, and she would probably feel bad if she only found out about it afterwards.

Tilly wondered if she could slip the subject of birthdays into a conversation with Pippa and Chelsea on the weekend. Maybe she should ask about everyone's birthdays. Her knowledge of this family – *her* family, half-family or whatever – was so limited it was practically zero. She didn't even know if Kate was the cake-making type.

Some of the mothers in Cairns had been unbelievably competitive when it came to over-the-top, elaborate birthday cakes. Tilly's mum had just rolled her eyes and said she never had time for such nonsense. Angela had never been ashamed to buy cakes from the cake shop and of course they'd looked gorgeous and had tasted totally delish.

'So what kind of cake do you think you'd like?' Olivia asked.

Tilly almost said chocolate cake, because, well, why wouldn't anyone want chocolate cake? But she also loved salted caramel, or white chocolate and strawberry and, actually, she didn't mind surprises and it was really nice of Olivia to even care. 'I love them all,' she said.

Olivia laughed. 'You really are quite the little diplomat, aren't you?'

'Am I?' Tilly wasn't totally sure she knew what this meant, but Olivia was now reaching into an overhead cupboard for a Tupperware container.

'You'll have to take these extra pikelets with you,' she said. 'I hope Kate won't mind that we've added cooking lessons to our sessions.'

'I'm pretty sure she'll be cool.' Tilly was totally proud of her pikelets and she was pumped about telling Kate her plan to make them again on the weekend.

'So do you do a lot of cooking and baking?' she asked Olivia as they transferred the freshly made batch into the tea-towel lined container.

Olivia seemed to hesitate for a moment, but then she shook her head. 'No.' Her mouth tilted in an awkward smile. 'Hardly ever.'

'Not for your kids? Or grandkids?'

Now Olivia's mouth twisted even more tightly and she seemed to flinch, almost as if she'd been hurt. 'No,' she said. 'I don't have any children or grandchildren.'

After this admission, the pain in Olivia's face disappeared quite quickly, but Tilly knew she was a highly experienced actor. And although her mouth curved into the serenest of smiles, the ghost of her pain lingered in her eyes, and Tilly was sure she shouldn't have asked such a personal question.

CHAPTER TWENTY-ONE

On Friday night Kate and Tilly had everything ready. The house was spotless, the wood heater lit, the spare beds made up and the pantry well stocked. This included a good supply of wine and cheese in anticipation of companionable girly chats, with soft drink, of course, for Tilly – and for Pippa, who would have to be careful now that she was pregnant.

Tilly had even plucked a few of the precious crimson blooms from the mandevilla plant in her hanging basket and she'd arranged the flowers in little green glass vases that had been her mum's. 'They probably won't last long, but you have to have flowers in Pippa's and Chelsea's bedrooms,' she'd insisted.

Kate assured her it was a lovely idea. The girls would be touched. And now, excitement was building in the little house on the hill. Pippa and Chelsea had left Townsville just before four that afternoon, and they planned to stop for a bite to eat at the halfway point, so it would be eight-thirty, or perhaps closer to nine, before they arrived.

Kate was familiar with the journey up the Bruce Highway and could picture the girls having dinner at Cardwell, a town nestled on the coast, with Hinchinbrook Island just offshore. From there, as they headed north, they would pass through Tully, surrounded by cane fields and with a spectacular mountain backdrop, and then continue on through the little town of El Arish until they were just south of Innisfail. The point to turn off the highway and head for the hills was marked by a building that had once been a grand Italian farmhouse, now two storeys of crumbling stone, standing tall in the middle of cane fields.

This drive was always spectacular with lush tropical scenery, but with night closing in, Kate supposed the girls would miss the dramatic sight of Mount Bartle Frere towering so close to the coast. But they weren't on a sight-seeing trip, after all, and at least the Palmerston Highway that climbed into the mountains was smooth and safe and wouldn't be too busy.

It was almost eight when Chelsea rang. Tilly was in her bedroom, finishing off her homework, so that she could have the weekend free, and Kate was trying to keep herself calm by playing a game of sudoku on her phone. Kate's heart kicked with excitement as she answered the call.

'Chelsea, darling, where are you?'

'We're just at the top of the range. Not quite at Millaa Millaa.'

'Oh, that's great. You'll be here in —'

'Mum, I think we need to head straight on to Atherton.'

Atherton? Why on earth?

'They have 24-hour Emergency there, don't they? It looks like Pippa might be having a miscarriage.'

'No!'

'She's having cramps and bleeding. It's pretty bad, Mum.' Chelsea sounded quite shaken, which was hardly surprising.

Kate was shaken, too, hit by a cyclone of emotions. Disappointment. Shock. Fear for poor Pippa. She struggled to think straight. 'Yes, you'd better go to Atherton,' she said. 'They definitely have an Emergency there. I'll come over, too. The hospital's not hard to find.'

'Yeah, I've already got it on Maps on my phone.'

'Great. I'll – I'll see you there then.'

'Okay.'

'Take care, Chelsea. The road isn't too misty, is it?'

'It's pretty bad, but I've found the fog lights.'

'Good girl. You're a safe driver. Take it easy. You'll be fine. Give my love to Pippa, won't you?'

'Yeah, sure.'

'I'll see you soon. Oh, and Chelsea?'

'Yes?'

'Have you rung David?'

'No. Pippa wanted to, but I thought it might be best not to worry him until we know for sure what's happening.'

'I suppose that's sensible. All right then. Take care.'

As Kate disconnected, Tilly came out of her bedroom into the hallway. 'Was that Pippa and Chelsea? Are they nearly here?'

'Yes, but there's a problem.' Kate tried to speak calmly, but it was hard to hide her distress. 'It looks like Pippa might be having a miscarriage.'

'Oh, my God.'

'I know. It's —' Kate couldn't quite finish the sentence. 'They're going straight to Atherton, to the hospital.'

'Really?' The girl's desolate face was a mirror of Kate's own anguish.

'I'm going to head over there now, too,' Kate said next. 'I feel I should. Do you think you'd be okay to stay here for an hour or two?'

'Can't I come?'

'You could come, I guess, but we might be sitting around in the hospital waiting room for ages, in the middle of the night. You'll be bored and tired.'

'But they're my *sisters*.' Tilly's mouth quivered, as if she might cry at any moment.

Kate hesitated.

'I won't say anything stupid, or get in the way. I just want to be there.'

'All right. Grab a jumper and maybe something to read.'

* * *

As Kate sped along the dark, mist-shrouded roads, Tilly couldn't help feeling scared. This was so messed up, not at all how the night was supposed to have happened. Right about now, she and Kate should have been welcoming Pippa and Chelsea into the warmth of the cosy cottage.

She had pictured that moment so many times during the past week – her sisters climbing out of their car, the introductions, the smiling hellos and hugs. Now, instead, Pippa was in hospital, possibly losing her baby, and Kate was worried and panicky and driving in total silence, probably battling a thousand worries.

Tilly supposed she should have known the whole 'getting to know you' weekend was too good to be true. Life generally sucked. And right now, poor Pippa was facing one of the biggest disappointments of all. Losing her baby would be heartbreaking.

Like losing your mum. Tilly tried not to think about that now.

Ahead of them, the lights on the hill at Atherton twinkled and, as they drew closer, Tilly could feel herself tensing all over. She'd never been in a hospital, not even after her mother's accident. They'd made her wait till they'd taken her mum to the funeral home and then Jed had gone with her, and her mum had been wearing her best dress and lying in a satin lined casket —

No. Stop. It didn't help to remember that now. It was time to remember Olivia's message about inner strength.

The streets of Atherton were quiet and many houses were already in darkness. They came to an intersection where a huge building loomed and Kate found a spare parking space in a side street.

'Okay,' she said as she opened her door. 'Have you got everything?' It was the first time she'd spoken since they'd left home.

'Yep.' Tilly had both her phone and her iPad in her shoulder bag.

A bitter wind whipped at their faces as they crossed the road. From the footpath, they walked down a ramp with railings on either side till they reached glass doors that slid open to reveal an empty, brightly lit corridor. The place was deathly quiet.

'This way.' Kate spoke in a kind of hushed awe, then promptly took off, while Tilly's sneakers squeaked on the shiny linoleum as she hurried to keep up. The corridor seemed to smell of medicine or disinfectant.

They reached a point where the corridor forked into two and in front of them was an office lined with glass windows. Again, this space was brightly lit and Tilly could see desks, wall charts, filing cabinets and computers inside. A woman in a uniform was sitting behind one of the windows.

'You wait over there,' Kate told Tilly as she nodded to where people were scattered on rows of seats. Then Kate headed over to speak to the woman behind the glass.

Somewhat warily, Tilly scanned the people already waiting on the seats. An old couple. A tired-looking woman with a baby in her arms that she kept jigging up and down, while a toddler slept in a curled-up ball on the chair beside her. Further back was a young guy in ripped jeans and muddy boots, with messy hair and straggly beard. He looked totally spaced out. There was no sign of anyone who might be Pippa or Chelsea.

Taking a seat at the end of the first row, Tilly looked up to a TV screen on the wall. It seemed to be showing some kind of interview, but she couldn't recognise the faces and the sound was so low she couldn't hear what it was about. Meanwhile, the woman behind the glass was making a phone call and Kate was standing extra still and straight as she waited.

Tilly squirmed in her seat. This hospital was too quiet. It totally creeped her out.

At last, the woman at the window put down the phone and spoke to Kate. A short discussion followed, before Kate nodded then finally turned and crossed the floor to Tilly.

Taking a seat beside Tilly, she leaned in and spoke extra quietly. 'They've taken Pippa to have an ultrasound.'

'Is Chelsea with her?'

'Yes. Holding Pippa's hand, I imagine.' As Kate said this, she reached into her bag and extracted her phone. 'There's no message here from Chelsea. I think I should ring David.'

'He's Pippa's husband?'

'Her partner, yes.'

'He'll freak.'

'Probably.' Kate frowned and stared at her phone, as if she was tossing up what to do. A brief sigh escaped her, but then she got to her feet again. 'It feels wrong not to let him know what's happening. I'll just pop around the corner. Won't be long.'

Then she was gone again, disappearing back the way they'd come and leaving Tilly alone. Tilly considered checking her own phone, but now that she'd stopped Snapchatting with her friends in Cairns, she didn't use it much. She tried to cheer herself up by thinking about the little theatre group in Burralea. She'd been surprised to find herself really enjoying being a member of the cast, polishing her small part and watching everyone else become more and more confident in their roles.

She was thinking about Hamish Kirk when a young man dressed in a pale blue top and trousers came down the opposite corridor from the one where Kate had disappeared. He called out a name.

'Susan Jeffries.'

The woman with the baby got to her feet and gave the sleeping little boy beside her a shake. The toddler was obviously sound asleep and Tilly couldn't imagine how the mother was going to be able to carry both her children.

Tilly was wondering if she should offer to help, when the uniformed guy stepped forward and took the baby from the woman, so that she was free to lift her sleepyhead. The kid was obviously heavy and the mother looked exhausted as she headed off with him in her arms.

Which one of them was sick? Tilly wondered. Mother, baby or little boy? She hoped Kate would come back soon.

A new face arrived around the corner. A young woman with shoulder length, golden-brown hair. She was dressed in jeans and a loose white shirt, topped by a floaty black velvet vest. Her high-heeled boots made a smart tapping sound as she walked. She stopped and stared at Tilly.

In response, Tilly's heart started to thump. She'd recognised her from Kate's photos.

'Tilly?' the young woman asked.

'Yes.' Tilly's heart banged even harder as she stood.

'Hello!' The woman flashed a smile and a gold charm bracelet tinkled at her wrist as she held out her arms and hurried forward. 'I'm Chelsea.'

'Hi,' Tilly said shyly.

It was only now that they were quite close, Tilly could see that Chelsea had green eyes. *Oh, my God. They're the same green as mine. Exactly!* Fine hairs lifted on Tilly's arms.

And now, Chelsea was staring at Tilly, staring at her eyes, and possibly making the same discovery. She didn't comment on this, though. She simply said, 'It's so good to see you at last.' And with that, she pulled Tilly in close for a fierce hug, the kind of sisterly hug she'd been hoping for and dreaming about. Chelsea smelled of shampoo and an exotic perfume, and Tilly thought she was as glamorous as a movie star.

'Where's Mum?' Chelsea asked.

'She's phoning David.'

'Pippa's just called him, too.'

Even as Chelsea said this, Kate reappeared, looking more stressed than ever.

'Chelsea, darling,' Kate cried and now there were more hugs. 'How's Pippa?' she asked as she released her daughter. 'Has she had the scan?'

Chelsea nodded, and her smile vanished. 'It's not good news, I'm afraid.'

'She's lost the baby?'

'Yeah. Or at least she's lost whatever was there. They seem to think the baby hadn't really started developing.'

'But the pregnancy tests were positive, weren't they?'

'Sure.' Chelsea shrugged. 'That can happen apparently.'

'But Pippa's okay?'

'She's devastated. But yeah, she's not in any kind of danger.'

'Can I see her? Are they keeping her in?'

'They'd like her to stay here for a bit longer – just to make sure that —' Chelsea shot a cautious glance to Tilly, who'd been trying to take this in, although she didn't totally understand. Chelsea sent her a gentle smile. 'Don't worry. Pippa's going to be okay.'

'I'd like to see her,' said Kate.

'Of course.' Chelsea pointed. 'Down that way. On the right – the third door, I think it was. They know you're here.'

'Thanks.'

'Before you go, Mum,' Chelsea said next. 'Did you get through to David?'

'Yes, he'd just finished talking to Pippa. The poor man's had a terrible shock. He's jumping straight in his car and rushing up here.'

'Tonight?'

'Yes. I tried to suggest he'd be better to wait till morning, but he insisted he had to come straight away.'

Chelsea frowned. 'It'll be well after midnight by the time he gets here.'

'I know.' Kate gave a helpless little shrug. 'I was worried he might be too upset to drive, but I couldn't talk him out of it.'

Chelsea pulled a face. 'I wonder what Pippa will make of that.'

A knowing glance passed between Kate and Chelsea, as if there might be a little more to their concern about David than they were prepared to share in front of Tilly. But Tilly supposed it wasn't really her business. And she certainly wasn't about to ask.

***

From the doorway, Kate could see her daughter. She was completely alone and lying on a trolley. Lying very still, with her eyes closed. Even from the doorway, Kate could see that her eyelids were red and her cheeks damp, as if she'd been crying very recently, or perhaps was still crying.

Kate stepped forward cautiously. 'Pippa.'

Her daughter's eyes flashed open. 'Mum!' Her voice cracked and on the single syllable her eyelashes glittered with tears.

A sob broke from Kate as she hurried closer. 'Sweetheart,' she said as they hugged. 'I'm so sorry.'

At first Pippa couldn't speak, she was crying again, her tears accompanied by gulping sobs. It was some time before she calmed down and Kate found a box of tissues on a nearby bench, and then waited patiently while Pippa mopped at her sodden face and blew her nose.

'My poor little baby,' she said, her voice squeaky with sorrow.

Perhaps it was for the best and similar clichés floated around in Kate's head. She gave Pippa another hug, wishing she could think of something wise and helpful to say.

Pippa spoke again. 'I rang David. I told him I'm sorry.' Her face creased with pain. 'I feel so guilty.'

'But there's no need to feel guilty, darling. This wasn't your fault. These things happen. It's just terribly bad luck.'

'But I was sneaky. I took a risk on getting pregnant without even telling him. I knew he thought we weren't ready, that we hadn't saved enough.'

Kate had her own opinions about this, but again, she held her tongue.

'I don't suppose I thought I'd get pregnant so quickly,' Pippa said and she sniffled and reached for another tissue. 'We had a horrible fight. I said some pretty bitchy things, I'm afraid.' Now, Pippa drew a noisy breath, as if she was fighting yet another urge to weep. Her mouth twisted. 'And now, all this time, there wasn't even a baby. How's that for karma?'

Kate took her daughter's hand. 'You mustn't be too hard on yourself. I've spoken to David, too, and he certainly didn't sound angry. I'm sure he's just upset and worried about you.'

Pippa gave a weary nod, and then another sigh.

'He's driving up here,' Kate said.

'To the Tablelands? Tonight?'

'Yes, he's already on his way.' Kate gave her daughter's hand a gentle squeeze. 'He loves you very much, Pipps.'

* * *

'We have the same colour eyes.' Now that she and Chelsea were alone, Tilly couldn't resist commenting on this amazing fact.

'We have, haven't we?' Chelsea was sitting next to her and she smiled. 'We can thank our dad, Stan, for that.'

'What's he like?' Tilly hadn't planned to ask this, but Chelsea had mentioned their father without any sign of uneasiness and she'd aroused the girl's curiosity.

'What's our father like?' Chelsea repeated. 'Now, *that* is a very good question.' Folding her arms and settling as comfortably as the metal chair allowed, she gave a wry smile. 'The thing is – Stan Sheridan's a lot of things – I guess we all are, but with him, the extremes are exaggerated. He's a bit like that little girl in the poem. When he was good, he was very, very good, and when he was bad he was —'

'Horrid?' supplied Tilly.

'Maybe stupid's a better word. Or foolish. Even careless. He's certainly made reckless choices in his life.'

This was closer to the picture Tilly's mum had painted on the rare occasions she'd mentioned Tilly's dad. But Chelsea had hinted there was more to the man than a list of faults. 'Can you tell me about his good points?'

Chelsea grinned, clearly pleased to be asked. 'When Pippa and I were younger, Dad was a ton of fun. Fun in capital letters. And he gave us lots of his time. He taught us how to swim, and he took us bike riding and sailing, and he put on the very best barbecues – letting us invite all our friends. Oh, and he loved reading aloud. At night, Pippa and I just adored lying in bed and listening to Dad read. He never got tired of reading our favourite stories over and over and he was so good at doing all the voices.'

Her smile was wistful now, as if she was caught up in the happiest of memories. 'Honestly, Tilly, I can totally understand why our mothers fell for him.'

CHAPTER TWENTY-TWO

After several misty, drizzly days, Saturday morning dawned fresh and clear, the kind of blue-sky Tablelands morning that beckoned both locals and visitors outdoors – hiking in the forests, canoeing on the lakes, riding mountain bikes, gardening, fishing, searching for platypus and tree kangaroos.

When Liam woke, his first thoughts were about Kate. No surprises there. Since her supposedly accidental phone call, she'd been on his mind, more or less constantly.

At the time, Kate had sounded flustered and she'd said the call was a mistake, but Liam couldn't shake off the feeling that it had been an attack of cold feet rather than a pocket bump. Of course, there was every chance Kate was nervous about getting in too deep with him and Liam understood that. Totally. The last thing he wanted was to dive into a relationship that led him on a merry goose chase to nowhere. But although he was fifty, jaded and world weary when it came to romance, Liam also knew that the morning he'd spent with Kate had been way more than a mere itch they'd needed to scratch. Together they'd discovered the unexpected.

For Liam, there'd been a surprising, heart jolting connection that went way deeper than surface sparks. He was pretty sure Kate had felt this, too. Was that her problem?

Mulling over this, he made himself coffee and scrambled eggs and then took his plate and mug out to his tree-shaded back verandah where a bottlebrush in bloom played host to noisy honey-eaters and rainbow lorikeets.

The birds made intriguing company as they squabbled and flitted from branch to bloom, but despite their noise, there was a certain peace that came with a tree-filled backyard. By the time Liam had finished his coffee, he'd reached a decision. But he would wait till later, around mid-morning, before he phoned Kate.

* * *

It had been a long night for Kate and the girls. They hadn't left the hospital until after eleven. By then the doctor who'd been looking after Pippa had decided that she shouldn't need dilation and curettage. There would be normal blood loss over the next week or so, but of course, she was to report back if she was worried.

Kate had been exhausted by the time they finally got home. She made hot chocolate and packed a somewhat reluctant Tilly off to bed, taking her warm drink with her.

Kate also tried to insist that Pippa should be in bed, but although Pippa had enjoyed a long warm shower and a change into a snug tracksuit, she'd stubbornly stayed up, curled somewhat forlornly in an armchair, as she waited for David.

'You're supposed to be resting,' Kate told her.

'I'm resting here.'

No point in arguing. Kate relit the fire and considered a glass of wine, but she knew it would only make her even sleepier. So she and Pippa drank hot chocolate, while Chelsea helped herself to a hefty glass or two from a bottle of shiraz, but no one seemed in the mood for chatting.

David texted Pippa when he reached the turn-off from the highway, which meant he was now just an hour away. They watched a late night TV show, without really paying attention, and they continued to wait.

Time limped along.

Kate might even have nodded off when Pippa gave a sudden shout.

'He's here.'

Sure enough, the purr of a motor vehicle could be heard coming up the track and Kate sent up a silent prayer of thanks. This was one worry she could strike off her list.

Hot on the heels of her cry, Pippa was out of her chair and rushing to the front door. Kate and Chelsea remained discreetly inside while the greetings took place.

'Cathy and Heathcliff,' Chelsea commented out of the side of her mouth, and she rolled her eyes to the ceiling.

Kate pretended to ignore this.

It wasn't long before Pippa and David came inside. David was tall, with angular features and shiny black hair that flopped over his forehead from a side part. Nice looking. Kate had always thought he looked more like an artist than an accountant, which was his actual profession. Fortunately, he didn't have the notorious artistic temperament to match his looks. He'd always seemed calm and steady. Just right for Pippa.

This evening, the pair made their way into the house with their arms tight around each other, and from their pale faces and bleak expressions, it was clear they'd both been crying.

Kate covered her own dismay by diving straight into hostess mode. 'What would you like, David? Tea, wine? I've made soup that I can heat if you'd like.'

He said he was grateful for the soup offer, as he hadn't stopped for any dinner. While Kate was heating it, Pippa came into the kitchen.

'Mum, I was wondering? Would it be possible for David and me to sleep in your van?'

This was a question Kate had been tossing around, too. She hadn't raised it before David arrived, as she wasn't sure how the land lay between the young couple. Quickly considering the practicalities now, she knew she'd already put a good quality waterproof protector over the new mattress and the hospital had armed poor Pippa with all the sanitary gear she might need.

Cooperative Chelsea had commented earlier that she didn't care where she slept, and now Kate sensed that the privacy of the van could suit Pippa and David rather well. If they wanted to discuss sensitive matters, they could do so without being overheard.

'Of course,' she told Pippa. 'The van's all ready. The only problem might be that I haven't put any bathroom facilities in there yet. You'd need to come inside. Is that okay? I could move the van closer to the house, of course.'

'That would be wonderful.' Pippa gave her a hug. 'Thanks, Mum.'

It was quite late when Kate woke next morning. Bright sunlight streamed around the edges of her bedroom curtains and she could hear someone moving about in the kitchen. Oh dear, she was the hostess. Action was required. A quick splash of cold water on her face, a brush through her hair, dressing gown, slippers.

She smelled coffee as she reached the kitchen. 'David!'

'Good morning.' David was dressed in jeans and a black jumper and his jaw was rough with a day-old beard. In front of him on the counter stood a freshly filled coffee jug and two mugs. 'I've helped myself. I hope that's okay.'

'Yes, of course. I'm glad you could find all you needed. How's Pippa this morning?'

'Still rather sleepy, but not too bad, really.'

'That's good news. It's going to take her a little while to get over this, of course.'

'Yes.' David nodded to the toaster. 'I thought she might like toast and jam to go with the coffee.'

'Please, go ahead.' Kate went to the breadbox. 'There's a fresh loaf of sourdough and I bought a new cherry conserve that I'm sure Pippa will love. I have eggs and bacon and all the trimmings, too. But I'm afraid I didn't think to stock the pantry in the van.'

'Please don't apologise,' he said. 'We're just so grateful you were willing to share your beautiful space with us.'

Kate smiled. 'So you like the van?'

'We love it, Kate. It's amazing. *You're* amazing. Pippa and I can't believe you've done all that work by yourself.'

'Thanks. I'm so pleased. It's been hard work, but very satisfying.'

'All that timber lining on the walls.'

'Yes, that was the tricky part, but once the walls were done, the rest has been so much easier. You will have noticed there's still a way to go. I have to put doors on the cupboards and I need to figure out the best way to set up the toilet and shower.'

'Would you get a plumber to help with that?'

'Probably.' She grinned. 'You'll be relieved to hear I used a professional electrician for all the wiring.'

'That's wise, I'm sure.'

'Yeah, he's been very helpful. I'm afraid anything electrical is out of my league.' Kate was grateful that David had turned his attention to the toaster as she said this, so he didn't notice the silly flash of heat that scorched her cheeks.

'Can I pour you a coffee?' he asked.

'Thanks. I'm not sure if Chelsea's awake, but I think that pot holds plenty.'

'I can always make more.'

What an obliging young man. Kate hoped Pippa appreciated his qualities.

Kate perched on a stool and sipped her coffee as she watched David butter two slices of toast. 'Last night, I wasn't sure you were wise to rush straight up here, but now I realise it was the right thing to do.'

David nodded. 'I had to see Pippa.'

'Yes.'

'We've both been on major guilt trips. I imagine she's told you the gist of it.'

'I know she felt bad about not telling you she'd been trying to get pregnant.'

'There was that, but maybe I should have been more prepared to listen to her in the first place.'

Kate supposed this might be true and it was promising that both Pippa and David were admitting to mistakes. 'I think the best listening usually involves a two-way conversation.'

'Exactly. And I'm pleased to report we've already started a better conversation.' David had been poised to scoop jam out of the newly opened jar, but now he turned to Kate, a happy light shining in his eyes. 'I reckon your van might have a touch of magic. It's got such a cosy and intimate vibe. Like the very best kind of gentle hug.'

'David, I had no idea you were so poetic.'

He laughed. 'Maybe it's the van? I told you it was magic.'

How lovely. His compliment filled Kate with unexpected happiness. She wondered why she'd ever minded that she wouldn't be the first to sleep in the van. All the old sayings about gifts and giving were true. The best gifts were usually those things you would really like for yourself. And giving brought its own rewards.

David had gathered up the mugs and a plate of toast, but now he paused and turned back to her. 'Actually, this might be as good a time as any to ask you an important question.'

'Sure. How can I help?'

His smile turned shy and his Adam's apple rippled in his throat. 'I'd like your permission to ask Pippa to marry me.'

'Oh, David.' Kate was so touched she wanted to hug him, but she was in her dressing gown and he was holding hot mugs and toast. 'That's just the loveliest news.' Privately, Kate had been wondering if the lack of certainty about their relationship's future had pushed Pippa to make her rash pregnancy gambit. 'I couldn't be happier.'

'Thanks, Kate.' Her prospective son-in-law looked pleased and flushed and shy all at once as he turned for the door. 'Anyway, I'd better get this coffee and toast out to Pippa before it goes cold.'

Kate was still smiling over this happy turn of events when her phone began to ring. She had left it in her bedroom, so she had to run down the hallway to try to catch it before it rang out, which meant she was already a little breathless when she saw Liam's name on the screen.

'Hello?' Her voice was little more than a whisper as she lowered herself to the edge of the bed.

'Good morning, Kate. How are you?'

'Fine thanks. And you?'

'All good. I'm calling because I wondered if you and Tilly might be free to join me for lunch today. At the Lake Barrine Teahouse.'

Kate swallowed quickly to cover her gasp of surprise. The teahouse at Lake Barrine was a beautiful, rambling, old-fashioned building, set amidst gorgeous gardens. Not only did it serve delicious food, but its extensive balconies looked out over the serene lake, a volcanic crater, that had filled with water thousands of years ago and was now rimmed by towering rainforest. And here was Liam offering a lunch date that included Tilly. Such a thoughtful, *safe*, enticing invitation.

'Liam, I would have loved that,' Kate assured him. 'But I'm afraid I'm busy this weekend. My daughters are both here.'

She realised now that she should have mentioned the girls' impending visit when she'd seen Liam at the theatre rehearsal on Wednesday night. Regrettably, she'd been too busy wielding paint brushes and avoiding any sniff of a personal conversation.

'I'm sorry,' she said and she wondered if he could guess how many levels of apology she was trying to convey with those two overused words. Sorry she couldn't join him today. Sorry that she'd been blowing hot and cold. Sorry she wasn't the woman he needed, that she was looking for freedom, when he wanted to put down roots.

'No worries.' Liam's tone was casual. Too carefully casual?

'Maybe another weekend?'

'Sure,' he said. 'Enjoy your daughters' visit.'

'Thank you. And – and thanks for the invitation.' It was pathetic that she wished she could keep him talking. His warm, deep voice was addictive, but of course he wouldn't want to waste time chatting just for the hell of it.

'Bye, Kate.'

'Bye.'

'Was that your new boyfriend?'

Startled, Kate looked up to find Chelsea in her doorway, eyeing her with an all-too-knowing smile.

'Good morning,' Kate replied with as much dignity as she could gather. The last thing she needed was a conversation about Liam with this ultra-confident and way too shrewd city-lawyer daughter. 'How did you sleep, Chelsea? David's made coffee. It should be still hot enough.'

Chelsea merely chuckled. 'It's okay, Mum. No need to get your knickers in a twist. I've already grilled Tilly and wrangled interesting info about your electrician.'

It was hard not to rise to this bait. With magnificent restraint, Kate resisted. 'Then I'm sure Tilly's told you that Liam's helped me with the van and he's also helping her little theatre group with their props.'

'Mum, you're not in your dotage. You're entitled to a little fun.'

'Thanks, but if I need your Agony Aunt advice, I'll ask for it.' Ignoring the amusement in her daughter's if-you-say-so smile, Kate rose. 'Come on, now. What would you like for breakfast? Perhaps we should make it a nice big brunch? We have to make the most of what's left of this weekend.'

CHAPTER TWENTY-THREE

Margot had another of her 'freaking out' moments when Olivia turned up at the next Wednesday night rehearsal. Olivia was perfectly entitled to show up, of course, but this was an important rehearsal, the last run-through for the cast before they moved to full dress rehearsal – the final chance to iron out any problems in presentation before they had to perform the whole show without interruptions, and with costumes and lighting and backdrops in place.

Thankfully, Margot was quicker to recover from her dismay at seeing Olivia than she had been on the previous occasion. Each week, she'd been gaining a little more confidence in her own acting ability and it helped that Josie had gone to great lengths to assure her there was no chance Olivia would resume the Lady X role, even though she was now free of the moon boot.

'Olivia's been surprisingly gracious about it,' Josie had admitted. 'But I know for a fact that she would never have been so amenable if she hadn't seen with her own eyes that you were perfectly up to the task.'

In recent weeks, actually, there'd been other evidence that Olivia might have mellowed. Margot's daughter, Bridie, had relayed surprising news about the weekly coaching sessions Olivia was giving young Tilly.

'I was sure Tilly was going to hate it,' Bridie had told her mother. 'I mean, Olivia always seems so up herself. And she's so old. But Tilly reckons she's actually really cool when you get to know her. Olivia even taught Tilly how to make pikelets, so Tilly could show off to her half-sisters when they visited on the weekend.'

'I thought Olivia was supposed to be teaching Tilly about acting.'

'I know. I think that was the plan. Actually, don't say anything to Josie about the cooking.' Bridie had given a guilty little smile. 'Tilly made me swear I wouldn't tell anyone. I shouldn't have even told you.'

A spot of cooking instruction was certainly a side to Olivia that Margot had never imagined. Clearly, quite a deal of mellowing had occurred and tonight, as soon as Margot had recovered from the shock of seeing Olivia sail through the doors of the Community Hall – how *did* she always manage such a grand entrance? – Margot made sure she gave the woman a friendly welcome.

'Lovely to see you again, Olivia. How's your ankle?'

Olivia smiled. 'Coming along nicely, thank you.' She patted the handle of a woven cane basket she was carrying. 'I'm looking forward to catching up with everyone's progress tonight, and I've brought a little something for supper at half time. I'll just pop it into the kitchen.'

Good heavens. More cooking? Margot hoped she didn't look too shocked. 'How – how lovely,' was her tame reply.

* * *

Kate almost didn't bother going to Wednesday night's rehearsal. She had plenty of editing work to catch up on after the busy weekend with her girls, and she was fairly confident there would be little for her to do now that the sets were built and painted, and props either acquired or made to Josie's and Rolf Anders's satisfaction. But Kate had always been a team player and the dress rehearsal was just a week away, so she supposed there might be last-minute requests for changes or additions, and it was probably best to have all hands on deck.

As it turned out, however, there was very little for her to do. While Liam was busy giving instructions and checklists to the lighting crew, Kate and Geoff were able to sit in the theatre and watch the rehearsal.

She found herself picturing Opening Night, the time-honoured suspense of a theatre's closed curtains, waiting for the big reveal . . .

And wow! Even at this rehearsal, without costumes or props, what a surprise it was. So fascinating to see these ordinary, everyday Burralea residents transformed into completely different characters. And such an intriguing, futuristic storyline! As for Tilly – my goodness – Tilly's part in the play was small, but her voice was as clear as a bell and from the moment she stepped onto the stage, her presence was mesmerising. All right, Kate knew she was biased, but still, the kid had talent.

Kate stole a glance in Olivia's direction and could see her nodding and smiling as she watched Tilly, so clearly the grand dame approved. It was pretty obvious that their coaching sessions had been deemed worthwhile. Not that Kate knew the woman very well. She and Olivia had chatted briefly on the first day Kate dropped Tilly off and Kate had made sure Olivia knew how grateful she was for these special classes. Mostly, however, when she collected Tilly, there was a simple wave of acknowledgement, or a call of, 'Thank you.'

Tonight Kate couldn't help marvelling that this confident young person on the stage was the same sullen and uncommunicative child who'd arrived on her doorstep just over a month ago. She wouldn't have been at all surprised if the poor kid – a grieving thirteen-year-old, dragged away from Cairns and from everyone and everything she'd ever known – had remained depressed and withdrawn for ages.

Kate realised how wise the schoolteacher Imogen Kirk had been when she'd suggested that Tilly might join this little theatre group. It had certainly provided a fast track to the kid feeling both inspired and connected to her new surroundings. Then again, it was also possible that Imogen's attractive son, Hamish, was a significant source of that inspiration. However it had happened, though, Kate couldn't have been happier with the result.

Tilly's progress had been particularly noticeable on the weekend. She'd been on her best behaviour, offering to help Kate in the kitchen, fussing over Pippa, asking both her half-sisters genuinely interested questions as she'd excitedly pored over the family photo albums that they'd thoughtfully brought with them, Kate's albums still being in storage in Cairns.

On Sunday, Tilly had also made her surprisingly delicious pikelets for afternoon tea. She'd topped these with jam and cream and everyone had made a fuss, telling her how clever she was, and then, to cap off the happy occasion, David and Pippa had announced their engagement.

Such a joyful celebration they'd had then, with the young couple blushing and sharing besotted grins and everyone else cheering and hugging them, and Chelsea opening champagne she'd found in Kate's fridge and insisting that even Tilly should have at least one glass of bubbles.

Family time at its best – and an event that would never have happened without Tilly's arrival. Incredible, really, the little twists life could take.

*

The rehearsal reached the halftime point with surprising speed, and as usual, the players and crew congregated in the kitchen, setting out mugs, tea bags and jars of coffee. Kate caught Liam's eye across the room and sent him a deliberately friendly smile. And when he responded with an especially warm smile of his own, she had the whole fireworks thing happening.

While she was filling her tea mug, he managed to work his way closer to her, and she was happily anticipating a convivial conversation, when the players were silenced by the sound of a spoon being sharply tapped against a glass.

Olivia was demanding attention.

'Good evening, everyone,' Olivia called in a superbly projected voice that no doubt marked her as an actor of huge repute. 'Tonight is a rather special occasion and I've brought a cake to celebrate.' On the table in front of her was a cake covered in deliciously thick, creamy icing and decorated with pink roses.

Of course everyone gathered around, captivated by this surprise.

'I'm afraid I couldn't manage fourteen candles,' Olivia said next. 'But I knew we couldn't let our newest member's birthday pass without a small celebration. So . . .'

Olivia was smiling directly at Tilly, who had gone bright pink.

Kate, on the other hand, felt as if she'd been tackled to the ground. She heard a huge groaning gasp erupt from her. She might even have cried out Tilly's name. She couldn't be certain. The people around her turned to stare at her and Tilly looked worried, but Kate was too busy dealing with an avalanche of emotions.

Today was Tilly's birthday? Why hadn't she known this? Why had Tilly told Olivia about this important date and not Kate, who was caring for her?

'Happy birthday to our Tilly!' Olivia exclaimed and, thankfully, the players stopped frowning at Kate and began to sing.

Kate did her best to join in, but it wasn't easy when she was fighting tears and her mouth kept pulling out of shape. She knew Tilly could see that she was upset. The poor kid was enjoying the attention and the singing and the hip-hip-hoorays, but she kept shooting worried glances in Kate's direction.

Olivia must have picked up on this as well. She also fired a quick glimpse back over her shoulder to Kate and although the moment was fleeting, Kate caught a spirited flash that might have been concern. Or annoyance. It was enough to make Kate feel even more guilty and wretched. She didn't want to spoil this. She mustn't. If only she was as skilled at acting as everyone else here.

With the last hooray, Josie moved in to help Olivia, producing a stack of small plates and a bundle of teaspoons and an offer to cut up the cake. Soon this was being handed around and people were wishing Tilly many happy returns and congratulating Olivia on her delicious cake. And by a supreme act of willpower, Kate managed to squeeze out a smile and to hold it in place.

'Your Tilly's certainly made a big impression on Olivia.'

Kate turned to find Liam standing behind her. She nodded, hanging on fiercely to her smile, but she mustn't have been very convincing.

Liam frowned. 'Are you all right, Kate?'

'Yes.' Her response was automatic, but she realised no one else was close enough to overhear, so she corrected this. 'Not really.'

At least, Liam was wise enough not to expect an immediate explanation. 'Can I fetch you a slice of cake?'

'Thank you,' she said, although she feared she might choke on it.

As Liam joined the cake queue, Margot approached. 'Well, well,' she murmured, lifting her plate of half-eaten cake. 'Who would have thought?'

'It's so good of Olivia,' said Kate.

'Mmmm.'

Kate couldn't quite bring herself to look Margot in the eye.

'Tilly's a dark horse, though,' Margot said next. 'I don't think Bridie knew it was her birthday.'

That makes two of us. Kate scanned the hall for Tilly. There were questions that needed to be asked, but already Tilly was back in another apparently animated conversation with Hamish Kirk.

Perhaps that was just as well. Awkward questions were best saved for later, not now in front of everyone. And Liam came back then, so they turned their attention to tasting and complimenting Olivia's cake, which was utterly delicious. Kate knew she should also do the gracious thing and thank Olivia, but the woman was busy chatting to a group of players, and by the time Kate had managed to eat most of her cake, Josie was asking everyone to finish up and head back to the stage.

There was a rush to dump mugs and plates in the sink and soon the players were either back on stage or hanging around, awaiting their cue. Olivia was free now, however. Kate straightened her shoulders.

'You want to step outside?' Liam asked her.

There was nothing Kate wanted more than to escape this scene. 'I should thank Olivia,' she said.

Liam smiled. 'I've already done that.'

'Yes, but —' She owed Olivia a special vote of thanks, surely. And she was also conscious of the piles of dirty dishes.

Following her gaze, Liam said, 'That's not your job.'

This was true. Washing up wasn't any specific person's job, but usually some good natured volunteer pitched in.

'I think you need a little fresh air,' he said.

'Sounds good.' Kate was relieved to follow him through a side door out into the night.

* * *

Neither Tilly nor Hamish was needed in the next scene and they were sitting to one side in the hall when Kate and Liam slipped out.

Catching sight of their retreat, Tilly let out a small groan. 'As if that's going to help.'

Hamish frowned. 'What's the problem?'

'This disaster of a birthday, that's what.'

Hamish gave an exaggerated, frowning blink. 'Is there a disaster? I haven't noticed one.'

'You didn't see Kate's face when Olivia produced the cake?'

'Well, yeah, she looked surprised, but so did you. Everyone was surprised. That's the general idea of a surprise birthday cake.'

'Yeah, except —' Tilly drew a deep, shuddering breath. She was feeling so guilty. She had to get it off her chest, had to share her shame with someone. 'I kinda stuffed up,' she said. 'Kate didn't know it was my birthday.'

Hamish stared at her now and an uncomfortably long moment ticked by before he spoke. 'Wow,' he said at last. 'That's pretty heavy.'

'I know. She'll be so mad at me. The thing is, I never really planned to keep my birthday a secret, but stuff kept happening and – I don't know – I just never found the right moment.'

Tilly had been going to say something about the birthday when she and Kate had been shopping in Atherton – make a joke perhaps, suggest that the op shop clothes could be her birthday present – but she'd been worried Kate might then feel obliged to get something else, something expensive. And then Tilly had planned to say something on the weekend, with Pippa and Chelsea. But first there'd been the whole hospital drama, and so she'd decided that her special afternoon tea might be the right moment. But Pippa and David had beaten her with their big engagement announcement.

'I actually thought Olivia was just going to do the cake thing on Monday,' Tilly told Hamish. 'You know, when we have our coaching session. But she didn't say anything about my birthday, so I figured she'd forgotten. She's pretty old, after all. I never dreamed she was going to produce a cake here in front of everyone.'

'And now you feel guilty,' said Hamish.

'Hell, yeah. Wouldn't you?'

'Dunno. Probably.'

Up on the stage the play had stopped. Josie and the players were discussing various options for moving about during the scene.

'But I do know it's very easy to load yourself with guilt and get yourself seriously messed up,' Hamish said quietly. 'Even when it's not really your fault.'

Something about the way he said this made Tilly wonder if he was speaking from personal experience, and when he looked her way, just for a beat or two, he looked deeply worried, kind of haunted.

But before she could work out a question that wasn't too obviously nosy, Hamish turned back to the stage. The play had resumed and he jumped to his feet. 'Sorry, gotta go. I'm on next.'

Watching Hamish stride away, tall, cool and confident, Tilly decided she must have imagined his haunted look. And now her own cold, grey misery returned. *Crap*. Birthdays were supposed to be happy occasions and she'd totally stuffed this one up.

Sorry, Mum. After all, it was thanks to her mum that she even had a birthday. But she mustn't think about her mother now, or she'd bawl her eyes out in front of everyone. *Inner strength*.

Hastily, she looked around the hall, expecting to see Olivia, but there was no sign of her. Maybe that was just as well. Tilly wasn't quite sure what she would say to her. She knew Olivia had meant well, but it had all been a little too much.

She looked over to the kitchen and saw the pile of dirty dishes on the sink. Plates with bits of icing still clinging to them. She thought of her mum again, and she knew exactly what she needed to do.

CHAPTER TWENTY-FOUR

It was the following afternoon when Olivia drove to Kate's place. Thankfully, her ankle was strong enough to allow her to drive now, although moral courage was what she mostly needed if she was to accomplish this difficult mission.

Such an uncomfortable night and morning she'd spent wrestling with guilt and remorse. Olivia couldn't quite believe she'd allowed herself to get so carried away with the birthday cake idea. What on earth had possessed her to barge into that rehearsal, as if she had some kind of special ownership of Tilly?

How could she have been so insensitive?

She had only caught a fleeting glimpse of Kate's reaction to the cake, but that glimpse had been enough to show her the woman's raw shock and pain. A pain that cut deep.

But by then, Olivia had already started with the presentation, and unlike a bad script that could be rewritten or edited, she couldn't undo her rash announcement. She'd had no choice but to carry on.

She'd hoped that she might be able to speak to Kate later, once the players had returned to their rehearsal – a private word, an apology, even an attempted explanation. When she'd noticed Kate slip outside with Liam Flint, she'd followed, hoping for this chance.

The last thing she'd expected was to find Kate sobbing in the man's arms, her face buried against his shoulder, while he gently stroked her hair.

Devastated, Olivia had beaten a hasty retreat, without even returning to the hall. It was the second time she'd run away from a rehearsal and this time she'd felt even more desolate and embarrassed than the last.

Again, she had cried most of the way home. Again, she'd cried herself to sleep, although the sleep had taken several hours to achieve. But this morning, as soon as she'd woken, she'd known she must try to make amends.

She had to visit Kate and she had to find the courage to do something she'd never done before. Ever. Her sense of self-worth, her friendships, and her crucial connection to the Burralea Little Theatre were all at stake.

* * *

Kate was sure that the recent weeks had brought her enough surprises to last her a lifetime. When she opened her front door, however, she realised she was wrong. Here was yet another surprise. Olivia Matthews on her doorstep.

'Good afternoon, Kate.'

'Olivia.'

With a careful smile, Olivia said, 'If you don't mind, I've come to apologise.'

This was so unexpected, Kate wasn't quite sure how to respond.

'Apologise about the cake, of course,' Olivia continued. 'I can't believe I handled it so badly.' Now, she paused and looked down at the container she was holding. It was clearly quite old and round in shape. *Not another cake, surely?* Olivia said, 'Would you mind if I came in?'

Kate did mind, actually. She'd been trying to put last night's gruelling experience behind her. After she and Tilly had arrived home from the rehearsal, they'd cried and talked and hugged. And then they'd talked some more. Tilly had explained how she'd never meant to keep the birthday a secret, but other things kept getting in the way and Kate could see how this might have happened, given the twists and turns their lives had taken recently.

They'd also had another chat about Tilly's mum, Angela.

'Mum always acted like my birthday was even more important than Christmas,' Tilly had told Kate. 'She wasn't big on baking cakes – not after one year when she made me a snowman cake with meringue icing and Smarties for eyes and the Smarties slid down the cake and freaked me out.'

They'd both managed a little smile over this.

'But Mum always tried to think up a special surprise. Tickets for a new show or movie I wanted to see. A trip to go snorkelling on the Reef. One year we even went skydiving at Mission Beach.'

These memories had involved another little weep, but eventually, they'd gone to bed, way too late for a weeknight. This morning, however, when they'd woken, bleary-eyed, they'd greeted each other with smiles and with a definite sense of facing a new day, ready to move on.

Now, here was Olivia, after causing her damage last night and sailing off without a care, wanting to rake the whole sorry business up again.

If you'll allow me, I've come to apologise.

Kate supposed she had no choice. She had to be gracious. They were grown-ups, after all, and Olivia did look quite pale and strained.

Kate nodded and stepped back. 'Of course. Come on in.'

'Thank you.'

It was only a few steps to the lounge room. Kate gestured to the sofa and Olivia sat, placing the container on the cushion beside her.

It mustn't be a cake, Kate decided. 'Can I get you a drink?' she asked. 'Water? A cup of tea?'

Olivia cast a meaningful glance to the nearby dining table where Kate's laptop was set up. 'I don't want to take up too much of your time. Perhaps a glass of water?'

Having fetched two glasses of water from the kitchen, Kate set them on coasters on the coffee table, then lowered herself into an armchair. She wondered if she should try to break the ice, but Olivia was clearly keen to take charge.

'The first thing I wanted to say is that I hadn't realised you were going to be at the rehearsal last night, Kate. I suppose I should have known. Tilly had mentioned that you were helping with the sets, but it slipped my mind. Even so, when I *did* see you there last night, I should have given you a heads up about the cake.'

This was delivered with such convincing sincerity, Kate found her opposition faltering. 'Actually, it's probably just as well that you didn't speak to me,' she said. 'You see, I had no idea it was Tilly's birthday, so there's no knowing how I might have reacted.'

'You didn't know?'

'No.'

'Oh, my goodness. Tilly hadn't told you?'

'Perhaps more importantly, I hadn't asked her – or paid enough attention when forms were being filled in. I've had a lot of distractions, but that's no excuse, really.'

'But it certainly explains why you were both so upset last night. Goodness, what a mess.' Olivia took a sip from her water glass. 'I should have been more thoughtful. I'm afraid I got quite carried away.'

Kate decided it was best not to comment on this.

'I've become very fond of Tilly, you see.' Olivia's smile was complicated now. 'Much to my own surprise, I must admit. I never expected to make friends with a teenager. And the last thing I wanted was to upset the girl. Or you, Kate. And yet, last night I managed to upset both of you.'

As Kate wrestled with the best way to respond, Olivia hurried on.

'In my defence, there's something I'd like to explain.' Now, Olivia set the glass back on the coaster and sat a little straighter.

Almost as if she was getting ready to deliver an important monologue, she clasped her hands neatly together and set them on her knees. 'There's something from my past I never talk about,' she said. 'Something I've never really shared with anyone.'

'Olivia, are you sure?' Kate certainly wasn't sure that she should be the recipient of an incredibly significant personal revelation.

'Bear with me, please, Kate. I'm afraid I've reached a point where I need to talk about this.'

With a careful nod, Kate also reached for her water glass. She wished she could check the time and she hoped Tilly wasn't about to arrive home on the school bus.

'Many years ago, I had to give a baby up for adoption,' Olivia said quietly. 'Or at least, at the time, I felt I had to give him up.'

'Oh, dear.' And just like that, Kate's lingering resistance began to loosen its hold.

'There probably hasn't been a day since then when I haven't regretted that decision.' Tears glittered in Olivia's eyes, but she made a very dignified attempt to smile, and then she turned to the container on the sofa beside her.

* * *

What am I doing?

For fraught seconds, Olivia was frozen. Now that the moment had arrived, she wasn't sure she could go ahead with this. She wasn't sure that she *should* go ahead. And poor Kate looked as if she might agree. Surely this was too deep and personal for two women who barely knew each other?

But Kate was caring for Tilly, someone else's child, and Olivia had told herself this gave them a reasonable point of connection. Hours ago, the reasoning had made sense, and she'd wanted Kate to understand.

Now, she wasn't so sure. But she was here. She'd brought the hat box. She couldn't stop now.

By itself, the box was simply a marvellous antique that had belonged to Olivia's grandmother. Deep claret in colour, it was round and made of varnished cardboard. It had a metal lock, and was lined with paper decorated with drawings of leaves. The lock no longer worked and the paper lining was stained with age, but it was the contents of the box that were so profoundly significant.

Olivia set the box on the coffee table between them. She lifted the lid. *Oh, dear. Oh, help.*

She willed herself to be strong, but the tears arrived, so that at first, she couldn't really see the collection of birthday cards. Fortunately, she'd brought tissues, tucked in her jumper's sleeve. Retrieving these now, she quickly dabbed at her eyes and then drew a steadying breath.

'I have forty-nine birthday cards here,' she said. And then, taking another breath, she spoke quickly, needing to get her story out. 'Back in the early seventies, rules about adoption were still very strict. I had no idea who my baby's new parents were, and the only time I ever saw him was in those first few hours after he was born. But I have bought him a birthday card every year since then, every July – hoping, imagining, that the card might match whatever stage he had reached.'

'Oh, my goodness, Olivia.' Kate had leaned forward and was staring intently into the box. 'If your son's forty-nine, he's almost as old as I am.'

'I daresay.' Olivia managed to smile. 'I've been buying these for a long time. Of course it was easy enough to picture him that first year – a chubby little fellow, perhaps taking his first steps.'

She frowned now as she lifted out the top cards, searching. 'I'm not sure where that card is. I suppose it doesn't really matter. At one time, I had the cards all stacked in order, but I've sifted through them so often, they're a jumble now.'

'May I?' Kate asked, reaching out to touch a careful fingertip to one of the top cards.

'Yes, be my guest. Here.' Olivia lifted out several cards and spread them on the table. Among these was one of her favourites – a mouse driving a little red sports car, with a surfboard in the back.

Another card showed a little boy in a forest, dressed in medieval armour and holding a sword. *Happy Birthday Little Warrior.* Yet another card had a boy dressed as a cowboy, complete with leathers and boots and a gun in his holster. Of course, there was also a Superman card. And an old, rather faded one of a toddler on a rocking horse.

'These are so lovely,' said Kate. 'Such an amazing record – through your son's childhood.' She lifted out more cards. 'And his teenage years, his twenties and thirties.' She looked up, her eyes bright with tears.

Olivia nodded. 'My imagination went overboard, of course, trying to picture him growing out of babyhood, losing his front teeth, getting taller, playing football perhaps.'

Becoming a man . . .

Every one of those birthdays had been a cruel kind of agony for Olivia. Now, thinking back on the many careful purchases, she tried for a smile, but it felt very lopsided. 'Somehow, buying these cards helped.'

'It's a beautiful idea,' said Kate. 'And I don't suppose you had an address, so you couldn't post them.'

'No, never. I had no idea where my boy lived. I don't even know what name they gave him.' For Olivia, he'd always just been her Boy.

'But it meant you were able to keep this wonderful collection. A record of an imagined life. I love it.'

'I just had to guess what might have interested him.'

'I can see you've covered a huge range of styles and moods.'

'Yes. All sorts of animals, of course. In every shape and size. Sometimes touching, sometimes humorous.' Olivia picked up a card with a koala in a top hat, set it down again. 'Somewhere in here there's an adult card with a fellow playing a saxophone. That was just in case my son inherited any musical talent from my father.' She gave a wry smile. 'But I have to accept there's a chance he's more like *his* father, so there's another card in there that's just a champagne bottle popping its cork.'

'Oh, dear!' At this, Kate gave a short chuckle. 'That sounds rather similar to my children's father. Tilly's father, too, for that matter.'

'Ah, yes. Tilly's father was your husband, is that right?'

'He was, yes, with the emphasis on the "was". For me, he's very much past tense. He's in Cambodia now.'

Olivia nodded. 'I get the picture. Anyway, I'm so pleased you like these, Kate. I was overwhelmed by a need to show you. I hoped they might help to explain why I went a little overboard with Tilly's birthday.'

'Of course they do,' Kate said softly as a tear spilled down her cheek.

Oh, dear. Don't cry, or you'll start me off, too. But this unwelcome possibility was quickly dispelled by a voice calling from the front doorway.

'Is that Olivia's car?'

Tilly, home from school.

CHAPTER TWENTY-FIVE

Tilly had run all the way up the track, so she was a little puffed by the time she reached the house. Admittedly, running to the front door was not her usual MO, but today there'd been a parcel in the letterbox and it was addressed to her. A parcel from Jed, which meant he must have remembered her birthday. How amazing was that?

Tilly had only received a handful of text messages from Jed since he'd left. He'd told her he was working on an offshore gas rig in the north of Western Australia. This meant living out at sea where they sometimes had extremely wild weather and the job kept him pretty busy – doing twelve-hour shifts and sleeping on the rig. But he also got decent breaks back on land and it seemed he'd been shopping. Yay!

Tilly hadn't allowed herself to open the package until she got back to the house, which was why she'd run.

But Olivia was here. And after last night's stuff-up, Tilly had no idea whether this unexpected visit was good or bad news.

Stopping in the doorway, she peered cautiously inside. No one was yelling. Kate and Olivia seemed to be working together, actually, busily stacking bits and pieces back into some sort of old-fashioned container.

As Olivia put the lid on this container, Kate turned to Tilly and smiled. 'Hey there, how was your day?'

Tilly's usual response to this 'home from school' greeting was an offhand 'good'. She had even answered her mum this way, mostly, because it saved being probed with further questions. But today deserved better than a mere 'good'. After all, Bridie had turned up at school with a lovely set of silver star earrings for Tilly's birthday. And now Tilly had this parcel from Jed.

'Today's been awesome,' she said, holding Jed's parcel triumphantly aloft.

'Was that in the letterbox?' asked Kate. 'How exciting.'

Olivia, smiling, got to her feet. 'Hello, Tilly. It's lovely to see you, but I was actually just about to leave.'

'There's no need,' Kate quickly intervened. 'Why don't you stay, Olivia, and I'll make that cuppa?'

A hard-to-read vibe passed between the two women, almost as if they'd been cooking something up. Yikes. Last night, they'd been on the brink of World War Three. Whatever was going on now, Tilly was relieved to see they weren't fighting.

And after a short moment of hesitation, Olivia nodded. 'Thank you, Kate. I'd love a cup of tea.'

As Kate headed for the kitchen, Tilly was itching to follow her and find out what was going on, but opening Jed's present was an even more pressing priority.

For Olivia's benefit, she explained, 'This parcel's from my mum's boyfriend, Jed.'

'Ah. How exciting.'

It was. Massively exciting. Even if Jed sucked at choosing gifts for fourteen-year-old girls, Tilly was really stoked that he'd bothered to think of her.

Wow. Even better. When she opened the outside packaging, she discovered not one, but three presents and an envelope inside.

And the gifts were all wrapped in different coloured paper. Who would have thought Jed might go to so much trouble?

Kate came back into the room. 'I've put the kettle on, and the tea tray's sorted, but I always think you need an audience when you're opening presents. It makes it more fun.'

'Absolutely,' agreed Tilly and she happily made a little performance of setting the gaily wrapped gifts on the coffee table and then opening the first one extra slowly, carefully peeling back the sticky tape and trying not to make a single tear in the pretty paper.

Kate laughed. 'There are two types of people in the world. The slow gift openers and the ripper openers.'

'I vary, depending on my mood,' Tilly responded coyly. But she soon forgot about performing. She was too busy oohing and ahhing over the first of her lovely gifts. The bracelet of pretty aqua-coloured stones had a little stone turtle clasp, and it came with an internet tracking card linked to a real sea turtle that was apparently swimming somewhere in the ocean off Florida.

Such an amazing, perfect gift. Tilly nearly cried. 'Jed and I used to go to the Turtle Rehabilitation Centre in Cairns,' she explained and Kate and Olivia looked seriously impressed.

The next gift was a starter set of coloured crystals in all different shapes and sizes. 'Oh, wow.' This was almost too much for Tilly. Her mum had been a huge lover of crystals and this gift was exactly the sort of thing her mum might have bought for her.

A hard lump lodged in Tilly's throat, and her eyes stung, but she'd done enough crying last night and she didn't want to spoil these lovely gifts with tears. She hurried on quickly to the third parcel. Small and wrapped in purple tissue.

Oh. My. God. The other presents had been amazing, but this was beyond perfect – a necklace with the sweetest, simple pearl droplet on a delicate silver chain.

'This boyfriend has class,' observed Olivia.

'Yeah.' Somewhat stunned, Tilly stared at the array in front of her. 'It's like Christmas.'

'Jed's certainly made up for the rest of us slackos,' commented Kate. She pointed to a blue envelope. 'Don't forget this one, Tilly. I'll finish making the tea while you check that out.'

Sitting cross-legged on the floor next to the coffee table, Tilly opened the envelope. 'It's a letter,' she told Olivia, and then she began to read it silently.

Dear Tilly,

Happy Birthday! I'm sorry I can't be there to celebrate the big day with you. I hope you have a good one. I'll be thinking of you, kiddo.

I also thought you might like to know that I've organised a plaque for your mum. It should be in place by now, so next time you're down in Cairns, you might be able to check it out at the Forestry View Cemetery. They should send me a photo soon and I'll forward it to you.

Miss you and Ange heaps,

Jed. xx

'Tilly?' Olivia was leaning forward, looking worried. 'Is something wrong?'

Tilly couldn't speak.

'Sweetheart?'

Tilly shook her head. She knew that if she tried to say anything, she would burst into horrible sobs. She handed the letter to Olivia.

'You'd like me to read this?' Olivia asked.

Tilly nodded and then held her breath as she watched Olivia put on her reading glasses and study the page.

This didn't take long, of course, and when Olivia had finished, she set the letter back on the coffee table and she sat for a moment in silence. After a bit, she said, 'Would I be right in guessing that the mention of the cemetery has upset you?'

Tilly nodded.

'That's totally understandable.'

I'm just missing her so much, Tilly wanted to say, but her throat was too tight and sore.

She looked from the letter that Olivia had placed back on the table to the lovely presents Jed had sent – the bracelet, the crystals, the necklace. So gorgeous. So generous.

A few minutes ago she'd been on top of the world. Now, all she could think about was her mum and their special bond and everything she'd lost.

Tears spilled. Hot and heavy. Tilly couldn't help it.

'Sweetheart,' said Olivia. 'I'm too old to get down on the floor beside you. Come here.'

Tilly stumbled to her feet and onto the sofa. She bumped against Olivia and the old woman slipped her arm around Tilly's shoulders and Tilly could smell the comforting scent of her flowery perfume.

'I'm sorry,' she spluttered. 'I'm trying to remember inner strength.'

'You can't be strong all the time,' Olivia said gently. 'Feeling angry and sad and confused is part of the grieving process.'

Tilly gave a grateful nod. Already, she was beginning to feel calmer. 'The thing is,' she managed to say, 'I know my mum's dead. I understand that, but it's like I can still *feel* her. Inside. I can still think of her as close to me somehow. And these presents – it was almost like Mum helped Jed to buy them.'

Her mouth trembled as she let her gaze shift to the letter, the single blue sheet of paper. She shivered. 'But that plaque – it kind of spoils everything.'

'It's too definite?' asked Olivia. 'Too final?'

'Yeah. Maybe. Something like that. I just hate the idea that they want to stick Mum behind a metal sign. I'm scared she won't be with me anymore.'

Olivia gave Tilly's shoulders a gentle squeeze. 'The thing to remember is that you'll always have your mother with you. She'll always live in your memory. She'll always be there in your heart.'

'But the plaque —'

'The plaque is for everyone else,' said Olivia. 'It's an acknowledgement of Angela's life, and it's there for the rest of the world to see. It's a place for Angela's friends to visit, to take flowers. And for you to visit, too, of course, but only when you feel ready. And you never know, one day you might have children of your own and you could take them to see it.'

Tilly did quite like that idea. As she wiped her face on the sleeve of her jumper, she could almost imagine her grown-up self with a little girl of her own, or maybe even a boy. If she tried hard she could just about see them, carrying bunches of flowers and listening solemnly as she told them about their grandmother.

As she imagined that possibility, she did feel a bit better. Looking up, she saw Kate standing in the kitchen doorway holding a tray loaded with afternoon tea things.

Kate had probably been listening to Olivia, too. Her eyes shone with tears, but she was also smiling. She sent Tilly a smile of sympathy, and then another smile for Olivia that seemed to convey an extra message – quite possibly one of thanks. Then Kate came forward. 'Can we make room for these on the coffee table?'

'Sure.' Tilly scooped up her presents and put them on a spare armchair.

Kate's tray held a teapot and mugs, a small milk jug and sugar bowl, as well as a glass of lemonade for Tilly and a plate piled with choc peppermint biscuits.

Tilly realised she was starving.

They settled to enjoy their afternoon tea and to marvel again at Tilly's lovely presents. She extracted Bridie's earrings from her schoolbag and these were duly admired, and she added them to the haul and reminded herself how awesome this day had been.

Kate, lifting the lid to see how much tea was left in the pot, said, almost causally, 'This is just an idle thought, Tilly, and feel free to knock it on the head, but I was wondering if maybe we should go down to Cairns on the weekend. You could catch up with some of your friends, and I could do a spot of shopping. Olivia, you could come too, if you wanted to. And Tilly – only if you felt like it – we could buy a lovely bunch of flowers and check out Jed's plaque.'

The idea would have horrified Tilly earlier, but now it didn't feel quite so bad.

'Can I think about it?' she asked.

'Of course. Take as much time as you like. There's no rush.'

Tilly smiled at the two women sitting side by side on the sofa. Tilly, Kate and Olivia. A moody teenager, a divorcee with dreams to take off in a van, and an ageing actress. Such an unlikely combination. An odd bunch. Like pieces taken out of different jigsaw puzzles. They didn't really belong together. And yet somehow they managed to fit. How strange was that?

CHAPTER TWENTY-SIX

On Saturday night, Margot and Jack fired up their barbecue and invited a few friends to join them for dinner on their back deck. This initiative in itself was unusual, but what was even more unusual about this occasion was that Jack was the prime motivator.

Until recently, Margot's husband had been in the habit of arriving home from the hardware store each night and pretty much collapsing in front of the TV. He'd had next to no social life, apart from the occasional game of golf. But since Margot had taken on the Lady X role, growing in confidence and paying more attention to her appearance, Jack seemed to have undergone a transformation of his own.

Not only had Jack begun to help more with general housework, but he'd also taken a keener interest in Bridie's and Nate's school and sporting activities. He'd even spent more time in the garden, mowing lawns and pruning hedges, without having to be nagged. *And* he'd repainted the back deck, much to Margot's astonished delight. So now, a barbecue was planned for the last free weekend before everything got really busy at the theatre.

Jack had invited Tim Fielding, one of his golfing mates, and his wife, Karen, and Margot had invited Josie and Hector.

In a burst of courage, she had also invited Olivia and Rolf, as she knew they were good friends, but Olivia was having a day in Cairns and Rolf was heading off for another quick trip to Sydney, ahead of the big southern production of *Next Stop Mars*.

So there would be six for Saturday night. They would keep everything simple and manageable. Bridie and Nate were more than happy to stay inside with takeaway pizza and their favourite Netflix show. The adults would dine on the deck. There'd be barbecued lamb racks, potatoes baked in the coals and a salad, plus a nice selection of wine and cheese, with poached pears in spiced red wine for dessert.

Margot bought smart, black and white striped cushions for the outdoor furniture and Jack set up a new cast-iron fire pit on the paved area next to the deck. Their guests would be able to enjoy the warmth and ambient light of flickering flames while sitting outdoors.

Luckily, the weather gods were on their side. Saturday delivered a beautiful, cloud-free evening. The air was crisp and clear and silver stars made a spectacular splash across the night sky. The table was set, the food prepared.

Margot and Jack had hasty, last-minute showers. Jack shaved, while Margot attended to her makeup, a task she paid careful attention to these days. They changed into fresh clothes – casual jeans and hand-knitted jumpers and a pair of extra snazzy earrings for Margot. With perfect timing, they were ready to greet their guests.

Tim and Karen hadn't previously met Josie and Hector, but they were easy conversationalists and within minutes everyone was chatting like old friends. Margot couldn't believe how happy she was to be entertaining like this, especially as Jack was looking after the cooking, which left her free to pass around the cheese platter and to top up drinks and otherwise relax and enjoy the good company.

The cheese was mostly depleted and the lamb almost ready when she looked across their backyard, past the black silhouette of their neighbour's tibouchina tree, and saw an orange glow in the sky.

At first Margot thought her eyes were playing tricks. The glow was some kind of reflection from their fire pit. But no, it was definitely in the sky. She frowned, trying to gauge the exact distance. Was it beyond Burralea, out on a farm? Or was it coming from somewhere closer, in town perhaps?

Setting her wine glass down, she stood. The glow was growing bigger, climbing higher. 'That looks like a fire,' she said.

Now Josie jumped up beside her. 'Oh, my God. Tell me that's not coming from over near the community hall.'

'You think so?'

They shared a quick horrified glance. Now Tim and Hector joined them, with Karen close behind.

'That's only a few streets away,' said Hector.

'Do you think it's near the community hall?' A tremor of terror threaded Josie's voice.

'Hard to say. It's possible.' Margot comforted herself that at least it couldn't be the hardware store, which was on the outskirts of town and in the opposite direction.

Over at the barbecue, Jack was concentrating on the important task of lifting the perfectly charred lamb racks onto a serving platter.

Josie, meanwhile, gave a fretful wail. 'I'm sorry, Margot. I can't possibly wait here and wonder. I'm too worried about the theatre. I *have* to check where that fire's coming from.' She held out her hand to her husband. 'Hector, can I have the car keys?'

Margot totally understood Josie's fear. The very thought that the community hall might be in danger was horrifying. Already she was fighting a terrible vision of their theatre going up in flames – the stage and curtains, their sets and props, their costumes, the lighting board. Everything! 'I'll come too,' she said.

'I assume someone's already called the fire brigade.' This calm observation came from Hector as he handed Josie the car keys.

'Wouldn't hurt to give them another call.' Tim had already retrieved his phone from his pocket. 'Just to be doubly sure.'

'Dinner's ready!' announced Jack, turning triumphantly from the barbecue, only to frown when he discovered his guests in disarray.

Oh, dear. Margot felt bad to be undermining her husband's moment of glory, especially when he'd made such an effort.

'I'm so sorry, Jack. We're worried about that fire.' She pointed to the blazing heavens, which her husband was only now noticing. 'Josie and I will be back in no time. We just need to set our minds at rest that it's not the theatre on fire.'

At least Tim and Hector recognised a need for mateship. As Margot hurried off after Josie, she could hear them complimenting Jack on the magnificent-looking meal.

The news only got worse as Josie drove closer. The leaping flames and showering sparks were definitely in the same block as the community hall.

'Oh, God, I don't like the look of this.' Josie sounded close to howling, while Margot, beside her, was as tense as a bowstring.

No! she prayed silently. *Please no. Don't let it be the hall. Not when everyone's worked so hard. Not when we're so close. Not when I —*

Margot quickly jumped on that last thought. The possible end to her fledgling acting dreams was a minor concern. She was thinking of Rolf who'd written their wonderful play, of Josie who'd worked tirelessly to bring it to life, and her heart was aching for the whole cast, even young Tilly, their newest member. And Geoff and Kate and Liam – everyone who'd worked on the sets.

By now they were turning into Rose Street and there was no avoiding the terrible reality.

'Holy shit!' whispered Josie.

The fire was halfway down the street, exactly where the hall was situated. Two huge fire trucks were already there, as well as at least two police cars with their blue lights flashing. On the opposite side of the street, the footpath was crowded with spectators.

Josie had no choice but to park quite a distance away. She leaped out of the car, hastily snapped the remote and raced off down the footpath with Margot struggling to keep up.

As they drew near the blaze, Josie came to such an abrupt halt, Margot almost barged into her.

Oh, thank God.

It wasn't the hall on fire, after all, but the house next door, a somewhat ramshackle little timber cottage. Old Bill Gently had lived there for more than thirty years, before his son arrived last Christmas to move Bill into a nursing home in Mareeba.

According to the local grapevine, Bill's family planned to renovate the cottage and keep it as an investment property. Now, that investment was engulfed in monstrous tongues of hungry red and orange flames that climbed higher and higher into the black night sky.

The firefighters were doing their best as they manhandled the massive hoses, but it was pretty obvious the house couldn't be saved.

Still puffing from the dash down the street, Margot drew a deep breath of relief. She felt badly about the Gently family's house, but the loss of the hall would have been so much more tragic – not just for the little theatre group, but for the whole community.

And at least now they could return to their little party and Jack's meal wouldn't be ruined.

Margot was about to share her relief with Josie when the other woman took off down the footpath, like a small, determined hen chasing after an escaping beetle, head angled forward as she elbowed her way through the crowd of gaping spectators.

Margot was about to follow when her phone buzzed and vibrated in her pocket. Not surprisingly, it was Jack.

'What's going on?' He didn't sound particularly pleased, which was understandable.

'It's the Gently house,' Margot told him as she lost sight of Josie in the crowd. 'You know, the cottage next to the community hall?'

'So the hall's okay?'

'Yes.' Margot had been following Josie, making her way, ducking and weaving at a much slower pace. 'Oh, no,' she gasped as she caught up and realised the source of Josie's concern.

'What is it?' snapped Jack.

'The timber window frames on the side of the hall have caught fire.'

* * *

Olivia was glad Kate was behind the wheel as they left Cairns and the coast behind and climbed the range to Kuranda.

There weren't enough seats in Kate's van for the three of them to travel to Cairns together, so they'd taken Olivia's car, and it had been a very enjoyable day. But now, as the road curved and climbed, rather like the vines that twisted their way up the rainforest tree trunks on either side of the bitumen, Olivia sank back against the headrest and closed her eyes.

She had plenty to think about. It had been quite an education to drive to the humble flats in Edmonton where Tilly and her mother had lived, and to not only visit with Tilly's former neighbour, Mrs Kettle, but to admire the beautiful pot plants Tilly's mother had left behind, and also to witness Tilly's joyous reunion with her cat, Josephine.

Admittedly, Tilly had seemed more rapt about the reunion than the cat had, but cats were like that, weren't they? After this,

Tilly had visited Zara, the best friend she'd missed so much. The meeting had been arranged, thanks to earlier deft diplomacy on Kate's part, and Zara's mother, Eleanor, had been very happy for the girls to enjoy the afternoon together, much to Tilly's rapturous delight.

This had also left Olivia and Kate free to take themselves off to the Cairns Pier for a little shopping, a delightful lunch and long conversations, while relaxing on the waterfront. Surprisingly revealing conversations they'd had while dining on a delicious seafood chowder and enjoying the lazy, warm breeze and the salty smell of the sea.

Olivia, having shared so much about her own past, had been interested to learn more about Kate's marriage to Tilly's black sheep father. She'd also ferreted out details of the travelling plans that Kate had been forced to put on hold. Tiptoeing carefully, Olivia had even tried to raise the topic of Liam Flint, the electrician.

She didn't mention that she'd witnessed Kate weeping in Liam's arms, of course, and Kate had cleverly deflected any suggestion that Liam was anything more than a tradesman who'd helped with the wiring in her van, as well as assisting the Burralea players with their lighting plan. Olivia was convinced there was more to this story, but she didn't push.

And the day had ended on a very satisfying note. Tilly was bubbling with excitement when they picked her up from Zara's.

'We've had the best time,' Tilly exclaimed. 'I've caught up on *all* the gossip and Zara's totally changed her room. Come and have a look.'

Fortunately, Zara, a smiley, freckled redhead, didn't seem to mind Tilly dragging Kate and Olivia inside to inspect her bedroom.

'This room used to have purple walls and strings of glittery lights,' Tilly explained. 'I thought it was awesome then, but now Zara's gone for all these gorgeous new colours.'

Indeed, the bedroom now had pretty, pale grey walls with fresh white windowsills and trims, while a set of bookshelves had been given a fun and funky makeover with frames painted white while the shelves and insides were pink. The rosy hue really popped and looked gorgeous, while a white dressing table had pink legs, and the drawer fronts on Zara's desk were all in different hues of pink and pale grey and charcoal.

'It's very clever,' Kate agreed, as she admired a macrame wall hanging decorated with beads to match the new colour scheme.

'Zara's going to be an interior designer,' Tilly told them proudly.

'Well, you certainly have an eye for colour, Zara.' Olivia was delighted to see Tilly looking so happy.

'And Mum and I are coming to see Tilly in her play,' Zara told them. 'It sounds awesome.'

After farewelling her friend, Tilly had announced that yes, she was ready to visit the cemetery. By then it was almost dusk and the air was cool, the lawns painted with gentle shadows. They stopped at a florist and Tilly chose a lovely bouquet of cream roses with pink edging on the petals.

'I almost got the lilies,' she told Olivia and Kate. 'I love how smooth lilies are and I love their smell, too, but Mum would never have them in the house. She said they can make cats sick.'

Understandably, though, there were tears when Tilly placed her roses beside her mother's plaque, and when Olivia read the words Jed had chosen, she was rather choked, too.

Angela Dent, mother of Tilly

1974 – 2021

Your presence we miss

Your memory we treasure

Loving you always

Missing you forever

Tilly was trying to smile through her tears. 'It's beautiful, isn't it?'

'It is indeed,' Kate and Olivia agreed.

'Jed was right,' the girl said. 'Mum deserves something really lovely like this.' She let out a shuddering little huff of breath and then managed a slightly stronger smile. 'Thanks for bringing me to Cairns.'

Coming forward then, she'd hugged both Kate and Olivia, and she'd seemed hearteningly calm by the time they left.

Now in the car, satisfied with these reflections, Olivia must have drifted off. When she woke, she discovered, to her surprise, that the day had given way to night and they were already on the outskirts of Atherton, where Kate had stopped at a service station.

'Good heavens,' Olivia said as she blinked. 'I've been asleep for ages. I hope I haven't been snoring.'

'Like a chainsaw,' declared Tilly from the back seat.

Kate laughed. 'Don't take any notice of her. She's had earphones in for the entire trip. I'm just topping up your petrol,' Kate added. 'You've been so kind as to lend us your car, it's the least I can do.'

'Oh, but the pleasure was all mine,' Olivia protested.

Kate ignored Olivia's attempts to contribute to this cost and soon the petrol was attended to and they were on the road again, heading to Burralea. The night was lovely and clear with a fat, bright moon that lit up the landscape as they skirted around hillocks, swooped down over rippling creeks, and whizzed past farms with pretty cottages and massive storage sheds and rows and rows of crops.

It was as they crested the hill just before Burralea that they saw the blazing fire.

Oh, my goodness. Olivia's first reaction was fear for her own little home. Had she left the stove on? Forgotten to turn off the heater? But as they drew nearer, she realised that while the fire was scarily close to her place, it was actually coming from the block behind hers.

'You don't think it might be the theatre on fire?' asked Kate as she slowed the car almost to a stop.

'No!' wailed Tilly from the back seat.

Olivia stared hard, piecing together the familiar landmarks. 'If it's not the theatre, it's very close,' she observed, but her words brought a sudden, bleak chill of despair. And it seemed, all at once, that their happy day of healing might have come, alarmingly, undone.

* * *

It was only a little after ten when Margot finished stacking the dishwasher and Jack, having tidied up the barbecue and doused the fire pit's embers, came back inside.

Their interrupted evening hadn't been a total disaster. Jack had managed to keep the meat warm enough and when Josie and Margot returned from inspecting the fire, they'd all topped up their wine glasses and dived into the meal, which was universally declared to be utterly delicious.

The conversation had been a little stilted at first. Josie was clearly distracted, but they'd tried to talk about things other than the fire. Tim politely enquired about Hector's latest conservation schemes and Hector was only too happy to rattle on about a project in place to record the population, distribution and health of Lumholtz's tree kangaroo.

Tim and Karen talked of their hopes to travel to the tip of Cape York before the next wet season. Josie, when quizzed, shared a few of her ideas for an end-of-year Christmas pantomime. All in all, the night rolled along happily enough, although Josie and Hector left earlier than they might have normally, as Josie wanted to get back to the hall to find out the latest damage report.

Margot had waved off Tim and Karen and was rinsing wine glasses when Josie rang her.

'So, how bad is it?' asked Margot.

'Bad enough, although you wouldn't think so to look at that wall. The firies got onto it quickly, but there's been damage to the timber framing on that side wall and the building inspectors have decided the entire hall's structurally unsafe.'

'Oh, no.'

'Yes, I'm afraid so. The whole area's been cordoned off.'

Margot didn't even try to hold back her groan of despair. 'I suppose that means we won't be able to go ahead with the play?'

'Certainly not in the community hall. And I don't imagine we'll find an alternative at such short notice.'

It was alarming to hear the usually optimistic and energetic Josie sounding so hopeless and defeated.

A wave of suffocating despair swamped Margot. Just like that, her acting debut had gone up in smoke. But this fire didn't only mean disappointment for the actors. As a committee member, she was also thinking of all the pre-sold tickets. There had been such a buzz throughout the district. Opening Night was already sold out. And now there'd be the hullabaloo of people asking for refunds.

'Anyway,' Josie said next. 'There's nothing we can do tonight. I suggest we try to get a good night's sleep and tackle this with fresh heads in the morning.'

Jack was surprisingly miffed when Margot told him this news. He looked like a dog that couldn't find its bone as he stood in the kitchen doorway, hands on hips, shaking his head. 'But your play is too important. It's a world premiere. It's got to go ahead.'

Despite her own disappointment, Margot couldn't help smiling. 'You just want to see me on stage.'

'What's wrong with that?'

As she gave a coy shoulder shrug, Jack came closer, slipped his arms around her waist. She sensed a whiff of barbecue smoke clinging to his clothing and the cool night air on his skin.

Jack smiled. Up close, she could see the mix of blue and grey flecks in his eyes, could remember falling in love with those flecks when she was just nineteen.

'Of course I want to see the spotlight on my wife,' he said. 'I've been hearing what a damn fine actor she is.'

'Really?' Silly how important this was to her.

'Too right. You know how word spreads in this town.' Jack was still looking into her eyes, his expression warm, with a hint of smoulder. 'I'm not surprised, of course. My wife has been surprising me throughout our married life.'

He kissed her then, and the kiss was brief, but tender enough to set Margot aglow with a kind of giddy, buzzing joy that she hadn't experienced in quite a while.

As Jack released her, however, he was frowning again. 'We've got to do something about this.'

'About the fire? Or *this*?' she asked, quickly returning his kiss.

Jack smiled. 'Maybe both.' He noticed an unfinished bottle of wine on the kitchen counter, picked it up. 'Want to polish this off?'

Their kids were still in the lounge room, watching the last of some sci-fi fantasy.

'Why not?'

They took the bottle and two glasses back onto the deck. With the firepit doused, the air was noticeably chillier, but not unpleasant and the sky was still clear and ablaze with stars.

Dropping her head back, Margot stared at the silvery dazzle. Tonight might have been perfect . . .

She sighed. 'Josie didn't sound very hopeful about finding anywhere else at such short notice.'

'She shouldn't give up without having a darned good try.'

'I'm sure she'll try, Jack.'

'And I reckon she'd have plenty of local support. After all, people in this region are used to adjusting to setbacks. There's been deregulation of the dairy industry, the forestry closed down, and now small businesses all over the place are having to diversify and get smarter.'

Margot was thoughtful as she sipped her wine. 'I wonder if the high school gymnasium is an option?'

'It's a possibility, I guess. Might be a problem if you're trying to charge money for a show in a state government building. Dunno.'

'Hadn't thought of that. Yes, I've no idea.'

'I don't suppose the play has to be in a building. Remember that time in Cairns when we saw *A Midsummer Night's Dream* in the park?'

'Mmmm,' mused Margot. 'But the director had planned from the start to use an outdoor venue. I think it would be a nightmare for us to try to set up our lighting and everything for *Next Stop Mars* without even a roof over the stage. What if it rained?' She gave an impatient shake of her head. 'I think Josie's right. We can't solve this problem tonight. Maybe, after a night's sleep, we might come up with a few bright ideas.'

'Fair enough.' As Jack drained the last of his wine, he looked back over his shoulder to the house. 'Those kids of ours in bed yet?'

'Just about, I reckon.'

'How about we hurry them up?'

Margot knew exactly what her husband had in mind. She smiled. 'Good idea.'

CHAPTER TWENTY-SEVEN

Sunday morning was normally Imogen Kirk's chance to sleep in. If she was lucky, Jamie came back from his morning session in the dairy and brought her breakfast in bed.

This Sunday, however, it wasn't even eight o'clock before she was stirred from sleep by a phone call.

Yawning extravagantly, Imogen flopped an arm sideways to fumble for the phone on her bedside table. Ah, there it was, with her caller's name evident on the screen. 'Good morning, Josie.'

'Imogen, I guess you've heard the news?'

'News?' Still fogged by sleep, Imogen tried to recall the events of the previous evening. A quiet dinner at home with Jamie. They'd watched a Scandi noir movie, shared a bottle of wine. Made love. 'No,' she said. 'I don't think so.'

'So, you haven't heard about the fire at the theatre?'

'Good heavens, no.' Now Imogen was wide awake and sitting bolt upright. 'Not the Burralea theatre? The community hall?'

'Yes.' With that single word, Josie managed to sound quite desolate. 'It actually started at the old Gently place next door. That house was completely gutted and then the side of the hall caught fire as well.'

'Good heavens. Is the hall badly damaged?'

'Just the side wall framing really, but it's bad enough. It's been designated as unsound. We can't use it.'

'Josie, that's terrible. You're so close to your new production.'

'Tell me about it.'

Imogen wondered if Hamish knew about this. He'd spent most of last night at a party in Ravenshoe, but that was in the opposite direction from Burralea, and he'd come home quite late. More than likely he hadn't heard about the fire and was still asleep.

'Is there any chance of having the repairs done in time?' she asked.

'I very much doubt it. The community hall's a council building and that always means a mile of red tape even before any kind of work can get underway.'

'Yes, of course.' Imogen gave a noisily sympathetic sigh. 'How frustrating.'

'At least our sets and props and costumes weren't damaged,' Josie said next. 'They might smell a bit smoky, but I got permission to check and they look okay.'

'Well, that's one blessing, I guess. So, are you thinking about an alternative venue?'

'I'm not sure if it's possible, but yes, I'd love to find somewhere else. That's partly why I'm ringing you, Imogen. I don't suppose you have any bright ideas?'

Imogen tried to think if there was anything at the school that would suit. The gymnasium perhaps? But it was little more than a roof with open sides. The acoustics were terrible. And she wasn't sure she could get the principal on side. 'I suppose you'd be looking for some kind of shed?'

'Yes, a nice big one – not too far out of town, if possible. Not asking for much, of course.'

'Ah . . . you're thinking of the Hetheringtons' shed.'

'Well, yes, I must admit I was wondering. It's perfectly situated on the outskirts of Burralea and Alec has at least two massive sheds on his property.' After a brief pause, 'What do you reckon?'

'I'm honestly not sure. I – I've seen very little of Alec lately.'

'I know. He used to be so outgoing, but we never see him anymore. Margot says he doesn't even come into town to place his orders. He just phones them through and he's so brusque. He hasn't been the same since . . .'

Josie didn't need to finish the sentence. Imogen knew only too well that Alec Hetherington, who'd been widowed ten years earlier, was still grieving for his son, Ben, who had drowned just last year in a terrible flash flood.

Josie's loud sigh vibrated in Imogen's ear. 'It might be asking too much of him. I'll keep thinking.'

It was almost midday before Hamish emerged, tousled and sleepy and quite possibly hungover. Imogen was in the kitchen making a spiced apple cake. It was one of Jamie's favourites and he worked so darned hard every day of the week, she liked to make an effort on the weekends.

The oven was ready and she was sprinkling spices and sugar over slices of apple when Hamish appeared in the kitchen doorway, yawning.

Imogen almost bade him good afternoon in the schoolmarmish tone that she knew annoyed him, but she had a tricky subject to raise, so she sent him a smile instead, and went about the business of slipping the cake into the oven.

'How was the party?' she asked.

'Good.'

Of course. This was the standard, automatic response. Imogen wondered why she'd even bothered to ask.

Still yawning, Hamish went to the sink and filled a tumbler with water, while Imogen began to stack the mixing bowl, spoons and beaters into the dishwasher.

'Fuck!' exclaimed her son.

Looking up, she realised Hamish was staring at his phone. No doubt he'd just learned the bad news.

'Did you know about the fire?' he demanded.

'Yes,' she said. 'But not till this morning when Josie rang.' She went to the kettle, sure that coffee was needed, while Hamish sagged against the pantry door, scrolling through his messages. There seemed to be quite a few.

'We're not going to be able to use the hall for the play,' he said. 'Bloody hell. Is Josie having a fit?'

'She's upset, of course. But I'd say she's commendably calm, all things considered. She's trying to find an alternative venue.'

'Any luck?'

'I'm not sure that she's approached anyone yet.' Carefully, Imogen added, 'She was wondering about one of those lovely big sheds on the Hetheringtons' farm.'

Her son seemed to blanch at this. Which was not at all surprising. Ben Hetherington's death was the main reason Hamish was still at home, taking a gap year instead of heading off to university.

'Here,' Imogen handed her son the freshly made mug of coffee. 'It's only instant, but I've added plenty of milk and sugar.'

Hamish grunted his thanks. And Imogen kept herself busy, fiddling at the sink, giving him time to drink the coffee, while fretfully wondering if he was coming to terms with these latest developments, if he would cope.

The thing was, Ben Hetherington and Hamish had been best friends throughout their school years. Just last year, when they were both in Year Twelve, they'd been invited to a party in town. Ben had offered to pick Hamish up in the battered old ute his father let him use.

It had been raining all week, with quite seriously heavy falls in the catchment areas further to the north, but there'd been no warnings about the possibility of flash flooding.

Ben had been on his way to collect Hamish, and when he'd come to the swollen creek at the bottom of the Kirks' hill, he'd decided to check it out on foot before trying to drive across.

The tragedy had been a blow for the entire district, but poor Hamish had blamed himself. He knew Ben would never have drowned if he hadn't been coming to collect him.

Imogen and Jamie had done their best to comfort and support their son, but the poor kid had been inconsolable. They'd organised counselling, which had helped, but there was no way Hamish had been ready to head off to university and carry on with his life, when his best mate's life had been cut so tragically short.

Instead, Hamish had stayed at home, helping his father on the farm, and ever so slowly picking up the pieces of his social life, playing soccer, joining the theatre group. In recent weeks, he'd been starting to talk about his future again.

Now.

This.

And Imogen realised she'd been terribly remiss in not encouraging some kind of contact between Hamish and Alec Hetherington during the past year. Yes, there was a private reason why she and Alec had always maintained a polite distance. But there'd been a time when Hamish had practically lived at the Hetheringtons', after school or on weekends, fishing with Ben in the creek that bordered their land, riding quad bikes, kicking a soccer ball, setting up hay bales as archery targets.

'Surely there must be somewhere else we can take the play,' Hamish cried angrily. 'The Tablelands is covered in sheds.'

Imogen gave a sympathetic nod. 'I know. I've been trying to think of an alternative, but I'm afraid I keep coming back to Alec's place. His sheds are so new and clean and big and so conveniently close to town.'

'Couldn't we clear one of our sheds?'

'Hamish, sweetheart, even if we managed to clean out the tractors and the hay and get those oil stains off the floor, do you really think people would want to traipse all the way out here?'

He scowled. '*We* do it every day.'

'True, but we're dreamers and Josie needs to be practical. And it's not just the audience she needs to consider. It would be an awful long way for the players to have to lug all the sets and equipment and everything.'

Imogen might have offered an encouraging smile if her son had been looking her way instead of staring hard into his coffee mug. Very gently, she added, 'I've actually been thinking I might ring Josie back and offer to go with her when she talks to Alec. I know she'd like the support, but I wouldn't do that if the idea really upset you.'

Hamish's expression was bleak. 'Whatever.' With that, he thumped his mug down on the counter so heavily it was a wonder it didn't crack. And then he stormed back to his room.

* * *

Olivia wasn't entirely surprised to receive a phone call from Rolf on Sunday afternoon. Calls had been running hot between the Burralea players. 'Are you still in Sydney?' she asked him.

'Yes, flying back on Tuesday.'

'I suppose you've heard about the fire?'

'Yes, I have. A terrible business, isn't it? Poor Josie. But I think the Hetherington shed will be a good option.'

'Oh, so Josie's already spoken to Alec?'

'It's not settled. But she's arranged a meeting with him. I believe she and Imogen Kirk are seeing Alec in the morning. And I've already offered to hire any trucks needed for transporting sets and whatever, and I'm looking into hiring a demountable stage from Cairns. I'm feeling confident.'

Olivia refrained from commenting, but she couldn't help questioning Rolf's confidence. She felt it was asking a great deal of Alec Hetherington to expect him to welcome half the district onto his property.

She was surprised Rolf wasn't more sensitive. After all, Rolf had three sons of his own and his imagination was more active than most. He must surely comprehend the suffocating burden of Alec's loss? A year hadn't yet passed since Ben's death and Alec had been living like a recluse ever since.

Olivia was still pondering this when Rolf said, 'I'm actually ringing you about some other news. Are you sitting down?'

'Yes,' she replied cautiously. She was sitting fairly and squarely on a kitchen chair, but Rolf's question still managed to make her reach to the table for support. *What on earth . . .?*

'I told you that Michael Carruthers is taking on the Lord X role for the Sydney production.'

'Yes,' Olivia said even more cautiously.

'So, now he also wants to come up to Burralea to watch the premiere.'

Good God.

'It's a pity you won't be Lady X, but still —'

A weak, hiccuping, half-laugh escaped Olivia. Suddenly, for the first time since her accident, she was incredibly grateful that she was *not* playing Lady X. The very thought of Michael Carruthers in the audience was enough to rip her confidence to shreds and to reveal the extremely thin veneer of a front she'd been hiding behind for decades.

'Are you there, Olivia? Are you okay?'

'Yes, I'm fine,' she lied.

'That's good. I was concerned that a reunion with Michael might be a little awkward for you.'

Yes, the reunion would be excruciating. Olivia's feelings for Michael were so complicated. Her memories of their exciting romance, their shared hopes and dreams, were tangled with memories of sharp and bitter disappointment and heartbreaking, unbearable loss. Meeting with the man now was the last thing she wanted. But it seemed she'd somehow have to find the courage.

The players would have to find courage, too. She hoped they weren't all starstruck.

'I thought you'd at least appreciate a private meeting with Michael before he turns up at the Opening Night,' Rolf said next.

'That – that would be best, yes.' Olivia couldn't possibly handle a public reunion.

'We don't need to lock it in now, of course,' said Rolf. 'Give it some thought. Michael could come to you, or I'd be happy to host a little dinner at my place.'

Olivia didn't need to think twice about this. She'd seen the photos in glossy magazines of Michael's luxurious mansion over-looking Sydney Harbour. Marble floors and walls of windows with stunning, panoramic views, a state-of-the-art kitchen, a fireplace imported from France. No way did she want him to visit her in her humble little cottage in Burralea.

She had to clear her throat before she could speak. 'Something at your place would do nicely, thank you, Rolf.'

CHAPTER TWENTY-EIGHT

A rather grand avenue of liquidambars marked the entrance to the Hetherington farm. Alec's wife, Kristen, had liked to display her sense of flair and she'd planted the trees many years ago. They provided a spectacle in autumn and a green haven in summer. But now in June they were almost bare.

Watching them from the passenger's seat in Josie's car, Imogen found herself fascinated by the last of the bright leaves that still clung to branches, almost as if they were afraid to let go.

Fear, it seemed, came in many guises.

She was reminded of Hamish's morose farewell earlier that morning. Her son hadn't tried to stop her from attending this meeting, but she knew he was afraid of the outcome, of having to turn up here at this farm and face his mate's grieving father.

Hamish's fear was not unwarranted. No one really knew how Alec might react to the Burralea players' request to invade his domain. He'd barely shown his face in town since the funeral. And now, as Josie drove past the impressive sheds that were the reason for their visit, Imogen couldn't help thinking about her own history with Alec Hetherington.

Decades earlier, when she'd first arrived on the Tablelands, Alec had been her boyfriend. Until she'd met Jamie Kirk and had fallen head over heels, knowing almost immediately that she needed to spend the rest of her life with him.

So long ago . . .

Imogen had never felt guilty about the breakup with Alec. She'd been honest with him and not unkind. Even so, there were times she woke in the middle of the night and relived the difficult conversation when she'd told him about Jamie. Lying there in the dark, she could still recall the way Alec had flinched, could still hear the rasp of his sharply indrawn breath, could still remember the way he'd driven her home without another word.

Alec had recovered, of course. Quite quickly, actually. He'd married Kristen and they'd been very happy by all accounts. Hayley had arrived quite early in their marriage and then Ben. And when their sons became good friends, Imogen and Alec had renewed their connection . . . although there'd always been a cautious distance.

'Okay. All set to go?'

Imogen's thoughts were scattered by Josie, who had now parked her vehicle at the front steps of the farmhouse. It was time to shut down the memories and focus on here and now. Imogen wished she felt calmer as she unclipped her seatbelt.

'Right,' she said. 'Here goes. Fingers crossed.'

Josie's blue eyes were as hopeful and bright as ever. 'At least Alec has agreed to see us, so that's a start.'

'Yes, but does he have any idea what we're asking?'

'I suspect he must. He knows we're representing the little theatre and he's bound to have heard about the fire.' Josie shot Imogen a searching glance. 'I should have asked. How does Hamish feel about this?'

'Not great.'

'Poor lad. He's been doing so well. He's really helped the new girl, Tilly.'

'Yes.' As Tilly's teacher, Imogen had been impressed by the girl's pleasing progress. That was something to be grateful for at least.

And her son wasn't short on courage. Hamish would find a way to handle this new challenge. Imogen straightened her shoulders. She would follow Josie's example and think positively.

The door opened before they could knock. Alec Hetherington was a tall, well-built man, but he'd aged in the months since the funeral. His dark hair and beard were now heavily flecked with grey and his shoulders were more stooped than Imogen remembered.

He didn't smile as he bade them, 'Good morning.'

'Good morning, Alec.' At least Josie was bright and focused. 'Thanks ever so much for making time to see us.'

Alec grunted a response and then nodded to Imogen. 'So they let you out of school on a Monday morning?'

'Yes,' she said. 'Luckily, I have a spare on Mondays just before morning break.'

'A spare?'

'Oh, it's a period when I'm not needed in the classroom. Normally I use it for marking and preparation.' She smiled. 'Or for meetings.'

'Right.' He offered no answering smile. 'Well, I guess we'd better not waste your time then. Come on in.'

Imogen knew that Alec's daughter, Hayley, was no longer living at home and she'd half expected the inside of his house to be a shambles, but it was surprisingly tidy and dust free. Perhaps he'd hired a housekeeper? Perhaps he was just naturally tidy? She was rather ashamed that their kids had been best friends and she didn't know these things.

Alec didn't take them to his lounge room, but to the kitchen where four chairs were set around a scrubbed pine table. There was no offer of tea or coffee, which was fair enough. Alec was a busy farmer and this wasn't a social call.

The three of them sat somewhat stiffly.

Josie opened her mouth, no doubt ready to deliver her carefully prepared lines when Alec spoke.

'So, I heard about the fire. A bad business. I'm guessing you want to use one of my sheds for this Rolf Anders play you're putting on.'

Josie's eyes and mouth popped so wide with delighted surprise she looked like a sideshow clown ready to swallow a ball.

Imogen responded on her behalf. 'Yes, Alec, we *were* wondering if you could spare us a shed.'

'How much time would this involve?' He was still looking down, his expression shuttered.

Josie, having somewhat recovered, was best placed to answer this. 'We were due to open on Friday night, actually, and we'd planned to run the play over two weekends. Friday and Saturday nights and a Sunday matinee.'

'And there'd be rehearsals?'

'I'm afraid so, yes. At the very least we need one full dress rehearsal. And there's the bump in and bump out. We'd have to get moving pretty quickly, actually. I realise it would be quite intrusive, but if people could park their cars in your front paddock, they needn't come anywhere near the house or the dairy. We'd hire portable toilets and it would be good if we could set up tents near the shed as changing rooms for the players.'

Josie was in full swing now, barely pausing for breath as she presented her case. 'We'd also be happy to pay you rent, Alec – take it out of the proceeds. That's only fair, given the inconvenience.'

Alec was frowning, tapping his fingers against the tabletop. 'If I was to consider this, I'd need help with clearing the shed.'

'Of course,' said Josie and Imogen together. Imogen had already figured that one of Alec's sheds must hold his tractor and other hideously expensive farming equipment, but the other probably housed hay bales.

'I assume you've got the muscle power?' Alec asked next. 'I have my hands full with the farm.'

'Yes, I'm sure we could rally enough helpers.'

At last, Alec nodded. 'Well, you're in luck. I shipped a big load of hay bales south just last week. So that second shed's almost empty.'

Josie looked as if she wanted to leap out of her seat and hug him. 'So does that mean . . .?'

Another nod followed. 'You can have the shed.'

Alec was showing them to the door when he made eye contact with Imogen. His eyes were very dark, his gaze piercing. 'How's Hamish?' he asked.

The question caught her unprepared. 'He's okay, thanks.'

'He didn't go away to university.'

'No.' What else could she say? Alec didn't need an explanation.

'And he's involved in this play?'

'Yes, he is.' She wished she could manage words of more than one syllable.

An uneasy silence followed. Imogen waited in case Alec made further comment, but he simply nodded and opened the door for them to leave.

* * *

Very soon after Liam caught up with the little theatre's latest developments, he rang Kate. 'Have you heard it's to be all hands on deck to move the theatre gear out to Hetheringtons' farm before the weekend?'

'Yes, Tilly was full of the news when she came home from Olivia's just now,' she said. 'She's so excited that the play's still going ahead.'

'Yeah, it's great. Everyone's pulling out all the stops. I believe Imogen Kirk is taking a group of students over to the farm tomorrow to clear the shed and hose it out ready for a major effort on Wednesday.'

'Right. I'd be happy to help on Wednesday.'

'Good to know.' Liam knew he was smiling. Could Kate tell? As soon as they'd started talking, he was picturing her, wondering where she was. In the house, preparing dinner perhaps? Working late in the van? Outside on that beautiful hillside, admiring the view of the setting sun?

He was imagining her smile, her lovely brown eyes, the soft golden sweep of her hair.

'I've told Josie I can clear my schedule on Wednesday,' he told her. 'My clients were very understanding, once I'd explained the deal. So I'll be helping to transport sets and set up the lighting. Rolf Anders has hired two trucks, and Jack Cooper from the hardware store is lending us a couple of his young chaps to help with loading and unloading. Peter Hubbard can't get away. He's an accountant and it's too close to the end of the financial year, so he's tied up at work. But Derek's wangled the morning off and Geoff, Heidi and Hamish are all free.'

'Sounds wonderful. Should be a proper working bee.'

'It's great, isn't it? Feels like the whole community's getting behind the players.'

'The joys of a small country town.'

'Exactly.' Not for the first time, Liam was glad he'd come back to the Tablelands. He loved that the Burralea folk were so unpretentious and down to earth, warm-hearted and friendly. Everything he'd been hoping for.

'I think they're hiring seating as well,' he said. 'So that will need setting out and there'll be tents to erect, and trestle tables for serving wine and cups of tea at interval.'

Kate laughed. 'I'm sure I'll find plenty of ways to pitch in and help.'

'For sure. You'll be handy. Might be an idea to bring your toolkit, just in case there's a dodgy hinge needs fixing or – who knows? Something that needs banging together.'

Far out. Liam couldn't believe he'd actually said that. Now, all his one-track brain could think about was Kate with her legs wrapped around him. It didn't help that her breathless little laugh sounded in his ear.

'It'll be good for me to have a day mixing with other people,' she said. 'I'm sure I spend way too much time on my own.'

Hell. Was he reading too much into everything she said? Or was there a subtle double meaning in her comment?

'I guess I should probably bring a packed lunch,' she said next.

'Nah. Don't bother. My place isn't far from the farm. We can duck back there and grab a quick bite to eat.'

'Oh?'

A stretch of silence followed this invitation. Liam told himself he hadn't been hinting at a chance for another of their 'flings'.

He hadn't, surely?

'That would be lovely,' Kate said at last and she sounded genuinely pleased.

Liam realised he'd been holding his breath.

CHAPTER TWENTY-NINE

Kate couldn't help thinking that good luck sometimes arrived disguised as bad luck. The fire had been a terrible blow for the little theatre group, but when she arrived at the Hetherington farm early on Wednesday morning, ready to help, she decided there was something rather special about the new venue.

It wasn't just the impressive avenue of trees at the front gate. The big sheds stood tall against a panoramic backdrop of gently undulating, grassy paddocks sparkling with dew, and there were ducks swimming in a small dam that reflected the morning blue of the sky, as well as quietly grazing black and white dairy cows. This setting lent an air of novelty and country glamour to the theatre's temporary location, she decided.

She was soon busy, of course. First she helped Geoff to erect the two tents that would be used as dressing rooms for the players and another where Tammy the hairdresser would preside, taking care of makeup and hair. Meanwhile, a great deal of heaving and hammering could be heard from inside the shed where the portable stage was being erected.

With the stage in place, the flats then had to be carefully carried in from the truck. The fellows from Coopers' hardware store were used to heavy lifting, but they were supervised by a very stern Josie, who gave them precise instructions.

'Okay, so we need one man on each side of the flat, and then you carry it with one hand high, and one hand low, so you're mirroring each other's position. Also, you only need to lift the flats an inch or so from the floor. And they need to be carried as fully upright as possible. That's the easiest and safest.'

Following them, Josie kept up the instructions. 'Keep walking slowly backwards now! Make sure you keep supporting that flat. Okay, Derek, Hamish, are you ready? We're going to need extra hands to help lift and support the flat onto the stage. Luckily it's not a very high lift, but slowly, slowly. That's it.'

The flats were certainly a challenge, but the guys did well. Nothing was dropped and there was hardly a scratch on the paint. And once these were in place, Josie and Kate began to set out the rows of plastic chairs for the audience, while the others brought in the rest of the set and props.

Geoff had found glass desks in a second-hand store that were perfect for the spaceship's bridge. On these they arranged the computer screens that Heidi had cleverly made out of cardboard magazine holders fastened together and set on their sides, so that they had the correct slant. Someone else had made more display panels with dustpans turned upside down, painted silver and edged with electrical tape. And the buttons made from bottle caps painted in various colours looked surprisingly realistic.

Kate found it all rather exciting. Yet another magazine holder was placed over the arm of a swivel desk chair. With a calculator glued onto it, an actor could punch numbers and look like the real deal.

Later, Liam would set little LED light systems on these desks, just to give a bit more atmosphere. So, along with Liam's starscapes and Kate's portholes on the viewing platform, the set was going to look just as good here in the shed as it had at the theatre.

'Are you going to have curtains for your stage?' Kate couldn't help asking Josie. She'd always thought there was a special magic about waiting in the theatre for the curtains to open.

But Josie was shaking her head. 'Curtains are a bridge too far, I'm afraid. But I believe Liam has ideas for something clever with the lighting – something to give a sense of anticipation for the audience.' She laughed and her bright eyes flashed. 'The man's a genius and it's so good of him to pitch in and help us. Good of you, too, Kate. Thanks so much.'

'No problem,' said Kate. 'I'm having fun.'

'Careful,' Josie warned with a sly wink. 'You'll find yourself hooked like the rest of us.'

Yes, thought Kate. She could see how easily that might happen. Small country towns had a dangerous way of gathering you in, making you feel as if you belonged and were needed. But settling down had never been part of her plan.

Perhaps it was fortunate that she was distracted from this quandary by Josie. 'Hamish and Derek have set up the trestle tables and the urns. So maybe you can help me to bring in the crates of mugs for the tea and coffee?'

'Sure.'

By lunchtime, much of the work was accomplished. Most of the other helpers had brought a thermos or cold drink and a snack, but no one seemed to mind that Liam and Kate planned to slip away.

Kate had never been to Liam's house, so she was interested to discover a simple but attractive weatherboard cottage of pumpkin orange – painted by the previous owners, he explained – and shaded by lush native trees. Her only problem now was the whole proximity thing. Sitting beside Liam as he drove back to his house, walking up the front path with him and waiting while he unlocked the door, she was alight with a wild, zinging tension.

'Are you okay with a corned beef and pickle sandwich?' he asked, as he gestured for her to precede him into the house.

'Sure,' she replied a little breathlessly, although in all honesty, she wasn't really hungry. She was too conscious that she and Liam were alone for the first time in what felt like ages. Too long.

She wouldn't have minded in the least if he decided not to head for the kitchen, but pulled her into his arms instead. Just imagining this possibility made her skin all tight and hot.

They were halfway along the polished timber hallway when Kate stopped and looked back over her shoulder. 'Do I keep going?'

She wasn't sure what message she signalled, but rather than answering her, Liam also came to a halt. She thought how damn desirable he looked, standing there, with his smiling dark eyes, filling the hallway with his big shoulders and workmanlike clothes. She was remembering the out-of-this-world pleasure of getting naked with this man.

Should she say something? Let him know how desperately keen she was?

Perhaps this wasn't necessary. As their gazes connected and held, there was a stillness about Liam, a heart-stopping intensity that echoed Kate's own tension. She could feel her heart thumping in her chest. And then, all other thoughts faded away. Lunch, the theatre, the shed.

Nothing else mattered, but this. This trembling moment. This all-consuming need.

'Kate.' His voice was little more than a whisper and when he took a step towards her, she silently willed him to come even closer.

Lifting a hand, he reached out, traced her cheek ever so gently with the backs of his fingers. An exquisite tremor shimmied through her. And then he leaned in to kiss her, placing his hands against the wall on either side of her, trapping her. It was exactly where she wanted to be. Lost in his kiss, drowning in a whirlpool of longing.

'Maybe lunch can wait?' he murmured.

'Please.' This was the only response she could manage, the only response Liam needed.

* * *

'Do you think you could make me look a little more glamorous?'

'Olivia, you always look glamorous.'

Olivia smiled at the reflections in the hairdresser's ornately framed mirror. Tammy was poised behind her, scissors and comb at the ready. 'It's very kind of you to say so, Tammy, but this time I really need to raise the bar. I'm going to a reunion with an old beau.'

Tammy's eyes widened. 'Wow. Tell me more.'

But Olivia wasn't prepared to give details. 'Sorry, you'll know soon enough, but I need to keep this under wraps for the time being.'

Unsurprisingly, Tammy's eyes widened with almost desperate curiosity and Olivia knew she'd disappointed the hairdresser, who loved nothing better than a good, juicy gossip. Usually, the tales Tammy spread were harmless enough, but word of Michael Carruthers in town would send the entire district, not just the gossipers, into an absolute frenzy.

Olivia looked again at the image of herself presented by the mirror. Until now, she'd accepted the inevitable signs of ageing – the silver hair, the crow's feet, the crepey neck and slackening jawline. But now she was seeing herself as Michael might see her.

She knew it was silly to mind. Michael had aged too, of course, and no one could expect her to still look as she had in her twenties. But Michael had spent his entire career surrounded by extraordinarily beautiful young women, or by older women who'd endured countless rounds of cosmetic procedures.

Unfortunately, while Olivia had always admired sensible older women who accepted their wrinkles and sagging bits as a badge of endurance or courage, Michael's uninvited return had channelled her focus onto everything she'd lost. Her looks, her career . . .

No, not the other. She mustn't think about their son. In all these years, Michael wouldn't have given him a thought.

'I don't know,' she told Tammy now. 'I just hoped you might have an idea or two to give me a little pizzazz.'

'Of course.' Lifting strands of Olivia's silvery blonde hair, Tammy smiled. 'I'm thinking an updo. Maybe with a little Scandi braid tucked down one side?'

'Oh, yes, I like the sound of that.' Bless Tammy. Olivia felt brighter and more confident already. 'Now, what sort of clothes do you think would work best with that look?'

* * *

Kate and Liam lay in a lazy tangle, luxuriating in an amazing after-glow, enjoying the sunshine that streamed through the bedroom window and the honeyeaters squabbling in a bottlebrush just outside.

Liam lifted a strand of Kate's hair, admiring its golden gleam in the sunlight. 'You do know you're very beautiful, don't you?'

She smiled shyly. 'You're not so hard on the eye yourself, Flint the Sparkie.'

'I'd love to stay here all afternoon,' he said next. 'But I'm afraid people might already have noticed we've taken a rather long lunchbreak.'

'Yes, I daresay.'

'They'll probably jump to the right conclusions. Do you mind?'

A rosy warmth tinted Kate's cheeks. 'Not really. I can't imagine Geoff or Josie madly gossiping. They're more likely to be anxious about whether you're coming back to finish their lighting set-up.'

'That's very true.' Dropping a light kiss on her forehead, Liam hitched forward to a sitting position. He tried to tell himself this rendezvous hadn't been planned, that it had been entirely spontaneous. But the whys and wherefores weren't nearly as important as the result – that he had fallen for Kate way too deeply and he had no idea how he was going to handle this going forward. Not without trampling all over her dreams.

'Sorry I haven't fed you,' he said. 'Are you hungry?'

'Not really.' A small shrug. 'Maybe a little.'

'Would a couple of apples be enough for now? You could eat one on the way back.'

'Perfect.'

CHAPTER THIRTY

When Olivia set off for Rolf's place that evening, she was happy enough with her appearance. Tammy had managed to make her hair look quite elegant and interesting and she'd decided to wear a loose cream silk shirt over black trousers. Her main accessory was a pearl pendant on a heavy gold chain, the very last gift her dear Gerald had given her, and she'd brought a black and gold woollen pashmina to ward off the chill.

Alas, being comfortable about her appearance was only half the battle this evening. Olivia was ridiculously nervous, which was annoying, given the level of maturity she believed she'd achieved, and the life lessons she'd supposedly learned.

She couldn't even pin down a reason for her nerves. She was quite certain Michael wouldn't want to dredge up their past and she didn't resent his success. She was truly content with the far quieter trajectory that her own life had taken. She needed to remember that now, as she came to the stone wall that marked the entrance to Rolf's place – a wonderful timber and glass affair, set on a tree-studded acreage on the shores of Lake Tinaroo.

As she climbed out of her car, she was pleased that she only had a small limp now. When she knocked at Rolf's open front door, she heard him call out.

'Hello there, Olivia. I'm in the kitchen. Come on through.'

Once more unto the breach. Pinning on a fresh smile, Olivia crossed the beautiful open-plan living area, admiring, as always, the magnificent red gum flooring, the natural stone fireplace bright with glowing logs, and the huge windows offering views through the trees to the lake. She was surprised she couldn't hear voices as she approached the kitchen, but then she discovered that Rolf was alone, standing at the island bench, cheerfully chopping cherry tomatoes and tossing them into a salad bowl.

'Hello there!' Rolf's smile was especially warm when he saw her. 'Don't you look wonderful?' Abandoning his chopping, he hastily dried his hands and greeted Olivia with a hug and a kiss. And then, holding her by the wrists, he leaned back to run an admiring glance from her head to her toes. 'Bravo, my dear!'

She was grateful for his approval, but she was too nervous to bask in it. She couldn't help looking around, half-expecting to find Michael Carruthers about to make a grand entrance through another doorway.

Rolf nodded to the window. 'Michael's down there, admiring the lake before we lose the last of the daylight.' He reached for a bottle of red wine and a spare glass sitting on the kitchen counter. 'Here, why don't you take a drink down there and join him? The track's quite smooth. I think your ankle should be okay.'

'Thank you.' As Olivia accepted the glass, she realised that a meeting with Michael in private and without an audience was probably a very good idea. Even so, she hesitated. 'Are – are you sure you don't need help here?'

'Olivia.' Rolf's smile was a gentle reproach. 'This is a barbecue. A simple salad and a few marinated Tolga steaks tossed on the hotplate. And I'm almost done.' He dismissed her with a wave of his hand. 'Now, off you go.'

*

Rolf's comment about the last of the light had been spot on. As soon as Olivia stepped outside, she could sense dusk closing in. The setting sun was behind her, but it cast a soft glow through the trees and lit the lake with touches of pink, mauve and gold. So beautiful.

Her heart picked up pace as she made her careful way down the track. And when she saw Michael, the drumming in her chest beat even harder. He was standing at the edge of the water, an almost empty wine glass in his hand.

His thick hair was now quite silver and he was dressed simply in blue jeans and a blue checked shirt, with a grey jumper draped over his shoulders. There was the hint of a softening paunch, but for the most part, he'd aged well – although Olivia had already known that, thanks to regular photos in the media.

Now, when Michael saw her, he smiled and waved, so that was a helpful start. He even came forward and gallantly held out his hand to guide her down the last of the stone steps at the bottom of the track.

'Liv,' he said and with that one syllable, uttered in his famous, deep baritone, he took her back fifty years. To Sydney. Their loft apartment. That dazzling final season.

Helpless tears arrived. Such a nuisance. And Olivia wished she wasn't carrying a wine glass. It felt awkward, as Michael greeted her with a kiss on each cheek.

'Hello, Michael.' At least her voice worked.

'How are you, Liv? You look wonderful.'

'I'm very well, thanks. And you?'

'Way fitter than I deserve to be.' He gave a short, self-deprecating laugh. 'I was so surprised when Rolf told me that you live up here now. But good for you.' He swept an arm to acknowledge the trees and the lake awash with fading pink. 'It's spectacularly beautiful country, isn't it?'

'Yes, I love it.' She was still blinking tears, so perhaps that was why she hadn't noticed that Michael was not alone. But now she realised there was another man standing only a few metres away in the shadow of a grove of pines. He was a similar height and build to Michael, but younger. He wore glasses and had dark brown eyes, and his jaw was stubbled by a trendy, closely trimmed beard. His dark hair was slightly receding.

Impossibly, he seemed somehow familiar.

Olivia couldn't help staring.

'Let me introduce Luke Brady,' said Michael. 'He's travelled up here with me from Sydney.'

Ah, thought Olivia, Luke was probably a fellow actor. Perhaps she had seen him on television. She acknowledged him with a small nod. 'Nice to meet you, Luke. Will you be joining Michael for the Sydney production of *Next Stop Mars*?'

The younger man shook his head. 'Only as a member of the audience. I'm not an actor, I'm afraid.' He made no attempt to approach Olivia and he didn't offer a smile, but he seemed to return her stare, his gaze unnaturally intense.

A shiver roused goosebumps on her skin, and she wished she hadn't left her pashmina in the house. There was a table near the water's edge, a round concrete affair with curved benches, but there was no suggestion they should sit. Perhaps this meeting was only intended to be very brief, before they returned to the warmth of the house.

Night always fell swiftly in the north and already it was darker. Olivia gave up trying to place the newcomer as she searched for a suitable conversation topic. 'I suppose you've heard about the fire in the community hall. Such a blow for the local theatre.'

'Yes,' said Michael. 'Although Rolf's quite excited about the new shed they've found.' He grinned. 'A unique setting could be a plus for a world premiere.'

'Let's hope so. As I'm sure you must know, it's a very clever play.'

'Brilliant,' agreed Michael and now he sent what seemed to be a cautious glance in Luke Brady's direction.

A fresh ripple of unease stirred in Olivia's chest. Why was Luke here? Why did this feel like some kind of set-up? Perhaps she needed the wine after all. She took a deep sip. As with all the wines Rolf offered, it was rich, smooth and delicious.

Watching her with an expression almost as intense as Luke's, Michael drew a deep breath. 'Olivia, Luke and I have something to tell you.'

Oh, dear God.

Just like that, she knew.

She could see it so clearly now. Luke looked like her father. He had the same dark hair and intelligent eyes, the same jaw, although it was now disguised by his beard. And when she really looked, she could see, showing just above his collar, on the side of his neck. That mark . . .

The tip of a bird's wing.

Her boy.

Her baby.

The wine glass fell from her hand, red wine splashing like blood, glass tinkling as it hit stones. Her mouth trembled and pulled out of shape. Tears filled her eyes and she was shaking all over. At any moment she might sink to the ground.

'Liv.' Michael's arm was around her, supporting her. 'I'm sorry if we've given you a shock.'

She couldn't speak.

'Here, why don't you sit down?' Michael had turned in the direction of the table and seats.

But shock had rendered Olivia incapable of walking and she couldn't see through her tears. She was helpless.

'God, Liv,' Michael said now. 'I'm sorry.'

And so you should be, she wanted to scream. Had he really thought he could spring this on her? Here? Now? While having a casual glass of red by the lake?

'Come on,' Michael urged again, giving her elbow a nudge. 'Sit down.'

'No, thanks!' Olivia snapped, shaking him off.

'Don't be angry.'

'Don't be angry?' she cried. 'Why shouldn't I be angry, when you – when he —'

Oh, help. This was her baby boy. Luke. His name was Luke and her heart was breaking. She longed to hold him. Her thoughts were spinning.

Once again she was overtaken by tears and she had to wait, to swipe at her eyes and to take several deep breaths before she could speak. 'How – how long have you known?'

'Luke came to me several months ago,' Michael said. 'It was only when his father died that he discovered he'd been adopted. His mother had died a couple of years earlier and it was all revealed in his father's will. Including our names.'

Our names.

Luke had known her name and Michael's, but he'd only bothered to find Michael. Of course, Michael was incredibly famous and wealthy, so perhaps it made sense. But the knowledge hurt.

Oh, dear Lord, it hurt. Olivia couldn't bear it. Her baby, her boy. She'd loved him so deeply and for so long and he hadn't even tried —

Her impulse was to turn and flee. But then she caught sight of tears shimmering behind Luke's glasses.

'Luke.' It was the first time she had said his name.

'I'm sorry,' he said. 'You were the one who gave me away and I assumed —'

'You thought it was *my* decision?' Olivia turned to Michael, glaring. 'You let him think that?'

'Ahh – I – I guess —' Looking shamefaced now, Michael scratched at his chest. 'I guess I did kinda dodge that question.'

Luke had been staring from one to the other and Olivia saw the moment when realisation dawned.

Shock flared in his eyes and then his face was crumpling, as if the moment was too big for him. And as Olivia stood there, taking him in, recognising so many details – the shape of his ears, the breadth of his hands, the chocolate brown of his eyes – all the ways he looked like her father, or like Michael and even, incredibly, like that tiny babe she'd held in her arms so many years ago, she couldn't remain angry. Not when he was here, alive and well. At last.

So many things she needed to know. Where had Luke lived? What work did he do? Did he have a family of his own?

She tried to smile. And they were happy tears now that ruined the last of her carefully applied makeup. 'You have no idea what this means,' she said. 'A day hasn't passed when I haven't missed you.' She had to bite her lower lip to hold back a noisy sob.

Nervously, she held out her arms and Luke smiled shyly. For a moment she thought the lopsided smile was all he had to offer, but then he came forward and after only a moment's hesitation, they hugged. Olivia closed her eyes as she breathed in the scent of him – the hint of aftershave so different from that long ago newborn baby smell. She sensed strong muscles beneath his jumper and remembered the little limbs that had kicked against her belly.

Her heart was so full she thought it might burst, but she was brought back from this life-changing moment by the very ordinary everyday sound of tinkering on metal. It was Rolf at his barbecue on the stone paved terrace outside his house.

'Dinner will be ready very soon,' he called to them. He had lit lamps and a patio heater and it all looked very inviting.

Olivia turned to Michael and Luke. 'Does Rolf know?'

They shook their heads.

At last she was able to smile through her tears. 'Well, if anyone loves a good story it's Rolf Anders, and we certainly have one to share with him. Actually, I'm desperate to hear it, too. I need to know every last detail.'

CHAPTER THIRTY-ONE

Tilly thought it was incredibly exciting to be transferring their play to a farmer's shed. This evening was to be their dress rehearsal and the players had been asked to arrive extra early. The sun hadn't quite set and the countryside was all soft and pearly as Kate drove up to the shed.

The new space was even bigger than the community hall, and although the walls were unlined corrugated steel and a lingering whiff of hay remained, Tilly thought it looked very professional, with a stage erected and all their sets and props in place.

Kate was going to stay on for tonight's rehearsal. She'd been involved in helping with the big shift and she'd brought her toolkit, just in case anything fell apart at a last, inconvenient moment. But Tilly suspected that Kate had mainly come because Liam would also be there to supervise the lighting.

Tilly had seen the way those two looked at each other. Jeez, Liam might be an electrician, but the glances between him and Kate gave a whole new meaning to sparks. They reminded Tilly of how gooey and smiley her mum and Jed had been when they'd first started dating.

These thoughts were soon swept away, though, by the excitement of getting into her costume. Tilly had never been camping, so the very idea of getting changed in a tent was cool. Her costume was a short blue jacket with two rows of shiny silver buttons, and a tiny, pleated silver skirt, plus her sneakers covered with foil to look like silver boots. Kate said she looked like an old-fashioned marching girl, but Tilly reckoned she looked exactly right for a robot servant.

Her jet black hair was already straight, but Tammy the hairdresser used electric tongs to make it extra blunt at the ends. After that, Heidi put on Tilly's makeup, applying it heavily, so that it gave her the slightly unreal look of an AI. So awesome! Tilly was stoked.

Hamish looked amazing, too. He was dressed entirely in shiny black, a brilliant contrast to his rich red hair. Tilly thought he looked more striking and handsome than ever. The only problem was, he seemed a bit 'off' tonight, not his usual relaxed and confident self. There was no sign of his customary welcoming smile. Not even a teasing dig about Tilly's costume. He didn't seem to be talking to any of the other players either, which was weird.

Tilly had no idea what Hamish's problem was and she didn't like to ask. At one stage, she saw Josie talking privately to him and giving him a pat on the shoulder, as if she was trying to reassure him about something. But when he was on stage, the special energy that was his trademark seemed to be missing. It was almost as if he was taking the whole robot thing a step too far.

This bothered Tilly. Hamish was her hero and she hated to see him like this. She almost said something to Heidi and Derek, but she'd feel silly if they hadn't even noticed. They might think she was being overly sensitive, or maybe they'd tell her to mind her own business. She was a newbie and still at school, a baby really, so what would she know?

Apart from her concern about Hamish, though, everything else seemed to be going really well. The set looked amazing now, especially with all of Liam's lighting giving it an extra sci-fi, outer space vibe.

At the halftime interval, the players had their usual break. The urns had been brought over from the hall and set on trestle tables along with mugs, tea, coffee and powdered chocolate, with milk kept in an esky.

'You're doing so well,' Kate told Tilly. 'You all are. It's really exciting. This play is going to be amazing.'

This was great to hear, especially as Pippa and David had texted Kate a few days earlier, saying they planned to come up to catch the show. They wouldn't make the opening, but would definitely be there for the following weekend and could they please stay again in the van? Tilly loved the idea of having family in the audience.

But what do you think about Hamish? Tilly wanted to ask Kate now, but she was afraid one of the other players might overhear her.

Then Liam approached, obviously hoping for a chat with Kate, so Tilly left them to it and plucked up the courage to take her mug of hot chocolate over to Hamish. He was sitting by himself on one of the plastic hire chairs. He hadn't bothered with a hot drink and was sipping from a water bottle.

'Hey,' she said.

'Hey.' The brief glance he gave her wasn't very welcoming.

'What do you think of our new venue?' Tilly asked, not wanting to give up at the very first hurdle.

Hamish let his gaze roll up to the high pitched roof and gave a shrug. 'It's fine.'

Something was definitely wrong with him and Tilly wished she was wise enough to know how to help.

There were spare chairs all around, but she remained standing, aware that if she sat and Hamish upped and left her, she'd feel totally pathetic. She was busily trying to work out another, not too poxy question, when she realised someone else was approaching. A man she didn't recognise.

He was tall and gruff looking, with a beard speckled with grey and wearing old-fashioned braces to hold up his jeans. It was soon clear he intended to speak to Hamish, and Tilly took a polite step backwards. As she did so, Hamish looked up. He saw the man and seemed instantly scared.

Worried, Tilly wished she could tell this stranger to eff off. Hamish already had enough problems.

'Hamish.' The man actually spoke quite gently, but Hamish still looked scared as he got to his feet.

'Hello, Mr Hetherington.'

Yikes. Hetherington was the name of the farmer who owned this place.

'I heard you were involved in this play,' Mr Hetherington said next.

'Yes.' Muscles rippled in Hamish's throat as he swallowed.

Mr Hetherington nodded and almost smiled. 'Good for you.'

Now Hamish's eyes seemed to widen with surprise. 'Thanks.'

For the first time, the farmer let his glance slide to Tilly, just briefly, before he looked at the stage, his faint smile lingering as he took in details. 'That's quite some set-up.'

'Yes,' Hamish said again, but he didn't seem so upset now.

'I'm looking forward to the show,' Mr Hetherington said next. 'And I wanted to make sure I found you first, so I could wish you all the best.' Now he held out his hand to Hamish. 'It's good to see you, son.'

Tears shone in Hamish's eyes. 'You, too, Alec.'

Tilly was strangely moved as she watched them shake hands. The look they shared was so filled with emotion, she realised she was witness to a very private moment. She might have scurried away, except that Mr Hetherington was smiling properly now.

'That's some costume they've got you in,' he said, giving Hamish an almost fatherly slap on his shiny black padded shoulder. 'I'm sure you'll make us all proud.' And when he glanced Tilly's way, he surprised her with a wink. 'I was going to wish you all good luck, but I believe the correct term is break a leg.'

'Thank you,' said Tilly and Hamish together and then Mr Hetherington gave them a brief wave that was almost a salute before he turned and left.

Hamish, watching him go, let out his breath in an audible huff. He took a long draught from his water bottle and wiped his mouth with the back of his hand.

Then, to Tilly's surprise, he gave a rough little laugh. 'I suppose I just wiped off half my makeup.'

'No,' she assured him. 'You're fine.'

For the first time this evening Hamish looked at her properly, and he smiled. 'Yeah,' he said. 'I think I just might be.'

Tilly had no idea what he was talking about. She was just glad the old Hamish was back.

The second half of the rehearsal went really well. Hamish was pretty much his normal self and everyone else remembered their lines, the set held together – and Josie seemed happy, which was the main thing.

Josie had made notes while she was watching the rehearsal and now she gathered everyone around her while she ran through her comments. She complimented people on the scenes that had gone really well – Tilly was thrilled to get a mention – and Josie also pointed out a couple of places where she wanted more movement, or particular lines that needed more emphasis, or more emotion.

'But on the whole,' Josie told them, 'I couldn't be happier.

Well done, everyone. I know Rolf is going to be thrilled with you, and you're going to blow Burralea away with his wonderful play.'

Everyone was grinning at this, a couple of people gleefully elbowing each other, or giving the thumbs up.

Josie went on to remind them to hang their costumes up carefully and to arrive in plenty of time tomorrow evening for their all-important Opening Night.

'Speaking of which,' she added. 'I do have one other rather exciting announcement.' She allowed a dramatic pause before she continued. 'We'll have a surprise guest tomorrow evening. Someone rather famous.'

'A politician,' muttered Derek, clearly unimpressed. 'On the hunt for a photo opportunity.'

'Before I tell you who this person is, let me say, you shouldn't be intimidated,' Josie went on. 'Every single player here is a darn fine actor and I'm proud of you.'

The players were sharing puzzled glances now. A couple of people looked worried.

'Put us out of our misery, Josie,' called Peter Hubbard. 'Who is this person?'

'Michael Carruthers.'

Tilly gasped along with everyone else.

'Not *the* Michael Carruthers from *Gods and Goddesses*?' cried Derek.

'And *Revenge Mountain*?' added someone else.

'Yes,' Josie affirmed. 'Michael's going to be playing Lord X in the Sydney production of *Next Stop Mars*, so he's keen to see our show. He and Rolf are quite good friends, but it seems he's also an old friend of Olivia's.'

Wow. Michael Carruthers! Tilly couldn't believe Olivia had never told her that she knew such a famous actor. Tilly's mum had been a real fan of him in *Gods and Goddesses*.

But now there was an anguished wail. 'Why the hell didn't someone warn us?' Margot cried, and without waiting for an answer, she turned and raced out of the shed and into the night.

CHAPTER THIRTY-TWO

For Olivia, it had been the most amazing day. Mid-morning, Luke had come to her house – an event momentous enough to finally obliterate any hang-ups she had about the modesty of her cottage – and they had enjoyed a delightful getting-to-know-you session over tea and croissants.

Even though Olivia had already discovered a great deal of Luke's story on the previous evening at Rolf's, she was keen to go over it all again and in more detail. It was so comforting to know that her boy had been adopted by a good, honest and caring couple – a dentist called Simon Brady and his wife, Nerida.

A year or so after Luke had joined this pair, Nerida Brady had discovered that she was, somewhat miraculously, pregnant, and so Luke also had a younger sister called Mary. The family had lived in Sydney, in the upper North Shore suburb of Turramurra and Luke had enjoyed a thoroughly respectable middle-class upbringing.

Of course, Simon Brady had hoped Luke might follow in his footsteps and become a dentist, but Luke had inherited an artistic and adventurous streak, which was no real surprise to Olivia. In his early twenties, he'd taken off to backpack through Asia and then later had continued on through Europe and America, where he'd had various jobs – bartending, picking fruit, working in ski resorts and in hostels.

Their conversation hadn't really included a discussion about his biological father, although Luke had commented that Olivia was quite different from Michael.

'I suppose that's because we've led very different lives,' she'd suggested and she was pleased that Luke hadn't felt compelled to continue this comparison. She might have found herself confessing that she had only come to terms with her own less than stellar career in her later years.

She did mention her marriage to Gerald, happily recounting what a sweet and fun companion he'd been. But it was during this conversation that Olivia and Luke had shared a rather astonishing, skin-prickling moment of synchronicity, when they'd realised that they had both been living in York, in the north of England, at the very same time.

They could only shake their heads and wonder whether they might have passed each other in the famous, cobblestoned Shambles. Or whether Olivia might have dined in the very café where Luke had washed dishes.

They would never know, of course, but she'd been especially pleased to hear that on returning to Australia, Luke had established a successful career as a freelance cinematographer. For almost two decades now, he'd been working in Sydney and on the Gold Coast and he'd had a wonderful range of experiences in film and video production, working with most of the television channels and with Tourism Australia, as well as a range of international filmmakers.

But although Olivia was thrilled about Luke's interesting and successful career, the very best news had been that her son was also happily married and that he and his wife, Erin, who was a librarian, had two young children, Toby and Isabella.

Luke had shown her photos and they were the most adorable children ever – Toby slim and dark like Luke, and Isabella with the most amazing dimples and curly golden hair.

I'm their grandmother.

'I think Isabella looks like you,' Luke said.

'Really?' At first, this suggestion was almost too astonishing to take in. 'But I've never had such beautiful curls.'

'Maybe not, but look at those expressive eyes.'

'You think?' Olivia felt ridiculously choked.

'Definitely.' With a fond grin, Luke added, 'Bella's a cheeky little scamp.' And then, 'Would you like me to forward these photos to you?'

'Oh, yes, please. And you must tell me when their birthdays are.'

Not long after this, Olivia had bravely shown Luke her hat box filled with the birthday cards, and they'd both shed a tear over these.

'I've only ever shown these to one other person,' she told him. 'And that was to explain something very foolish that I'd done. I'm afraid I've become far too sentimental about birthdays.'

With lips tightly compressed, Luke picked up the card of the mouse in the little sports car, with the surfboard in the back.

Watching the play of emotions on his face, Olivia felt compelled to at least try to explain, or perhaps defend the fateful choice she'd made all those years ago. 'I should never have given you away, Luke. But back in those days, becoming a single mother wasn't nearly as acceptable as it is now. And I suppose, if I'm brutally honest, I was still rather dazzled by Michael and our Hollywood dream. By the time I understood what a terrible mistake I'd made, it was too late.'

Swallowing quickly, she managed a shaky smile. 'I've had to live with that regret ever since. But I'm very grateful to finally know that you've had a happy life.'

'I have. I've been lucky.'

After a small silence, Olivia said, 'And who knows how bizarre your life might have been if I *had* tried to take you to Hollywood with me? Perhaps it was for the best after all.'

'And we've found each other now.' Luke's smile was so affectionate, she was fighting another round of tears.

At lunchtime, Michael had arrived, driving a flash sportscar he'd hired in Cairns and, on Rolf's advice, he'd taken them to the lovely teahouse at Lake Barrine.

Michael's arrival at the teahouse had caused quite a sensation, of course. A waitress carrying a tray loaded with bowls of soup almost dropped the lot when she saw him, and the customers sitting at various tables all turned to stare. But a fellow who seemed to be in charge had appeared and although he'd seemed somewhat overawed, he'd ushered Michael, Luke and Olivia to a relatively private table out on a little deck overlooking the lake, and people hadn't come out there to bother them.

So, they'd spent a very pleasant afternoon enjoying a leisurely lunch and a bottle of wine. Luke had been blown away by the beautiful lake framed by rainforest. Watching a black duck come into land with barely a ripple on the water's surface, he vowed that he must come back to film this place.

So gratifying for Olivia was the discovery that the more she saw of Luke, the more she genuinely liked his shrewd and amiable personality. Meanwhile, Michael had entertained them with stories, both fascinating and hilarious, from his experiences with all manner of famous people.

'So, tell me,' Olivia had felt compelled to ask at one point, 'I'm dying to know more about how you two met up and what that first meeting was like.' Michael and Luke seemed to get along quite well now, but surely their initial contact had been awkward?

The two men exchanged wry smiles.

'To be honest, I was dead scared,' said Luke. 'I half expected it was some kind of joke, that my dad – my adoptive father – had made a mistake when he left your details in the letter attached to his will. I was sure there had to be another Michael Carruthers. Dad had the wrong guy.'

'And I was full of trepidation,' admitted Michael. 'I'd spent a lifetime pretending the kid – sorry, I mean our *son* – never happened. Mind you, over the years, I've had my guilt-ridden moments, when I felt bad about deserting you, Liv.' His mouth twisted into an awkward grimace that was almost an apologetic smile. 'But I'd never been ready to own up to that embarrassing truth.'

'And the initial meeting?' prompted Olivia, surprised that Michael's confession had less impact now than she might have expected. 'I still can't quite picture it.'

Michael nodded. 'Luke first contacted me via my agent, and I have to confess I told Vince it was a load of bull, a scam, but I also told him to forward me the email. Then I got in touch with Luke privately and invited him to my place.'

At this, Olivia was once again picturing the beautiful apartment overlooking Sydney Harbour. 'So then, it was pistols at dawn?'

The men chuckled.

'It was pretty bad for the first five minutes or so,' said Luke. 'I was so nervous and Michael was sure I was fortune hunting.'

'Yeah, I played the tough guy at the start,' admitted Michael. 'But deep down, I could sense that Luke was a good'un.' The look he sent Luke now was unmistakably fond. 'I soon realised he was decent and honest – and modest.'

Olivia swallowed to ease the painful rock in her throat. 'His parents brought him up well.'

'They did,' Michael agreed and there was a moment or two when everyone around the table had extra shiny eyes. But then Michael refilled their glasses. 'And now I've been handed a second chance that I never deserved and I'd like to propose a toast.' He raised his glass. 'Here's to the future. We might not be able to make up for my past mistakes, but we can have a damn good try.'

There were smiles all round as they clinked glasses.

Now, it was evening and Olivia was home again, alone, happy and at peace in a way she had never imagined possible. She was also utterly exhausted. For her supper, she had made a simple cup of soup, and for once, she was confident she would sleep well. She was heading for her bedroom when the phone rang.

'Olivia.'

It was Josie. Guiltily, Olivia remembered that tonight had been the all-important dress rehearsal for *Next Stop Mars*. 'Hello, Josie,' she said. 'How was the final rehearsal? And how's the shed? Are you happy with it?'

'Yes, the shed's fine, and the rehearsal went well.' Despite this good news, Josie sighed rather dramatically. 'But in the wrap-up, I told the players that Michael Carruthers will be coming to the show tomorrow night. I thought they should be warned, but I tried to make light of it and to bolster their egos first, so they wouldn't freak. But I'm afraid Margot's had a meltdown.'

'Oh, dear. So she's still feeling insecure about that role?'

'I'm afraid so. She's in a bad way, Olivia. I was wondering . . .'

For a moment, Olivia thought Josie was going to ask her if she would resume the Lady X role. It had been ages since she'd learned that part, though, and she wasn't sure she could manage a refresher in under twenty-four hours, especially without a dress rehearsal.

'I was wondering if you might be able to help Margot,' Josie said. 'With all your experience, I hoped you might have a few techniques for dealing with stage fright? I'm afraid Margot's past listening to anything I might suggest.'

'Oh.' Hastily, Olivia pivoted from worrying about getting herself onto the stage, while she considered possible strategies that might help Margot. She'd never really suffered from stage fright, but she'd certainly witnessed it. And since working with Tilly, she'd been rereading old textbooks and articles about various approaches to acting. 'I can try, I guess.'

'That would be wonderful, Olivia. I'm really worried that Margot won't be able to sleep tonight unless she calms down.'

'Tonight? You want me to go to Margot's place now?' Olivia asked, somewhat dismayed.

'Would you mind?'

On any other evening, Olivia might have minded a great deal. But today she'd been blessed with such a wonderful gift, she was sure she owed the universe a little generosity in return. 'Of course I don't mind,' she said, and, despite her exhaustion, she was already heading back down the hallway to find her coat and car keys.

It felt ridiculously late to be knocking on someone's front door, and it didn't help that a bitter wind was howling, or that Olivia had rarely visited Margot's house in all the years she'd known her.

When the door opened, Margot's very worried-looking husband greeted her. 'Good evening, Olivia. It's so good of you to come.'

'How's Margot?' she asked as she stepped out of the cold into the pleasantly heated house.

'She's a mess, I'm afraid. I've tried to get through to her, but she keeps telling me I could never understand.' Jack gave a helpless shrug. 'I guess she's right. What would I know about acting?'

'Well, I might be an actor, but I'm no psychologist. I'll certainly see if there's any way I can help, though.'

'Thanks, Olivia. Margot says Michael Carruthers is here in town because he knows you?'

'That's true, but it was many years ago.' She didn't add that it was Rolf who had invited Michael.

By now they were halfway down the hall and had reached a doorway to what appeared to be the main bedroom. Olivia could see Margot sprawled on her back across a queen-size bed that was covered by a quilted, emerald-toned spread. She was fully dressed, staring at the ceiling. She hadn't removed her stage makeup after the rehearsal and her face was streaked with black mascara.

'Margot,' said Jack. 'Olivia's here.'

'Olivia?' Margot repeated rather dazedly. And then, frowning and squinting, she managed to prop herself up onto her elbows. 'What are you doing here?'

'I heard you were in a bit of a panic,' Olivia said. 'I hoped I might be able to help.'

'You can help by taking back the Lady X role.' Margot was sitting up properly now, trying to push away untidy strands of hair that had stuck to the makeup on her cheeks. 'I can't possibly play that part with Michael Carruthers watching.'

'Of course you can.'

'I can't,' Margot cried. 'I absolutely can't.'

'Maybe not while you're panicking. But I'm going to help you to calm down.' Olivia prayed she wasn't punching above her weight as she made this claim.

'How can I possibly calm down?' Margot persisted. 'I'll be terrified. I'll make such a hash of that role.'

'To begin with, you need to stop talking like that. If you think negatively, your panic just keeps spiralling. You need to stop that now, and breathe and focus on positive things.'

'But there's nothing positive about *me* acting in front of such a famous actor.'

Olivia could certainly sympathise with this fear. She was recalling her own panicked reaction to the news that Michael was coming to Burralea. 'Do you mind if I sit down?' she asked.

'No, of course not.' Margot wriggled backwards to make room and Olivia sat, carefully, on the edge of the bed.

In front of her was a rather pretty antique dressing table – polished timber, a swing mirror, photos of children in silver frames, a cut-glass dish holding jewellery, a small vase with crepe paper flowers. Olivia might have felt like an intruder in this very private domain if her mission hadn't been so important.

'Okay, to begin with,' she said, almost as if she was feeling her way into a role, 'you're putting on this play for the Burralea community, not for Michael Carruthers. He's only another body in the audience. And before you give me any buts – the other thing to remember is that all the other players will be in the same boat as you.'

'Th-that's true.'

'Michael will be caught up with Rolf's clever storyline and he'll be watching every one of you up there on the stage. So, your goal – or, at least, one of your goals – should be to work as a team with the others. You need to support each other.'

'I – I guess.'

At least Margot had stopped throwing up protests. Encouraged, Olivia said, 'Why don't you start now by taking a couple of lovely deep breaths? You know, the way Josie gets us breathing when we're doing our warmups.' Olivia offered a reassuring smile. 'Oxygen is magic. But when you're nervous, you breathe shallowly and that can make you dizzy and even more nervous.'

Margot nodded.

'Now, put your hand on your belly and close your eyes, and then breathe in deeply through your nose, and out through your mouth. Push your belly out. That's it. Now another deep breath.'

Obediently Margot followed these instructions and when she was done, she actually managed a small smile. 'The breathing does help, doesn't it?'

'Always,' Olivia agreed. 'And you should make sure you keep up the deep breathing tomorrow, especially tomorrow night. But I suspect that your next step now should be to try to clear your head of those negative thoughts and think about goals instead.'

'Goals?'

'Yes. Imagine you're stepping onto the stage right now. What is your goal? What is your hope?'

'That I won't stuff up. That I won't let Josie down.'

Olivia smiled gently as she shook her head. 'Sorry, Margot. They're still negative thoughts. Don't focus on *not* making mistakes. How can you turn that around, so you're only thinking positively?'

'You mean – things like – um – play my part. Support my fellow actors.'

'Yes, that's exactly what I mean. That's great!' To Olivia's relief, she could see that Margot was already sitting straighter. 'What else?'

'I want to hit the right notes,' Margot said. 'And I want to become Lady X.'

'Exactly! Focus on that. On becoming Lady X. You'll be wonderful. I know you will.'

'You think so? Really? You're not just saying that to make me feel better?'

'I know so.' Olivia was glad she could say this convincingly. 'I've seen you as Lady X, remember? And I was very impressed with how you overcame your fear that night when I was watching you. You managed so well. I was totally envious.'

Margot's jaw dropped. 'You? Envious of me?'

'Yes. I could see Josie was right. You deserved the role.'

'Oh, my God.'

'And the other thing, Margot, is that you learned all your lines so quickly, on top of everything else you do – looking after your family and helping Jack to run the hardware store. I'm in total admiration.'

'Gosh.'

Olivia waited for a moment, letting this tribute sink in. 'Now, how are you feeling?'

Margot gave this some thought before she nodded. 'Better.'

'Good for you.' Olivia drew a deep breath of her own. She hadn't realised how nervous she'd been, but now she was warmed by a growing sense of confidence. 'Tonight, I suggest you keep concentrating on relaxing, on letting go and allowing yourself to only think positively. Stamp on anything negative.'

'All right. I think I can do that.'

'You can tell yourself that your anxiety is just excitement.'

'I guess.'

'And it might also be helpful to think about what Lady X might be feeling. What's her basic mindset?'

Margot answered quite quickly. 'Basically, she's up herself?'

Olivia laughed. 'Of course she is. Lady X is so up herself she would simply look down her nose at an ageing Hollywood has-been like Michael Carruthers. She'd probably say, Michael *who*?'

Now, Margot's giggle was almost a proper laugh. 'Perhaps I should say that to myself when I step on to the stage. Michael *who*?'

'You should. That's exactly what you should do. Focus any nervous energy into being Lady X.'

'Okay. That sounds – doable – I think.'

'If you like, I'll come backstage with you tomorrow night, just to check you're okay and we'll do some more breathing. But I'm sure Josie will take the cast through her usual relaxing exercises. You know – progressively relaxing your body. Relaxing your feet, your shins, your thighs.'

'Yes.' Margot took another deep breath and let it out in a happy huff. 'Oh, my God, Olivia. I really am starting to feel better.'

'That's wonderful.'

'Thank you.'

Olivia nodded. 'I'm only too happy to help – but you've done the hard work by pulling yourself together.' She gave Margot's hand a heartening pat and then she stood.

Margot also got to her feet. 'I know I shouldn't have let myself get into such a flap. I suppose it's just that I've always loved the theatre, but I've never really seen myself as an actor.'

'And that's another negative thought you need to strike out.'

'Yes, ma'am.' Margot gave a cheeky mock salute. 'Okay, it's gone. And now, I might be able to tell poor Jack he can stop tearing out the last of his hair. But maybe I should wash my face first. I know I look a mess.'

'War paint,' said Olivia.

'Yes, I do feel like I've been through the wars.'

'And emerged triumphant.'

Impulsively, Margot reached for Olivia's hand. 'Can I give you a hug?'

Olivia had never really been a great one for hugging, even though hugs were pretty much a compulsory form of greeting in most theatrical circles. But now she knew that another hug was the perfect way to end this better than perfect day.

CHAPTER THIRTY-THREE

It was around lunchtime when Kate rang Liam. She knew she would be seeing him at the theatre in just a few hours' time, but there was bound to be so much buzz and excitement about Opening Night there'd be little chance for a private conversation. And since she'd been thinking about the guy more or less nonstop since their last time together, the impulse to call him was irresistible.

'Kate, how are you?' At least he sounded pleased to hear from her.

'I'm fine,' she said. 'I hope I'm not interrupting anything important.'

'Not at all. I'm on a lunchbreak. Are you looking forward to tonight?'

'Absolutely – and you?'

'Sure, especially now the lighting crew are clued up and should be able to handle everything without me.'

'Great. So you can sit in the audience and relax and enjoy the show?'

'That's the plan. There's been a last-minute rush on tickets, of course, now everyone knows about Michael Carruthers. But luckily the shed can hold extra seating, and Rolf's set aside tickets for us.'

'Us? But I've already bought my ticket.'

'No worries. I'm not sure how Rolf reorganised things, but he's got you and me sitting with him and Olivia and Michael.'

Gulp. Kate certainly hadn't expected this honour. 'And Luke?' she asked.

'Is that the other guy's name? I knew there was someone else.'

Kate decided it wasn't her place to elaborate on who this someone else was, but earlier in the morning she'd received a phone call from a very excited Olivia with the most incredible news. Michael Carruthers wasn't the only surprise in town. Olivia had finally, amazingly, after almost fifty sad, regret-filled years, been reunited with her son. Her boy was no longer the imagined recipient of birthday cards that were never posted, but a grown man, alive and well. And here to spend time with Olivia in Burralea.

Kate had been so moved and entranced by Olivia's story of Michael and Hollywood and Luke, she'd almost missed her friend's deft change of subject. But it had been an unexpected suggestion by Olivia, actually, that had prompted this phone call to Liam.

'I don't want you to take this the wrong way,' Kate said now. 'But I was talking to Olivia this morning, and she's offered to have Tilly to stay overnight some time – if I ever need a little more – social life.'

Liam made no audible response to this courageous suggestion and Kate immediately wished she'd given more thought to the actual message she'd wanted to convey.

Perhaps she should have written it down first. She was an editor after all, and she'd always been better at expressing herself via the written word. Speaking, she was inclined to get tangled up, especially if she was a bit nervous – her original flirting conversation with Liam being a prime example.

'Liam?' she asked now. 'Are you there?'

'Yes, I'm here.'

It was hard to gauge his mood from this curt response.

Kate tried again. 'Did – um – what I said just now make sense?'

'I think so. Basically, you're hinting, or perhaps suggesting, that you might be free for us to spend an evening together?'

'Yeah.'

'Perhaps a whole evening? A sleepover?'

'Yes. I guess.'

'Okay. But you don't want me to take this the wrong way. That's the part of your very appealing suggestion that I'm struggling with. What wrong way might I take this?'

'Sorry. It – it's just – you know – I just meant the whole not getting too serious part.'

'Ah, I see.' Now there was another pause. Was Liam playing with her? 'I don't think one night sounds too serious, Kate.'

'Well, no.' She winced. 'I do manage to complicate everything, don't I?'

'Not everything. But maybe us.'

'Mostly when I'm talking.'

'That's possibly true. When we're together and *not* talking, things do seem to be much clearer.'

Now she was sure he was teasing her and Kate blushed as she remembered the delicious spontaneity of their latest lovemaking.

She sighed. Falling for Liam was so easy. He wasn't just sexy and fun, he was everything else – thoughtful and kind – not to mention an expert handyman. The whole package. And deep in her bones, Kate just knew he would never do anything to hurt her, and that, in itself, was a priceless gift.

But the lure of independence and an adventure in her van had been the goal that had sustained her over the past two years and she hated to let it go. She already had one road bump in the form of Tilly. If she took on a meaningful relationship as well —

'If I cut to the chase,' Liam said, breaking into her thoughts, 'my answer is yes, I think it's a brilliant idea, Kate. Work out whatever date and time suits you and Olivia and I'll be ready.'

* * *

I can do this, Liam told himself as he disconnected. Yeah, he was besotted with Kate, but he could play this any way she wanted.

He understood that she needed a clear and uncomplicated vision for her future – just her and the van and an adventure of her own making – and she'd certainly earned it. Even if she had to put the dream off for a while until Tilly was more settled and secure, Liam didn't want to place an extra obstacle in her way.

Mind you, Liam had also tried the freedom thing and it wasn't all it was cracked up to be. He'd found a lonely side to freedom, a wandering star restlessness that hadn't sat well with him. But maybe that wouldn't bother Kate.

At any rate, it wasn't his job to cast doubts on her quest. Perhaps she really did need to head off and explore before she found her own answers.

* * *

The dress code for the Opening Night was a mystery to Kate. Burralea was a small, rural community town, after all, and the play was being held in a farmer's shed, and although a few of the locals loved to wear multi-layered and colourful hippie-style gear, most people dressed quite conservatively. It was possible that tonight's audience could arrive in anything from jeans and flannel shirts and work boots to black satin dresses with strings of pearls and ultra-high heels.

But this evening should be all about the players, and Kate opted for low-key – a long-sleeved, emerald-green midi dress and low heels that didn't draw attention, but still felt attractive, especially with her hair freshly washed and blow-dried and the addition of dangly copper earrings. It was the first time she'd dressed up since she'd left Cairns and she felt good.

'Oh, yes,' Tilly said, when she saw Kate emerge from her bedroom. 'You look perfect. I'm sure Liam will approve.'

'I'm not dressing for Liam.'

'Yeah, right.'

Ignoring Tilly's look of unveiled disbelief, Kate held out her arms and walked towards her. 'Tonight is all about you,' she said giving her a hug.

Tilly grinned. 'Thanks.'

'Are you excited?'

'You bet.'

'Got everything you need? You're supposed to be there nice and early.'

'Yeah. I'm ready.'

'Okay. Let's go.'

A mist tinged with the pink of sunset was rolling in over velvety hills as they set off.

'How gorgeous,' said Tilly.

Kate smiled. 'I thought you didn't like all this misty, moist weather.'

'I guess it's not so bad. I really missed the Cairns sunshine when I first came up here. Maybe I'm getting acclimatised. It's all about what you're used to, isn't it?'

'Well, yes, oh, wise little one. How long have you been here?'

Tilly sent her a sly grin. 'You know Hamish Kirk, my friend at the theatre? He's doing a gap year and he had a couple of months out west on a cattle property earlier in the year. It was all red dust and bright blue skies. Proper outback country. But he reckons he really missed the misty mountains.'

'The green, green grass of home.'

'I guess.'

Liam had mentioned a similar reaction, Kate remembered. Nostalgia, homesickness . . . whatever the emotion was, it had been the drawcard that had brought him back to the Tablelands.

She wondered if she would ever feel that kind of connection to a particular place. Unfortunately, Stan had cast a shadow over the fondness she'd once felt for Cairns and a need to escape had been the original reason she'd been so keen to take off in the van. To travel anywhere and everywhere. No one place. No ties.

But was it possible, or even desirable, to stay forever disconnected and free?

Or was it selfish?

For an uncomfortable moment, Kate wondered if she was being just as selfish as Stan – unprepared to accept the negative impact of her own goals on others, primarily on this sweet, innocent kid. Wouldn't Tilly feel happier and more secure if Kate just sold the van, or – or handed it over to Pippa and David?

'Oh, wow!' Tilly's sudden exclamation brought Kate back from her wandering thoughts.

They were approaching the Hetherington farm now, and they could see lanterns hanging from the bare-branched avenue of trees, while more lanterns had been erected on poles in front of the shed, along with huge tubs filled with potted plants. Kate wondered if she'd missed a last-minute working bee.

'Doesn't it look great?' Tilly was beaming like a full moon as Kate carefully angled the van into a parking spot.

'I wonder if they've done this to impress Michael Carruthers?' Kate said.

'Maybe. I'm totally impressed.'

'By the lanterns or Carruthers?'

'Both, I guess. I mean, everything looks great, but how can I *not* be impressed – make that terrified – about having such a star in the audience?'

Kate wished she'd raised this matter earlier with Tilly. Was this a case of last-minute nerves? She'd been about to unclip her seatbelt and climb out, but now she turned to Tilly. 'You're not going to let that man overawe you tonight, are you?'

'I hope not.'

'Don't. From what Olivia's told me, he's not worth it.'

Tilly's lovely green eyes widened. 'What's Olivia told you?'

'Never mind. Just remember all the things she's taught you. And remember you're a very talented actor and you're here to have a jolly good time tonight. Okay?'

To Kate's relief, Tilly smiled. 'Okay. Anyway, Michael Carruthers is old. It would different if he was Timothée Chalamet or Joel Courtney. Then I'd totally freak. I'd die.'

Kate laughed now, and having unclipped her seatbelt, she gave Tilly another hug. 'You'll be wonderful. Off you go and break a leg.'

She watched the kid run to the dressing tents and thought again about her own indecision, her frustrated goals, her responsibilities. A familiar, uneasy pang stirred deep in her chest. But tonight was about other people's efforts and ambitions coming to fruition on the stage. Her problems would have to wait for another day.

CHAPTER THIRTY-FOUR

Deep breath. Deep breath. In and out. You can do this. In and out.

All day, Margot had conscientiously followed Olivia's instructions and, for the most part, they'd worked. Every so often negative thoughts had crept up on her, like pouncing spiders, bringing flashes of panic, but she was beginning to see that Olivia's theory might actually work.

As long as she stayed positive and paid attention to her breathing, she was okay. *Just* okay, mind you, but hopefully that was enough to get her through the first, nerve-wracking performance.

Of course, all the players were excited and nervous tonight. The air in the dressing and makeup tents seemed to carry an extra level of electricity and there was less chatter than usual and more focus on checking and re-checking costumes.

Nervous smiles were exchanged and without even being asked, people were rolling their shoulders, shaking out their arms, practising deep breathing. Several people made extra trips to the portable toilets that had been set up.

From outside the tents, vehicles could be heard coming along the drive, their headlights flashing as they turned into the nearby field set aside for parking. Excited voices called greetings. Jack, Bridie and Nate would be out there somewhere and Margot pictured them waving to their friends. She imagined all the locals filing into the shed, tickets at the ready, expectant and eager. So many of them would be customers she knew from their store.

What would they think of her after tonight?

Stop that. Stay positive. Focus. Put all your energy into Lady X.

Margot's makeup didn't take as long to apply as the AIs' and when Tammy had finished with her, she made her way from the tent to the assembly point – a patch of grass at the back of the shed. It was quite cold there and her costume wasn't exactly cosy, but at least there wasn't a wind. Peter Hubbard was already there as well. He'd grown a goatee for his Lord X role and it suited him, especially now he was in full costume.

'Hey there, Peter.'

Peter nodded curtly. 'Margot.'

She rubbed her arms against the chill. 'It's a bit nippy out here, isn't it? I'm going to need Josie's warmup exercises tonight.'

Peter glanced at her again more closely. 'Apart from the cold, how are you feeling?'

'So-so.' She smiled shyly. 'A lot better than I was last night when I went hysterical. I'm sorry about that.'

'I'm glad you've recovered.'

'Olivia helped me, thank heavens. She's been great.'

'Olivia?' Peter made no attempt to hide his surprise. 'Olivia Matthews came down from her high horse?'

'Not only that. She came to my house. I'm sure Josie sent her, but she was lovely. Truly kind and encouraging. And she got me deep breathing and focusing. Thinking positively.'

'I could do with a bit of that myself.'

'You, Peter? But you're unflappable.'

'Tonight I'm flapping.'

Now that Margot paid closer attention, she could see that Peter was twisting his hands, over and over, and his Adam's apple kept jerking as if he had trouble swallowing. 'You're not nervous about Michael Carruthers, are you?'

'I wasn't until I saw the TV cameras.'

'TV?' Margot squeaked. 'They're not going to film the show?'

'No,' he said. 'I'm sure they're just here to get a news story with Carruthers. But – I don't know – it kinda feels like this is getting out of hand. We're just a little theatre in a country town, but suddenly there's movie stars and cameras and all this talk about a world premiere. I'm feeling right out of my comfort zone.'

'No, you're not.' Margot surprised herself with the sudden authority she managed to convey, but she couldn't let Peter fall apart. He'd always been as steady as a rock. 'This is totally *in* your zone, Peter. We're still just the Burralea players and we're putting on a play written by a local guy we all know. Besides, you're one of our longest playing members and a pillar of the community.' She was channelling Olivia now, trying to pass on the positive thoughts she'd been telling herself all day.

Peter's mouth tilted. It wasn't quite a smile, but he did look a little less stressed.

'And when we get on that stage,' Margot added. 'We're going to look up at that starscape and say to ourselves, Michael *who*?'

Now, just as the AIs began to file out of the tents, Peter smiled properly.

'You've got this,' Margot whispered.

To her surprise Peter slipped his arm around her and gave her shoulders a squeeze. 'Thank you, Lady X,' he said. 'You're right. We've got this. We're both going to be absolutely fine.'

* * *

'This is brilliant,' exclaimed Michael as he walked with Olivia and Luke to the shed.

Olivia had to agree and she knew Michael wasn't talking about the TV camera operators, or the grinning fans lined up, as if there was an actual red carpet. Michael was appreciating the entire, lovely rural setting – the impressively big shed, the massive sky arching overhead like a giant curtain stitched with stars, the lanterns and pot plants. It was all so very different from Sydney, and exciting and unexpectedly uplifting.

Another unforeseen element for Olivia this evening was how she felt about being a member of the audience and not one of the cast. Only a matter of weeks ago, she'd been in a fit of depression over her inability to play Lady X. She felt quite embarrassed now, when she remembered the way she'd insisted poor Josie must allow her to play that role in a moon boot. Oh dear, the hubris.

Clearly, Josie was far wiser than Olivia had ever given her credit for. And now, thanks to Josie's suggestions, Olivia could count Tilly and Kate as close friends and she'd had a chance to help Margot. Just ten minutes earlier, she'd slipped around the back to check that Margot was coping and the woman had seemed as calm as could be expected, which was wonderful, and surprisingly rewarding for Olivia.

And now, as Olivia made her way down the centre aisle, accompanied by Michael and Luke, Kate and Liam – and countless, wide-eyed stares and whispers of excitement from the rows of seated onlookers – she felt perfectly relaxed about being a mere viewer and not a performer. She was looking forward to the play with the same eager and breathless anticipation as everyone else.

She was tense, of course. She knew the Burralea players were quite capable of putting on a good show and she just hoped they'd stay on top of their nerves. At least the set looked absolutely brilliant and Liam's special lighting effects were very classy.

As she shifted a little restlessly in her seat, crossing and then uncrossing her legs, she wondered if this new apprehension was how it felt to be a mother watching her child perform. Or was this what it was like for Josie, as director, watching from the sidelines, knowing that her work was done and it was now up to everyone else?

* * *

It was almost time. The players had finished their warmups and were ready and waiting. There was no proper backstage set-up, so they gathered just outside the shed's back door. Derek, who'd snuck in and peeked around the set, reported back that the place was packed, the audience seated and eager for the show to begin.

Tilly thought about all the people out there. Among that crowd were Kate and Liam and Olivia. Bridie and her father. Mrs Kirk. People who'd gone out of their way to help her and make her feel as if she belonged here. She wished her mum could meet them. Wished her mum could watch her tonight.

Oh, God. She wanted her mum so badly.

A massive wave of sadness threatened. Tilly knew she should remember Olivia's lesson about inner strength, but it seemed, all at once, too hard.

'Are you okay, Tilly?' Hamish was beside her, looking concerned.

'Yes,' she said, but then, because it was Hamish, she felt brave enough to add, 'But I've been thinking about my mum.'

'She passed away, didn't she?'

Tilly nodded.

'It's so hard,' he said. 'My best friend died last year.'

'Really?' Now, when Tilly looked more closely, she could see her own pain mirrored in Hamish's face. 'That's awful.'

'Yeah. He was Alec Hetherington's son.'

'The farmer who owns this place?'

'Yep.'

It occurred to Tilly now that this probably explained why Hamish had been so tense at the rehearsal. She was remembering Hamish's stilted conversation with Mr Hetherington, the pat on the shoulder that the farmer had given him and the way it had seemed to heal a hidden pain. Had that puzzling exchange been all about their grief?

'Did you know Alec hung all those lanterns outside and organised the pot plants and everything?' Hamish said. 'He told me it's his private tribute to Ben and to his wife who died some time back. His way of remembering them, but it's about getting on with his own life as well.'

'Wow,' Tilly whispered. 'That's actually a very cool idea.' Already, she felt a little stronger and the threat of tears was receding. 'We should do that with this play, don't you reckon? Make it awesome. For my mum and for your friend.'

Hamish nodded slowly. 'That sounds like a very good plan.' He raised his hand. 'It's a deal,' he said, and they were both smiling as they high-fived.

'Okay, everyone.' Josie, having ducked quickly out the front to greet the local mayor and other distinguished guests, was back. 'Silence, please,' she said. 'You need to file inside the shed, quietly now, and wait on the chairs behind the set. You know the drill. Geoff will give you your cues.'

With that, Josie disappeared again.

This was it. A thrill zapped through Tilly. Not nerves, just pure excitement. After the weeks of rehearsals, it was happening.

The players obediently filed in, Margot and Peter taking the chairs nearest the set, as they were in the first scene. Margot didn't seem to be freaking – apparently Olivia had worked some kind of magic – and she and Peter looked splendid in their Lord and Lady X costumes.

The music that had been playing over the sound system stopped and a breathless silence fell throughout the shed.

Geoff, wearing a headset linked to the lighting desk inside, delivered his first cue. 'Okay, here's the warning.' Margot and Peter rose from their seats and made their way to makeshift steps that led onstage.

Tilly was sitting so very still now, she almost forgot to breathe.

'Standby,' ordered Geoff, and Margot and Peter exchanged a quick smile.

And then came their final cue. 'Go.'

They disappeared through a door onto the stage. The play had begun.

CHAPTER THIRTY-FIVE

'Olivia, it's Michael.'

'Oh, hello. Are you back in Sydney?'

'Yes, got back last night.'

Olivia, sitting in her little front room in Burralea, pictured Michael calling from his apartment, no doubt admiring his magnificent water views, the stunning Sydney architecture that edged the harbour and the beautiful bridge that spanned it.

'I was wondering if you've read Charles Bingham's column in *The Sydney Morning Herald*?' Michael said. 'It's a great story about Burralea and the play.'

'Good heavens. Really? I didn't even know there was a media person at the play, apart from the TV promotion you managed to attract. But *The Sydney Morning Herald*? That's astonishing.'

'Bingham's doing some kind of roving report around Australia. He's one of those columnists who likes to operate under the radar.'

'I'm not sure our local newsagent carries *The Herald*.'

'I thought that might be the case. I'll send it through to you then. What's better for you? Email or a text to your phone?'

'Oh, email, please.' Olivia much preferred to read on her laptop, rather than struggling with the tiny print on her phone.

'No problem,' responded the surprisingly affable Michael. 'I was really chuffed when I read it. I think you will be, too.'

'That's nice to know. A good review's always better than a kick in the teeth. Thanks for thinking of me.'

'No probs. And listen, Liv, I was wondering, now that your ankle's almost healed, would you be interested in playing Lady X down here?'

It was just as well Olivia was already sitting down. She was suddenly quite dizzy with shock. Could this be real? Michael, after all this time, asking her to act in a Sydney show? In the Sydney Opera House? 'With you, Michael?'

'Of course with me. Why not? We'd make a great Lord and Lady X combo. Rolf tells me you're brilliant.'

'That's very kind of him.'

'Not that he needed to tell me that. I already knew it.'

Olivia was tempted to borrow one of Tilly's classic responses – *as if*. After all, there was little point in trying to disguise her disbelief.

'I know what you're thinking,' Michael went on, before Olivia could dredge up an appropriate reply. 'You can say it, Liv. I've been a total arse and I don't deserve you.'

'That's not what I was going to say.'

'You might as well. It's the truth.'

Michael's self-flagellation was an even bigger surprise than his invitation, and Olivia was very aware that there'd been a time, not so long ago, when she would have given her eye teeth for this chance to prove to herself and to the general public that she truly was an actor of note. Now, she was more concerned about the unfortunate actor Michael might have elbowed aside to make room for her.

Strange how quickly one could change. Olivia's reunion with her dearest Luke, her budding friendship with Tilly and Kate, and the experience of sitting in the audience and watching the players pour their hearts and souls into their performance had shown her a truth she'd always known, but had chosen to overlook. Fame and recognition were self-centred goals, bringing a hollow version of happiness that she no longer needed. 'It's very generous of you to offer me the role, Michael.'

'But you're going to turn me down.'

From outside came the sound of a vehicle pulling up. That would be Kate dropping off Tilly. The girl had made it clear she was very happy to spend the night at Olivia's while Kate and Liam went off to a restaurant and enjoyed a well-earned evening to themselves. In fact, Tilly and Olivia were also plotting to free Kate up at some point in the future, so she could take off in her van. Kate had been making noises about passing her van on to her daughter Pippa, who was coming to watch the play on the following weekend. But both Tilly and Olivia were dismayed by the thought of Kate missing out on her dream.

'I have commitments here,' Olivia told Michael now, quite firmly. 'So thank you, but I'm not actually available.'

'That's a shame.' He sounded surprisingly disappointed, but Olivia, who'd experienced her own disappointments at his expense, found it difficult to feel much sympathy.

They said their goodbyes and she went to open her front door. Tilly was already there with a small, bulging backpack that held her school gear and overnight things, plus a clothes hanger with the school uniform she would wear in the morning. Kate, a few steps behind, looked very elegant in a soft, mushroom pink blouse and black trousers.

'I have two assignments due at the end of this week,' Tilly announced importantly. 'So I'm going to be rather busy tonight.' She sounded quite grown up and proud of her new responsibilities.

'That's all right,' Olivia assured her. 'I have a little room I set aside as a study that you're welcome to use.'

Kate held out a small container. 'I've given Tilly money for tuckshop tomorrow, but I've made you a lemon slice, Olivia – just as a thank you.'

'Goodness. How delicious. My tastebuds are already tingling. There was no need, but thank you, Kate.'

Tilly sniffed at the air. 'Something smells amazing. Is that our dinner cooking?'

'Oh, it's just a sauce I'm making for pasta,' said Olivia.

'Awesome.'

It seemed they were set for a satisfactory evening. With Kate farewelled, Olivia showed Tilly to the room where she would sleep and then to the small study. The girl settled to her homework and Olivia pottered in the kitchen, enjoying a little classical music on the radio, turned down low.

It wasn't until much later, after they'd eaten their dinner, had chatted at length about the play and Tilly was finished with her homework and almost ready for bed, that Olivia remembered that she hadn't looked for the news column Michael had sent through.

'You should come and read this, too,' she called to Tilly. 'It's an article in a Sydney newspaper about our Opening Night. Michael said it was rather good. Grab that chair,' she added, and as Tilly came into the room, she pointed to a spare chair in the corner, an antique balloon back with a delicate tapestry seat, one of the few pieces she'd inherited from her family.

'It looks too pretty to sit on,' said Tilly.

'Nonsense. Pull it over here. There's room for both of us at this desk and we can read this piece together.'

Taking great care, Tilly sat at the desk and they both began to read.

Off the Beaten Track
with Charles Bingham

After sending in last week's story about Cairns and the Great Barrier Reef, I drove up the Kuranda Range to the Tablelands, prepared to tell you about stunning rainforest scenery, framed by waterfalls, crater lakes and tree kangaroos.

I did not expect to be moved and uplifted by a group of amateur players taking to a makeshift stage in a tractor shed outside the town of Burralea. Nor did I expect to join in a standing ovation, almost choked with emotion, as if I'd been with these people throughout their creative journey.

I might have missed finding this hidden gem if I hadn't heard locals in a coffee shop in Burralea talking about a celebrity visiting town for what was being cheekily promoted as 'the world premiere' of a locally written and produced play.

My journo nose twitched even more when I discovered the play had been written by Rolf Anders, one of our more enduring authors, who has won popular domestic and international readership, and claims local citizenship by residing for a good part of the year beside a picturesque Tablelands lake. The term 'world premiere' is not a misnomer for someone of Anders's stature.

I bought a ticket at the coffee shop and was told that the visiting celebrity was none other than Michael Carruthers, veteran of Australian film and television, who has returned to the boards and will play the lead role in this same production at the Sydney Opera House next month.

That's right dear readers, *Next Stop Mars* is headed for the big smoke, not only because it has influential backers such as Anders and Carruthers, but because the script is so good. It's new and refreshing, full of insight into the foibles of the human spirit and brilliantly spiced with humour.

The play, cleverly billed by a wordsmith up here as
'*Downton Abbey* meets *Star Trek*', shows a dysfunctional, priv-
ileged family in the future, escaping from a rapidly overheating
Earth to a colony on Mars. They're forced to share a cramped
spaceship with their servants, an advanced form of robot whose
artificial intelligence makes them smarter and more humane
than their human masters.

Anders has written a play that resonates with many of
today's political issues and environmental challenges at a time
when billionaires are paying big money for space flights and
the concept of humans travelling to Mars is no longer science
fiction.

If the Sydney production, cast and crew put as much effort
and passion into this work as the Burralea amateurs have, it's
bound to be a hit. Anders has created great scope with his characters, from bumbling pompous elders to ultra-cool youngsters.

Burraleans are used to setbacks – droughts, floods, fires,
cyclones and deregulation of the dairy industry – and they also
managed a crisis when their community hall was damaged by
fire and they were forced to find an alternative venue in a hurry.

This wasn't their only trial, though. A theatrical 'break a leg'
became a painful reality for the nominated lead actress, Olivia
Matthews, a NIDA graduate, who spent most of her performing career in the UK and has retired to Far North Queensland as
an icon and mentor for amateur theatre.

With Matthews no longer available, they pulled first-timer
Margot Cooper from her counter at the local hardware store
and gave her a crash course in acting. Hard to believe and I'm
no theatre critic, but Cooper's performance was close to flawless
on the night.

The Sydney professionals are unlikely to contend with
their venue being seriously damaged by fire a few days before

opening, and the Sydney community won't have to rally in support. That's what happened up here at Burralea, however, and the locals were determined that the show would go on. I'm told there were also chook raffles and bingo nights and even a tractor art union that helped stage this premiere.

Don't try to tell me that the arts and the pursuit of creative excellence are limited to the cities and their famous venues. I have just been entertained, uplifted and refreshed by theatre in its most spontaneous form, and it all happened in Alec Hetherington's tractor shed on Boar Pocket Road.

Tilly jumped from the chair as soon as she finished reading and danced a little jig. 'Did you read that about the ultra-cool youngsters?'

'I did,' said Olivia. 'And he's right. You *were* ultra-cool.'

'How about that?' the girl cried, punching the air. 'The Burralea players are famous.' She paused then, frowning, 'Or maybe we're *almost* famous.' Now she added a grin. 'But that'll do me.'

'It's certainly not a bad wrap for your very first show,' Olivia agreed. 'Imagine what the future might hold.'

* * *

The café was intimate, with natural stone walls and romantically flickering candles set on deep windowsills. Kate and Liam had enjoyed a delicious meal, keeping the conversation light and safe. But now, as they finished their mains, Liam smiled across the table to Kate. 'I understand Olivia and Tilly are plotting to free you up, so you can take off on your big trip.'

'Yes, Olivia mentioned that to me, too. It's very generous of her, isn't it?'

Liam nodded. 'I suspect she would really enjoy having Tilly's company.'

'They certainly seem to get on well. Tilly's never actually met her grandparents, so I think she sees Olivia as the grandmother she never had. I've been thinking . . .' Kate paused. She'd been doing rather a lot of thinking since Olivia had taken her aside at the party after the show on Opening Night and suggested her plan to mind Tilly while Kate travelled in her van. At first Kate had felt a little bulldozed, but since then she'd been warming to the idea.

'I've been thinking,' Kate went on now. 'Tilly would probably enjoy living in town. She'd be able to walk to school from Olivia's place. I guess she'd most likely walk with Bridie and her friends and hang out with them in the afternoons.'

'Sounds like a neat arrangement all round.' Liam set his knife and fork together and picked up his wineglass. 'So, does this mean you're starting to make plans for your trip?'

Kate didn't answer straight away. She had no idea how Liam might really feel about her taking off, and she didn't want to spoil this night. Then again, he was the one who'd raised this. 'I'm getting closer,' she said. 'I've almost finished fitting out the van, but I'd like to get the whole guardianship business sorted first. I need the court order giving me official parental authority. I think that's important for Tilly to feel secure. It means tracking down Stan in Cambodia, though. Or trying to, at least.'

'And if you can't?'

'If I can't find him, or if he refuses to respond, I believe the court process can still go ahead. But it takes around six months.' She smiled. 'So I'll be here till the end of the year at least.'

'And then there's Christmas.'

'And then there's Christmas. Exactly.' Kate's smile gave way to a helpless little laugh. 'Tilly's keen to be involved in the players' Christmas panto, and Olivia will have her son, Luke, and his family visiting. And now Pippa and David have decided they want to be married at New Year's.'

'That'll keep you busy.'

'Yep. Luckily, Pippa and David only want something small and intimate on a beach on Magnetic Island, but I'm sure I'll be needed to help with all the planning. Then soon after that it'll be the new school year, and I'd like to see Tilly happily settled in Year Nine.'

'And by then, you will have well and truly earned time for yourself.'

By then, Kate would probably be so deeply in love with this man, she'd never want to leave. She dropped her gaze, afraid he might read this message in her eyes.

'Which direction would you take?' Liam asked.

Okay, so she would play this his way. She would miss him terribly, but she knew she should be grateful that he'd never wavered from supporting her travel plans.

'South,' she told him now. 'I'll definitely head south. I've lived my whole life in the tropics and I have this vision of being way down at the bottom of Oz, maybe somewhere on the Great Ocean Road. Perched on a lookout over Bells Beach, perhaps. Somewhere where it's all cold and blustery, but I'm in the van and I'm snug.'

Liam smiled. Oh, God, she loved his smile.

'I'm going to miss you so much, Liam.' There, she'd said it now.

At first, he didn't respond, but as he dropped his gaze, his smile was replaced by a more serious expression. 'I won't try to hold you back, Kate.'

'I know and I'm grateful. Or, at least, I think I'm grateful.' With a small shrug, she added, 'It's not as if I'll be gone forever. I think six months should get me to most of the places I want to see.'

'And I've been wondering . . .' Liam paused, shifted his wine-glass a few careful centimetres. 'I have all this experience in fly-in fly-out, you see, and a ton of leftover frequent flier points.'

Kate blinked. 'Are you suggesting you might come and visit me?'

'Only if it fitted in with your plans.'

She would make her plans fit. This was the best idea ever.

'I wouldn't want you to think I was stalking you.'

'Oh, Liam, I know you're not a stalker.'

'But maybe we could plan for a weekend on the Sunshine Coast? Another when you reach somewhere like the Northern Rivers in New South Wales?'

'That's the best idea! I love it. I flippin' *love* it.' Kate realised she'd become a little over-excited and people at nearby tables were now looking her way. Lowering her voice, she leaned across the table. 'Might you come to Sydney?'

'If you like. I'd love to. And perhaps I could bring Tilly with me for that trip.'

'Oh, wouldn't that be amazing? The three of us could stay near the harbour, take Tilly on the ferry to Taronga Park Zoo and to Manly. Maybe to a play at the Opera House. Gosh, Liam, that's brilliant. Can't you just see Tilly posing for a selfie on the steps of the Opera House, then shooting it off to her friends?' This was such an exciting idea.

A waitress arrived to clear their plates and enquire if they would like to see the dessert menu. Kate wasn't sure she needed dessert. If visits from Liam were now part of her travel plans, she was already a woman who had her cake and planned to eat it, too.

They opted for coffee, and it arrived, rich and aromatic and brewed from locally harvested beans. Shortly after, as they left the restaurant, walking out into the misty night, Liam took Kate's arm, tucking it inside his. They were only a couple of streets from his place and they walked home through the sleepy, silent town.

Looking up at him, Kate felt her heart lift, as if it had grown wings. 'You know you're too good to be true.'

'Of course,' he quipped. 'It's a very well-known fact.'

'I mean it, Liam. I feel so lucky.'

Now he smiled at her. 'My beautiful Kate, you wouldn't be flirting with me, would you?'

'You'd better believe it.'

He pressed a warm kiss to her forehead. 'Then I'm quietly confident that the luck works both ways.'

ACKNOWLEDGEMENTS

I've been lucky enough to have worked with Ali Watts at Penguin Random House Australia for almost ten years now and I'm truly grateful for the enthusiastic support and wise advice she has offered, along with the welcome freedom to write the books that seem to call to me (with a nudge from my sometimes bossy muse). So, a huge thank you to Ali and also to the others who make such important contributions to the final product – Melissa Lane, Nikki Lusk, Lily Crozier, Veronica Eze and Jordan Meek. Thank you to cover designer Laura Thomas and to proofreader Meaghan Amor for their work on this book too.

In this story I've also drawn on advice from friends, who patiently answered my pesky questions. Most importantly on this occasion, I'm grateful to Julie Bligh, who pointed me in the right direction regarding wills and guardianship. Also hugely helpful was Jacqui Stephens, president of the Atherton Performing Arts. Jacqui has produced many wonderful amateur shows that I've thoroughly enjoyed, not only while we were living on the Tablelands, but when we've returned for visits to that beautiful part of the world. Kirsty Veron probably has no idea how she helped in this regard, but her acting and comments about performing were also part of my inspiration.

My granddaughters were also helpful, whether it was giving me advice about 'teen speak' or about acting classes. Perhaps I should also be thanking the teachers who inspired and encouraged me to step onto the stage and perform in school concerts many moons ago, most notably Tom Brady (not the American footballer, but principal of The Gap High School back in the sixties).

As always, my husband Elliot was my first reader, giving me the encouragement to push on, just as he has done ever since my first attempts to write a publishable manuscript almost thirty years ago. Thanks again, mate. xx

Discover a
new favourite

Visit **penguin.com.au/readmore**